DIVIDED WE STAND

Book One

Fractured Union Series

ROBERT COLE

DIVIDED WE STAND

By
Robert Cole

Divided We Stand

© 2024 Robert Cole
All Rights Reserved

No part of this publication may be reproduced, distributed, or transmitted in any form or by any means, including photocopying, recording, or other mechanical or non-mechanical methods, without the prior written permission of the copyright owner. For permission requests, please contact Carentan Publishing at info@carentanllc.com.

The story is a work of fiction, and as such all names, characters, and incidents portrayed in this production are fictitious. While the author used the description of real places throughout the novel for ease of reading, many of these descriptions are altered with details added or subtracted for purposes of storytelling. All characters in this book are the product of the author's imagination and no identification with actual persons (living or deceased), is intended or should be inferred.

Ebook ISBN: 978-1-964981-99-4
Paperback ISBN: 978-1-964981-98-7

This ebook is licensed for your personal enjoyment only. This ebook may not be re-sold or given away to other people. If you would like to share this book with another person, please purchase an additional copy for each recipient. If you're reading this book and did not purchase it, or it was not purchased for your enjoyment only, then please return to Amazon.com or your favorite retailer and purchase your own copy. Thank you for respecting the hard work of this author.

Also By Robert Cole

<u>The Matt Sheridan Series</u>

Cataclysm

Breaking Contact

Standing Ground

Bounding Overwatch

<u>Fractured Union Series</u>

Divided We Stand

United We Fall - *coming Summer 2024*

To Melanie, Liam, and Clare
Whose love and support mean everything

Author's Note

On June 9, 2023, former President Donald Trump was indicted on thirty-seven felony counts in the Southern District of Florida. The charges included conspiracy to obstruct justice, corruptly concealing a document or record, and willful retention of national defense information. On August 1, he was further indicted in Washington D.C. federal court on four counts of alleged attempts to subvert the results of the 2020 election.

As a professor of political science, I've been fascinated by the continued polarization of American politics in recent years and the inefficiencies created by the stalemates within and between our three branches of government. As a writer of fiction, I simply asked myself: what if Donald Trump refused to attend his arraignment on felony charges in federal court? What would happen? What *could* happen?

This last question is the entire premise of this novel—this fictional novel.

While you may find similarities in certain characters with real people, every character in this book is a creation of my own mind and is purely fictional. I say this not out of any fear of liability but rather to establish your expectations as the reader. This novel is not meant as a political commentary, nor is there any agenda other than to attempt to weave an interesting story that readers will find engaging and enjoyable. The backdrop for this novel is the current state of affairs in American politics, but that is where the similarities end.

My goal is for readers of every political view to respect some characters and loathe others—all based on the reader's personal views, not on mine. If you are hoping to read a book that aligns perfectly with your image of how this country should be, I can assure you now that you will be sorely disappointed. Likewise, if you are seeking validation to support your views of current political candidates and officials, this book offers nothing. In furtherance of my goal of telling a good story, the fictional characters in this book act exactly how I want them to, not how you think they should— and they are certainly nothing like the person in real life you may associate them with. Some are very good at what they do, and some are terrible. Some are luckier than any person alive, and some have misfortune after misfortune. The plot is entirely a figment of my imagination, and while it does mimic certain aspects of the current divide in American politics, this fictional story is not intended to take sides or portray one side as superior to the other.

It is my sincere hope that readers of all political persuasions will find this novel enlightening, entertaining, and enjoyable.

Robert Cole
May 2024

Part I

Lewis Rothschild: You have a deeper love of this country than any man I've ever known. And I want to know what it says to you that in the past seven weeks, 59% of Americans have begun to question your patriotism.

President Andrew Shepherd: Look, if the people want to listen to-...

Lewis Rothschild: They don't have a choice! Bob Rumson is the only one doing the talking! People want leadership, Mr. President, and in the absence of genuine leadership, they'll listen to anyone who steps up to the microphone. They want leadership. They're so thirsty for it they'll crawl through the desert toward a mirage, and when they discover there's no water, they'll drink the sand.

President Andrew Shepherd: Lewis, we've had Presidents who were beloved who couldn't find a coherent sentence with two hands and a flashlight. People don't drink the sand 'cause they're thirsty. They drink the sand 'cause they don't know the difference.

—Excerpt from the movie "The American President" (1995)

Prologue

Tuftonboro, NH
August 5, 2023

JASMINE ORTIZ HAD the patience of an assassin.

She lay unmoving and expertly hidden behind a wood pile near the shoreline, a position she'd held since before the sun set over Lake Winnepesaukee behind her more than two hours ago. She was close enough to the couple sitting on the wooden dock to hear the sound of their voices but too far to make out their words. It didn't matter. Jasmine had watched the couple intently for the last two evenings and felt confident that the empty wine bottle on the table signified the completion of her mission was approaching.

The man and woman, whom Jasmine knew to be in their late fifties and married for thirty-one years, were dressed in shorts and short-sleeved shirts on this warm August evening. They were lounging on deck chairs placed to capture the stunning views across the breadth of the lake and the Belknap Mountains to the west. The wind blew gently from the east, keeping this side of the lake calm, with just the lapping of tiny waves along the rocky shoreline a few yards to Jasmine's left. The large dock upon which the couple sat was L-shaped, thirty feet on a side. The top pointed out into the lake, with the base paralleling the shoreline. Facing the dock was a boathouse shingled in gray clapboard siding to match the 6,000-square-foot home situated more than a hundred feet back from the water's edge. Muted deck lights discretely edged the perimeter of the dock.

Jasmine waited for her cue to act. While she knew many intimate details about the two people she was watching, she had no feelings for either. This was a job. There had been many assignments before this, and she expected to receive a new one as soon as this job was complete.

As Jasmine predicted would happen, the man stood up, leaning down to kiss his wife on the forehead before grabbing the empty bottle of wine. He sauntered off past the boat house, following the wooden path up to the well-lit house. As Jasmin anticipated, the man was fetching a second bottle of wine. The couple's evening ritual started with a couple of glasses of wine. Upon finishing the bottle, they'd agree to open a new one. Two bottles down, the couple would stumble up to bed. Jasmine wondered if this was what getting old was all about.

On each of the last two nights, when the husband had retreated to the house to retrieve more wine, the woman had stood up and walked out onto the dock's pier, enjoying the view of the lake at night. This was the moment Jasmine had been waiting for.

Quiet as a cat, Jasmine stood up and moved onto the deck. She was barefoot so as to move silently and wore only a skin-tight wetsuit colored in woodland camouflage. She kept her dark hair in a military buzz cut, and with her lean, muscular build, she was often mistaken for a male at a distance.

Jasmine knew the man would only be gone for a few minutes. Moving steadily, Jasmine closed the distance to the woman walking lazily along the dock. The woman seemed to sense Jasmine's presence when she was still a few steps away.

"That was quick," the woman said without turning, assuming it was her husband approaching with a fresh bottle of wine.

Two more steps.

Jasmine spent considerable time each week training in Brazilian Jiu-Jitsu and Krav Maga. Although only 5'7", she had the build of a champion MMA fighter: thick, ropy muscles along her shoulders and back, narrow hips, and steel legs. She'd spent several hours earlier that morning rehearsing this specific takedown maneuver, and Jasmine pounced as soon as she came within striking distance.

As if she were about to tackle the older woman, Jasmin bent at the waist, twisting to duck her head along the woman's left side and reaching her right arm forward so that it swept across the woman's upper chest. Simultaneously, Jasmine's left arm scooped under the back side of the woman's thighs. As Jasmine's head cleared the woman's left hip, Jasmine propelled her legs to sweep the woman off her feet. As soon as the woman's feet left the dock, Jasmine launched herself upward and off the side of the dock. She knew instantly that she'd timed her jump perfectly.

The woman yelped in surprise, having no clue what was happening. Jasmine didn't care. The man in the house was well outside of hearing range, and a scream at this point wouldn't matter.

Jasmine kept her body upright, flipping the woman parallel to the ground. As Jasmine's feet hit the water, her eyes swept down to find the side of the dock while her right arm, braced across the woman's upper chest and neck, levered forcibly downward. The two women plunged into the water—Jasmine feet-first and the woman on her side. As Jasmine had choreographed, the woman's head was over the edge of the dock, and as their bodies' plunged downward, the woman's head slammed into the edge of the wooden decking with a sickening crunch, a large gash immediately visible on the side of her head.

Jasmine knew the water here was about six feet deep. Taking a deep breath as she submerged, Jasmine pinned the stunned and concussed woman to the sandy bottom, forcefully kicking her feet to keep them both underwater.

The hope had been that the fall would knock the woman unconscious, but Jasmine knew from her training that hope was not a course of action. While somewhat incapacitated by the blow to her head, the woman was definitely not unconscious. Jasmine adjusted her grasp to keep control of the struggling lady. Jasmine could hold her breath for over two minutes and gave her panicking victim fifty seconds at best before the woman involuntarily inhaled water.

Jasmine crushed the woman in a tight bear hug, finding purchase with her feet along one of the dock's pilings. This ensured Jasmine had more than enough leverage to keep the woman underwater. It was now just a waiting game—a short waiting game.

At the thirty-second mark, the woman made a furious attempt to break from Jasmine's grasp. Unfortunately for her victim, Jasmine was prepared for this. Knowing the end was near, Jasmine pressed her face close to the woman's, hoping to get a glimpse of her terror-stricken face, but the nighttime water was too dark to see the lady's facial features.

People often die silently in the movies—not so in real life. Even underwater, Jasmine could hear the woman's unintelligible screams. The high-pitched whine cut off abruptly, and Jasmine could both hear and feel the woman choking on water.

Seconds later, the woman went limp.

Holding the woman tightly, Jasmine poked her head slowly above the water's surface while keeping the woman's body fully submerged. She heard no signs of activity, and saw no one as she looked up the length of the dock towards the house.

Excellent. Still a few minutes before the husband returns, she thought.

While treading water, Jasmine counted to sixty; the woman remained unmoving in her arms. Quickly, Jasmine maneuvered the woman a bit farther down the length of the dock, tucking the body so that it floated partially submerged under the edge of the dock.

Perfect. The head wound and alcohol, along with the absence of any physical marks on the woman's body, should convince any investigator to conclude this was an accidental drowning. If foul play were ever suspected, all fingers would point to the drunk husband. It was inconceivable that anyone would suspect the woman was murdered for political reasons.

Jasmine swam silently away from the dock and further into the lake, her dark skin and wetsuit maintaining her invisibility. Her getaway boat was moored a quarter mile north around Millstone Point. Now, several hundred meters away, she saw the lights come on in the boat house and someone with a flashlight frantically running up and down the dock.

They'd find Sylvia McDowell soon enough. The Democratic U.S. Senator from New Hampshire was dead and drowned.

1

Osprey, Florida

Sunday, February 4

NATHAN GREENE EYED his daughter as she tapped her foot impatiently. He wondered why exposure to the sun had the effect of bleaching hair but bronzing skin. While he could admire its effect in highlighting his daughter's natural beauty, he wasn't thrilled with the bare midriff and tight shorts that seemed to be the current fashion. Tall, at almost 5'9", Maeve was fifteen and trying hard to look twenty. Nathan was thankful that his daughter had yet to become infatuated with boys, seeming content to socialize with friends and chase her dream of becoming a Division I collegiate swimmer. At the moment, Maeve's complete attention was on getting her mother to hurry up and drive her to the beach to meet up with friends.

"I know this sounds silly, Maeve, but you do know we live right on the beach," said Nathan, gesturing to the room's large bay window with expansive views over the Gulf of Mexico. "Why don't you have your friends come over here instead of meeting them at Siesta Key?"

"Dad! You know why! Everyone is already at Turtle Beach. Besides, my friends came over last weekend."

"Okay. I get it," said Nathan, not getting it at all. A jam-packed beach was second only to a teeming shopping mall as one of Nathan's least favorite locations. Their family's 6,000 square-foot beachfront home on one of Florida's most exclusive barrier islands still left Nathan in awe, and he couldn't fathom why anyone would want to brave the masses at the public beach several miles up the coast.

Nathan's wife, Emily, walked into the family room, jiggling her car keys. "Let's go, Maeve. I'll drop you at the beach, and then I have a couple of errands to run." Eyebrows raised, she looked at Nathan sitting in his leather chair, a novel splayed on his lap.

"Taking the afternoon off?" Emily asked him

"Yeah, I think I might," Nathan smirked, reaching for the remote control to turn on the television. "I can even foresee a nap in my future."

"Good. I might join you when I get back. I plan to hit Trader Joe's after I drop her off at Turtle Beach and should be back in an hour."

"Sounds good," said Nathan, apparently to himself, as he realized his wife and daughter were already halfway to the garage. The eighty-four-inch flatscreen television came to life before him, opening to CNN. He reflexively rolled his eyes as he heard the CNN host rambling about the ongoing saga of former President Benjamin King's legal woes. King, the former divisive President continued to contend that he had, despite all evidence to the contrary, won the previous Presidential election three years prior. Most recently, King had become the first U.S. President ever indicted. That said, listening to a news anchor babbling on about King and President Fulton was not high on Nathan's list for Sunday afternoon television watching.

Switching to a channel showing the final-round action of a PGA golf tournament, Nathan opted to keep the book on his lap and instead folded his hands across his stomach and closed his eyes. As he attempted to cleanse his mind and take a nap, Nathan's brain would not comply, and his thoughts kept creeping back to the story on CNN. *Let it go*, Nathan thought to himself. *That isn't your world any longer.*

Despite the self-admonishment, Nathan opened his eyes and used the TV remote to switch back to CNN. In previous years, headline news stories involving a current or former U.S. President were core to Nathan's career. However, in January, Nathan had taken a sabbatical from teaching, and despite being only forty-seven years old, he was leaning strongly toward formally retiring. While he thoroughly loved his position as a Senior Fellow at Stanford University's Hoover Institution, Emily and Nathan had decided that Sarasota County, Florida, offered their daughter a better small-town high-school experience than Palo Alto, California. While Maeve saw herself swimming for the Stanford Cardinal in college, Emily and Nathan agreed that four years away from the Bay Area would benefit everyone.

Nathan watched the news broadcast for less than ten minutes before turning the television off in disgust. CNN was closer to a daytime soap opera than an unbiased news program. With zero new information to impart, the CNN anchor had resorted to interviewing pundits who had no first-hand knowledge of the situation but were equally forceful in their prediction of what would happen next. Nathan was reminded of Will Roger's definition of an expert as someone with a briefcase more than fifty miles from home.

Fox News and MSNBC were just as bad, in Nathan's opinion— cable news networks had become entertainment masked as information.

Bored but no longer interested in a nap, Nathan decided to go for a jog. Standing up from his comfortable chair and stretching to his full height of 6'4", Nathan caught his reflection in the large decorative mirror mounted on the living room wall. At 190 pounds, his weight was almost exactly as it had been upon graduating from Dartmouth and being commissioned a 2nd Lieutenant in the Infantry twenty-five years prior.

He attributed this to his commitment to an active lifestyle during the intervening years. While he'd never developed a genuine love for running, he embraced pushing himself physically as often as his work and family schedule allowed. As he walked closer to the mirror on his way upstairs to get changed, Nathan took note of his three-day stubble that, like his wavy brown hair, now showed a bit more gray than he was comfortable. *You're becoming an old man*, he thought to himself, even though he knew he was fitter and more capable than most men half his age. While he may have spent the last twelve years as a college professor, his former life as an Infantry and Special Forces officer sharpened his internal steel and gave him a honed edge he'd never allowed to dull.

Sixty minutes and a little over six miles later, as he approached the turnoff to Blackburn Point Road, Nathan found himself unable to resist the urge to turn towards the bridge. Just before the old, single-lane steel drawbridge, Nathan slowed his pace and veered to the right into the crushed-shell parking lot of the Casey Key Fish House.

Sweaty and wearing only shorts and a t-shirt, Nathan wasn't presentable for the restaurant, but he'd fit right in at the small outdoor tiki bar. Already thirsty from his run, the sound of Jimmy Buffett playing through the outdoor speakers called to Nathan, and he soon found himself sitting on a stool along one side of the bar.

Catching the eye of the mid-forties barkeep, he said, "The coldest Landshark you've got, please."

She looked at him for a second, smiling as she took in his running attire and glistening skin. "Comin' right up, Nathan."

Nathan watched as the bartender turned and bent over to reach deep into the beer cooler. She had the body of a 20-year-old CrossFit enthusiast, the skin of a sixty-year-old tanning booth addict, and the bleached, stringy red hair of someone who spent most of their free time at the beach. She turned back to Nathan, a glistening bottle of Landshark beer as well as an ice-cold bottle of water held expertly in one hand.

"Thanks, Donna," Nathan said as she placed both drinks before him. "I'm not sure which of these I should drink first." He noticed the narrow tribal tattoo ringing her well-defined bicep. He met her eyes, deep brown and full of bad decisions but few regrets. She smiled at him, more friendly than flirtatious.

"Out for a run? Haven't seen you here in a couple of weeks," Donna asked. Over the last year Nathan and Emily had become regulars at the Casey Key Fish House, especially enjoying its outdoor tikki bar. Donna was the lead bartender and they had developed the type of friendship one seeks in a neighborhood beach bar—friendly recognition, quick service, and the occasional witty banter.

Nathan nodded in the affirmative as he placed the open mouth of the water bottle to his lips. He'd decided the best course of action was to drain the entire bottle of water and then savor the cold beer.

Donna turned to help another one of the dozen customers scattered around the circular outdoor bar. Nathan reached down, pulled his iPhone from the thigh pocket of his running shorts, and typed a text for Emily to join him at the tiki bar when she returned from shopping. He took three long pulls on his Landshark, finishing it, and signaled Donna for another round. Savoring another ice-cold sip of beer, Nathan glanced up at the television hanging behind the bar.

Former President Benjamin King was on the screen, giving what appeared to be a live, impromptu press conference from the front of his now infamous beach club/residence. Nathan smirked, realizing that King was standing no more than eight miles away from where Nathan was sitting. King's Lido Club was located on Lido Key, the barrier island offshore of downtown Sarasota.

The tiki bar's outdoor performer switched from Jimmy Buffet's "Son of a Son of A Sailor" to CSN's "Southern Cross," and the music made it impossible for Nathan to hear what was being said on the television. However, as the screen was at least sixty-five inches across, he could easily read the captions scrolling across the bottom.

As you know, the 2020 election was stolen from me, and now Bewildered Bill Fulton is intent on persecuting me because he knows he can't beat me in the November election. These indictments by his lackey Justice Department and the crooked FBI are a joke.

On the television screen, King paused, looking up at the crowd of reporters gathered around him. The camera took advantage of the pause and panned out to capture the entire scene. King was standing on the grounds of the Lido Club, wearing a golf shirt emblazoned with the King brand logo. His skin was an artificial orange, and his artificially dyed blond hair fluttered in the Gulf breeze. King acknowledged someone in the crowd with a wink before continuing his speech.

After careful consideration and upon the advice of my very capable team of attorneys—the best attorneys in the world—I will not present myself before the federal court tomorrow morning as this fake indictment requires.

King held up a stapled sheaf of papers to accentuate his point.

This indictment isn't worth the paper it's printed on. The only paper I care about is the great Constitution of the United States, and President Bill Fulton has failed this country and violated our Constitution. The indictments of me and my staff are nothing but a witch hunt, and I will not participate. You hear that, Bill? Or is he taking a nap? I hear he takes naps all day long now. That's not very presidential, Bewildered Bill.

King held the papers in front of him and, without warning, tore them in half. He then folded them and tore them in half again. Completing the theatrical performance, King tossed the pieces of paper into the air in front of the lectern.

The reporters sitting in front of King jumped up, blasting the former President with a barrage of questions. Nathan was glad the volume was turned off. He felt a warm hand on his shoulder and sensed someone sitting on the open stool to his left. Turning, he saw the broad smile of his wife, Emily.

"Hey! Glad you got my text," Nathan said, leaning over to kiss his bride of over twenty years on the lips. "How was shopping?"

Emily laughed. "Well, you seem to be in a good mood. Since when have you cared about my shopping?"

"You're right. I don't. But I am glad you're here. What'll you have?"

She looked around the bar, then down to the nearly empty bottle in Nathan's hand. "I'll have what you're having. That looks refreshing."

Nathan turned to signal to Donna, but the bartender had

already noticed Emily's arrival and was standing before them. "Oh, hey, Donna. Two more, please."

"Sure thing. Hi, Emily. Nice to see you again."

"Hi, Donna. Busy, I see."

"Yeah, can't complain. Livin' the dream!" She answered, turning and grabbing two ice-cold beers from the cooler. She set them on the bar before the Greenes and moved on to another customer.

"So, dear, I thought you were taking a nap. What brought you to the Fish House? You look like you went out for a run."

"I did. And somehow, my internal compass pointed me here."

"Well, this *is* why we live here, I suppose. The Salt Life and all that." Emily laughed, referring to the ubiquitous bumper sticker seen on cars and trucks throughout Florida. She pointed her bottle at the television and said, "What's King up to now?"

"From what I can read," Nathan replied. "It looks like he's going to ignore his indictments and not present himself at the federal courthouse tomorrow."

"Jesus," said Emily. "Is he really that obtuse? I mean, he's a self-promotional genius, but does he think he can go head-to-head with the Justice Department? He's gonna find himself in jail."

"Yeah," said Nathan, thinking. "It's an interesting situation. We don't want to be anywhere near the Lido Club tomorrow when he fails to appear in court."

Nathan felt his cell phone vibrate in the interior pocket of his running shorts. Pulling out his phone, he saw the call was from an unfamiliar number with an 850 area code. Having served as a professor at the University of Florida for eight years prior to accepting a position at Stanford, Nathan knew the 850 area code represented Florida's panhandle.

"Hello, this is Nathan," he said after pressing "Accept" on his iPhone.

"Is this Nathan Greene?" an unidentified male voice said.

"Yes. Who's calling?"

"Please hold for the governor."

2

Lido Key, Florida

Sunday, February 4

CAPTAIN BUTCH KREMER stood next to the hood of his white Sheriff's SUV and assessed the more than a half dozen Sheriff's vehicles forming a defensive cordon around the front entrance of the Lido Club, each with a deputy Sheriff standing behind his or her vehicle. Unlike the deputies forming the cordon, who were each attired in the standard green polyester sheriff's uniform complete with a leather gun belt, Captain Kremer was wearing the uniform befitting his position as commander of Sarasota County's special operations division—olive-drab cargo pants, matching green top and heavy-looking, bulletproof plate carrier festooned with rifle magazines and a radio. The bead of sweat trickling down the left side of his forehead made him realize he'd forgotten his OD-green baseball hat on the passenger seat of his vehicle. He forgot all about his hat and the unseasonably warm February day as soon as he spotted the two oversized, dark-gray armored trucks emblazoned with SWAT along their sides approaching down Benjamin Franklin Drive.

Divided We Stand

Reaching for the radio handset clipped to his vest, Kremer dipped his chin to his left to speak into the handset. "Kilo-33 and Kilo-34, bring your trucks in through the opening in the barricade and park on each side of the portico at the front of the club. I'll meet you there for a quick briefing in five."

"Roger," came the reply from the drivers of his two SWAT trucks.

What a shit show, Kremer thought to himself as he watched the sheriff's deputies move an SUV blocking the entrance to the Lido Club to allow the SWAT trucks to enter. *I sure hope the Sheriff knows what he's setting us up for.*

Kremer's thoughts summed up his feelings regarding the meeting he had attended earlier that afternoon with Doug Knight, the elected Sheriff of Sarasota County and Kremer's ultimate boss. Knight had been Sarasota's sheriff for all sixteen years that Butch had been on the force, during which time Butch had developed a high level of respect for the man. As the commander of Sarasota County's special operations division, Butch had almost daily interactions with Sheriff Knight and had always found him to be a thoughtful, reasonable man who worked hard to shield his deputies from county politics and media interference.

This was why Butch had such difficulty understanding the orders Sheriff Knight had given Butch this afternoon—orders that would most definitely place Sarasota County deputies at the forefront of what was sure to be the biggest political and media shitstorm the country had ever seen.

Using the palm of his hand to wipe the sweat forming on his closely shaved head, Kremer once again contemplated grabbing his hat from his vehicle. Figuring he'd be in the shade or indoors momentarily, he turned away without the hat and walked over to where his two SWAT trucks had parked, one on each end of the portico. A dozen members of his SWAT team, all fully geared up in combat fatigues, armored vests, and helmets, were unloading crates of equipment from the SWAT trucks. As Kremer approached, he saw several men in dark suits and sunglasses walk out of the club's entrance and begin speaking with members of his SWAT team.

These were undoubtedly members of former President King's Secret Service detail. Both the Secret Service and SWAT members looked a bit confused, and Kremer realized he was going to have to break the news.

"Good afternoon, gentlemen," Kremer said as he approached the group. "I'm Captain Kremer with the Sarasota County Sheriff's Office."

"I'm Agent Adams, Secret Service," replied the taller of the three men in suits. He stood about 6'2", the same height as Kremer, and had the stocky build and thick neck and shoulder muscles of an ex-college linebacker. "This is Agents Burns and DiNozzo. I'm in charge of President King's security detail. We weren't informed of any special equipment needed at the Lido Club. Your men here tell me that they're sending a team of snipers up on the roof and also establishing additional measures on the grounds here. I think there's been a misunderstanding."

"I understand," said Kremer, keeping his voice calm. He had a tremendous amount of respect for the Secret Service and knew that if he were in Adams' position, he'd be ticked off with all these SWAT guys showing up announced. "I was told by Sheriff Knight that you'd been informed. I'm sure that…"

"Been informed?" Adams interjected, his voice rising in annoyance. "The Secret Service is in charge of every aspect of security at the Lido Club. While we appreciate your deputies helping us with manpower at the front gate, we take our orders directly from President King. Not the Sarasota County Sheriff."

"Yes, I understand, Agent Adams," Kremer replied in his most diplomatic voice. "I wasn't implying that the Sheriff was giving the Secret Service orders. What I should have said was that your orders have changed and that it's my understanding you'd been informed."

"What are you talking about, Captain? I've received no change to my orders, and I just spoke to my Special Agent-in-Charge less than an hour ago."

As Kremer was about to reply, he noticed a short young man, mid-twenties and wearing a light gray suit with a red bow tie, jog out the front door, quickly descend the entryway steps, and head in their direction.

"Agent Adams!" the young man shouted as he approached, a bit winded. "I'm sorry. I tried to catch you upstairs, and it took me a few minutes to realize you'd already come down here. There's been a change in plans."

"What kind of change?" Adams sighed wearily. Kremer could tell by Adams' reaction that he disdained the young man, and Kremer couldn't argue based on his own first impression. Despite the young man's swarthy complexion and what looked to be a perpetual five o'clock shadow, the slicked-back hair, red bow tie, and overpowering odor of cologne screamed junior political operative with an oversized ego. Kremer had seen the type while escorting King's entourage on occasions and always tried to keep his distance.

"Well, Agent Adams, President King has decided to terminate the Secret Service's protection detail. He has notified your SAC directly, and I've been instructed to let you know. Your team is free to go. The Sarasota Sheriff's Office will handle all security matters going forward."

"What are you talking about, Bout?" Adams asked. "The Secret Service is required to protect all current and former presidents. No offense to your deputies, Captain Kremer, but the Secret Service is responsible for protecting former President King."

"Captain Kremer?" asked the young man, turning towards the SWAT commander and ignoring the Secret Service agent's question. "I'm Gregor Bout, special assistant to President King and your primary liaison. President King has been expecting you. Please take the time you need to get your deputies in position, and I can escort you up to meet President King whenever you're ready."

Kremer and Agent Adams stared back at the young man, silently absorbing what was happening. Both men noticed that Bout had not once made eye contact with either of them and instead seemed to be speaking to the center of their chests. Kremer shifted his gaze to the lead Secret Service agent and watched as Adams' expression turned from annoyance to resignation.

Before Adams could speak, Bout snapped, "You have one hour, Agent Adams, to vacate the Lido Club. Please confirm your orders with your SAC, who I'm confident will instruct you to conduct your handover in a professional manner. Captain Kremer, I'll be in the lobby whenever you're ready to go upstairs and meet President King. Please don't keep me waiting long. I have important matters to attend to."

Not waiting for a reply, Bout turned on his heels and headed back up the stairs to the club's plush lobby.

"That guy's all sunshine and rainbows, huh?" Kremer said to the three Secret Service agents. "I'm sorry for any confusion, gentlemen. I learned about this myself less than an hour ago."

"I can tell you this, Captain Kremer," said Agent Adams. "I've been on King's detail for over a year, and there's hardly a dull moment." Adams paused, taking a deep breath and collecting his thoughts. "Please give me a minute to confirm things with my SAC."

Kremer nodded and watched as the three agents walked ten yards away while Adams pulled a cell phone from the pocket of his suit coat. Adams held a brief phone conversation, then raised his wrist to his mouth and began speaking. Kremer could tell Adams was issuing orders to his men over the radio. Adams then walked directly back to where Kremer was standing under the portico.

"As unbelievable as it may seem, the former President of the United States has formally terminated the protection offered to him by the Secret Service, effective immediately. I've been instructed to have my men retrieve all of our equipment, get their personal items from their rooms, and leave the premises as soon as possible. I've also been told to wish you good luck."

"I'm sorry," said Butch. "I'll send some men up to your command post to coordinate a handover."

Adams looked coldly at Kremer for a second, then his face softened. "I know this has nothing to do with the Sarasota County Sheriff's Office, and I don't envy you at this moment, Captain Kremer. But I don't think you quite understand; there is no transition. We're simply leaving. I've been told to take anything we can remove quickly, including all computers, weapons, and documentation. We'll leave any cameras that are permanently installed in the building." Adams paused for a moment, searching for the right words. "You're on your own. The director of the Secret Service has ordered me and all of my men not to speak with anyone outside the Secret Service. I'm sorry. Good luck to you and your men."

Kremer looked on incredulously as Agent Adams turned and, accompanied by his two sidekicks, walked back into the lobby of the Lido Club. *Well,* he thought to himself, *that wasn't how this was supposed to go.* Sheriff Knight was very specific in his instructions to conduct a proper transition, especially related to the surveillance systems and access control. I need to get my men into their command center to learn as much as we can about the security in place.

Kremer jogged over to where his second-in-command, Lieutenant Jim Jacobs, was supervising the unloading of the SWAT trucks along with more than a half dozen of his SWAT deputies.

"Hey, JJ, this thing's about to become a goat rodeo," briefed Kremer. "King's assistant has a bit of a Napoleon complex, and the Secret Service has been completely blindsided by our arrival. It seems like this is turning into a pissing contest between King's people and the Secret Service, which we want to stay as far away from as possible."

Kremer paused, looking around the grounds and attempting to absorb the layout of the building and various access points. "I want you and Smitty to head up to the Secret Service's command post. Figure out as much as you can, then determine what we're going to need to monitor the entire property and gain full control over all access points. Get the snipers on the roof, and at a minimum, put people on every ingress or egress point you can. Sheriff Knight is coming in an hour, and we can put together a more comprehensive plan at that time."

"Got it, boss. We're on it."

"Oh, and JJ?" Kremer said. "Be careful. This thing is all about politics. Make sure everyone keeps their mouths shut."

"Affirmative," JJ replied, turning to address the SWAT deputies behind him.

Having issued orders to get things rolling, it was now time to meet former President King.

3

Tallahassee, Florida

Sunday, February 4

"WELL, Sam, you know what they say—go big or go home," said Florida governor Vince Marino, sitting back into the plush cushion of the patio chair and putting his cowboy boots up on the glass-topped wicker table in front of him. Never a big drinker, Governor Marino took a long pull from an ice-filled glass of sweet tea. Across from him sat Sam Stryder, his chief of staff and best friend since their college baseball days at Duke. Both men were similarly attired in slacks, sport coats, and open-necked dress shirts, having just flown back on the state-owned private jet from Sarasota, where they'd met with former President King at his Lido Club residence.

Mirroring the governor, Sam took a long sip of his own glass of sweet tea while he considered how best to advise his former college roommate.

"Vince, we need to prepare for the absolute chaos that's going to unfold tomorrow morning. This is a bold plan, and it's the right thing to do, but we need to decide now how far we're willing to take this."

The governor looked across the table, then down at the sweating glass in his hand. What he lacked in height, he more than made up for in cunning, ruthlessness, and the firm belief that God was on his side. Placing his drink on the table, he reached down and unzipped the sides of his leather boots, pulling them off and putting his stocking feet back onto the table. Normally, the governor was very private about removing his boots in front of anyone for fear of them seeing the specially made lifts that added two inches to his five-foot six-and-three-quarter inch frame. But Sam was his closest friend, and despite being six inches taller than the governor, Marino trusted Sam implicitly.

"We planned this all out yesterday, and today's meetings with King and Sheriff Knight added even more detail to the plan. This is it, Sam! This is why we're sitting here in The People's House—the governor's mansion for the third largest state in the country. Fulton and the libtards in DC are completely ruining this country. We have the Constitution on our side, and I'm willing to go as far as it takes."

"Including civil war?" Sam asked.

"It's not going to get to that. Trust me. But to answer your question, yes. You heard the governors of Texas and Georgia on the phone yourself; they fully support this. I've no doubt all the other Republican governors will also support us."

"Like I said," reiterated Sam. "I agree this is the right thing to do. I just want to make sure we've thought through every contingency. King is a bit of a wild card."

"Screw, King," shouted the governor, in a rare use of semi-profanity. "He's doing this to save his own hide and could care less about the country. We're doing this because it's the right thing to do, and history will show that you and I had the guts to put our nation back on the right path and keep it from circling the drain due to Fulton's misuse of Presidential authority."

The governor took another sip of his drink and pulled out his iPhone to check his email, something he often did in mid-conversation. Used to this idiosyncrasy, Sam sat back and thought about the whirlwind of the past forty-eight hours.

What if former President King simply refused to go to federal court this week, and the governor of Florida, exercising the authorities granted to the States by the Tenth Amendment of the Constitution, refused to allow federal law enforcement to arrest him? What would happen?

That was the question Sam had proposed to the governor and his wife as they dug into their chef-prepared supper of grouper and lobster freshly caught from Florida's coastal waters. Both the governor and his politically astute first lady had seized on the idea, and the three of them had talked late into the evening, refining a plan and thinking through all the potential events and repercussions of the answer to Sam's question.

The final amendment to the U.S. Constitution's Bill of Rights, the Tenth Amendment, seemed straightforward: the powers not delegated to the United States by the Constitution, nor prohibited by it to the States, are reserved to the States, respectively, or to the people.

Simply stated, the Founding Fathers outlined specific powers for the three branches of the federal government and also forbade the states from doing certain things, such as issuing their own currency or entering agreements with foreign countries. Any powers not specifically granted to the federal government or that states were specifically prohibited from doing were reserved powers belonging solely to the states.

In Governor Marino's opinion, nothing in the Constitution gave the federal government law enforcement powers, and the Founding Fathers certainly would never support the federal courts being used to further partisan political agendas.

Governor Marino, an attorney by profession and a self-proclaimed Constitutional law expert, believed firmly in the rule of law and the historically proven benefits of the separation of power. Trumping these beliefs was the governor's absolute certainty that he was put on this Earth to make a difference in the lives of others. Therefore, he held the moral imperative to do what was right for society, no matter the difficulty or the cost.

Sam, on the other hand, was a bit more skeptical and pragmatic. He had grown up the son of a long-time U.S. Congressman from North Carolina and, as such, had been privy to the backroom bargaining common to all politics. His father, one of the noblest people he'd ever known who had died in a plane crash more than ten years ago, had taught him to be wary of politicians asserting their moral high ground.

Politics was about power, pure and simple, and the key to power was understanding when to compromise and when to hold firm. Similar to high-stakes poker, the best players knew how to read their opponents and discover their "tell"—the subconscious visible response to how good their cards were. In politics, Sam's father had always said, a politician's "tell" was his confidence in being re-elected by his constituents. Those with less confidence were more likely to compromise and were more susceptible to being bullied, while those politicians who knew they would be re-elected could stand firm on their position and play their cards more shrewdly to build power.

The strongest player in the poker game of politics was the politician who didn't care about reelection. For it was this individual who could truly vote his conscience and do what was right, as the fear of losing power held no sway.

Reviewing the conversations that had taken place over the last forty-eight hours and the decisions that had been made that would irrefutably change the course of the United States, Sam wondered what his father would think.

While he was confident his father would be proud of all that Sam had accomplished, deep down, he knew his father would not support the path they were embarking upon.

"The press conference is starting," said a young man, entering the lanai from the large pool house that ran at the back of the Governor's mansion. He was one of several members of the house staff who was always on duty, and Governor Marino had requested to be reminded when King was starting his televised press conference. The young man used a remote control device stored beneath the large flatscreen television mounted on the wall directly behind where Sam and Governor Marino were sitting. In seconds, an image of former President King standing in the lobby of the Lido Club appeared on the screen.

For the next five minutes, both men watched intently. King's speech was exactly as they'd scripted earlier that morning, and even the answers to the cleverly placed questions from allied reporters seemed genuine.

"The man can certainly fire up an audience," said the governor. "I mean, twenty years ago, people thought George W. Bush came across as a buffoon. King has no business whatsoever being President, but people love his straightforward, off-the-cuff way of speaking. I'll definitely give him that. He has a gift."

"Half the country might be applauding," said Sam. "But the other half are absolutely losing their minds right now. If things go as we think, King won't be the center of attention for long. He has no power, and the election isn't for another nine months."

"Agreed," said the governor. "Should we call Greene now?"

"Yeah, that's the plan. Are you sure you want to reach out directly? He was my professor at UF, and I've kept in loose touch with him over the years. I could easily set up the call."

"Thanks, Sam, but I think it's important the call comes directly from me."

"Understood."

4

Osprey, Florida

Sunday, February 4

"HELLO, Professor Greene, this is Vince Marino. How are you doing this beautiful Sunday afternoon?"

Nathan pressed the phone tightly to his ear as he quickly walked away from the tiki bar's noise towards a shaded area at the rear of the shell parking lot. "I'm well, Governor. How can I be of service?"

"Well, I'm calling about former President King's recent press conference. Did you, by chance, watch it? It was just a few minutes ago."

"I'm actually at a restaurant with my wife, and we happened to see flashes of it on the bar's television. I wasn't able to hear the full details, but as I understand, he's decided not to submit himself to the jurisdiction of the federal court."

"Yes, that about sums it up from my understanding. I was hoping you might have a few minutes to advise me on the constitutional impact of President King's decision."

Nathan paused, attempting to understand why the governor of Florida would be calling him with such a request. "To be frank, sir,

Divided We Stand

I'm not an attorney. I would think you are eminently more qualified than I to understand the nuances of federal and state law and the specifics of former President King's indictments."

"Yes. Yes. That would be true if I were seeking your opinion on the law. What I'm seeking, though, Professor Greene, is a greater understanding of the Founding Father's intent with the Constitution, and specifically the Tenth Amendment. As one of the country's pre-eminent constitutional scholars, not to mention a war hero, I would greatly value your insight. Sam Stryder, one of your former students, is my closest friend and advisor. He's convinced me there is no one more knowledgeable than yourself on this subject."

As Nathan was about to reply, he noticed Emily walking towards him. She had paid the bill and was holding up her car keys, a signal that they should move to the car, which would be much more convenient than standing in the parking lot. Nathan nodded and began following Emily to their car.

"I'm flattered, sir, but I can think of many more learned scholars than myself. Sam was a breath of fresh air in my class—it's not often I see a former Navy SEAL pursuing a graduate degree." Nathan opened the passenger door of Emily's Audi Q7 and slid into the front passenger seat while Emily started the car, and more importantly, the air conditioning. "I'm happy to be of service. What specifically are you interested in knowing about the Tenth Amendment?"

"Do you mind if I call you Nathan?"

"Not at all, sir."

"And would you mind if I placed you on speakerphone? I have Sam here with me, and I'd like him to hear your comments." Before Nathan could answer, he could hear the background noise of the call shift to that of being on speaker.

"Ah, sure. Hello, Sam. I trust you've been well."

"Hi, Nathan," said Sam loud enough to be heard by the iPhone the governor had placed on the table in front of them. "Great to hear your voice. Yes, I've been very well. Busy, but doing well. Yourself?"

"I've been great, Sam—although definitely surprised to get this phone call."

Emily drove the car out of the shell lot and turned left towards Casey Key and home.

"Nathan," said Governor Marino. "As I'm sure you're aware from the media, President King believes that the indictments against him are the result of a political witch hunt. The offenses that are alleged are nothing more than an attempt to get political payback and prevent him from winning the nomination and the Presidency this Fall. The Justice Department and the FBI are no longer impartial purveyors of justice, and therefore, these federal indictments are not valid, nor can he possibly receive a fair trial. President King has asked me to use the power of the state of Florida to protect him until a political solution can be worked out."

"Okay," said Nathan tentatively. "I understand both sides of this argument, but I am not an attorney. The specific case law surrounding the jurisdiction of the federal courts is not something I'm familiar with, nor do I feel comfortable commenting. I'm—"

"Let me be blunt," interrupted the governor. "Does the Constitution, specifically the Tenth Amendment, allow the States to remove the authority of federal law enforcement officers from carrying out their duties within the state? President King has terminated his Secret Service detail, and I have authorized the Sarasota County Sheriff to protect him. This includes protecting him from federal law enforcement agents attempting to arrest him."

Nathan thought carefully, his mind racing to find the most appropriate answer. His leisurely afternoon of a jog and a couple of beers had suddenly turned into a complex game of high-stakes national politics. Nathan knew his next words could have a profound effect on how the governor acted and desperately wanted to give a straightforward answer to an immensely complex question. An attorney would give useless two-handed advice—on the one hand, you can do this, but on the other hand, you could do that. Nathan wanted his answer to be clear and concise.

"I don't want to be wishy-washy with my answer, governor, but you've posed a complex question that touches on a variety of constitutional issues. The direct answer to your specific question, as stated, is *no*—you do not have the authority to remove law enforcement officers from the state. The Articles of Confederation codified the right to free travel between the states and is generally thought to have been incorporated as part of the Privileges and Immunities clause of the Constitution's Article IV, Section 2. That said, what I think you're really asking is: can the federal government exercise police powers within the state against the state's wishes? In 1800, the answer would have been *no*, as these powers were reserved solely to the States by the Tenth Amendment. However, over the last 200 years, relying especially on the Fourteenth Amendment, the Supreme Court has greatly expanded the powers of Congress to include state and local issues that would have appalled the Founding Fathers. As I said, this question is more appropriate for an attorney rather than a political science professor."

"So correct me if I'm wrong," replied the governor. "Under a strict interpretation of the Constitution of the United States, all police powers reside at the State level. Correct?"

"Yes, I would say that is correct. Excluding regulating interstate commerce, punishing felonies committed on the high seas, and prosecuting treason, which are specifically mentioned in the Constitution as powers belonging to Congress. But short of that, I would say you are correct from an academic perspective."

"What do you mean by academic perspective?"

"Sir, I don't think I need to point out that we have almost 140,000 federal law enforcement officers throughout the country, and I imagine more than 5,000 of them are in Florida. There is a difference between powers delineated in the U.S. Constitution and the authority and power you have as governor of Florida in 2024. You may be able to cite the authorities provided by the Tenth Amendment, but the Justice Department has over 10,000 attorneys who would argue differently. As for your power as governor, I think it would be quite difficult for you to go head-to-head against the President of the United States and win this argument."

"Excuse me, Nathan," interjected Sam. "I seem to recall a lecture you gave on this very subject years ago at the University of

Florida. If I remember correctly, you specifically outlined a situation where the federal government could encroach upon the powers of a State to such an extent that the State simply said: enough. At that point, the governor could either declare martial law and rule by decree or if he had the backing of his state's Supreme Court and legislature, he could issue an executive order limiting arrest powers within the state only to those law enforcement personnel authorized directly by the Governor. Isn't that right?"

Nathan shut his eyes and squeezed the bridge of his nose, wishing he were back sipping his Landshark at the tiki bar. They had arrived back at their house, with Emily parking the Audi in the shade of their four-car garage. He nodded to her as she put the keys in the cupholder, leaving the car and air conditioning running, and quietly closed the car door.

"Sam, your recollection is correct, but the context is important for the governor to understand. That lecture was designed to get the class to think about the tug-of-war between the powers of the federal and state governments and to think *philosophically* about how this has changed over time. It was not a blueprint for insurrection."

"Who said anything about insurrection?" Governor Marino asked sharply. "This isn't insurrection. This is protecting the legal authorities granted to the state of Florida by the Constitution of the United States."

"Yes, Governor," replied Nathan. "I understand that is your point of view. I can assure you, though, that the President of the United States and the Attorney General will undoubtedly view this as an insurrection. Under the Insurrection Act of 1807, there are a host of powers granted to the President to respond to such situations —none of which would be good for you or the people of Florida."

"I'll be the judge of that," stated the governor. "I take it from your tone, Professor Greene, that you're not on board with my decision to protect President King."

"Well, sir, to be honest, I haven't given it much thought. It seems to me that this situation is one of authority versus power."

"What do you mean by that," asked Sam over the speakerphone.

32

Divided We Stand

"There is an inherent difference between authority and power. The former grants one legal permission to do something, while the other is the actual ability to make that something happen. For example, you can issue a legal order, but can you actually make someone comply? In this case, it seems to me that you are creating one hell of a pissing contest between you and the President of the United States. I'd have to give it more thought, but I'm not sure protecting the former President is worth the risk of civil war."

"I thought you had disdain for the federal government and were a strong supporter of State's rights," said Marino. "Apparently, your personal convictions are not as strong as your published articles and lectures."

"Governor, I understand this is a tense time for you. If Sam has told you anything about my background, you would understand that my personal convictions are not something you should ever question." Nathan paused to tamp down his growing anger. "This entire discussion seems to me to be a legal one, and I've already told you: I'm not an attorney. That said, while I've met thousands of attorneys in my life, I've never met a single one with any moral backbone. I've often wondered if there's a surgical procedure in law school that removes morality and the ability to stand up for what's morally right versus what's legally correct."

"You do realize I'm an attorney, don't you?" asked the governor.

"Yes, sir. I'm fully aware of that."

Sam watched the color drain from Marino's face. The governor was not used to being spoken to in such a blunt manner, and Sam wanted desperately to keep the conversation on track. "Nathan, would you mind waiting for a moment while we put you on hold? We'll be back in thirty seconds."

"Sure, Sam," replied Nathan, who was immediately put on hold. Nathan wondered if he had enough time to dash into the house and take a seat in his office but decided against it. The car was cool, and the vehicle's audio speakers handled the call well.

In twenty seconds, the governor and Sam came back on the line.

"Nathan," started Governor Marino. "I'm sorry for springing this difficult scenario on you without notice, and I appreciate your obvious expertise on the subject and willingness to be frank with your opinion. I do not like yes-men, and your bluntness is refreshing. I'm going to be in Sarasota tomorrow for a meeting with President King. Would you be available for a private meeting with Sam and I?"

"Of course," Nathan replied without hesitation. "I'm not sure what value I can provide, but I'm happy to meet with you."

"Great," said Marino. "Sam will be in contact with the details. I hope you enjoy the rest of your day. Good-bye."

Before Nathan could say anything, he heard the click of a terminated call.

5

Lido Key, Florida

Monday, February 5

CAPTAIN BUTCH KREMER knew there'd be trouble today as soon as he approached St. Armands Circle. The large traffic circle was located over the bridge from downtown Sarasota and was a half-mile short of the Lido Club and the beaches of Lido Key. Surrounded by dozens of shops and restaurants, the area was a popular destination for both Sarasota residents and the mass of beach going tourists who flock to Sarasota throughout the year. At 7:45 a.m., Butch would normally expect the circle to be virtually empty, as almost all of the shops and restaurants had yet to open for the day.

Not this morning.

As he entered the traffic circle in his Sheriff's Suburban, he stopped his vehicle at the crosswalk to let more than a dozen people cross. If he didn't know better, he'd have assumed a Grateful Dead concert or music festival was in the area. The pedestrians were all wearing tie-dyed T-shirts, shorts, and sandals, with some carrying large posterboards mounted to wooden sticks.

Butch continued driving counter-clockwise around the circle, noting more large groups of people all walking in the direction he was traveling. Unlike the first group, the other groups contained myriad stereotypes: senior citizens, clean-cut college kids, and moms with strollers, to name a few.

The unifying theme among all groups seemed to be the posters and placards they were carrying, all plastered with anti-King slogans.

Damn! Thought Butch. *The only easy day was yesterday.*

Butch had first heard that quote more than twenty years ago as a young Navy SEAL going through Basic Underwater Demolition/SEAL school training in Coronado, California. Back in the day, Butch had been a record-setting quarterback at Sarasota High School and had accepted an appointment to the U.S. Naval Academy in Annapolis. He'd loved the military training of his plebe summer. The football team was everything he'd hoped it would be, and he was looking forward to becoming a Naval officer. On the eleventh day of his first September at Annapolis, nineteen Islamic terrorists hijacked four commercial airplanes, changing the United States and the world forever.

Two things happened in May of his plebe year that would also profoundly impact Butch's future. First, Butch failed Calculus and earned a lowly 2.2 grade point average for the year. At a minimum, he would be required to attend summer school instead of touring the fleet with his classmates, and it was likely he would go before an academic board to determine whether he should be dropped from the Academy. Second, on May 31st, Pat Tillman, a defensive back with the NFL's Arizona Cardinals, enlisted in the U.S. Army to become an Airborne Ranger. After speaking with his Dad, Butch decided to voluntarily resign from the Naval Academy and enlist in the Navy with the goal of becoming a Navy SEAL.

SEAL training was the most mentally and physically demanding thing Butch had ever done—and he loved it! The mantra *"the only easy day was yesterday"* was something he'd continued to embrace well after his six years in the SEALs had ended and throughout his career with the Sarasota County Sheriff's Office. In the military, the mantra often referred to extreme physical exertion, whereas with the Sheriff's Office, it more often than not was in reference to a complicated situation that required patience, perseverance, and outside-the-box thinking.

Butch had met yesterday afternoon directly with former President King and the man's personal aide, Gregor Bout. Butch found King to be very pleasant to deal with, grateful to have Butch's team on board, and generally uninterested in the details of his protection. The only question King asked of Butch was whether King would be able to play golf on a regular basis.

Gregor Bout, on the hand, was a bit of a control freak and demanded he be continuously updated on Butch's plan for securing the Lido Club. Butch noted that Bout was very careful not to seem intrusive while in the presence of the former President, his boss, but once outside King's earshot, he became very difficult to deal with. Adept at dealing with difficult people, which was basically the job description of a Sheriff's deputy, Butch nodded his head at Bout's requests while paying little attention to the specifics of his questions.

Continuing through St. Armands Circle onto Ben Franklin Drive, the gathering activists on the sidewalk closest to the beach seemed denser. Butch had watched the broadcast news last night and this morning, whose coverage of President King's refusal to show up in federal court had been the lead story and Butch was well aware that a significant percentage of the population, probably a majority, greatly opposed King's flaunting of the federal courts.

As Butch neared the blockaded entrance, the Sheriff's deputies moved a vehicle out of the entrance to let him pass. At the same time, the deputies standing in front of the entrance blockade motioned for the gathering crowd of several dozen protesters to disperse from the roadway. While only a few dozen protesters currently stood chanting anti-King slogans, Butch estimated from the numbers of people walking from St. Armands that the total protester count would swell to several hundred by mid-morning.

Butch steered his SUV through the narrow path created by the deputies. Looking to his left, he saw three older ladies in their late seventies or eighties, one of whom reminded him of his late grandmother. They were holding placards that read *No One's Above the Law* and *Don't Make King a King*. Butch smiled and waved politely. Acknowledging his greeting, one of the older women stepped forward and raised her middle finger toward him.

Oh man, he thought. *It's going to be one of those days, isn't it?*

6

Washington D.C

Monday, February 5

SHARYN GRAY FOLLOWED her boss into the Roosevelt Room and placed her leather portfolio in front of a chair farthest from the head of the long conference table. Unlike the Cabinet Room, where she would normally sit directly behind her boss in the seats reserved for "seconds," meetings in the Roosevelt Room were smaller gatherings, and the only chairs in the room were directly at the long, walnut table. A half dozen attendees were already seated, and Sharyn recognized the Attorney General, Deputy Attorney General, and the Director of the FBI. She had dealt with each of them on many occasions in her role as Chief of Staff to the Vice President of the United States, Serena Moore.

The youngest in the room by decades, at twenty-eight, Sharyn exuded a quiet self-confidence that was forty percent real and sixty percent acting. Tall at 5'9", she walked with the lithe grace and assurance of an avid runner and former volleyball player. Despite her attempts to hide it through conservative attire, her natural beauty was impossible to dampen. Unblemished light-brown skin, emerald green eyes, and curly brown hair turned the heads of both men and women.

Sharyn took her seat closest to the fireplace, above which was a portrait of the room's namesake as a Rough Rider on horseback. She watched her boss, Vice President Moore, shake the hands of the Attorney General and his deputy while the FBI director sat huddled in conversation with the two men next to him across the table from where Sharyn sat. The door behind her opened, and she immediately stood up, knowing that particular door led directly from the Oval Office. Sharyn turned to see the President of the United States, Bill Fulton, walk unsteadily through the door, a huge smile on his face. Both VP Moore and the Attorney General walked over to shake the President's hand warmly, with Moore seeming to direct him to his chair at the head of the conference table. The President sat down immediately, motioning for everyone else to sit.

Behind the President strode two men and a woman, the three continuing a hushed conversation as they walked. The first man entering behind the President was John Reynolds, the White House Chief of Staff. An NCAA champion wrestler nearly fifty years previous, Reynolds looked fit enough to go a few rounds on the mat, with a permanent scowl on his face that looked like he'd love to do nothing more than just that. As the Chief of Staff for VP Moore, Sharyn dealt with Reynolds on a daily basis and knew him to be a sweet, highly intelligent man whose passion was sharing pictures of his six grandchildren with anyone who seemed remotely interested. Reynolds had earned the reputation of never stabbing anyone in the back but one who would gladly stick the knife in your chest with a smile. Sharyn continued to be amazed at his ability to navigate the most cutthroat political dealmaking while almost always maintaining the respect of friends and foes alike.

The same could not be true of the younger man sticking closely to Reynold's heels. Brad Nesbitt was John Reynold's deputy and a person Sharyn attempted to avoid at all costs. Tall, slim, and with the dark good looks and chiseled jawline of a Hollywood actor, Brad was loved by his superiors and almost universally despised by his peers and subordinates. A recent *Vanity Fair* article had described him as "one of Washington's most eligible bachelors who was scaling the Democratic ladder at breakneck speeds." Sharyn thought womanizing, deceitful ass-licker was a much more appropriate description, but who was she to judge.

Lastly, Geraldine Fox, the White House Communications Director, entered the room. She disengaged herself from her whispered conversation with Nesbitt and put her hand on Sharyn's shoulder as she took the seat next to her.

"Hey, sister, glad you could make this," Geraldine said quietly as she pulled her chair up to the table. "I told Maggie specifically to add you to the invite list."

The Maggie she was referring to was the President's executive secretary, who handled all matters relating to the President's calendar and who'd phoned Sharyn earlier that morning to tell her about this 8:00 a.m. meeting in the West Wing's Roosevelt Room. Sharyn usually worked in the Vice President's suite of offices in the Eisenhower Executive Office Building next door but attended meetings in the West Wing on a regular basis.

Geraldine was twelve years Sharyn's elder and Sharyn had been one of the select few invited to Geraldine's fortieth birthday bash at the exclusive Pinneaple and Pearls restaurant over by the Marine Barracks on 8th and I Streets. Six feet tall in her stockinged feet, strawberry blond hair, and the figure of a swimsuit model, she had a penchant for nerdy glasses to downplay her beauty and accentuate her Ivy League master's degree and genius IQ.

Sharyn smiled, but Chief of Staff Reynolds started speaking before she could reply.

"Thank you all for coming on short notice and moving whatever else you had planned for this Monday morning." He paused and made eye contact with everyone at the table. The President sat at the head of the table, with VP Moore to his right, along the same side of the table as Sharyn. Next to the Vice President sat the Attorney General and Deputy Attorney General, followed by Geraldine and Sharyn herself. Chief of Staff Reynolds sat directly to the President's left, with the FBI Director, Assistant Director, and a man Sharyn assumed to be a senior FBI agent arrayed on that side of the conference table. "The President wanted to convene a small working group to determine how best to deal with Benjamin King's latest antics. I think you're all aware of Mr. King's speech yesterday afternoon, in which he stated his intended refusal to submit himself to the jurisdiction of the federal court at his arraignment scheduled for 11:00 a.m. this morning. Neil, we spoke last night, but if you could please tell the group your current plan to deal with this, it would give us a starting point from which to comment."

Reynolds nodded at the Attorney General sitting in the middle of the conference table down from Sharyn. Neil Krueger had been appointed Attorney General by President Fulton as part of his original Cabinet and navigated the position's difficulties well over the past three years. A former federal judge who had spent most of his career before becoming a jurist working in the US Attorney's office, Krueger was a trim, dignified man in his late sixties who normally was very thoughtful in everything he said.

"Thank you, John," said Krueger before turning his attention to the head of the table. "Mr. President, as we've spoken about many times, it is important that we treat Mr. King as an ordinary citizen as much as possible. You appointed a special prosecutor to investigate the former President's involvement in several issues, and that independent investigation returned two indictments against Mr. King. That process was undertaken without any interference or cooperation from my office. Mr. King is scheduled to be arraigned on those charges in a little less than three hours. As I told John last night, despite Mr. King's words at his press conference, he has not violated the law until he fails to show up for his arraignment as scheduled."

"And what then, Neil? Will the judge in this case simply issue a warrant for his arrest?"

"In a normal situation, Mr. President, that would be the case. However, as you know, there is nothing normal about this situation. The federal judge in Tampa was appointed by then-President King, and it is unclear how she will react to Mr. King's absence."

"Well, has anyone called her and asked her?" President Fulton asked. "Why don't we get her on the phone right now?"

"Ahh, Mr. President," cautioned the Attorney General. "That would be highly prejudicial behavior on our part. As with any case, I think it's important that there be no collusion between the parties and the judge. As in all federal criminal cases, the Justice Department is the prosecuting party, so it would be inappropriate for anyone in the executive branch to phone the judge directly."

"So what do you suggest, Neil?" asked the President. "Should we just sit here while that fool makes a mockery of our entire criminal justice system?"

"No, Mr. President, that's not what I'm suggesting at all. I received notice last night that the independent prosecutor will be at the arraignment this morning and is prepared to request the judge issue an arrest warrant for Mr. King. It would be highly unlikely for her to deny this request unless Mr. King's attorneys ask for some sort of continuance or provide a valid reason for Mr. King's absence. To be honest, Mr. President, from a legal perspective, King has just shot himself in the foot. After his public press conference, any attempt by his attorneys to explain King's absence this morning would hurt King with his constituents."

The President looked at Krueger for a minute before turning to his Chief of Staff. "Who's that attractive young lady at the end of the conference table?" The President asked in a voice loud enough for everyone to hear as he pointed down toward Sharyn. "Why, hello there, young lady. What's your position?"

Sharyn looked on in horror as most around the table rolled their eyes. Over the last three years in the Fulton administration, Sharyn had attended more than a hundred meetings with the President, although, in fairness to him, she rarely found occasion to speak with him directly. This was now the second time in the last month that he had singled her out during a meeting. At eighty-two years old, President Fulton was the oldest president ever to sit in office, exceeding Ronald Reagan, who was 77 at the end of his second term in 1989.

The White House senior staff had grown accustomed to the President's frequent ruminations, and VP Moore leaned in as an elder daughter would. "Mr. President, that's Sharyn Gray. I'm sure you remember her from the campaign and our efforts on the Infrastructure and Jobs bill—she led that push for us."

President Fulton stared directly at the Vice President for a solid three seconds, a blank look on his face. Everyone watched silently. Like the flip of a light switch, the President came to life and almost seemed offended by the Vice President's motherly tone. "Of course, I know who Sharyn is, Serena. We go way back, don't we, girl? I remember when I first met her on the campaign…Michigan, I think it was…we had ice cream cones."

The Vice President, Sharyn, and Geraldine all smiled, knowing that this was actually accurate. Sharyn had first been introduced to the President while on a campaign stop walking the streets of Dearborn, Michigan and the President had steered all of them into an ice cream shop, as he was wont to do.

"Mr. President," said his Chief of Staff, attempting to get the meeting back on track. "I think you already have a good handle on the situation. Why don't you brief us on your plan to manage this potential political situation going forward."

"Yes, John. That's a good idea," said President Fulton, now seeming as sharp as ever as he reviewed the stack of index cards his staff prepared for him before every meeting. "As you all know, I started out as a prosecuting attorney in Philadelphia before working my way up to U.S. Attorney for the Eastern District of Pennsylvania. My office window looked right out at the Liberty Bell and Independence Hall, and I know what this country stands for. King is openly flouting the federal court's jurisdiction over him on these matters. In essence, he is…flouting; that's a word, right? Did I use that right? Or is it flubbing?"

"Yes, Mr. President, flouting is correct."

"Right as rain. Just keeping you on your toes, John," the President continued, smiling his grandfatherly smile and glancing down at his index cards. "We won't stand for it. King is attempting to sell the American public a bill of goods, and I have no doubt this is just the beginning. At the same time, we can't let this man distract us from running the country. I'm creating a special working group—called Working Group Delta. The D in Delta stands for deputies.

Serena here," the President said, turning towards the Vice President. "She will chair the working group. She's a former District Attorney, State Attorney General, and U.S. Attorney, so no one knows these issues better than her. Justice, FBI, the deputies you brought here this morning will be on this group, as will my chief of staff and the vice president's chief of staff, young Sharyn, down at the end of the table. Am I missing anything, John?" The President turned once again to his Chief of Staff sitting to his left.

Before he could reply, VP Moore asserted herself into the conversation. "No, Mr. President, I think you've covered all you need to at this point. For everyone's full benefit and protection, prior to this meeting, the President signed an executive order naming the individuals in this room to Working Group Delta and authorizing us to take the action we deem necessary to ensure former President King receives fair and impartial treatment under the law, while also not being able to skirt the law as he is currently trying to do. Our group will meet regularly in the Eisenhower Executive Office Building next door. If the Vice President, Attorney General, and FBI Director met daily with the President here in the White House, the press would think we're running scared. No one will take notice of the deputies convening over at the EEOB. Lastly, the President's executive order has classified the existence of our working group, as well as anything we produce. Is that clear?"

Everyone around the table nodded their head in the affirmative.

"Boy Scouts?" Queried President Fulton.

"Excuse me, sir?" Replied the Vice President, unsure what in the world the President was referring to. She immediately glanced over to John Reynolds and his deputy to see if they could interpret.

"Boy Scouts," insisted the President. "I thought we are meeting Boy Scouts today."

"Ah, yes," interjected Brad Nesbitt, the deputy chief of staff who had remained entirely silent throughout the meeting so far. "I told the President earlier that a group of the top Eagle Scouts from every state will be visiting with him in the Rose Garden. It's not for another couple of hours."

John Reynolds nodded briefly, pulling out his iPhone and

sending a quick text. In moments, the door behind the President opened, and a bearded man in his late twenties walked in. He looked harried, carried a sheaf of thin binders, and had a lanyard tucked into the pocket of his suit coat. Sharyn nodded at him, but the young man was too focused on the President. This was Anthony Best, personal aide to the President of the United States—otherwise known as his bodyman. Sharyn and Anthony had developed a strong friendship, and Sharyn often went to dinner and socialized with Anthony and his husband as they lived in the same apartment building as her, along the edge of Dupont Circle.

"Mr. President," said Anthony quietly, leaning down to speak in President Fulton's ear. "Maggie has some paperwork for you to sign in the Oval Office before we meet with Senators Robbins and Conrad."

"Of course," said the President. "Great work here today, folks. You're all great Americans. Keep your eye on the ball, and I'm sure you'll keep me updated." The President stood up abruptly, and Anthony pulled out his chair. As the President turned from the table, his head swiveled between the two doors. To his left was the door to the Oval Office, through which he had entered fifteen minutes prior. To his right was the door leading to the hallway used by the staff, down which was the President's dining room and the Chief of Staff's office.

Seeing his hesitation and uncertainty, Anthony stepped forward and tenderly took the President by the elbow, steering him to the left. "I believe Maggie's in the Oval Office, Mr. President. Right this way."

As soon as the door to the Oval Office closed behind the President, VP Moore said, "Okay, everyone. It's game time. Secretary Krueger and Director Tracy, you are welcome to stay, but I know you may have other pressing matters. Please feel free to leave whenever you need. For the rest of us, let's figure out what we're going to do with King before he makes a laughing stock of the entire justice system and the Constitution.

7

Lido Key, Florida

Monday, February 5

NATHAN HAD DRIVEN past the entrance to the Lido Club on countless occasions, but he'd never had a reason to venture onto its property. He approached along Ben Franklin Drive, the public beach to his right with multistory condo buildings and houses all around. Nathan raised his eyebrow at the number of protesters gathered along the street. Numerous Sheriff vehicles formed a barrier across the front of the property, and as he turned into the entrance, two large, white Sheriff's Suburbans with red-and-blue-light bars blocked his path, looking like two big horn sheep ready to butt heads.

A uniformed deputy approached his vehicle, and after verifying his identification, Nathan proceeded onto the grounds, parking near the entrance. He smiled at how out of place his twelve-year-old Jeep Grand Cherokee looked, parked next to the other vehicles in the valet parking area. To his right was a line of several black Suburbans, several with Florida State Police license plates. Nathan knew these were likely Governor Marino's, at whose request Nathan had come. To his left was a sleek dark-gray Mercedes Maybach limousine, as well as several Maybach sedans and what appeared to be a vintage Rolls-Royce.

"Professor Greene?" said a voice behind him, causing Nathan to turn. Standing under the portico was a slim man in a suit, complete with gelled hair and a bow tie. The man extended his hand as he approached Nathan. "It's a pleasure to meet you, sir. My name is Gregor Bout, and I'm President King's assistant. If you'd be so kind as to follow me, everyone is gathered on the Garden Terrace."

"Good morning, Gregor," said Nathan, shaking the young man's hand. "Lead the way."

Without another word, Gregor turned on his heel and began walking briskly back towards the Lido Club's main entrance. He made no effort at small talk, seemingly content to walk and text at the same time and completely ignoring Nathan. Nathan dutifully followed, taking in the opulence of the private club as he walked. Nathan knew the historic building set on six acres of Gulf-front property had been built in the late 1920s at the height of the pre-Depression boon, around the same time the Ringling brothers made Sarasota their home. As he followed Bout's quick pace through the massive main lobby, Nathan was reminded of the Ringling Museum several miles up the coast. With twenty-foot ceilings, ornately carved glass-paned doors, and marble everywhere one looked, it was easy to appreciate the opulence of the club's decor. Through massive windows to the front, acres of intensely groomed gardens stretched towards the white sugar sand beach and the aquamarine waters of the Gulf of Mexico. Ebullient, manicured, borderline pompous, and one hundred percent over-the-top, the Lido Club seemed to Nathan a perfect match for what he knew of Benjamin King's personality.

Point man Gregor turned sharply along a side corridor, and in seconds, Nathan had entered a large sunlit room, a minimum of forty feet on a side, with a placard in the doorway naming this the Garden Terrace Room. The far wall was dominated by floor-to-ceiling glass windows and doors, providing a stunning view across a large swimming pool and the beach. On the far side of the pool, toward the edge of the property, Nathan could see a large Sikorsky executive helicopter resting on a helipad. Nathan saw a half dozen men standing near a buffet table on the far side of the room. The men were all dressed in business suits, and most had a cup of coffee in their hands. Years ago, Nathan had sworn never again to wear a tie, so he was dressed smartly in a linen olive blazer, open-necked light-blue dress shirt, and khaki slacks. He momentarily felt slightly underdressed but realized it wasn't as if he were trying to impress anyone.

Gregor stopped at the open door to the room, motioning for Nathan to enter on his own. Nathan watched one of the men detach themselves from the group conversation and walk towards him.

"Nathan! I'm so glad you could come," said Sam Stryder, Nathan's former graduate student and current governor's right-hand man. The two shook hands warmly, with Sam tugging Nathan towards the group of men on the far side of the room. 'C'mon, let me introduce you to the Governor and President King."

As Nathan and Sam approached the remaining men, Governor Marino stepped away from the group and took several quick steps toward Nathan.

"Professor Greene!" Exclaimed the governor, extending his hand in greeting. "It's a pleasure to meet you finally. I'm so glad you could join us this morning."

"My pleasure, Governor," replied Nathan.

"Please, call me Vince. You're among friends. Let me introduce you to President King." As the governor turned toward the remaining three men in the room, Nathan couldn't help but notice that Governor Marino was taller than he'd anticipated. People had always joked about the governor being 5'7", but to Nathan, he appeared at least 5'9". Nathan stole a quick glance at the governor's shoes—polished black cowboy boots under the cuff of his tailored navy suit pants.

Shoe lifts? He thought to himself and smiled.

"President King? I'd like you to meet Professor Nathan Greene," said Marino.

"Ah, Dr. Greene," said King as he shook Nathan's outstretched hand. "It is indeed a pleasure to meet you. I've been told so much about you."

"The pleasure is all mine, President King. But I caution you not to believe everything you hear!" Nathan replied with a sly smile.

Nathan had actually met King's predecessor once at a ceremony at the White House a decade previously but had been unsure how to properly address a former President. He and his wife, Emily, had joked about it over breakfast earlier that morning, and Emily had actually looked it up. According to Emily Post, the revered etiquette expert, former presidents are supposed to be addressed as "Mr." However, in most settings, especially informal ones where the current President is not present, former presidents are almost always addressed as "Mr. President."

"No need to be modest, Nathan. You don't mind if I call you Nathan, do you? Please feel free to call me President King," the former president replied with a chuckle. "Just kidding, Nathan. Forgive me. A little presidential humor."

"Nathan's fine, sir." Nathan was instantly disarmed by the man's charm. Despite all he'd read and seen on television, especially all the rants and rhetoric, the man was instantly engaging on a personal level.

"It's not every day I get to meet a former Army officer with Delta Force who's been awarded the Medal of Honor. And a constitutional law professor at Stanford as well. Your parents must be very proud of you, son."

"Yes, sir, they are," Nathan replied, not feeling it necessary to divulge that both of his parents had passed away several years prior.

"Do you know Orlean here?" King asked, nodding to the older of the two gentlemen standing next to President King. "Orlean's a true patriot as well."

Orlean Brumback was the founder of the most successful conservative media group in the country, Bunker Hill Media. Over the last twenty years, Brumback had turned his syndicated radio show into a media empire worth hundreds of millions of dollars, complete with disciples on TikTok, countless well-funded political action committees, and a behind-the-scenes political machine that was influential in conservative elections at the local, state and federal level across the country. Nathan knew that Brumback had been an unofficial advisor during King's previous administration, but he had no idea Brumback was involved in King's current legal situation.

"Only by reputation," replied Nathan as Orlean Brumback stepped forward to shake Nathan's hand. Brumback was six feet tall, soft, and had a closely trimmed full gray beard that compensated for his shiny pate, which was almost completely bald. His perfectly capped white teeth fell well short of a movie star smile and appeared to Nathan more like the grin of a conniving carny. "Nice to meet you, Mr. Brumback."

"The pleasure is all mine, Professor Greene. And as you just said, don't believe everything you hear."

"I never do," said Nathan.

Not waiting to be introduced, the last man in the group thrust his hand forward toward Nathan. Marathon-runner lean and of medium height, the man appeared Nathan's age and had Slavic features—high cheekbones, chiseled jaw, and piercing blue eyes. So severe was his look that Nathan expected the man to speak with some form of Eastern European accent.

"And I'm Alex Treacher," the man said in as accentless a voice as a California newscaster. "It's nice to meet you." No further information about the man was provided, and Nathan didn't have time to ask.

"Shall we get started, gentlemen?" Governor Marino suggested, motioning for everyone to take a seat at one of the long tables in front of the glass windows. "It's 9:30, and President King is expected to be at his arraignment in Tampa in ninety minutes. Obviously, he won't be going, but we need to have our strategy agreed upon before our press conference. Please, have a seat. Nathan, if you're hungry, there's coffee, water, and plenty of food."

The six men sat down at the table, King at the head of the

table. Governor Marino, Sam, and Nathan sat on one side, with Orlean Brumback and Alex Treacher on the other. Nathan had never heard of Treacher and had no idea of the man's role this morning. At first glance, the man seemed almost irrelevant, surrounded by several of the most powerful conservative men in American politics. Upon closer inspection, Nathan wasn't so sure. The man's suit was impeccably tailored and of the finest quality, while the IWC Portugieser watch on his wrist was worth north of $100,000.

Governor Marino started the informal meeting: "In less than two hours, the world will know that President King stands up to bullies and that the United States Constitution is no longer fodder to be watered down and dissolved by the woke agenda of President Fulton and his merry band of misfits up in D.C. We will no longer tolerate this President and his party using the FBI and the Justice Department to exact personal retribution and steal another election from the American people.

"President King's press conference yesterday afternoon put people on notice, as did his termination of his Secret Service detail. The Lido Club is under the full protection of the Sarasota County Sheriff's Office, and Sheriff Knight answers to no one but me. We've called a press conference for 10:30 this morning. We'll keep the press waiting an extra fifteen minutes, and at 10:45, President King and I will jointly address the assembled media. Orlean and Nathan, we'd like you on the dais with us but standing off to one side. We won't be fielding any questions, so there's no need for either of you to speak, but your presence will show that we have conservative America fully behind us as well as the nation's foremost expert on the Constitution."

"Not to mention a certified war hero," added President King.

Nathan successfully kept the surprise from his face. He'd agreed to this meeting mostly due to his respect for Sam Stryder but also out of a sense of duty to provide advice to his governor when requested. No one had mentioned participating in a press conference, and Nathan had no intention of doing so.

"Orlean, what do you think Fulton's most likely response will

Divided We Stand

be? A half-hearted speech telling the country that no man is above the law?"

"Well, if I were him, I'd say nothing. However, as soon as the Special Prosecutor gets the judge to sign an arrest warrant for President King, which I have no doubt Judge Carney will do, I would send several dozen U.S. Marshals to arrest the former President and physically bring him before the judge. The deputies manning the front will have no option but to comply as they are sworn to uphold the law."

"That's where you're wrong, Orlean. The deputies out front are sworn to defend the Constitution and enforce the laws of the *state of Florida*. With my executive order this morning, acting under powers granted to me by the Constitution's Tenth Amendment, federal law enforcement officers in the state of Florida no longer have arrest powers."

"Bravo," said Alex, clapping his hands together lightly. "I love it."

"I agree," said Orlean. "But do you think Fulton is going to just stand by and watch President King give him the finger? The American people are going to love this—it's exactly what they have always loved about President King. Do what's right, damn the politics, and drain the swamp."

"What do you think, Nathan?" President King asked. "Does the Constitutional argument hold up? Does this Tenth Amendment give the governor this power?"

Nathan paused before answering, not wanting to alienate everyone in the room. "As I told Governor Marino last night, Mr. President, I'm not an attorney. This is a very nuanced legal argument that I am wholly unqualified to advise on."

"Then why are you here," asked Alex.

"I was asked by the governor, so I came. How about you, Alex? What's your role in all of this."

Alex sat back in his chair, assessing Nathan coolly. "I guess you could say I'm a substantial investor in Orlean's media group, and I have some experience providing advice to senior politicians. Like you, though, I'm not an attorney. Just a businessman."

"But I'm told you're one of the foremost experts on the U.S. Constitution, Nathan," said King, attempting to get an answer to his original question. "I keep hearing Tenth Amendment this, Fourteenth Amendment that. I'm not asking for a legal opinion. I'm asking what the Constitution means."

"Yes, sir. I know you're looking for a black-and-white answer. From the Constitution's perspective, and by that I mean the document ratified in 1778 with the first ten amendments, as well as the seventeen subsequent amendments. Under that document alone, Article Three provides for the establishment of the Supreme Court and such inferior Courts as the Congress shall, from time to time, ordain or establish. This means the Middle District of Florida federal court, located in Tampa, is a lawful court established by Congress, and as you are a U.S. citizen, it has jurisdiction to try your case. However, nowhere in the Constitution is the federal government expressly authorized police or law enforcement powers, which is a function of the Executive branch, not the Judicial branch of government. The Tenth Amendment states simply that the federal government has only those powers delegated in the Constitution and that all other powers reside with the States. Law enforcement, therefore, from a strict Constitutional perspective, is the sole domain of the state. In this case, in Florida, the domain of Governor Marino."

"Excellent," said President King. "Then what we're doing is not only morally right but also lawful under the Constitution."

"Sir, if I may," continued Nathan. "While I've provided an analysis as a political science scholar, we have over 230 years of Supreme Court decisions that would take exception to my conclusions. The Court has ruled consistently that federal law enforcement operates under the inherent powers of the Executive branch to enforce laws that Congress has passed. This began with the Judiciary Act of 1789 and has been in force ever since."

"But it's not in the Constitution, right?" Governor Marino asked. "That's the point. The Supreme Court, as we've seen over time, is a political beast that sways with the appointments of individual justices. Never in the history of our country has a sitting President unleashed the Justice Department and the federal court system on persecuting a former President. It's time we hit reset and go back to our founding document to guide our actions."

"So, Vince?" asked the former president. "This was originally Orlean's idea, but you seem to have taken the ball and run with it. What's going to happen when I don't show up in court later this morning?"

"I would assume that the judge is going to issue a warrant for your arrest, and the U.S. Marshals Service will drive here to Lido Key and attempt to arrest you and take you before the federal judge in Tampa."

"But your Sheriff deputies outside, under that Butch fellow I met yesterday, they're going to keep the Marshals out?"

"That's right," said Marino. "I have already signed the executive order rescinding the arrest powers of all federal law enforcement officers, as well as their right to carry open or concealed weapons without a properly issued permit from the State of Florida. I am personally going to hand a copy of the order to Lieutenant Kremer so he can give it to the first federal law enforcement agent who shows up at the Lido Club."

"I like it," said King. "I like it a lot. You're a good friend, Vince. And I take care of my friends."

"What then?" interjected Nathan.

"What do you mean?" asked Governor Marino.

"What do you think is going to happen after you confront the Marshals? Is the local sheriff going to arrest U.S. Marshals for carrying firearms? How do you think that is going to go down? What if President Fulton sends the FBI's Hostage Rescue Team to apprehend President King? What then?"

"That's not going to happen," said Sam, speaking for the first time and defending his governor. "Fulton doesn't have the balls or the political clout. It's going to be a standoff, and President King's going to use that standoff to propel him back into the White House this coming November."

"That's right, Nathan," added Orlean Brumback. "We've thought through this as carefully as a chess grandmaster. President

King is going to win in a landslide this November, similar to Reagan in 1984. Once he's President again, all of this will go away. Except, President King will ensure that state's rights remain intact, as our founding fathers had always intended."

"You don't seem to be on board," said President King, looking at Nathan. "Is that true, Nathan? Because I need people around me that are onboard."

Nathan thought carefully for a moment. "Mr. President, with all due respect, I'm not sure I add any further value to this discussion. I'm not partisan, nor am I political—not in any way. I have served my country, but I don't think my skills are of any use to you in this situation. I stand by my interpretation of the U.S. Constitution, but if there's nothing further, I should probably leave you gentlemen to continue your planning."

"But we wanted you at the press conference, Nathan," said Marino. "I understand your reluctance, but this is an opportunity to be a part of the inner circle."

"I appreciate that, Governor, I really do," said a cautious Nathan. "And I sincerely hope that what you are doing is what's best for the country. As you probably know, I've recently taken a sabbatical from my duties as a professor at Stanford, and I've committed to my wife and daughter that they will be my sole priority until my daughter graduates high school. I hope you can understand that."

Nathan noticed Alex Treacher eyeing him shrewdly from across the table. Something about the man raised the hair on the back of Nathan's neck. Over the course of numerous deployments and countless Top-Secret missions as a Special Forces officer in the Army and clandestine paramilitary officer with the Central Intelligence Agency, Nathan had developed a fine-tuned sense of danger. Looking at Alex, he had the sense that this was a very dangerous individual.

Orlean patted his palm down on the table, getting everyone's attention. "The man's mind is made up, and we thank you for your time this morning, Nathan. It was a pleasure to meet you. It's not every day we are graced with the presence of a Medal of Honor recipient. We trust that you will keep the details of this meeting in your utmost confidence." It was a statement, not a question.

"Of course, Orlean," said Nathan, standing up. "Mr. President, Governor, meeting you both in person was truly a pleasure and an honor. I wish you all the best of luck."

Sam stood as well, but Nathan noted the others lowered their eyes and didn't make further eye contact with him as he stood.

"I'll show you out, Nathan," said Sam.

8

Sarasota, Florida

Monday, February 5

BUTCH KREMER STOOD in the operations center that they'd commandeered from the Secret Service when his deputies took over responsibility for protecting former President King at the Lido Club. He leaned down behind one of the two deputies who continually manned the operations center tucked away in a small room behind the club's ornate lobby. The room was large enough to contain two computer workstations, a weapons storage locker, and a small break area that kept the on-site deputies fueled with caffeine and snacks throughout their shifts. The room smelled of bad coffee, stale sweat, and boredom. He let his gaze wander across the dozens of camera views depicted on the three flatscreen monitors on the wall to his front.

Each monitor was divided into a dozen boxes, with each box corresponding to a camera mounted somewhere on the property. The left monitor contained the cameras at the front of the club, around the entrance, and along Benjamin Franklin Drive. The center monitor showed the cameras arrayed along the rear of the property and the beach, while the right monitor showed cameras mounted throughout the interior of the club.

Butch focused his attention on the left-hand monitor as he was currently most concerned with what was happening at the entrance to the Lido Club. Six private security guards manned the width of the barrier erected at the front of the club while four of his deputies stood behind the two large, white Suburbans positioned across the entrance driveway, giving them the ability to move a vehicle out of the way when an authorized person arrived or departed.

On the left side of the entrance barrier, beyond the dense eight-foot hedge surrounding the front and sides of the property, gathered more than a hundred protestors. The protestors came in all shapes, sizes, and colors, and many held large signs or placards with derogatory slogans about former President King. So far, Butch's men had found the protestors peaceful, respectful, and willing to stay within the roped-off area designated for them to freely assemble and exercise their right to free speech.

On the right side of the entrance were the reporters, including clusters of television crews, print reporters from the major newspapers, and independent stringers. A line of vans topped with satellite dishes dotted the street as far as the security camera could capture.

It was almost noon, and Butch had put his men on high alert as soon as the former president and current governor held their press conference a little over an hour ago. The Sheriff was expecting the U.S. Marshals to present themselves at the front gate with an arrest warrant for Benjamin King and had told Butch that he was keeping at least two contingents of ten deputies in the area of Lido Key to respond to anything that Butch's on-site team of deputies couldn't handle.

In addition to the four deputies manning the front entrance, Butch had an additional four deputies roaming the grounds along the side and rear of the Lido Club, four snipers on the roof, and a quick reaction force of four SWAT deputies who were currently sitting in a spare room down the hall. These deputies augmented a private security force employed directly by King that numbered at least twenty armed security guards. These private contractors managed security within the Lido Club itself, especially President King's personal quarters on the top floor.

Butch's cell phone vibrated in his pocket. Grabbing it, he saw it was a call from Sheriff Knight.

"Hey, sir, any news?" Butch asked, not wasting time with pleasantries. It was the fifth call he'd received from the Sheriff in the last hour.

"Yeah, Butch. I just received a call from the U.S. Marshal for the Middle District of Florida. Judge Carney has issued an arrest warrant for Benjamin King, and the Marshal was giving me a courtesy call to inform me that two Marshal's vehicles would be arriving in the next ten minutes to arrest King. He assumed we would cooperate."

"Okay," said Butch. "And I assume you still want me to bar them access to the property. Is that still the plan?"

"You got it. Both the governor and former president are still inside the Lido Club, is that correct?"

"Yes, sir. They're up in the member lounge on the top floor. Should I notify them?"

"No, I'll do that. You focus on the front gate. I don't anticipate the Marhals pulling a fast one like trying to gain access through the beach, but make sure every deputy is on alert."

"Roger. I'm going to put two of my QRF outside the door of the member lounge with strict instructions to disarm and arrest anyone who may get through our security perimeter."

"Sounds good. And Butch? Remember, everything you do will be filmed by a dozen television cameras. All the deputies have been well-briefed, and your presence at the gate will provide a calming effect and keep this from getting out of hand. The Marshals are just trying to do their job, but it's now *our* job to see that they can't execute that warrant. That order comes directly from the Governor, and he's the one who ultimately signs our paychecks."

"Yes, sir. We're on it."

"I have complete confidence in you," said the Sheriff before ending the call.

Butch glanced once more at the monitors to confirm that nothing had changed anywhere on the property.

"Okay, guys," Butch said to the two deputies manning the workstations in the operations center. "That was Sheriff Knight. I'm heading out to the front gate. Keep a close eye on everything and ensure everyone is alert to what's happening. Looks like the Marshals should be here inside ten minutes."

Both men replied in the affirmative, and Butch grabbed his green baseball hat emblazoned with SCSO and headed out the door. He wore his usual SWAT uniform, complete with an armored plate carrier and pistol belt, and felt the surge of adrenaline he'd always felt before executing a mission. *Here we go*, he thought. *Don't screw it up.*

By the time Butch made his way to the entrance of the club, the Marshals had arrived. Walking out under the entrance's portico towards the barrier along Ben Franklin Drive, Butch could clearly see the two black Suburbans with U.S. Government license plates stopped in front of his deputies. Though unmarked, Butch knew from the extra aerial antennas and the blue lights embedded in the front grill of each of the vehicles that the U.S. Marshals had come to town. Butch was drawn to the contrast between the black Marshal's vehicles and the pure white Sheriff's vehicles. *I hope this isn't an analogy of good and evil*, thought Butch. *At least with our white trucks, we should be the good guys in all of this.*

As Butch walked up next to two of his deputies standing in front of the blockade, the front doors of both black Suburbans opened. Out stepped four men wearing khaki slacks and navy polo shirts with the emblem of the five-pointed star of the U.S. Marshals above the left breast.

Butch had expected the men to be wearing armored plate carriers similar to the one Butch and his men wore, but clearly, someone had made the decision to look less threatening when attempting to arrest the former President of the United States. Each Marshal wore a holstered sidearm on their belt, but other than that, the men had no additional equipment.

"Afternoon, deputy," said the taller of the four men as he

approached. He was a hair over six feet, wiry, with a steel gray crew cut. "I'm Deputy U.S. Marshal Wes Hanson. We are here to serve an arrest warrant for Benjamin King. I believe my boss has already spoken with the Sheriff. We'd appreciate you moving your vehicles so we can execute the warrant." He held up a stapled sheaf of papers, folded length-wise.

Both men were aware that they were being filmed by dozens of television cameras, at least several of which were likely broadcasting live. It was not lost on Butch that this was a historic moment for the country.

"I'm sorry, Marshal," said Butch, uttering the speech he'd prepared earlier based on his conversations with both the Sheriff and the Governor himself. "While I have the utmost respect for you and your men, I have been informed by the Sheriff that a recent executive order issued by the Governor of the State of Florida has suspended the arrest powers of all federal law enforcement officers, including the U.S. Marshals Service. Consequently, I am not able to provide access to this private property."

The Marshal looked at Butch for a solid five seconds without expression or reply. "I know you're just following orders, Deputy, but is that really how you want to play this? I can arrest you and your men on felony obstruction charges right now. I sincerely don't want to do that. Please step aside and let us do our job."

"My orders come directly from the Governor," replied Butch.

"And mine come directly from the President of the United States. You're way out of your league, Deputy. This is not a traffic stop or a domestic disturbance call, which I've no doubt you're well experienced. Step aside."

Butch looked at the Marshal and promptly realized he didn't like the man.

"I'll tell you what, *Mr. Hanson*," said Butch, taking two steps forward to get directly in front of the Marshal. "It is not my intention to publicly embarrass any of you, but I will if you force me. I strongly suggest that you and your compatriots keep your hands well away from your sidearms. I don't know what your contingency orders are from *your* boss, or from the President of the United States, but I can tell you that *I* have very specific instructions not to allow you onto this property."

Butch paused to ensure all four Marshals were paying attention. "I am going to count to three, after which I am going to arrest all four of you for unlawful open carry of a firearm. I will disarm you, handcuff you, and you will be transported to the Sarasota County jail. What happens after that is above my pay grade, but I can assure you, I *will* follow my orders."

"You're making a grave mistake, Deputy...uh," the Marshal looked down to read the name tape on the front of Butch's plate carrier. "Oh, I'm sorry...Lieutenant Kremer. You don't want to do this."

"It's not a question of want, Mr. Hanson. You no longer have any authority in the state of Florida. Please get in your vehicles and call your boss. You are not entering this property."

"You're committing a felony, Kremer, and on national television. I could arrest you right now."

"You can't, though. So stop the nonsense," said Butch. "I'm showing you respect, Marshal. Get in your vehicles. Leave and call your boss."

"One word from me, Lieutenant, and my men will arrest you at gunpoint. You'll then spend..."

"Stop!" Butch commanded, holding up his hand. "Enough with the idle threats, Marshal. Get in your vehicles. This is going to be resolved way higher up the food chain than the two of us."

"Idle threats? Who do you think you're talking to?" The Marshal responded. He turned to the two fellow Marshals on his right. "Billy, go ahead and..."

"Enough!" Butch growled. "The four of you are openly carrying dangerous firearms without authority in violation of Florida law. The last thing I want is for any of my deputies to have to live the rest of their lives knowing they took the life of a fellow law enforcement officer who was being stupid and pigheaded. The order has already been given, gentlemen. The four snipers on the roof will shoot you in the head should you so much as think about pulling your pistol on me."

Butch paused to let this sink in. He made eye contact with each of the four U.S. Marshals. The three, other than Hanson, seemed to want to be anywhere but at that location. "Let's stop the games, shall we? You don't want to be martyrs, and I don't want to be the hero who did his duty. So, Marshals, one…"

Butch paused.

"Two…"

He paused again.

"Three."

As he finished his count, the two deputies on Butch's left turned and walked back to their vehicle. Seeing this, Hanson and the driver of his vehicle quickly did the same.

Thank God, thought Butch. *This whole thing is getting out of control.*

Butch expected the two black Suburbans to reverse and drive away. However, the vehicles remained in place, and Butch could see Hanson speaking on his cell phone.

9

Washington D.C

Monday, February 5

THE VICE PRESIDENT WAS FUMING.

She sat behind her 19th-century wooden executive desk and watched the live feed on a television mounted in the bookcase to her left. To her front were two gray, paisley-patterned sofas positioned opposite each other, upon which Sharyn Gray sat with the same deputy attorney general who had attended the Working Group Delta meeting the day before.

His name was Brent Swartz, and while he was undoubtedly a very bright man and an experienced attorney, Sharyn found him to be the epitome of what was wrong with career civil servants in Washington. It seemed like his every comment, proposal, or decision was filtered through a cheesecloth of bureaucracy and politics to the point that what came out the other side was so watered-down and mild as to be completely ineffective or irrelevant.

Every new idea Sharyn proposed, Swartz inevitably met with a litany of reasons not to do something or a list of people who might take offense or be politically opposed. With a staff full of Brent

Swartzes on the team, Sharyn was amazed that anything actually got done at the Justice Department.

"What the hell stunt is that little runt trying to pull off?" Shouted Vice President Moore at the television. "This is complete and utter political bullshit!"

They were watching the live feed of the U.S. Marshals getting back into their vehicles after attempting to serve the arrest warrant on Benjamin King. An hour earlier, the Vice President had spoken directly with the U.S. Marshal for the Middle District of Florida and let him know, in no uncertain terms, how important it was for his best deputies to arrest Benjamin King and bring him before the Court.

VP Moore violently jabbed a button on the phone on her desk.

"Yes, Madame Vice President?" Came the voice of the Vice President's administrative assistant who sat at a small desk in the anteroom outside the vice presidential office.

"Imelda, would you please poke your head around the corner and see if the President's Chief of Staff is available? If he is, could you ask him to please join us here for a few minutes? It's very important."

"Yes, ma'am. I believe he is in his office."

The Vice President's office in the West Wing was actually adjacent to the President's Chief of Staff's office, both just down the hall from the Oval Office. In less than a minute, the closed door to the Vice President's office opened. Imelda, the Vice President's assistant, entered first, followed closely by John Reynolds and Brad Nesbitt, the chief of staff and his deputy. Both men walked in hurriedly and took seats on the sofa opposite where Sharyn and Deputy Attorney General Swartz sat. Imelda departed, closing the office door behind her.

"Thanks for coming, John," said Moore. "I assume you've been watching this?"

"Yes, Serena. King's always been out of control, but I thought Marino had more sense than this."

"Is the President aware?"

Divided We Stand

"Uh, not yet," answered Reynolds. "He's taking a nap in the residence."

"What the h—," she exclaimed, catching herself before finishing her outburst and looking at Swartz. "I'm sorry. I didn't mean to…" She gathered her thoughts, erasing whatever she was going to say. "Okay. I guess this is why the President authorized Working Group Delta. We're to handle this situation. Do you have any suggestions?"

Swartz swallowed before speaking. "Well, Madame Vice President, this is clearly a very complex situation, with significant political ramifications, both on setting legal precedent and impacting the upcoming Presidential election. I suggest we fly the U.S. Marshal and some of his folks up to DC immediately to interview him. I'll assemble a team of the best legal…"

The Vice President held up her hand, cutting the Deputy Attorney General off in mid-sentence.

"Thanks, Brent, but the time for convening strategy sessions is over. Benjamin King just said *Fuck You* to the President, the Constitution, and the American people. No man is above the law, yet King continues to believe that he is the exception. And now he has Governor Marino helping him. We can't let that stand. Not for one minute."

"What do you suggest, Serena?" This question came from the President's Chief of Staff, the only person in the room who would dare call the Vice President by her first name in front of others. Reynolds and Moore had known each other for decades, and their respect was mutual.

"Send in every U.S. Marshal in Florida as well as the FBI's goddamn Hostage Rescue Team. And if that doesn't work, we send in the 101st Airborne Division or Delta Force or whatever else it takes to bring that man before the court where he has been lawfully indicted."

Reynolds sat there in silence, thinking, while his head subconsciously nodded in agreement. Sharyn looked around the room, somewhat perturbed that no one seemed to be opposing the Vice President's suggestion.

"Ma'am," said Sharyn. "I'd caution us all to think through this carefully. We know King is a dolt, but Marino is a strategic thinker. He's currently several steps ahead of us, and there's no doubt he's thought through how he thinks this will play out. Creating an armed standoff outside the Lido Club will play right into their hands. They want to paint this administration as a politically-motivated Gestapo who will use its control of federal law enforcement to win the election."

"This has absolutely NOTHING to do with the election!" VP Moore shouted.

"Everyone in this room knows that, but a good portion of the American public doesn't. And King and Moore are just waiting for us to give them something so they can twist it to their advantage. They're baiting us. We need to be careful not to take the bait."

"Okay, Sharyn," said the Vice President, calming her temper. "What do you suggest?"

"First, I think we need to get Geraldine in here to get started on a media blitz. The President should speak from the Oval Office on the importance of the separation of powers and the ability of the Judicial branch of our government to ensure justice prevails. He can convince…"

"Sharyn?" Moore interrupted.

"Yes?"

"People think President Fulton shit his pants yesterday on national television while walking in the Rose Garden. They think he wears a diaper, for god's sake. Half the country hates King and everything he stands for, while the other half is not going to listen to a single thing anyone in this administration has to say. The only thing everyone agrees on is that the other side is wrong. There's no convincing anyone anymore. They've already made up their minds from TikTok, Instagram, CNN or Fox News."

"Serena's right, Sharyn," said Chief of Staff Reynolds. "Eight years ago, your suggestion would have been sound advice. Today, we're operating under a new set of rules. We need to put politics aside if we can and solve this problem. We have a fugitive from justice, and we need to treat it as simply as that."

"With all due respect, John," said Sharyn. "I think we're missing the whole point here. King is a distraction. This is not about bringing him before the judge to face his indictment. This is about the governor of the state of Florida issuing an executive order nullifying the federal government's powers to enforce laws in his state. We can't let that go unchallenged, nor can we afford to convene a round-table conference at Main Justice."

"Agreed," said Reynolds. Sharyn turned to see the Vice President nodding affirmatively as well.

"So I think the Vice President's plan to send in a force of U.S. Marshals is the initial step. It's what we would do with any fugitive attempting to skirt justice. We stabilize the situation. We keep things calm—and we keep King penned up in his private club."

"What else?" VP Moore said. "You said initial step. What's next?"

"We have President Fulton convene the leaders of the other branches of government, including the Chief Justice and the leaders of both Houses of Congress. Marino's executive order is a strict constructionist view of the Constitution. It disregards more than two hundred years of Congressional laws and Supreme Court rulings. Convening the leaders of all three branches of the federal government is the surest way to show the American people that our country remains unified and strong and that Florida's governor is the outcast."

"Okay," said Vice President Moore, clearly coming to a decision. She shifted her gaze to the deputy chief of staff, sitting quietly on the sofa next to his boss. "Brad, please take Mr. Swartz to your office and let him use the phone and whatever else he needs. Mr. Swartz, get the U.S. Marshal in Tampa on the phone and light a fire under his ass. I want enough deputy Marshals on site there to contain everything and let everyone know the U.S. Government is in charge. No cowboy shit, just lock down King in the Lido Club."

"Yes, ma'am," said Brad, standing. The Deputy Attorney General stood as well and followed Brad out of the office.

The Vice President waited until the door was fully shut before speaking.

"Okay, John, Sharyn," she said. "Sometimes I feel like it's just the three of us running this insane asylum. Let's think this through to the end. What are King and Marino really trying to accomplish?"

"King's strategy is easy," answered Reynolds. "His goal is to win the election in November. In his mind, if he wins, all his problems will go away. He gets to be king for the next four years, quashes the indictments against him, pardons everyone who's helped him and sets himself up financially forever. It was unlikely these indictments would have resulted in a trial prior to the November election, but by not even showing up for court, he's making that even less likely."

"Agreed," added Sharyn. "It's Marino I worry about. We all know his ultimate goal is to get to the White House. I think this state's rights thing he's hit on is a ploy to make him the new leader of the conservative movement in this country. King won't have the official Republican nomination until July, so there's still a chance Marino works his way into that position. But he also might be maneuvering to be added to the King ticket in November, which would put him next in line in 2028."

"Yes, I can definitely see that," concurred the Vice President, who'd ridden President Fulton's coattails along a similar path. "Speaking of November, how is the President holding up? Since he started actively campaigning, he's seemed much more frail in the last two weeks. Are we still sure we have the right strategy?"

"It's the only strategy that allows our party to keep control of the White House, Serena," said Reynolds. "We've been over this countless times. Bill still has all his faculties, and he's as sharp as a tack, but only for limited periods of time. He's the only Democrat with a shot at beating King, or any of the other Republican challengers for that matter. Every other Democrat with national name recognition either refuses to run or they are too progressive to swing the independent vote. You know this, Serena. Even you are polling so low that there is no likelihood you could beat King or Marino in a head-to-head election. TikTok and Instagram Reels have not been your friend."

"Me? What about Bewildered Bill? I mean, how many times can a man look so helpless on stage, John? I agree he's done an excellent job running the administration, and he has my complete loyalty, but how much is he actually running things now? You do all the heavy lifting, and if they need an authority figure, they ask me to do it."

"It is what it is," said John. "We have to play the hand we're dealt. Bill is eighty-two. He'll be eighty-three by the end of his term. We just need to get him elected in November, then he's said he'll step down when the time is right."

"I still worry about Marino. He's up to something we're not seeing. No governor in their right mind signs an executive order outlawing federal law enforcement from their states. It's tantamount to secession."

"I think you're right about Marino, Serena," said Sharyn, who'd been quiet for much of the conversation. Sharyn was careful never to address Vice President Moore by her first name in a public setting, but the VP preferred to be called by her first name in private. "I have a few things up my sleeve that I think might be helpful, but the focus now should be on the plan you both had laid out. We contain King, and we get the President on his A-game to rally the three branches of government and show a unified front for defining the Constitution."

10

Savannah, Georgia

Tuesday, February 6

JASMINE STEPPED off the Citation XLS jet as soon as the co-pilot opened the door after the jet came to a complete stop. The private jet was parked on the apron just in front of a modern, unmarked one-story building with large picture windows framed by red-brick siding. This was the fixed base operator at the Savannah-Hilton Head International Airport, and Jasmine had flown through here several times before.

The co-pilot quickly retrieved her two nylon bags from the cargo hold, and Jasmine began the short walk towards the private terminal. It was just after six in the morning, and there wasn't anyone else around. As she walked, she heard the small jet's door closing behind her as the engines spooled up to taxi back toward the runway, leaving her alone on the tarmac.

She knew the private terminal would have only a skeleton staff at this hour, and no one would approach her directly unless she went to the service counter. The hoodie from the sweatsuit she wore was pulled up over her head, and her face was covered with large sunglasses and a surgical mask. Covid-19 had done wonders for obscuring one's identity in public places, and Jasmine had found no one ever questioned why someone continued to wear a mask several years after the pandemic had subsided. Several locks of hair from the long, blonde wig she wore intentionally curled out from the sides of her hoodie. Should anyone ever bother looking at the security camera footage, she hoped she appeared as just one of the celebrities passing through the airport and attempting to retain their anonymity.

Not stopping in the terminal, Jasmine walked straight through and exited the automatic glass doors at the front. Familiar with the layout, she followed the sidewalk to the right toward a small car park. The gray Ford F-150 was parked exactly as she'd been informed, and she opened the rear door of the Supercab pickup and tossed in her two bags. The keys were in the cupholder, and within seconds, Jasmine was exiting along Product Support Road and following the signs for I-95 South.

The drive to Sarasota would take about six hours, depending on traffic.

This was just one more in a long series of assignments for her boss over the last two years. This one was expected to last less than twenty-four hours, and later this evening, she was scheduled to fly out of Sarasota after completing her mission.

Fifteen minutes down the highway, Jasmine pulled off at the exit for Richmond Hill. The blue amenity signs for this exit listed more than a half dozen fast food restaurants, and Jasmine pulled the pickup into a Burger King. After a quick trip through the drive-thru to get breakfast and caffeine, Jasmine pulled into the near-empty rear parking lot of the hotel behind Burger King. Pulling down her hoodie, she removed the blonde wig from her head. *God, I fucking hate wigs*, she thought.

She pulled down the visor to take a quick look at herself. While a stunningly beautiful, short-haired brunette stared into the visor's mirror, what Jasmine saw looking back at her was an emotionally-scarred, weak girl who had to prove to the world that she could take all the shit it could dish out, that she had a purpose in life, and that she was better than the system that had thrown her away like discarded garbage. Jasmine thought her own eyes looked soulless, and she wondered for a moment if they had always looked like that or if she'd changed in the last few years. She wondered briefly if her parents would still recognize her—still love her. Wiping that thought from her mind, she flipped the visor up to the roof, slammed the truck into gear, and pulled out of the parking lot toward the interstate.

As she ate her soggy ham-egg-and-cheese Croissan'wich while driving with one hand, the taste of the rubbery egg made her flashback to the mess hall at Camp Pendleton.

Jasmine had grown up in a patriotic Cuban family on the outskirts of Miami. Her grandfather had gone ashore at the Bay of Pigs, and her father had been a decorated Marine during the first Gulf War. A perennial straight-A student in high school, Jasmine had earned a Bright Futures scholarship to her state's premier public university and became the first in her family to attend college. However, after two years of college, Jasmine decided to follow in her father's footsteps and enlist in the United States Marine Corps. She would never forget the pride in her father's eyes as she took the oath of enlistment, and the only time she'd ever seen her daddy cry was when saying goodbye to her at the MEPS station en route to basic training at Marine Corps Recruit Depot Parris Island.

Partly because everyone said she couldn't do it, Jasmine volunteered for Infantry training and was one of the first women to earn the coveted 0311 military occupational specialty. She was assigned to the 5th Marine Regiment at Camp Pendleton, California and she excelled at every aspect of being a Marine. Her strength and conditioning placed her at the very top of her unit, and her devotion to exceeding every task or mission assigned to her allowed her to overcome the inherent bias many of her fellow Marines had toward women in the Infantry. After two years in the Corps and having been promoted to the rank of Corporal, Jasmine's application was accepted to attend the grueling Marine Special Operation Command Assessment and Selection Course, commonly referred to

Divided We Stand

as MARSOC A&S—the first step on a journey to become the first-ever female Marine Raider.

The first phase of A&S was a demanding three-week assessment course at Camp Lejeune, North Carolina. Only those who successfully passed Phase 1 would be invited to attend Phase 2, an even more grueling test involving extensive land navigation, obstacle courses, and small unit tactics. Graduates of Phase 2 of A&S went before a selection board, and those few selected would attend the seven-month MARSOC Individual Training Course.

Although less than a handful of women had ever successfully completed A&S Phase 1, Jasmine smoked this three-week assessment and was named the honor graduate of her course. She attended and successfully completed the next A&S Phase 2 course, held only three times each year at a secret location in North Carolina, becoming only the second female Marine to complete both phases of MARSOC Assessment & Selection. Unlike the previous female candidate, Jasmine was selected to attend the seven-month ITC, also held at Camp Lejeune. Embracing the course's motto, "the strength of the pack is the wolf," she continued to prove her mettle in becoming a Marine Raider by acing every graded event, despite many of her classmates and certain instructors consistently making fun of her as a woman.

Jasmine had witnessed and experienced significant sexual discrimination and harassment almost since her very first day in the Marines, and she knew exactly how to best deal with it—be better than all the men at everything she did.

The course seemed to fly by, with Jasmine loving every difficult task presented to her. She excelled in both the individual challenges and leadership roles she was given and finished the course near the top of her class, quite a feat considering more than sixty percent of those Marines starting her course washed out.

The night before graduation, when all that was left was to clean their gear and prepare for the actual ceremony where they'd receive the coveted winged-dagger badge of a Marine Special Operator, Jasmine went to an informal graduation party hosted by one of the instructors at his off-post house. It wasn't mandatory, but almost all of her fellow students attended, along with most of the instructor cadre for the course. Alcohol was served, and everyone had a great time. At the end of the evening, with just over a dozen Marines left at the party, Jasmine looked around the backyard gathering and realized she was the only woman remaining at the party—all of the wives and girlfriends of the instructors had departed.

She felt uncomfortable in the pit of her stomach and decided it was best for her to leave. She ordered an Uber on her phone and unobtrusively walked through the instructor's house to wait out front for her ride to arrive. As she walked into the kitchen, the instructor and two classmates stood there, blocking her exit.

"There she is!" Proclaimed the Staff Sergeant, who was a weapons instructor in the course. Memories of him making inappropriate comments to her throughout many iterations at the rifle and pistol range immediately came to mind. She looked to her left at the two Marines now leering at her. One was the honor graduate of her class, and the other was a Marine who should have washed out, having had to retake almost every test. Both of them had given her the creeps since Day One of the course.

"C'mon, Jasmine. Come have one last shot with us. It's not every day we get to graduate the next female Chesty Puller—and I do mean chesty!" He laughed, and the two Marines laughed with him.

It was an ugly laugh that Jasmine will never forget.

Just wanting to be done with them, she agreed to a shot of tequila so they would let her leave. Her Uber was due any minute. The Staff Sergeant turned to the far countertop and poured four shots, handing one to Jasmine.

"Wait," said the instructor. "First, a toast." He paused, clearly intoxicated and having trouble thinking of the words for his toast. "Okay," he said, holding up his full shot glass. "Here's to the hole that never heals; the more you use it, the better it feels…"

"What the fuck, Staff Sergeant?" Jasmine shouted. "That's some fucked up shit. I'll drink, but not to that fucked up toast. Be better, Staff Sergeant." Her fellow students just laughed and leered, but the instructor got a dark look on his face.

"Oh, I'll be better, all right. Drink up, Ortiz!" He downed his shot, and Jasmine did as well, figuring this was the best way out of the situation.

That was Jasmine's last memory of the evening.

The next thing she knew, she was being shaken awake by one of her fellow Raider students who was on fire watch at the student barracks. It was 4:30 in the morning, and she was passed out sitting at a picnic table outside the building. He had been on his nightly rounds to check on the barracks and had seen her asleep.

"Wake up, Ortiz," he'd said, gently waking her. "Did you drink too much last night? Go get in your rack. First call is in less than two hours." He shined his flashlight on her face. "Jesus, Ortiz! What the fuck happened to your face?"

"Wha...what do you mean?" Jasmine stammered, still in a fog and with blurry vision.

"Did you get in a fight?" The Marine asked. "Your eye is completely swollen shut."

"I, uh, I don't know," she replied. "I, uh, I'll be okay. Just gimme a minute."

He left her to gather her thoughts, and she did her best to remember how she'd gotten there. She had no recollection of how she'd returned to the base, and her entire body ached. As she attempted to stand, shooting pain lanced through her groin and inside her pelvic region. She buckled over, barely able to stand.

Breathing deeply, catching her breath after a few moments, the pain subsided to a dull ache, and she gingerly stood up and made her way to the female bathroom. Squinting into the mirror under the harsh white light of the bathroom, she could see that something was terribly wrong. The left side of her face was badly bruised, and her eye was swollen almost shut. She was wearing the same clothes that she had worn to the party, but her shirt was on inside out. She realized she was no longer wearing a bra, and when she unbuttoned her jeans, she could tell her panties were missing as well. The inside of her jeans was stained with what appeared to be blood.

She knew immediately that she'd been raped. Closing her eyes, she realized it was probably multiple times.

At first, she felt violated, but that quickly turned to anger. *How dare those fuckers do this to me*, she thought.

Instead of going to the base hospital, she looked at her watch and realized the Raider Individual Training Course chain of command would be arriving shortly if they weren't already in their office. Marine NCOs and officers tended to show up before dawn. Not changing her clothes, she walked over to the admin office where both the course's Commander and First Sergeant had offices.

The First Sergeant, a crusty Marine Raider from Alabama, was drinking coffee from a mug and standing next to the company clerk when she walked into the office.

"Jesus, Ortiz. What the hell happened to you?"

"I was raped, First Sergeant. By one of your instructors."

His eyes went wide with shock. After a second, he motioned for her to go to his office. "Have a seat, Marine. Let me get the Captain so you only have to tell this story once."

She gingerly sat down on one of the cheap vinyl chairs in his office and waited to be called to see the commander. The door was open, and she could hear the Captain's response:

"Are you fucking joking me, First Sergeant?"

Then, a few seconds later: "See! This is exactly why we don't need women Raiders. God-fucking-damnit!"

It was another two minutes before the First Sergeant came back through the office. Jasmine heard him instruct the clerk to take a smoke break and clear out of the office. A moment later, both the First Sergeant and Captain walked into the room where she was sitting. Normally, as a junior enlisted Marine, she would pop to attention. However, given the circumstances, Jasmine decided to stay seated. Neither the First Sergeant nor the Captain corrected her.

Over the next ten minutes, Jasmine recounted everything she could remember. The First Sergeant looked both pained and sympathetic, as she would imagine her own father would look should he ever find out. The Commander, on the other hand, looked pissed.

"This is some fucked up shit, Corporal," said the Captain. "So you're telling me you got drunk, passed out, and then woke up back at the barracks. And you think you've been raped? By one of *my* instructors? A staff sergeant who has served his country for over twelve years and has been decorated with the Bronze Star for valor in combat?"

As much as it hurt, Jasmine decided to stand up before replying.

"No sir," said Jasmine. "I wasn't drunk, sir, nor did I pass out. I was intentionally drugged by *YOUR* instructor, and I was raped by him and two of *YOUR* future Marine Raiders, *sir*. I don't believe I fucking stuttered, *sir*, so I'm assuming what I said was perfectly fucking clear. *Sir!*"

The Captain's face turned beet red, and for a second, Jasmine thought he might pop a blood vessel in his forehead. He took several deep breaths before answering. "Listen, Ortiz. I've spoken with the Battalion Commander. He agrees with me. This is not something you want to go public with. You were drinking. You don't remember exactly what happened or who did what to whom. You're about to be the first female in Marine Corps history to receive the 0372 Marine Special Operator military occupational specialty. I would strongly encourage you to consider how this plays out. You could have your choice of assignments, whichever one of the three Raider battalions—if you play this right. If not, you're likely in for a nasty he-said-she-said situation that will follow you your entire career. Understand, Corporal Ortiz?"

Jasmine stood there, seething. She couldn't bring herself to reply, nod, or shake her head. The Captain continued to lock eyes with her and then looked down. "Please handle this, First Sergeant. I hope to see you both at graduation."

With that, the Captain abruptly left, leaving Jasmine and the First Sergeant alone in the small office.

"I'm sorry, Ortiz. I really am," said the First Sergeant, sympathy oozing from his tired eyes. "Please, sit down, Corporal."

Jasmine sat, still too stunned and angry to speak. The First Sergeant sat on the corner of his desk, one foot on the ground and the other swinging freely.

"Look, Ortiz," he said in his Alabama drawl. "You're a Marine.

A damn fine one, as far as I've seen. I believe your story, and I'll support you one hundred percent. I will take you to the Naval Hospital right now and make sure you're seen by everyone you need to. They can do a rape kit, and I'll call the MPs and NCIS myself. But part of what the Captain just said is true. Your life as a Marine Raider will be over before it even starts. You get that, right, Ortiz?"

Jasmine looked up to see his sad eyes. She could tell he wanted to be anywhere but here, dealing with this. "I get it, First Sergeant. I go to the hospital and cry rape; those three fuckers are going to say I was drunk and begging them to pull a train on me cuz' they're such good-lookin', studly Marines. And when I point to my fucking eye that's swollen shut, they'll say that maybe I like it rough and agree that maybe, just maybe, in the heat of passion, one of them got a bit carried away. Is that about right, First Sergeant?"

He looked even more sad, if that were possible. "Yes," he said, his voice barely above a whisper.

"And if I don't say anything, then I get to be a good little Marine Raider and go to MARSOC where I'm expected to have those fuckers have my back and for me to have theirs. Right? And maybe the rumors start flying, and my fellow Raider teammates think I might want to pull another train. Is that how you see this going down, First Sergeant? Me being a good Marine?"

"Yes," he whispered, although hardly any sound came out of his mouth. "I'm sorry, Ortiz."

"Fuck you," she said, standing up and walking out of the office, her head swirling with thoughts of revenge and getting even.

She found herself back in the female barracks, and her thoughts became a bit clearer. Seeing no better option, Jasmine took a long, hot shower and dressed for the upcoming graduation ceremony. The ceremony was scheduled for 0900 hours, and as the hour approached, Jasmine just couldn't bring herself to walk out there with her classmates.

She stayed in her room, and an hour later, the First Sergeant knocked on her door and entered. In his hand was a piece of Manila cardstock and the winged-dagger metal pin of the Marine

Raiders. He walked up and handed it to her—it was her certificate of graduation.

"What do you want to do, Corporal Ortiz?" He asked. "I've spoken with both the Sergeant Major and the Battalion Commander. They sympathize with your situation and agree you should have any assignment you want. Just say the word."

Jasmine didn't even want to look the man in the eye. "I want out, First Sergeant. Today."

"I'll see what I can do," he responded, leaving her graduation certificate on her bed and retreating out the door.

11

Sarasota, Florida

Tuesday, February 6

THE DRIVE from Savannah to Sarasota was without event, and Jasmine continued to reminisce about the path that led her to be driving south on I-75 toward her next mission. She saw signs for the Ellenton Outlet Mall, crested a small bridge across the wide Manatee River, and knew her exit would be coming up in the next fifteen minutes or so.

The month after that fateful morning in the First Sergeant's office at Camp Lejeune had been a blur. The First Sergeant had returned and informed Jasmine she was being granted thirty days of leave, after which she could report back to her unit and receive her honorable discharge papers and outprocess the Marine Corps. She would be promoted to the rank of Sergeant/E-5 even though she didn't meet the time in grade requirements, and she would also receive a full one hundred percent disability. The reasons for her discharge had been classified.

Jasmine had spent that first thirty days driving up the coast of California and sleeping on the couches of friends she'd made while living at Camp Pendleton. She spent a week in Huntington Beach and then drove all the way up the coast to the San Francisco Bay area. She figured this was about as far away from the Marine Corps as she could get, spiritually if not geographically, and she spent time wandering amongst the local college campuses in the area, hanging out with some student protesters, smoking pot, and working out for hours on end as if it were her religion.

She was seriously considering doing just that, but only after she accomplished the task she had set for herself while sitting in the First Sergeant's office: revenge.

Returning to Camp Pendleton after her 30-days of leave was up, Jasmine outprocessed as quickly as she could and drove the sixty miles to Huntington Beach. One of the only female infantry Marines she knew had moved there with her husband to become cops after they were both honorably discharged. They had made their spare bedroom available to her for as long as she wanted.

Now a civilian for the first time in almost four years, Jasmine arrived in Huntington Beach in the mid-afternoon. Knowing her friends wouldn't be home from work until later, she stopped at Sushi on Fire for a late lunch. She had just taken her first sip of her crisp Asahi beer after ordering a couple of the restaurant's special sushi rolls when a sharply dressed man approached her table and asked politely if he might sit down and discuss a business proposition with her.

A bit taken aback but also intrigued, Jasmine motioned for the man to sit. They were in a public place, so Jasmine saw no harm in hearing the man out. In his mid-40s, he appeared extremely fit, and Jasmine could tell his linen slacks, blazer, and open-necked shirt likely cost more than she had made in a month as a Marine corporal.

Introducing himself as Alex, the man placed a thin manila envelope on the table between them—the kind with the two cardboard circles and a piece of red string woven between them to keep the flap closed. Intrigued, Jasmine had taken another sip of her beer and sat back to let the man speak.

"I'd like to offer you a position within my organization, Jasmine.

I think you would be very valuable to our cause, and you'd find the work extremely rewarding."

"I'm not sure I'm looking for a job at the moment, Alex. But I do appreciate your offer." Jasmine knew she'd have to do something —either school or a new career. She was torn between finishing her degree or possibly going overseas for a military contractor position. First, though, her focus was on exacting revenge upon the three men who raped her—she thought of little else these past thirty days. She wasn't quite sure how she was going to do it, but her mind raced with various possibilities.

Alex smiled and pushed the envelope toward her. "Please have a look. I hope this might convince you that we're the right organization for your talents."

Expecting a job offer with a salary figure written down on a piece of paper, Jasmine untied the red string, lifted the flap, and slid out the envelope's contents. Inside were four documents. The first appeared to be a printout of a news article dated yesterday with the byline of Myrtle Beach, South Carolina. Titled "A Brutal Seaside Execution," the story detailed the discovery of three bodies on the beach just south of the tourist city's boardwalk. The men were as yet unidentified, but there was some speculation that they might be American servicemen and that the killing was gang related.

Without reading any further, Jasmine flipped to the second document which she could tell from the paper's texture was a glossy 8.5 x 11 photograph. The picture was of three men, clearly dead, sitting side-by-side and propped up against a low concrete wall. The picture was taken at night with a flash, which made the colors harsh in the glare cast by the flash. The men appeared to be sitting on a sandy beach, except the sand around the three of them was drenched red with blood. While it was evident each man had died from a single bullet to the forehead, that was not the most shocking aspect of the photo. Each man's pants had been stripped to his ankles, his groin a bloody mess of sliced tissue and pooling blood. In each man's mouth, a penis and scrotum had been shoved. From the look of pain, shock, and terror on each dead man's face, Jasmine assumed their genitals had been severed premortem.

Divided We Stand

She recognized the three men as the Staff Sergeant and her two fellow ITC classmates who had drugged and raped her.

Jasmine thought she'd be shocked, but she found herself smiling. She knew Alex was watching her closely, but she didn't care. Her revenge problem had just been solved. She didn't feel any special loss at no longer being able to exact her revenge personally—she was just thankful these men could no longer prey on anyone else.

She flipped to the third document—an arrest warrant dated two days previously. She looked at the federal seal at the top of the page, the words Eastern District of North Carolina and Arrest Warrant clearly stamped in bold letters. Looking closer, she read the name "William D. Baldwin" and the offense as "knowingly receiving, producing and distributing visual depictions involving the use of a minor engaging in sexually explicit conduct." Not recognizing the name, Jasmine flipped to the final document, another 8.5 x 11 photograph.

Her breath had caught in her throat as she looked at the picture.

The photo appeared to have been taken with a telephoto lens, but the quality was outstanding, and the people in the photograph were clearly identifiable. A handcuffed man wearing Marine Corps cammies and with the silver railroad track insignia of a Captain was being led by a man on either side of him. One man wore a navy blue jacket with FBI on the left breast, while the other man's similarly colored windbreaker had NCIS emblazoned on it. The handcuffed prisoner was none other than the training commander who had "convinced" her not to go forward with her rape complaint.

Jasmine couldn't help but let out a small laugh. Catching herself, she looked up at Alex and realized this was a very powerful man sitting before her.

That lunch had changed Jasmine's life, and she'd never looked back.

Shaking off her daydream, Jasmine saw she was driving past a large shopping mall and a long, narrow lake, with signs declaring the next exit to be for Fruitville Road. She promptly angled the pickup truck into the right lane so she could exit. She traveled west on Fruitville Road, an unremarkable six-lane road lined with strip malls, medical offices, fast food chains, and apartment complexes divided every quarter mile or so by a traffic light—the result of a complete absence of suburban planning common to most Florida towns and small cities.

Fruitville Road ended at a complex of high-rise condominiums, and Jasmine navigated the small roundabout to head south on US 41. A few hundred meters later, after passing the Ritz Carlton, Jasmine merged to the right and headed due west over the Ringling Causeway—a sixty-five-foot tall bridge spanning Sarasota Bay and offering stunning views south to Siesta Key and north to Longboat Key. The bridge descended onto the tiny isle of Bird Key, and Jasmine continued on the causeway as the road quickly approached Lido Key and its famed St. Armands Circle.

The traffic around St. Armands Circle increased significantly, and Jasmine was forced to bring the F-150 pickup to a crawl while pausing for numerous speedbumps and crossing pedestrians. The restaurants and shops on the circle held no interest for her, and she slowly made her way halfway around the circle to continue towards the beach. Just after passing an ice cream parlor and Tommy Bahama's restaurant, Jasmine could see the sand dune barrier signifying the beach.

The clock on the dashboard read 12:09. *Perfect timing*, she thought.

Jasmine had spent the last twenty-four hours intently studying maps and satellite photographs of the area, and she felt as comfortable as if she'd been here before. The beach was on her right, studded with taller condos ranging up to twelve stories high. She passed the entrance to the Ritz Carlton Beach Club, and the road made a sharp curve to the right before turning back to the left as it approached the south end of the barrier island. In the distance, Jasmine could see the line of police vehicles, a mass of protesters, and numerous large television news trucks stacked in front of the famed Lido Club, home to former President Benjamin King.

Several hundred meters short of this morass of people, Jasmine made a quick turn toward the beach into the parking lot for a ten-

Divided We Stand

story condo building situated a hundred meters back from Ben Franklin Drive and positioned directly on the sandy shores of Lido Beach. As if she had lived there for years, Jasmine pulled the F-150 pickup truck into an empty spot under the metal shade structure built over the parking spaces in front of the building.

Turning the ignition off, she found her palms a bit sweaty and her heart rate slightly elevated—totally normal in the moments before embarking on the final stage of a mission.

"You got this," she said to herself. "Easy peasy."

Without further hesitation, Jasmine put on her blonde wig, zipped up her hoodie, and pulled the hood over her head. She then stepped out of the cab and opened the rear door. She pulled the smaller of the two black nylon bags in the backseat toward her, unzipped a side pouch, and removed a blue baseball hat with the orange logo of the Florida Gators. Pulling the hat low over her wig, Jasmine grabbed the bag, the size of a large briefcase, and closed the door. Leaving her larger duffel bag and locking the truck with the key fob, Jasmine strode confidently toward the entrance to the ten-story building in front of her.

The entrance to the condo building was not staffed, and required a passcode to gain entrance via a keypad located on the left side of the glass doors. Jasmine entered the code she had previously memorized. She walked straight to the open elevator on the far side of the small, empty lobby and pressed the button for the tenth floor —the top floor. No one else happened to be in the lobby on her arrival, but she wouldn't have cared if there were. She was just another snowbird enjoying her short-term VRBO rental.

The elevators opened onto a wide, carpeted hallway spanning the length of the building. Jasmine turned right and walked to the end of the hall to a door marked 10-D. On the door handle was a realtor lockbox. She entered the correct code, causing the device to open and reveal a brass key in the small receptacle of the lockbox. Jasmine used the key to open the door and immediately closed it behind her.

In the apartment, she took a moment to stand there, absorbing the sights, sounds, smells, and feel of the apartment. The apartment itself was immaculate and smelled of recently-applied lemon air freshener. A small galley kitchen was to her right, and directly to her front, the entryway opened to an expansive living room with large sliding-glass windows and a balcony overlooking the turquoise waters of the Gulf of Mexico. It was a truly stunning view, and Jasmine imagined how much this place must cost to rent. Whatever it was, she thought, it was about to become almost as famous as Dallas' Texas Book Depository.

She turned down the hallway to her left and followed it to the end. A master bedroom was on her right, with similar views of the beach and Gulf. To her left was a guest bathroom, and at the end of the short hallway was the second bedroom. The door was open, and she instantly knew the room would suffice. In addition to two twin beds, the room had two windows facing south, offering a beautiful view to the southern end of Lido Key all the way to Siesta Key across Big Pass.

She looked at her watch. 12:21 p.m. She had a couple of hours to kill. No pun intended. The President was due to give a national speech with Congressional leaders at 4 p.m. in the Rose Garden, and her instructions were to complete her mission at least an hour before that.

Reaching into the same side pocket of her nylon case from which she'd retrieved the Gator baseball hat, Jasmine pulled a slim leather folio slightly larger than the palm of her hand. The leather had seen significant wear, and the binding was frayed. Leaving her bag on the bed in the small bedroom, Jasmine retreated back to the main living area and took a seat on the overstuffed leather recliner facing the glass sliders. She found the button on the side of the chair to extend the footrest, and from this reclined position, Jasmine opened the leather folio, revealing a slim Kindle reader.

She'd just finished the last book of Jack Carr's *Terminal List* series, thoroughly enjoying a book about a military sniper gone rogue in reaction to his superiors' greedy self-interests. She couldn't wait to start Don Winslow's second book of the *Danny Ryan Trilogy*, having recently learned that his final book of the trilogy, due out in a couple of months, would also be Winslow's final book as an author. Her Kindle had become her favored companion over the last two years since leaving the Corps, and she loved the fact that there was always a new novel to immerse herself in with just the touch of a button.

12

Lido Key, Florida

Tuesday, February 6

THE AFTERNOON SUN WAS HOT.

It was an unseasonably warm day for early February. While the temperature may only have been in the low 80s, standing in the direct sunlight for any length of time was absolutely brutal. It's why Lt. Butch Kemer had taken the initiative to erect several open-air shade tents just inside the vehicle barricade at the entrance to the Lido Club. His Sheriff's deputies, now numbering more than a dozen, were spaced in pairs across the entrance.

Less than thirty feet away, a similar line of black U.S. Marshals vehicles with twenty-one deputy Marshals, at last count, faced the deputies. The difference was that the Marshals didn't have shade. And from the looks of some of them, they weren't used to the Florida sun.

At least a half dozen of the Marshals looked like they were melting. Sweat poured down their faces, their t-shirts underneath their body armor were drenched in sweat, and their bare forearms were turning bright pink.

Divided We Stand

Butch felt bad for them. Sort of.

Their boss was definitely a conceited prick, but Butch had sympathy for the average deputy Marshal. They were doing what they were told to do, just as Butch and his Sheriff's deputies were doing. That didn't keep Butch from making a show out of delivering ice-cold bottles of water to his men at the entrance.

"How's it going, Tripp?" Butch asked one of his deputies manning the center of the barricade. "Any issues?"

"Nah, boss," the deputy replied. "All good. The few people that have entered or departed were all cleared, and the Marshals don't seem to be interfering. Not really sure why they're even here."

"Yeah, me neither," replied Butch. "But clearly, someone in DC wants them here. Hopefully, the politicians will sort this thing out before it gets out of hand."

"Yeah, LT. Thanks for the water—." Before the deputy could finish his thought, both he and Butch saw the Marshal directly across from them crumple to the ground. Before anyone could react, the face of a second Marshal seemed to implode as a spray of bright red mist exploded from the back of his head.

The deputy sheriff next to Butch instinctively grabbed the M4 rifle slung across his chest, and this prompted a Marshal on the barricade opposite them to open fire. Bullets cracked passed Butch's head, and he saw Tripp take two rounds to his upper arm. Without thinking, Butch dove on top of his deputy and dragged him down behind the front wheel of the white Sheriff's Suburban in front of them. Butch turned to see several of his deputies returning fire toward the Marshals, and for a moment, Butch felt like he was back in Fallujah in the midst of a firefight. Hundreds of bullets were exchanged between the two sides in mere seconds, several of them thunking into the Suburban he and Tripp had sheltered behind.

"Cease fire! Cease fire!" Butch started yelling at his deputies. "Stop shooting!"

Fortunately, Butch could hear at least one other person from the line of Marshals echoing his commands. Within seconds, the firing stopped, leaving an ominous quiet to descend upon the sunbaked street in the middle of one of Florida's most popular tourist destinations.

Tentatively poking his head up to look through the front window of the Suburban, Butch could see that the Marshals on the other side had stopped firing and seemed to be gathering around several of their fallen comrades. Butch looked to his left and saw two of his deputies sprawled on the ground, with two other deputies sprinting toward them to render aid.

Putting his hand on the radio mic affixed to his vest, Butch pressed the toggle button. "Shots fired at Lido Club. Officers need assistance. At least six officers down. Roll everything."

Several immediate questions came back from the dispatcher, but Butch was relieved to hear the deputies in his Operations Center inside the Lido Club begin managing the flow of information. They had already vectored the quick reaction force to the front of the club and were now coordinating with central dispatch to get ambulances to the scene.

Looking down, Butch watched Tripp try to pull the tourniquet off his vest with his left arm. His right arm was saturated with blood, so much so that it was already pooling on the ground in significant quantities. Butch was fearful one of the rounds might have severed Tripp's brachial artery. Without immediate attention, he could bleed to death in minutes.

Pushing Tripp's hand aside, Butch ripped the tourniquet from Tripp's vest, pulling it open and sliding it over Tripp's bloody hand. Once he had the tourniquet positioned several inches above the highest bullet wound, Butch threaded the small plastic handle, twisted the tourniquet until the bleeding stopped, and secured it with velcro. The tourniquet seemed to cause Tripp more pain than the bullet wounds, but Butch knew that was actually a good sign—the nerves in his arm were still intact.

Leaving Tripp, Butch sprinted over to the two other wounded deputies about ten meters to his left. As he got to them, he saw that the wounded deputies were Jim Henry and Mark Lesniewski. Both were on Butch's SWAT team, and two additional members of his team were already performing first aid. Henry appeared to have taken several rounds directly into the front plate of his armored vest. He was in considerable pain and having difficulty breathing, likely with a couple of broken ribs, but otherwise, he appeared to be okay.

The same could not be said for Lesniewski. He had taken a bullet directly to his Adam's apple. His throat was a geyser of blood, and both Lesniewski and the other deputy had their hands clasped tightly around Lesniewski's throat. Butch yanked the pressure bandage from his first aid pouch and dropped to the ground next to Lesniewski. As Butch attempted to put the bandage and his own hands over the wound, he knew it was going to be too late. He had seen wounds like this in combat in both Afghanistan and Iraq. It wouldn't have mattered if Lesniewski'd been shot on the floor of a hospital's operating room. There was simply too much damage and too much blood loss.

Butch locked eyes with the wounded deputy, who was struggling to speak.

"It's going to be okay, Mark," said Butch. "We got you, man. The docs are on their way. We're going to have you in the OR in minutes. Just hang in there, buddy." Butch grabbed the man's hands and squeezed. Unfortunately, he knew what was coming next. Mark's breathing got faster and faster. Blood started to pour from his mouth. He was literally drowning in his own blood. Butch leaned in close as Mark tried to form words.

"Cath…" was all that seemed to come out of Mark's gurgling lips. Butch knew Mark's wife was named Cathy, and his heart just about broke.

"I'll tell her," Butch said. "I'll tell her you love her."

Butched watched Mark's eyes roll back into his head, and his chest started bucking. In seconds, the bucking stopped, and Mark was still.

"What the fuck happened?" Screamed Butch, standing up, covered in the blood of his dead and wounded deputies. He could hear the scream of multiple sirens in the distance and knew dozens of police, fire, and ambulance vehicles would be there in moments.

He wandered out into the no-man's land created between the line of Sheriff's Suburbans and Marshal's vehicles. "What the fuck did you guys just do?" Butch yelled, his voice deep with hurt and injustice and oblivious to the dozens of television cameras capturing his every word. "You trigger-happy thugs shouldn't even fucking be here. Go! Go now!" Butch pointed up the road as he yelled. "You're the problem, not the solution!"

13

Lido Key, Florida

Tuesday, February 6

JASMINE CALMLY EJECTED THE MAGAZINE, unscrewed the long suppressor from the barrel, and collapsed the folding stock of the B&T SPR300 Pro sniper rifle. The cacophony of the firefight was raging exactly 210 meters away. After closing the window, she expertly fitted each piece of the rifle into the specially made straps inside the black vinyl briefcase. She then collapsed the carbon fiber tripod, which had stabilized her rifle for the two shots she'd taken, stowing the tripod in a zippered compartment of the same briefcase.

Her heart rate was lower than it had been earlier that day in the parking lot. Killing had a calming effect on Jasmine, and she welcomed the sensation of being in total control.

Walking quickly but without hurrying, Jasmine carried the gun case out to the living room. She stepped out of her sweatpants and stripped off the t-shirt she was wearing. Reaching into the side pocket of the briefcase, she pulled out a light blue, sleeveless, wrinkle-free shift dress and slid it over her head and down along her slim hips. The Nike Air Force Ones she wore on her feet were just as stylish with the shift dress as the sweatpants, but it completely changed her look.

Tossing her blonde wig into the bag before pulling out a red-haired wig, she fitted it expertly over her closely cropped hair, completely changing her look.

Shoving her Kindle, Gator hat, and clothes back into the brief-case, Jasmine took one last look around the apartment. Knowing she'd left nothing behind, she quickly walked out the apartment's front door and took the elevator to the ground floor.

It had been precisely two minutes since she'd fired the first shot —down the road, Lt. Kremer was still performing first aid on his dying deputy.

Now outside, Jasmine walked directly to the parked F-150 pickup truck. She unhurriedly placed the briefcase in the back seat, started the vehicle, and pulled north onto Ben Franklin Drive just as a wave of several Sheriff's vehicles sped towards her at a high rate of speed, lights flashing and sirens wailing. An ambulance and fire engine were approaching at a similarly high rate of speed behind the Sheriff's. Several hundred meters down the road, Jasmine took a right turn away from the approaching vehicles.

Having closely studied road maps of the entire area, her route back to the mainland took her down Taft Drive to Boulevard of the Presidents. Maintaining exactly seven miles over the speed limit put her onto St. Armands Circle in less than a minute. From there, it was as simple as reversing her course from early that day and crossing back over the Ringling Causeway Bridge to mainland Sarasota.

She turned north on US 41, and in five minutes, she could see the runway of Sarasota-Bradenton International Airport off to her right. She continued for another minute to the turnoff for Dolphin Aviation. Similar to the streamlined process she'd encountered while landing in Savannah early that morning, Jasmine simply parked the truck in the small parking lot outside the private air terminal, grabbed her two bags, and walked through the small lobby. She knew someone from her organization would be arriving within minutes to move the pickup somewhere no one would ever find it.

Divided We Stand

While there were more than a dozen people in the lobby at this time of afternoon, only one person so much as gave her a second glance.

That person, a trim man in his early thirties wearing a pilot's uniform, stood up and motioned for her to approach.

"Good morning, ma'am. The plane is ready. If you'll allow me to take your bags, we can take off as soon as you board."

"Thanks, Glen," said Jasmine, having met this pilot on several previous occasions. She handed him the larger bag but kept the nylon briefcase. Glen was a different pilot from this morning, and this was a different plane. The Gulfstream G550 was a much larger plane than this morning's Citation, but they were both owned by the organization she belonged to.

In less than two minutes, Jasmine was seated with her Kindle and a refreshing glass of apple juice as the pilots taxied the jet for takeoff.

14

Washington D.C

Tuesday, February 6

SHARYN WATCHED the events unfold on the television as they happened. Dumbfounded, she felt an icicle of dread pierce deep into her stomach. As the television cameras zoomed in on the bloody and wounded law enforcement officers, dressed in either black or green uniforms, she couldn't help herself thinking maybe they should have been wearing blue or gray. *Was this the opening salvo in America's next civil war*, she thought.

She was sitting at the desk in her office in the EEOB—the Eisenhower Executive Office Building, adjacent to the West Wing on the White House grounds. With the crisis brewing in Florida, Vice President Moore had been spending more time in her West Wing office, and Sharyn knew the VP was currently in a meeting with several Senators regarding the President's initiatives on climate change.

This is bad, Sharyn thought, dashing out of her office to head to the West Wing. *Really bad.*

Minutes later, she walked into the West Wing and was immediately hailed by Brad, the President's Deputy Chief of Staff, as he was hurrying down the hallway.

"C'mon," he said without greeting. "We're meeting in the Situation Room. Your boss is already there."

She walked with Brad, maneuvering through the busy hallways to the stairs that would take them to the West Basement, where the Situation Room was located. They showed their badges to the uniformed Secret Service officer manning the vault-like door outside the Situation Room, who granted them entrance after securing their cell phones in a wall-mounted cubby. The secure conference room that everyone thinks of as the Situation Room also included a small warren of several small offices, a bullpen of computer workstations manned around the clock, and communications and other technology crammed into every available space.

Upon entering, Sharyn saw that the Vice President and Chief of Staff were already seated at the far end of the table, along with the President's National Security Advisor, Carl Tidhams. Tidhams had recently returned from a five-day visit through the Middle East, where he was attempting to broker relationships in support of an Israeli ceasefire in their war on Hamas in Gaza. Now that he had returned, he would likely be a participant in the Working Group Delta discussions, especially given what had just happened a few minutes ago.

The conference room was smaller than most people assumed, almost cramped, with fairly low ceilings and a large conference table and chairs that took up almost the entire room. On one wall was a bank of television screens, three of which were tuned to different news channels. Each channel was covering the situation in Sarasota live.

"Pull up a chair, Sharyn and Brad," the Vice President ordered, a note of disgust in her voice. "Welcome to our nightmare."

"The President will be along shortly," added Reynolds. "He was up in the residence after lunching with the First Lady, preparing for his upcoming speech with the congressional leaders."

It was common knowledge among the inner staff that the President took an afternoon nap on most days, but the Chief of Staff consistently maintained the facade that the President was working.

"And yes, the FBI Director and Attorney General are also en route," said Vice President Moore, anticipating Sharyn's first question. "Does anyone know what the hell actually happened down there? Has anyone spoken to Krueger or Swartz?"

"I called Swartz as soon as I watched it," answered Chief of Staff Reynolds. "He was also watching it but had no more information than what we've all seen on television. It's difficult to tell, but most media outlets are reporting that the U.S. Marshals opened fire on the Sarasota Sheriff's deputies. However, MSNBC has made the contrary claim that a Sheriff sniper on the roof of the Lido Club shot one of the Marshals first, who then returned fire in self-defense." He paused, looking at the news tickers sliding across the television screens. "What seems to be in no doubt, however, is that three U.S. Marshals are dead, along with one Sarasota County deputy. An additional deputy and another Marshal were wounded, but neither is life-threatening—at least according to the media."

"Goddamnit!" Moore said, smacking the palm of her hand down on the table in frustration. "We told the U.S. Marshal down there specifically not to do anything stupid. The President was all set to hold a press conference in less than an hour with the Chief Justice and Congressional leaders. We had both parties on board! We had the perfect solution to King and Marino's stupid game of chicken—and now this! Jesus! What an absolute goddamn shitshow this has become. We're going to get crucified!"

The door to the conference room opened, and Sharyn turned to see a large Secret Service agent push open the door and make way for the man behind him. She immediately stood up from her chair, along with everyone else in the room. The President, dressed in a crisp navy blue suit and regimental striped tie, walked into the room and took a seat at the center of the conference table, with his chief of staff to his right and directly across from where Sharyn and Brad were sitting.

"Please sit, folks," said President Fulton. "Sorry, it took me a few minutes to get down here. I'm sure you're doing important things.

Serena or John, could one of you please tell me what's going on down in Florida?" The President was facing the bank of television monitors, and he began reading the chyron on the bottom of the screen.

"Well, Mr. President," said Reynolds as soon as he realized the Vice President was remaining silent. "It appears that just ten minutes ago, at 3:04 p.m., the U.S. Marshals and Sheriff's deputies positioned outside King's Lido Club opened fire upon each other. We don't know exactly what sparked the firefight, but we do know that four people were killed and several others wounded."

The President looked sad. "How did we let this happen, John?"

At that moment Reynolds knew why the Vice President, normally the first to take charge in any conversation, had remained silent. Never be the bearer of bad news to your boss—rule number one for success in DC politics.

Rule number two, Reynolds thought. *Never take the blame for anything, even if you're to blame.*

"Well, sir," Reynolds replied. "We won't know exactly how this started until after an investigation, which I suggest we task the FBI to commence immediately. There appears to be a discrepancy as to which side initiated the shooting, but it's clearly the fault of the on-scene commanders. Hopefully, Attorney General Krueger will be able to shed more light on the subject when he arrives shortly."

"Okay, John. Let's do that," ordered the President, shifting his gaze to his Vice President. "Serena, what do you think about this mess? Do you think we can still salvage Congressional support against what Marino and King are trying to do?"

Before the Vice President could answer, the door to the conference room opened. In walked the remainder of Working Group Delta: Attorney General Krueger and his deputy along with FBI Director Tracy and his deputy. These men were followed by Geraldine Fox, the President's communication director, who rushed in as the door closed behind her.

"I'm sorry for being late, Mr. President," exclaimed Geraldine, taking a seat next to Sharyn while the four other newcomers found seats around the table. "As you can imagine, the press room is going bonkers. I took the liberty of postponing the scheduled 4 p.m. press conference. We'll need to get them an official statement as soon as possible."

"Thank you, Geraldine. On top of it, as always," the President commended. He turned to face the Attorney General. "Neil, what can you tell us that CNN already hasn't?"

"Mr. President, I just got off the phone with Brent Maloney, the US Marshal for that area, as you'll recall. He says that two of his men were shot by a sniper. They believe the shots came from the roof of the Lido Club, where there were multiple Sarasota County Sheriff's SWAT snipers protecting the compound. Without orders from the on-site team leader, several of the Marshals opened fire toward the Sheriff's deputies along the barricades across from them. As I'm sure you've seen on television, the Sheriff's deputies returned fire."

"Are they sure the Sarasota County folks fired first?" President Fulton asked.

"Sir," interrupted FBI Director Tracy. "If I may, I might be better able to answer that than the Attorney General."

"Okay, Barry. Please go on."

"As soon as this happened, Mr. President, our imagery analysis cell started looking at all of the available footage that was being broadcast. The FBI has a small office there in downtown Sarasota, and as this involved a potential crime against federal law enforcement officers, I immediately dispatched all available personnel to the scene. I've also ordered the Tampa field office's SAC—the Special Agent in Charge—to get down there as soon as possible with a complete criminal investigation and forensics team."

"Good, good," said the President.

"The FBI's imagery analysis cell has given me their initial opinion that they think the first sniper rounds may have come from a different direction than the roof of the Lido Club. Their initial analysis, which I must preface by saying is based solely on the broadcast television footage, seems to indicate the first two U.S. Marshals were shot from an angle that suggests a building to the north of the Lido Club."

Divided We Stand

"That would prove the Marshals didn't fire the first shot," said the Attorney General, desperate to get the blame out from under his Justice department, of which the U.S. Marshals were a component.

"Yes, Neil. My analysts feel comfortable confirming that—at least from what was broadcast," replied Director Tracy. "In the interest of cooperation, I phoned Sheriff Knight, the Sarasota sheriff, to ask him to dispatch personnel to seal off the three condo buildings to the north of the Lido Club from which my analysts say the sniper could have fired. He was not very receptive to my call, to say the least."

"Who does he think he is, man," said President Fulton, appearing to be on the verge of getting angry. "He's the sheriff, and you're the FBI. He damn well better understand who he takes instructions from."

"Sir, if I may," interjected Geraldine gingerly, attempting to use her role as Communications Director to keep the conversation moving in a positive direction. "It's that kind of comment that has led to us being here in the first place. There is a clear separation of authority between the local Sheriff and the FBI, but it is Governor Marino who has muddied the waters with his recent executive order. While I'm sure the appropriate law enforcement agencies, federal and local, will fully investigate this tragic incident to determine if a crime has occurred, it is our job here in the White House to reassure the American public that the pillars of our government remain strong. I think keeping the Chief Justice and Congressional leaders on board and presenting a unified front to the press remains our biggest priority."

"Agreed," said the President. "Let's get them on the phone right now. Can we do that?"

"I think that's a great idea," added Vice President Moore.

Sharyn watched as Reynolds and Brad scrambled to get the conference table's speakerphone positioned in front of the President. Cell phones were not permitted in the Situation Room, so they would have to route the call through the White House switchboard.

Reynolds pressed a button on the speakerphone, causing the

phone to spring to life and the voice of the White House operator to immediately answer.

"How may I place your call?"

"Please get Chief Justice Hudson Stevens for the President."

"One moment, please," the operator said in the nasal monotone common to all switchboard operators. In less than a minute, she was back on the line. "Mr. President, I have Chief Justice Stevens. Allow me to connect you." They all heard a distinctive click.

"Hello? Mr. President?"

"Hello, Justice Stevens. Thank you for taking my call."

"Absolutely, Mr. President. How can I be of help?"

"I'm sure you've been watching what's happening down in Sarasota. I want to ensure the three government branches continue to stand strong against Governor Marino's seditious executive order. You are in agreement, correct, Chief Justice?"

"Mr. President," Chief Justice Stevens answered cautiously. "I can unequivocally state that the Supreme Court has, and always will, faithfully support the Constitution of the United States. There is no specific issue on this matter currently pending before the Court, for if there were, it would be entirely inappropriate for me to comment. However, the law on this general matter is well-established, and the police enforcement powers of the federal government date all the way back to the Judiciary Act of 1789. I stand with you on this, Mr. President. Governor Marino's executive order is not a lawful one under the Constitution."

"Thank you, Justice Stevens. I look forward to speaking with you when our joint press conference is rescheduled."

"I'll keep myself available, Mr. President."

Reynolds reached forward, stabbed a button with his finger, and disconnected the call. He then repeated the process, this time asking to be connected to the Senate Majority Leader.

"Dick, this is President Fulton. I just wanted to give you a quick call to make sure you're still with us on displaying a unified front for all three branches of the federal government. I've spoken with Chief Justice Stevens, and he has given his full backing."

"Of course, Mr. President," said Dick Cohen, the Senate

Divided We Stand

Majority Leader and the senior Senator from New York. He was also a fellow Democrat and staunch ally of President Fulton. "I've spoken with the Minority Leader, and he continues to pledge the support of the Senate Republicans."

"That's great, Dick. Truly great."

"The issue, Mr. President, if I may be so forward, is going to be Speaker Jameson."

"Yes, Dick. He's always been the wildcard. Do you think he's wavering in his support?"

"Wavering? Oh, I'd say he's doing a bit more than wavering. Mr. President, please have someone on your staff show you the Speaker of the House's latest social media post. It's on Twitter, Instagram, you name it."

Without waiting to be asked, Geraldine sprinted out of the room. As cell phones were not allowed in the Situation Room, they were all in the dark when it came to browsing the latest social media posts. Geraldine returned in less than a minute.

"I've asked one of the techs to put it up on one of the monitors so we can all see it. It should be up any second," Geraldine said to the President while taking her seat. Leaning over to Sharyn, Geraldine whispered, "It's bad, girl."

The large projector screen at the end of the table sprang to life, and a moment later, an image appeared on the screen in high resolution. The image was a map of the mid-Atlantic area of the United States, including Maryland and Virginia, with the diamond shape of Washington, DC, centered on the screen. A burning flame icon was positioned directly over the city, with the flames leaping upward. On the left of the screen was a man riding a large elephant, appearing to march towards the Capitol. The man was dressed in medieval attire, complete with a long spear. Looking closely, the man's face was clearly that of former President Benjamin King. On the right side of the image was a cartoonish depiction of President Fulton playing the fiddle. In large block letters across the bottom were written the words "Rome Must Burn!" King was meant to be Hannibal, and the fiddle-playing president evoked an image of Emperor Nero fiddling while Rome burned.

"Wow," said the Vice President, giving voice to what they were all thinking.

"Mr. President," said Geraldine, "this image was posted by both Benjamin King and Governor Marino approximately ten minutes ago. Since then, it has been reposted more than 30,000 times with over 60,000 likes. That's in ten minutes, Mr. President."

Senator Cohen's voice came over the speakerphone. "Mr. President, the Senate is here when you need us. We understand what is at stake. I am available at any time, as always."

The President didn't respond, still staring at the image intently. John Reynolds said goodbye to Senator Cohen and ended the call. Everyone looked around the table, unsure what the President would say next.

"That's an interesting picture. Do you think they know that I don't know how to play the fiddle?"

Sharyn's eyebrows raised, and she noticed others around the table having the same reaction. *Seriously?* she thought.

The President smiled. "I'm joking, folks. I'm joking."

A sigh of relief went through every person in the Situation Room. The last year had been incredibly difficult, with the President seeming to become much more frail and often appearing to have slight dementia at times. He had fallen in public several times and had been cast by unfavorable media as bewildered on occasion. At other times, most of the times in Sharyn's experience, President Fulton was sharp as a tack, allowing his witty, if not corny, sense of humor to shine through. It was difficult for the staff, however, as the uncertainty of which President Fulton was going to show up constantly preyed on everyone's mind.

"So what's the plan?" The President asked, turning to his Chief of Staff and the Vice President. "Serena, I put you in charge of this. What do you propose is our next step?"

"Mr. President," VP Moore answered cautiously. "Without the support of the Republican-led House of Representatives, we still need to put out a statement. If John and Geraldine agree, I think you should give a speech this evening to reassure the American people that this is under control. It should be a similar speech to the

Divided We Stand

one you planned to give this afternoon, and we can have the Chief Justice and Senate leaders behind you. It should be quick—and lay the blame squarely at the feet of King and his refusal to allow due process to run its course. As for what's happening in Sarasota, I think Director Tracy has both the mandate and manpower to see that justice is served. We can take our time, flood the area with special agents, and thoroughly investigate the incident while keeping King bottled up in his private club. When the time is right, the FBI can go in and arrest him. Instead of a dozen U.S. Marshals, I'm thinking several hundred FBI agents."

"I like it, Serena," said the President. "I like it. Barry, are you good with that? How about you, John? And you, Neil? Are you on board with the Vice President's course of action?"

All three men nodded, with Barry saying, "Yes, sir."

15

Osprey, Florida

Saturday, February 10

LIKE MOST AMERICANS, Nathan had been following the events of the last week primarily through television news networks and online articles. Normally not a big fan of watching the incessant rambling of most 24-hour news anchors, Nathan found himself spending more and more time in front of the television to see how things were unfolding both on Lido Key and in Washington, D.C.

The shootout at the Lido Club had been heartbreaking to watch, but coverage over the last four days since it occurred had ceased to abate. The national news coverage had mostly focused on the rift that was expanding between the federal government in Washington and the state governments, which were exerting their Constitutional rights under the Tenth Amendment, especially in the domain of law enforcement. Hundreds, possibly thousands, of large protests had erupted across the country, with college campuses and public squares in cities of all sizes becoming ground zero in the battle for which side was right.

Living in Sarasota County, the local news coverage had focused more on the tragic consequences wrought as a result of the shootout that had caused the deaths of four law enforcement officers. The three U.S. Marshals had all resided in the Tampa area, but the one Sarasota County Sheriff's deputy who had died, Mark Lesniewski, had been born and raised in Sarasota. The officer left behind a wife and three children under twelve. Nathan's heart broke with such a needless tragedy.

Emily had told Nathan on Wednesday that the fallen Sheriff deputy's children attended the same school as his daughter, Maeve, and this brought the tragedy even closer. Maeve attended the Pine View School for the Gifted, a public magnet school that consistently rated in the top ten schools in the country. Covering grades two through twelve, the deputy's children were much younger than Maeve, but that didn't lessen the fact that the tragedy had impacted very close to home. Feeling strongly that it was the right thing to do, just that morning, Nathan had driven to Sarasota National Cemetary to pay his respects as Deputy Lesniewski was laid to rest with full military honors, having previously served in the U.S. Air Force before becoming a deputy sheriff. The funeral had been attended by thousands, with Governor Marino in attendance.

Nathan had just returned from the funeral and was still wearing a dark business suit as he sat in his family room watching the latest blather on CNN. He found himself constantly changing channels to see which news outlet might have something interesting—something other than the same pundits rehashing the same information while showing the same footage of the brief firefight at the Lido Club.

"Still watching this drivel?" Emily asked, walking into the family room after watering her flowers out by the pool.

"Yeah, it's addictive. Nothing new," said Nathan.

"Of course, there's nothing new," said his wife. "This was a tragic mistake that never should have happened. The news media will ride this horse until the next tragedy comes along. Hopefully, the politicians will sort everything out before anyone else is killed. I still can't believe you were almost a part of this fiasco!"

"I wasn't almost a part of it. Why do you keep saying that?" Nathan's defensive frustration was evident. "The governor asked me to attend a meeting with the former President of the United States. Who turns that request down?"

"I know, but you hate politics!"

"Absolutely, and I hate politics even more after this past week. But it doesn't mean I would turn down a request for a simple meeting. I had no idea they would ask me to be a prop on television."

"Politicians are users. It's what they do."

"Marino has a point, I just don't think he's going about it the right way," said Nathan. "Federal law enforcement officers have doubled since 9/11. Doubled! Now, a lot of that increase is in the Border Patrol and federal prison guards, but still."

"But a state can't just outlaw federal law enforcement, can they?" Emily asked. "I mean, you're the Constitution expert, but that's the very definition of sedition, right?"

"Sedition? I see you've been watching CNN!" Nathan laughed. "I smile every time I hear these legal experts describe Governor Marino as committing sedition. *Sedition* is inciting someone to rebel against the government. Marino's executive order isn't seditious."

"Then what is it, Mr. Professor?"

"It's based on the principle of nullification, which is sometimes called interposition. Simply stated, the Constitution is an agreement between the States to form a government with certain rules, procedures, and limitations. The very essence of the Constitution is the concept that it is the States who are forming the Union, and thereby, each state has an inherent right to judge the constitutionality of federal laws and refuse to enforce those laws the State deems unconstitutional."

"But doesn't that go against what's written in the Constitution?"

"No, actually, it doesn't do that at all. It goes against the Supreme Court's *interpretation* of the Constitution, not the actual *language* of the Constitution."

"What do you mean?"

"Well, think back to high school civics class. Does *Marbury vs. Madison* and *McCulloch vs. Maryland* ring any bells?"

Divided We Stand

"Kind of," Emily replied. "Hey, look, you're the Constitutional expert. I have an engineering degree, for god's sake."

Nathan laughed again. "It's okay, honey. No one but civics teachers ever remembers these Supreme Court cases. In a nutshell, *Marbury* was a case in 1803 that established the concept of judicial review—meaning the Supreme Court can declare the constitutionality of laws made by Congress and actions taken by the Executive branch. *McCulloch*, which was a case heard about fifteen years or so after *Marbury*, proclaimed that the federal government is supreme and that Congress can make laws upon the States, the President can enforce these new laws, and the States can't do anything about it."

"So who's right? I can't believe a governor can tell the President of the United States just to go fuck himself."

"Well, in the 1860s, a bunch of governors did just that. However, they didn't have the military might to get away with it— but they spent four very bloody years trying. For the last 150 years, Congress has continued to pass laws expanding its power, the Executive branch has continued to enforce this, and the Supreme Court has endorsed it legally."

"So you think Marino has the right to secede from the Union? C'mon, Nathan, this isn't some game of semantics; he's playing a game of chicken with the President, and a bunch of cops just got killed over it."

"I agree, but this isn't just semantics. It's about the State's rights to limit the expansion of the federal government, which the States ultimately have to pay for. Think of this for a second. In 2020, the federal government's budget was over thirty percent of the GDP— Gross Domestic Product—of the country. The GDP is our entire U.S. economy—the value of all the goods and services produced in the United States. Thirty percent."

"Okay," said Emily, never enjoying when her husband started spouting off facts and figures.

"In 1920, the budget size of the federal government was three percent of GDP. That's a ten-fold expansion in a hundred years, much of which has occurred since 9/11."

"That seems like a lot," agreed Emily.

"Because it is. Here's a better example, one everyone can understand. In 2000, Boston and Washington D.C. metropolitan areas were generally the same size. Each had a population of about 4 million people. Boston, which has become extremely popular, has grown to 4.4 million—a ten percent growth. Washington? Its population is now 5.5 million. That's over thirty-seven percent growth. In twenty years!"

"Okay, you make a good point, Professor. But this seems all about politics to me. Republicans versus Democrats. Red states versus Blue states. Rednecks versus libtards. Whatever you want to call it."

Nathan could always count on his wife distilling the most complicated problem to its essence. "You're absolutely right. It *is* about politics. *Everything* is about politics, but politics is just about power. It's a game of tug-of-war. And for a hundred years, the federal government has been pulling on the rope hand over fist, expanding its power. But recently, the states have started pushing back. Mostly because they are forced to deal with major problems that historically have been the federal government's responsibility.

Nowhere is this more evident than with immigration and border control. Everyone admits it's a huge problem, yet the federal government does little to slow illegal immigration. I mean, twenty years ago, Bill Clinton gave numerous speeches about cracking down on illegal aliens. Today, our government won't even use the word *illegal alien*, instead mandating the term *undocumented migrant*. That's like calling a speeding motorist an unticketed fast driver. There are 193 countries in the world—in 192 of them, you get arrested for entering their country without permission."

"So, what then?" Emily asked. "Governors like Marino can just tell the President and Congress to take a hike?"

"No, they can't," admitted Nathan with finality. "That's why I left the meeting with the Governor and former President King. I don't think what Marino's doing is ultimately legal, although I can see the rationale behind his actions and have some sympathy for his cause. The Tenth Amendment has been relegated into obscurity by

Divided We Stand

the federal courts when it should be one of the most important parts of our Constitution."

"And King? Do you support him not turning himself in? The guy's an idiot. How can you support him?"

"No, I don't support his position at all. He's a citizen of this country, and he needs to submit to the jurisdiction of our legal system. No man is above the law. For what it's worth, he seemed like a very nice person, but I don't agree with what he's doing. Frankly, after the officers were killed, I'm very surprised he hasn't just turned himself in."

"But it's politics, as you said. And that would mean he'd lose power." Emily pointed to the television, where an opinion poll just happened to be displayed on the screen. "Look. King's as popular as he's ever been. Marino is even more popular!"

"I know. Fascinating how this all plays out, isn't it?"

"Spoken like a true political scientist," agreed Emily. "Hey, listen. I'm taking Maeve and a couple of her friends to lunch and to shop for a dress. One of her teammates is having a birthday party down in Venice tonight. Maybe you and I could go to that new Greek restaurant that just opened. Sound good?"

"Sounds great," said Nathan. "Where are you going shopping? UTC?" Nathan was referring to the sprawling mall by the highway that Maeve and her friends seemed to spend so much time at.

"No, the girls wanted to try St. Armands Circle. There's a couple of cool shops that have dresses in the style they're looking for."

"Jesus, Emily, have you seen the news?" Nathan asked, somewhat alarmed. "I was downtown the other day, and there were about a hundred FBI agents walking around. Apparently, they took over several floors of the Holiday Inn on Lido to house everyone involved in their investigation. I really think you should stay away from St. Armands."

"It's fine, Nathan. The Lido Club is more than a mile away, and St. Armands is probably the safest place in America right now with all these federal agents. We'll be fine. The girls want a 1905 salad from Colombia as well."

Nathan nodded in resignation. Emily was probably right. Nathan also loved the chopped salad from the popular Colombia restaurant and thought for a moment of joining his wife and daughter. However, he knew his daughter would cringe at the idea of her father accompanying her and her friends on a shopping trip.

"Have fun. Be careful," Nathan shouted as Emily walked away down the hallway to get ready.

16

Sarasota, Florida

Saturday, February 10

ENRIQUE WAS grateful the voice coming from the GPS had been adjusted to speak Spanish. The woman's electronic voice told him to turn right, so he followed the car in front of him into the right lane, flipped his turn signal, and made the turn as instructed. The map on the dashboard screen showed him to be 5.7 miles and fourteen minutes from his destination.

Enrique smiled.

Fourteen minutes, and he'd finally be on his way home to see his wife and son.

Home was a small, ancient but tidy single-wide trailer on the outskirts of Arcadia, Florida. Arcadia was just over forty miles due east of where his current location was on the south side of Sarasota's city limits. With luck, he'd be home in an hour.

He hadn't seen his family in almost seven months, and the journey back to Florida had been wrought with difficulties and uncertainties. Although he had initially blamed his predicament on bad luck, Enrique took full blame for his situation and vowed to be extremely careful so it would never happen again.

Last summer, Enrique had been arrested for a DUI—driving under the influence. He had no recollection of his actual arrest, but he does remember drinking with his fellow farm workers at a local speakeasy in Arcadia. He had decided to take his battered pickup truck to McDonald's to get something to eat, and the next thing he remembered was waking up in a jail cell. His public defender told him he was accused of causing a head-on collision that put three people in the hospital—an older couple and their young grandson. Luckily, none of them were too seriously injured, and the lawyer was confident he could get Enrique off with no jail time.

Then his lawyer had told him the bad news: he would be deported back to Mexico.

Enrique didn't blame the American judge for sending him back to Mexico. Enrique knew the rules, and until that night, he had always been very careful to keep his distance from the police. Enrique's lawyer told him he could try to fight it, which could take more than a year, but Enrique knew how the system worked. The easiest thing to do was to volunteer to be deported. Then, he could come back to his family as soon as he'd saved enough money for the return journey.

The last seven months had been especially difficult in his hometown of Monterrey, Mexico. Enrique's parents had died years before, so he was forced to stay with an uncle and his extended family. Work was scarce and low-paying. Two weeks ago, Enrique's luck had changed for the better. An acquaintance of his uncle, knowing Enrique had family in Florida, offered to transport Enrique back across the border, all the way to Arcadia, as long as Enrique was willing to do a short job that was completely legal. Not only would the return trip not cost Enrique anything, but he would receive $2,000 for his time and efforts.

Enrique jumped at the opportunity.

After a dusty, bumpy, circuitous route across the border in various vehicles, Enrique made the long journey by road all the way to Florida. This morning, Enrique, along with several other undocumented immigrants, arrived at a warehouse somewhere east of Tampa after driving the length of the Gulf Coast all day and night in a beat-up passenger van. In Tampa, Enrique was separated from the others, given an opportunity to shower, and provided a new pair of khaki pants and a light-blue short-sleeved polo shirt with navy blue sleeves. Donning the shirt, Enrique was intrigued by the Amazon logo on the shirt's left breast.

A man introduced himself as Raul, the person who had paid for Enrique's trip. The man spoke Spanish fluently, albeit with a foreign accent Enrique had never heard before, and told him there was a straightforward task to perform before he'd be driven to see his family in Arcadia and paid $2,000 cash. It was a simple matter of driving an Amazon Ford Transit van from Tampa to Sarasota and parking it so the packages could be unloaded. That was it.

Enrique was not naive enough to believe this was a normal Amazon van. Why would someone pay for him to travel illegally from Mexico and pay him $2,000 for a job that they could hire just about anyone to do here in America? He assumed the van likely had drugs in it, but at this point, he was committed, and it seemed a simple task.

Minutes later, he was on the highway, following the female Spanish voice emanating from the van's GPS.

An hour later, Enrique was driving over Sarasota Bay's Ringling Causeway Bridge, which was less than two minutes from his destination. He had been given very specific instructions for leaving the van. As he turned onto St. Armands Circle, he was to look for a restaurant on the right-hand side called the Colombia Restaurant. There would be a loading zone in front, and he was to pull into the loading zone, put on his blinking hazard lights, and park the vehicle. Once parked, he was to leave the vehicle running, take the small cardboard box that was already on the seat next to him, and exit the vehicle. He was then to use the sidewalk by the Colombia Restaurant and follow it down to the end of the block. At this location, Raul would be waiting for him in a red sedan. Job complete, Enrique would be driven to his home in Arcadia.

Muy fácil, thought Enrique. *Demasiado fácil*.

The roundabout that was St. Armands Circle was extremely crowded this Saturday lunchtime, but Enrique had no problem finding the Colombia Restaurant after waiting for dozens of pedestrians to cross on the crosswalk. As instructed, he pulled into an empty spot by the curb, left the vehicle running, and exited while carrying the shoe-sized brown box that had been resting on the passenger seat.

Enrique felt conspicuous wearing his Amazon uniform but did as instructed. The Colombia Restaurant had dozens of tables, all full of patrons, positioned just off the sidewalk, several feet from his parked van. Looking at the tables, Enrique's body stiffened—at least three of the tables were filled with men wearing shirts with FBI stenciled on them. It was crazy to think that any of these police officers would recognize him as an illegal immigrant, but he immediately looked away and quickened his pace.

Distracted by the presence of the FBI agents, Enrique was oblivious to the mom eating a salad at one of the tables with her teenage daughter and her friends.

In seconds, he was at the end of the block looking for Raul driving a red sedan.

Looking back toward his parked van, about twenty meters away, Enrique saw a bright flash of light. He never saw the concussive blast that picked him up off his feet, throwing him backward, nor the chunk of the van's side-view mirror that flew directly at him at such speed that it sliced off his entire head above the bridge of his nose. Enrique never had time to realize he'd never see his family again.

17

Osprey, Florida

Saturday, February 17

THE CAR BOMB AT ST. Armands Circle killed thirteen people and wounded forty-three others. For Nathan, however, it erased every reason he had for living.

Emily and Maeve, sitting at a table within feet of the exploding van, had been killed instantly, their bodies so destroyed that formal identification was made through DNA. Both of Maeve's teammates who had been sitting at the table were also killed in the blast, along with three FBI agents and six other innocent bystanders enjoying their lunch at the popular tourist location.

The nation's outrage at the attack had escalated to such a boiling point that many feared additional acts of violence. Half the country blamed Benjamin King and Governor Marino for thumbing their noses at the legal system and creating an environment where people felt the need to take the law into their own hands. The other half of the country blamed President Fulton and his "Gestopo" FBI for flooding this small town with hundreds of agents and endangering the local citizens. Protests across the United States had turned from tense to violent.

Nathan was deaf to all this noise. He had not watched the news and had barely spoken to anyone over the last seven days since the bombing. His entire world had been shattered, and he had completely withdrawn from the world around him.

Nathan was an only child whose parents had both passed away years before, leaving him with no close family. Upon being notified by the Sarasota Sheriff of his wife's and daughter's deaths, Nathan had made two phone calls—and since then had barely spoken to anyone.

His first call had been to his brother-in-law, Dave Armstead. Emily had grown up in Sarasota with one younger sister in an old-money family. Emily's sister, Kristen, still lived in Sarasota, and Nathan thought it best that she heard the news from her husband rather than on television.

Emily's maiden name was Harkness, and somewhere along the line, she was descended from the great robber baron Henry Morrison Flagler, the founder of Standard Oil, who, at one point, owned most of Florida. Emily's father, whom Nathan had greatly respected, had become one of Southwest Florida's leading commercial real estate developers and had exponentially increased the family fortune. A story that Nathan loved but Emily's father kept private was that despite his family's wealth and prestige, he had refused to fight his draft notice for Vietnam. Emily's father had spent twelve grueling months in-country as a grunt with the 101st Airborne Division, stories of which he'd shared only with Nathan. Unfortunately, several years ago, Emily's parents had been killed in a tragic plane crash when their jet's landing gear malfunctioned. Emily and Kristen had each inherited an ungodly sum of money, hundreds of millions of dollars each.

That was how Nathan and his family had purchased the stunning beach-to-bay home on northern Casey Key, one of the most exclusive yet unpretentious enclaves in Florida. For the last seven days, since the moment he'd learned of his family's death, Nathan had spent almost all of his time sitting on the beach in front of this

Divided We Stand

house, staring into the distance. He didn't want consoling. He didn't want sympathy. He just wanted to be left alone.

The other phone call Nathan made was to Tim Spooner. Spooner—everyone, including Spooner's ex-wife, called him by his last name—had been Nathan's team sergeant during Nathan's two years with the Unit, often referred to as Delta Force. Nathan and Spooner had forged an unbreakable bond during several combat deployments, and Spooner was the only person other than Emily that Nathan confided in. Now retired from the Army as a Sergeant Major, Spooner had returned to his childhood home in Clewiston, Florida, where he'd taken over the historic marina his family owned on Lake Okeechobee. He'd also converted the two-hundred-acre sugarcane farm his family had owned for generations into one of the country's premiere combat skills training centers, providing tailored services to both law enforcement and special operations forces from the military and intelligence communities.

Spooner was two inches shorter than Nathan's 6'4", but his shoulders were twice as wide. As the Lynard Skynard song described, he was "lean, mean, big and bad" and, as many foreign bad guys had learned the hard way, when Spooner pointed his gun at you, he did not give you three steps—it was game over. He had a jagged scar running vertically the length of his left cheek, and while most women found it distinguishing, to Spooner, it was a constant reminder of the battle in which two of his men never made it home.

His physical appearance did not evoke the image of a retired Army Sergeant Major, for he had let his light brown, naturally curly hair grow into a shaggy mess, complimenting his bushy fu-manchu mustache. He was more apt to be confused for a member of a motorcycle gang rather than an ex-Delta Force operator.

Two hours after receiving the call, Spooner arrived at Greene's home on Casey Key. He'd promptly taken charge of handling every detail, allowing his best friend to grieve in solitude. The media was all over the tragedy, especially upon learning of both Emily's and Nathan's backgrounds. The death of a mother and daughter from one of the area's wealthiest families, combined with a grieving father who was a former Delta Force officer, recipient of the Medal of Honor, and renowned political science professor, made for great television and reporters were massing around Greene's Casey Key estate. Likewise, a steady stream of politicians and celebrities continually called or attempted to visit in order to pass on their condolences—or perhaps to gain some free television air time. Hell, Spooner had even turned away calls from the Vice President's office! Spooner made it his life's mission, as he had fifteen years previously in both Iraq and Afghanistan, to protect Nathan with his life.

Spooner saw to it that no one disrupted Nathan's grieving. No one.

This morning had been especially difficult as it had been the funeral for both Emily and Maeve. Hundreds of mourners had gathered at the church to pay their last respects, and Nathan had stoically given a heartfelt eulogy for the two women he loved more than anything else. The graveside ceremony had been reserved for close family and friends, and Spooner had put the fear of God into the Sheriff's department to ensure the location would remain private.

Upon returning home an hour ago, Nathan had gone directly to the beach where he was sitting in the chair Spooner had put there so that Nathan wouldn't sit in the sand, as he had the first twenty-four hours after Emily and Maeve's death. Spooner watched through the house's glass window as Emily's sister, Kristen, who'd been spending most of her time at the house, rubbed sunscreen onto Nathan's exposed face and neck. After the first day of constant sun, Nathan's face and neck had turned a deep red, and Kristen was trying to take care of her brother-in-law as best she could. While devastated herself, she could only imagine the utter sense of loss Nathan must be feeling after losing his entire family.

Walking back into the house, she looked up to see Spooner watching her. "How much longer are we going to let him sit there?" She asked.

"As long as it takes," Spooner replied. "As long as it takes."

"And how long do you think that'll be?"

"Mmmm," he calculated. "Not too much longer, I'd say. After watching his wife and daughter's caskets being lowered into the

Divided We Stand

ground, I'm guessing Nathan is fast approaching the switch from grief to revenge."

"Revenge?" Kristen asked. "What's there to avenge? It's a tragedy. The scumbag who did this was killed by his own bomb. Emily and Maeve weren't the targets anyway—they were just in the wrong place at the wrong time."

Spooner looked at her like he would a child. "You don't understand, Kristen. You can't kill a man's family and expect nothing to happen—especially a man like Nathan. The guy who was killed? He was just a pawn—just the driver of a van who probably had no clue about the bomb he'd been delivering. It's the people behind it that will pay. And to be honest, I would not want to be in their shoes at the moment."

"Jesus, what a mess!" she said with finality. "I need a drink. Would you care to join me?"

"Sure thing, darlin'," Spooner said. "I'll get it. What'll you have?"

Kristen's husband, Dave, arrived shortly after dropping off their three children at their home in Sarasota, and Spooner, Kristen, and Dave spent the next couple of hours nursing their drinks and telling stories about Emily and Maeve. It was cathartic, and at various points they were all either laughing or crying. The entire time, they kept an eye on Nathan sitting alone on the beach, barely seeming to move at all.

Just before dark, as the three of them were wondering what to do for dinner, Nathan suddenly stood up and walked back into the house, still wearing his dark charcoal suit from the funeral. He hadn't even bothered to loosen his tie.

Nathan walked in through the sliding glass door. He didn't acknowledge Spooner, Kristen, or Dave and instead walked directly to the flush-mounted double-door Viking refrigerator. He pulled out a bottle of water, opened it, and drained the entire bottle in one long gulp.

"Thank you," Nathan said, turning to face the three closest people he had left in the world. "Thank you for all that you've done for Emily and for Maeve this past week. I know it's been incredibly difficult for each of you. Most of all, thank you for letting me grieve in my own way."

Kristen came over and wrapped her arms around Nathan, hugging him close. She had the same lithe, athletic build as Emily, and holding her was a bit awkward for Nathan. He hugged her back with his arms but otherwise showed no emotion.

"You know we're always here for you, Nathan," said Dave. "You're family. Don't disappear on us."

"I'm not going anywhere, Dave. At least not for a little while. It's time to get to work."

"Work?" Kristen asked, looking up at him, somewhat baffled. "You don't need to work, Nathan."

Nathan looked down at her, then looked up and made eye contact with Spooner, who was returning Nathan's gaze with a questioning look on his face. Nathan nodded almost imperceptibly, and Spooner knew precisely what Nathan was saying. *"Go to work"* had a different meaning to the men of A Squadron of the Unit during their deployments to Iraq and Afghanistan. At the height of those wars in 2006-07, when Nathan and Spooner were in the thick of things on almost a nightly basis, it was a phrase they used often. It didn't mean *Go to the office*, as Kristen had interpreted. It meant *Go kill some bad guys.*

Nathan looked down and gently disengaged himself from Kristen's embrace. "I know, Kristen. I just meant that I have a lot to do." He looked up at Dave. "You two have been incredible. I really don't know what I would have done without you both. Why don't you guys go home and get some sleep? This has been hard enough on you and your kids without having to babysit me. I'll be fine. Trust me. Plus, I have Spooner to keep me in line."

Kristen and Dave said their goodbyes, happy to be going home to their children but still concerned about their brother-in-law. Nathan had mellowed out considerably over the last fifteen years, but when they had first met Nathan, while he was a Special Forces Captain in the Army, he was wound extremely tight. The first adjective Kristen would have used back then to describe Nathan was "dangerous." It wasn't that he was violent or that he was aggressive;

Divided We Stand

it was this feeling that, just under the surface, he was a man capable of extreme violence—someone you would never want as an enemy in a million years. That's the vibe Kristen had felt just now when she had hugged Nathan.

Spooner watched Dave and Kristen back their cars out of the driveway, then turned to Nathan. "You sure, brother?"

"Yes," said Nathan, drinking from another bottle of water. "As sure as anything in my entire life."

"You know I'm in. Who we killin'?"

"I don't know yet, but I know where to start."

"Tell me."

18

Washington D.C

Tuesday, February 20

SHARYN HEARD the commotion outside her office in the EEOB just before her door opened unexpectedly. In walked the Vice President, who normally summoned Sharyn rather than come to Sharyn's office.

"Hi, Sharyn. Do you have a minute?" The VP said, walking in and sitting down in one of the two armchairs before Sharyn's desk.

"Of course, Serena," Sharyn said, standing quickly and then re-taking her chair once she saw the Vice President sitting. "I was just reviewing your speech for tomorrow's event at the Smithsonian. I didn't know you needed it so soon."

"That's fine, Sharyn," said the Vice President dismissively. "I'm here about Working Group Delta and what's happening in Florida. Did you watch Marino's speech ten minutes ago?"

"I'm sorry. I didn't catch it. Anything new?"

"He's now clarifying his executive order and stating that federal law enforcement agents are not authorized to conduct business in

Florida outside the confines of federal installations. They can operate in airports, ports, courts, and military installations. Everywhere else is off-limits. He's instructed every Sheriff in the state to arrest any law enforcement officer who is armed or wearing a uniform or insignia of a federal law enforcement agency."

"That's ridiculous," said Sharyn.

"He's basically ordering the FBI to depart Sarasota. He gave them a week to collect any evidence they need regarding the terrorist bombing, but he wants them out."

"He can't do that," Sharyn stated flatly.

"You and I know that, but apparently, Vince Marino missed that day in social studies class when they covered the Supremacy Clause of the U.S. Constitution."

Sharyn stayed quiet, thinking. The best advice she'd ever been given was to keep quiet when she didn't have anything important to say.

"President Fulton is an honorable, intelligent man who's always held this nation foremost in his heart. A man I deeply respect," said the Vice President.

"Of course," Sharyn replied, not sure where this was headed.

"I'm worried about him," the VP admitted. "And I'm worried for the future of this administration."

Again uncertain what to say, Sharyn just nodded.

"I know he's the best hope the party has of retaining the White House, but I'm not confident he can keep it together for an entire election cycle," continued Moore. "I mean, you've seen how he gets in meetings after a while. And how Geraldine has to get them to edit every social media clip to cut out any parts where he looks frail or out of touch. Are you confident he'll be able to debate Benjamin King on live television for sixty minutes?"

"Yes, I definitely see your point, and your concerns are valid," Sharyn responded carefully. This conversation was borderline mutinous, and she wanted to be careful with her words. "What are you suggesting?"

"We need a win, Sharyn. The President needs a win to take

some of the heat off of this fiasco. First, King flips his middle finger at the legal system, then Marino neuters the FBI, then Ms. *Perfect Wife*, Emily Greene, and her daughter get blown up eating lunch. The President's polls are down considerably in the last ten days. Have you been able to get in touch with Nathan Greene?"

"No, I haven't. I've tried several times and have been told he's not taking any calls."

"Did you tell them you were one of his former students?" VP Moore asked.

"I did. And I even tried saying the Vice President was calling. No luck," Sharyn admitted. Professor Greene had been her favorite professor as an undergrad at the University of Florida, so much so that she'd actually applied to grad school at Stanford University just so she could continue studying under him. She'd spent many dinners at Greene's on-campus faculty residence at Stanford and had grown especially close with both Mrs. Greene and their daughter Maeve, who was in elementary school at the time. Sharyn knew Nathan would want to speak with her, but she didn't know how to get through his gatekeepers.

"I think maybe you should take a trip down there. Would you do that for me?"

"Of course," said Sharyn. "Whatever you need me to do."

"This week is a mess with the Smithsonian tomorrow and dinner at the British Embassy on Friday. You should fly down there on Saturday. Please pass on the sincere condolences of the President and Vice President, and do everything you can to get Professor Greene to agree to come to the White House. At a minimum, we need a photo op with him and President Fulton. Best case, he'll agree to a press conference. But if we can get him on the White House grounds, we can get photos with him and the President. Geraldine can spin that to make it look like we're the good guys, and Marino and King are the bad guys."

"I understand," said Sharyn, feeling a bit queasy, realizing she was being asked to leverage her friendship to use a grieving husband and father for political gain. "I'll do my best."

Divided We Stand

"As long as your best is getting Professor Greene to Washington," stated the Vice President, locking eyes with Sharyn to ensure she understood the gravity of the situation.

"Yes, Madame Vice President."

19

Jackson, Wyoming

Wednesday, February 21

"WHAT DO YOU THINK?" Orlean Brumback asked, sitting back in the oversized wingback leather chair, a rocks glass of amber liquid with a golf-ball-sized ice cube resting on his ample belly.

"Quite nice," said Alex Treacher, attempting to inject sincerity into his voice. "Very smooth, indeed." Alex much preferred vodka to bourbon, but he'd learned long ago to admire any alcohol his host preferred.

"You bet your sweet ass it's smooth," said Orlean in the deep, chesty baritone that had made him America's preeminent on-air radio personality in the 1990s. Over the last two decades, Brumback had parlayed his on-air success into building the country's largest conservative media group: Bunker Hill Media.

He ran Bunker Hill Media out of his mountainside retreat along Jackson Hole, just north of Jackson, Wyoming. Jackson Hole is the eighty-mile-long valley stretching from Yellowstone National Park and following the Snake River down to Munger Mountain south of the popular tourist town of Jackson. Brumback's twelve-acre estate included an 8,800 square-foot timber-frame lodge with every amenity known to the rich and famous, as well as several outbuildings, including a bunkhouse and a state-of-the-art radio and television studio. He owned a half dozen million-dollar homes lower on the mountain, which he offered rent-free to the various conservative media personalities that contributed to the success of his media empire.

Brumback and Treacher sat alone in the vast living room of the lodge, peaked ceilings rising at least twenty feet with the exposed Douglas Fir logs comprising the walls and ceiling. Two massive stone fireplaces bookended the room, logs simmering and providing heat against the cold February afternoon. An entire wall of glass windows offered majestic views toward the peaks of the Grand Tetons reminiscent of a postcard.

Orlean savored another sip of the Kentucky Bourbon, looking at his glass as the liquid provided a pleasant burn in his throat. "This is Buffalo Trace's Eagle Rare 25. They only produced 200 bottles at $10,000 a bottle. Lucky me, I was able to get ten bottles."

"Worth every penny," said Alex, not meaning it in the least.

"So, where are we with the plan?" Orlean asked. "We've done everything you've asked so far. Are we ready for Phase 2?"

"Close," said Alex. "Your people are doing a tremendous job stirring the pot on social media. Tik Tok, Instagram Reels, Facebook—the animosity across the country for the opposing view on the federal versus state issue has significantly increased over the last two weeks. We need to keep stirring until the pot boils over. That's when we initiate Phase 2."

"When will that be? And how will we know?"

"Oh, we'll know," said Alex. "And I think soon. Maybe two weeks. Maybe a bit longer. At some point someone on one side or the other is going to make a move, and it's going to increase the tension exponentially. It could be Fulton and his crew, or it could be King and Marino. For us, it doesn't matter."

"Don't we want it to be Fulton? If King screws up, it will hurt our chances in November."

"That's the old way of thinking about things. The reality is that the election is going to come down to a handful of states, and our ability to influence the votes in those states is unequaled. Trust me. Right now, though, the key is sowing as much chaos, discontent, and animosity as possible. It makes no difference if the spark starts from the left or the right. It's the spark itself that our social media engine spins to our advantage. Our goal is a bonfire—no one cares which side threw the match."

"Okay," said Orlean, seemingly satisfied. "You're the boss."

"That's right, my friend." Alex sipped his bourbon, wishing it were vodka. "How are you set for capital?"

"We're good until Phase 2. The $20 million infusion two weeks ago is more than enough to allow us to run the machine and to provide boosts where needed." Orlean referred to the underground worldwide network of cyber shops that specialized in pumping out social media memes and videos and then used a mix of bots and real people to make what they produced immediately go viral across targeted audiences.

Alex had been instrumental in helping Orlean's Bunker Hill Media establish this network over the last ten years, providing both funding and know-how. Orlean continued to be amazed at Treacher's deep pockets and ability to source qualified people internationally.

Orlean sometimes wondered at the source of Treacher's wealth but had been able to find very little about the man's background. *Sometimes, it's not wise to look too hard,* Brumback thought. *As my mother used to say, never look a gift horse in the mouth.*

20

Osprey, Florida

Thursday, February 22

NATHAN HIT SEND ON the email, firing the first shot in what he hoped would lead him to the people responsible for killing his family.

He was not naive to think this path would be simple, straightforward, or short. The puppet masters behind the St. Armands Circle bombing were well-organized, well-funded, and well-hidden.

They were also politically motivated, and that was their weak point. Their political motivation was how Nathan would root them out and uncover their den of iniquity, where they planned the murder of innocent Americans, and kill them. Every one of them.

These people were terrorists. And Nathan had at one time in his life been one of the very best in the world at killing terrorists.

Since the funeral, Nathan had devoted himself to the effort of finding who was behind the bombing. Spooner, who still had significant contacts in the intelligence and law enforcement communities, had reached out to these contacts and started gathering all available information. Together, Nathan and Spooner spent long hours organizing every scrap of intelligence, examining every possible lead, and starting the process of building a profile of the group behind the murder of Nathan's family.

Nathan knew that the perpetrators responsible for the bombing, the ones who called the shots and put everything in motion, were motivated by politics. They were clearly seeking to influence the outcome of the standoff between President Fulton and former President King, although it was unclear which side they were on. On the one hand, killing federal agents might be seen as an attempt to get the federal government to back off. On the other hand, the death of the agents and a major terrorist bombing on U.S. soil were bound to force even more federal involvement in what was happening in Sarasota.

So far, the information they'd gathered had amounted to a big pile of nothing. The FBI had matched the fingerprints of the decapitated bomber to those of Enrique Rosario, a Mexican national who had illegally lived in the United States for more than seven years before being deported last summer after being arrested for a DUI resulting in multiple injuries. There was no record of him having connections to drug cartels. No one had seen Enrique Rosario back in the United States prior to him parking an Amazon van and exiting it just prior to the van exploding.

The van itself was a dead end. It was not a real Amazon van—real ones have multiple GPS sensors that are centrally tracked. This Ford Transit van was stolen the week before from a Miami car dealership, and someone had professionally wrapped the vehicle to mimic an Amazon delivery van, as its original color was white.

The explosives used in the bombing offered some information, but the FBI and CIA were still attempting to identify the bomb maker. The bomb was a fairly sophisticated improvised explosive device using a large amount of Semtex plastic explosive. The explosive could be traced to the manufacturer in Czech, but no taggants were found, so it could have been legally exported just about anywhere in the world. It appeared likely the Semtex was initially manufactured for military purposes rather than civilian use—as

Divided We Stand

many countries require civilian explosives to have added chemical taggants to allow the identification of the batch.

The interior wall of the van had been lined with over a hundred pounds of nails and screws, the kind that could be purchased from any hardware store or Walmart in America. The detonator used was similar to some of the more sophisticated detonators used at the end of the Iraq War, and it seemed highly likely that the bombmaker had experience or was trained in the Middle East. This narrowed it down to hundreds of potential bombmakers and their countless disciples.

Nathan and Spooner had decided on a moniker for the group behind the bombing—the Cabal.

It seemed clear to Nathan and Spooner that the Cabal was well-connected—they had moved a Mexican national across an international border using known drug cartel routes, had access to military-grade explosives, and could tap into the expertise of an experienced bomb maker. The Cabal was well-funded—all of the previous things required a substantial outlay of cash. Lastly, the Cabal was well-led—most attempts to pull something like this off resulted in failure, and it was only through competent, effective leadership and supervision that this plan was executed flawlessly.

Spooner had pressed his federal and local law enforcement contacts and had learned another tidbit of information that was helping them piece things together. Both teams of investigators, the Florida team and the federal team, firmly believed that the first shot in the Lido Club shootout had been from a sniper position in a condo building a couple of hundred yards north of the Lido Club.

Using video analysis tools of the two U.S. Marshals initially shot, investigators from the Sarasota Sheriff's Office and the Florida Department of Law Enforcement found what they were certain was the specific condominium used as the sniper hide. Unfortunately, the only forensic evidence found in the apartment were traces of gunshot residue on the window sill facing the Lido Club. The FBI, whom the FDLE had reluctantly allowed brief access to the building, agreed.

The professionalism of everything that had happened so far

made Nathan think this was very likely state-sponsored terrorism—but which country? Was it a foreign state such as Iran, North Korea, Russia, or China? Was it rogue elements within the U.S. Government? Or could it possibly even be rogue elements in the King campaign or Marino's team that had deep pockets and access to some very unsavory people?

The potential for these actors to continue their terror campaign fueled Nathan's quest for revenge, and part of him was thankful this wasn't the result of some lone wolf crackpot. With the Cabal behind his wife and daughter's murder, Nathan at least felt a sense of mission and looked forward to the ability to inflict pain upon his family's killers.

Nathan also knew his thirst for revenge was not healthy—but it was all he had.

Spooner also recognized this and did his best to keep a close eye on his best friend. Spooner was grateful Nathan had broken out of his trance-like sessions sitting on the beach, but Spooner was now getting concerned that Nathan was becoming too obsessed with finding the Cabal. Nathan had hardly slept at all since the bombing, nor was he eating properly—only eating when prompted to by Spooner or Kristen. The one day Spooner had flown to Washington D.C. to meet with his contacts in the CIA and FBI, Spooner returned late that night to find that Nathan had been typing on his laptop for sixteen straight hours, not eating or drinking anything.

Grief continued its onslaught just beneath the surface. Nathan seemed engaged in the investigation, his mind working overtime to link pieces of the puzzle. However, Spooner watched as Nathan often slipped back into an almost catatonic state of grief, thinking about his wife and daughter and their horrific death that he had been unable to prevent.

This afternoon, Nathan was alone again at his home on Casey Key. Kristen had stopped by earlier to find Nathan fully immersed in typing on his laptop, and Spooner had been needed back home to Clewiston to handle some business issues for a couple of days. Spooner was loathe to leave Nathan alone, but Nathan had insisted.

Nathan's cell phone buzzed with a call. It had been turned off

Divided We Stand

for over a week, and he'd just turned it on a few minutes after sending his email.

He swiped the glass of the phone to answer the call.

"What did you think?" Nathan asked, without preamble or greeting.

"It's amazing, Nathan," answered the woman on the other end of the phone. "Timely, inciteful, groundbreaking—I can publish it on the website in a few hours and in the print edition at midnight. I can't guarantee it will be above the fold, but I've just spoken to the executive editor, and he says it's definitely front-page material."

"I want you to be honest, Jessica, and critical," said Nathan. "This is all based on research I've done over the last couple of years, but with everything that's happened in the past two weeks, I think America's politicians need a wakeup call."

"Honestly, this is one of the best Op-ed pieces I've ever read. To say that it will get the attention of the D.C. establishment is a gross understatement."

Nathan breathed a silent sigh of relief—the first step in his plan was starting to come together. This Op-ed was the equivalent of tipping a boulder from the top of a hill and hoping that it gathered momentum on the way down, starting an avalanche.

The woman on the phone was Jessica Dwyer. At thirty-six, she was one of three deputy managing editors of the New York Times —the youngest person ever to be named to the masthead of the esteemed newspaper. Jessica had been a Rhodes Scholar at Oxford at the same time Nathan was there completing his PhD. They had developed a strong friendship that had solidified over the years.

"Others have written before on the decay of democracy and the need for term limits," Jessica said. "But I don't think anyone has captured it quite like you have, especially with the data. Ten current members of Congress have served more than forty consecutive years; forty-eight members have served more than twenty years. While that may not be terribly surprising, your data matching Congressional length of service to personal wealth is astonishing! The Senate Majority Leader, who has only held jobs that were elected offices since he graduated law school in 1974, currently has a publicly disclosed net worth of between $9 million and $24 million, excluding the millions of dollars of real estate he owns. The Senate Minority Leader, who's also been in D.C. for more than forty years as well, had his wealth grow from less than $2 million in 2002 to more than $32 million in 2022. I mean, people will freak out when they read this on the cover of the New York Times. These politicians come to Washington as members of the middle class and leave as some of the wealthiest people in the country."

"And how about the office of the Presidency? Does that part make sense as well?"

"Nathan, I've been covering politics in Washington for over ten years, and I never really ever looked at this quite like you have. President Fulton has spent more than fifty-two years of his adult career as an elected official in Washington D.C. He's now worth well over $10 million, and he's running for reelection at the age of eighty-two! King, who's a relative newcomer to DC, had his family empire more than double in value during the four years he was in office. The average American simply can't grasp how much wealth our politicians accrue while serving in public office. Your editorial piece exposes this underbelly of politics in a way no one has done before. And with all that's going on down in Florida, this couldn't come at a better time."

"I've actually had a lot of this data for the last year but wasn't quite sure how to organize it all. The statistics about Fulton's age were alarming. He's almost eighty-three now and, if re-elected, will be eighty-seven at the end of his second term. According to the Social Security Administration, only fifty-seven percent of current eighty-two-year-olds will live to reach the age of eighty-seven. That means there is a forty-three percent chance a re-elected Fulton will die in office. Since the days of George Washington, only four of forty-six Presidents have died of natural causes while in office— that's about eight percent. Fulton's odds are forty-three percent of dying in office. Forty-three! Yet the Democratic Party still says he's the single best person in all of America to be President for four more years."

Divided We Stand

"Astonishing, I know," agreed Jessica, a lifelong member of the Democratic Party.

"And Benjamin King? Setting aside his buffoonery as an orator and a statesman, he had a ninety-one percent turnover in his A-team advisors—the people that make up the senior executives of the White House and Executive branch. Fourteen cabinet secretaries resigned—the average of the previous six presidents was just over four resignations, and that included three two-term presidencies. His supporters, whether you agree or disagree with their politics, ransacked the U.S. Capitol building—the first such occurrence since the British invaded in 1812. He's currently under indictment for failure to secure classified material, inciting an insurrection, and illegally interfering with the election process. Yet the Republican Party thinks he is the single best person in all of America to be President of the United States."

"You make some great points," said Jessica. "It's astonishing that the average business owner would never consider hiring either of these candidates, yet one of them is likely going to be President of the United States for the next four years. This is a great Op-ed, Nathan. It will be the talk of the town tomorrow. Probably the talk of the entire country."

"Good," said Nathan. "Thanks for your help."

"How are you holding up personally?" Jessica asked. "I can't even imagine what you're going through."

"It's been tough, but I'll be fine. Thanks for flying down for the funeral. I'm sorry I wasn't able to meet with you. I, uh, I wasn't in a very good place last week."

"No, no," Jessica said. "You don't need to apologize at all. I'm here if you need anything. But Nathan?"

"Yes?"

"Be prepared for a lot of press regarding your Op-ed. It's going to run through the D.C. elite like shit through a goose, and they are definitely not going to be happy. None of them. This is a house of cards that's been built over the last sixty years, and you're the guy turning the fan on. They are going to be very protective of their power, so be prepared to be the target of their ire."

"That's the whole point, Jessica," said Nathan softly. "That's the whole point."

Nathan disconnected the call. His feeling of satisfaction at getting his article published in the New York Times was quickly replaced with an overwhelming sense of grief at the loss of his wife and daughter—of his future, everything he looked forward to in life.

Nathan grabbed the Glock 19 9mm pistol lying on his desk, turned out the light in his study, and proceeded through the house and out to his chair on the beach.

The beach chair had become both his solace and his penance. It was where his thoughts were clearest. Looking out at the waters of the Gulf brought perspective to his place in the world. Without Emily and Maeve, Nathan realized he was just a tiny grain of sand on this endless beach, unable to exert any impact on the endless cycle of waves pushing and pulling at the sand.

He'd begun carrying the Glock the day Emily and Maeve had been killed. It wasn't for self-protection—it was for self-harm.

Nathan didn't consider himself suicidal. To him, suicide was a cop-out. He'd lost plenty of friends and fellow veterans to suicide over the last two decades, and in every case, Nathan felt the person was running away from pain and troubles that they just weren't able to cope with.

That wasn't how Nathan felt at all.

He was perfectly capable of coping with the pain and the loss—he just didn't want to any longer. His reason for living, his future, had been stripped away from him by the terrorist's bomb.

Would his wounds of grief heal over time? Sure. Could he develop new reasons for living, for feeling joy and happiness? Undoubtedly.

He just didn't want to. It was that simple. The world that had taken his wife and daughter was one he no longer wished to participate.

Holding the Glock inside the front pocket of his hooded sweatshirt, Nathan caressed the metal and polymer tool of death. Nathan had killed people before, and he held no belief in the afterlife. He'd watched closely as the life went out of people's eyes, and he was certain death was just an off-switch. He held out no hope of an afterlife, no green pastures where he'd get to spend eternity with his loved ones.

The opportunity to spend time with his family had been brutally severed from Nathan. He would make those people pay; then he'd opt to flip his own off-switch. It was that simple.

21

Washington, D.C

Friday, February 23

VICE PRESIDENT MOORE walked into the Working Group Delta meeting in the West Wing's Roosevelt Room with a scowl on her face and a folded-up newspaper under her arm.

"I assume all of you have seen this already?" The VP asked, slamming the newspaper down on the table.

Sharyn, sitting along the conference table with the other Working Group Delta members, smiled to herself, wondering if the Vice President was referring to Nathan Greene's front-page editorial or to the actual newspaper itself. Sharyn would bet that almost no one at the table had read the actual paper newspaper, but felt confident they'd all seen the article online.

"Something amusing, Sharyn?" VP Moore asked sarcastically. "Perhaps you find your former college professor's article funny in some way."

"No, ma'am," answered Sharyn, wiping the smile from her face. "I was thinking of something else entirely."

"Good," said the Vice President. "Because this article is not good. At all." She turned to face Chief of Staff Reynolds. "John, what do the latest polls show?

"Well, the polls regarding the matchup with King remained unchanged—virtually neck and neck. However, the answers to two questions have swung considerably since the article's publication. By the way, it's already the most-read article on the New York Times website in 2024, and the day's barely half over. The article has been reposted more than 500,000 times on Twitter, or X, or whatever they call themselves now."

"Jesus," said the Vice President.

"That's nowhere near the worst," added Geraldine Fox. In her role as White House communications director, understanding the impact of a news article was right in her wheelhouse. "Professor Greene, whose X account has 2,700 followers and has not posted anything in the last sixteen months, sent out a tweet this morning and attached the Op-ed piece published in the Times. It read simply: Time to stop drinking the sand."

"Okay," said Reynolds.

"It's been liked more than one million times and has been retweeted 400,000 times. John, the record is six million. Greene's tweet reached one million in a SINGLE day!"

"I assume the President has read this. What was his reaction, John?" VP Moore asked.

"He's pissed. You know how he gets when anyone questions his mental acuity or his commitment to leading the country. But he thinks it hurts King more than it hurts him, so he didn't seem too worried about it."

"Bullshit," yelled Moore, raising her voice. Sharyn knew that as soon as Serena Moore started using profanity, it was a sure sign that she was losing her cool. "Drinking the sand? This two-bit political science professor is telling the American public that the two people running to be President aren't worthy of the office and they need to pick someone new. Someone not from inside the Beltway. And they're listening to him! Every talk show today and through the weekend is talking about this. This could be disastrous, and I'll be damned if some misguided Army veteran with the Medal of Honor and a PhD is going to take the Presidency away from me!" She slammed her hand down on the newspaper for additional emphasis.

Clearly lost her cool, thought Sharyn.

"You mean taking the Presidency away from President Fulton, don't you, ma'am," interjected Geraldine, whose disdain for the Vice President's ambition was well-known.

"Yes, yes, of course," stammered Moore. "You know exactly what I meant."

"Do we think this is going to impact King and Marino down in Florida?" Reynolds asked the assembled group. "I mean, that's what this meeting is for. What is this going to do to that situation?"

"It depends on their ultimate strategy," said Geraldine. "King's platform of draining the swamp dovetails well with Greene's Op-ed's call for a Constitutional amendment for term limits on all federal offices. While Greene clearly exposed King's failures as a President, if King jumps on the term limit idea, he could significantly change the narrative of what the upcoming Presidential race is all about. Instead of the economy, inflation, and immigration, he could turn President Fulton's fifty years in Washington against him."

"Goddamnit!" VP Moore said. "Sharyn, we need to get Nathan Greene to the White House. We need to get him in front of President Fulton, and we need to put them both on display, having a meaningful conversation while walking through the Rose Garden. This will show that the President retains all his faculties and is much more presidential than King. We all know this, but it's critical the American people see this as soon as possible. You know Greene, Sharyn. Invite him to the White House. We'll send a damn plane for him, for God's sake!"

"Madame Vice President, I've tried phoning him more than two dozen times since his wife and daughter were killed. I've left messages. He's not taking calls—even from me."

Moore turned to the FBI director. "Barry, can you send some of your folks to go pick him up? I know your agents are keeping a low profile, but maybe a couple could go over there and get him on a plane to D.C. I don't really care if they arrest him."

"Uh, actually, there's something else you should know about

Greene before we decide on a course of action," said FBI Director Tracy.

"And what's that?" Moore asked.

"As part of our investigation into the shootout between the Marshals and the Sheriffs, our investigators have subpoenaed, collected, and reviewed all of the video footage shot by the television crews on-site in the days before the incident." The FBI Director paused, shuffling the paper in front of him to pull a specific sheet to the top. "The morning former President King and Governor Marino gave their press conference where King refused to be arraigned in federal court. That morning, Nathan Greene drove into the Lido Club. We have video footage of him being met at the entrance by King's personal aide, and it's presumed that he met with both King and Marino. He left one hour before the press conference.

The Vice President looked away from the FBI Director, her gaze settling on the portrait of Teddy Roosevelt on horseback hanging above the fireplace.

"That's interesting," she said. "Bring him in, Barry. Tonight. Arrest him if you have to, but I want Nathan Greene at the White House tomorrow morning."

22

Cromwell Island, Montana

Friday, February 23

"THIS IS the spark we've been waiting for, my friend," said Alex Treacher, sitting alone in his private library whose large picture windows looked out over the frigid waters of Flathead Lake in northwest Montana.

"You think so?" replied Orlean Brumback, sitting in his much smaller study almost 400 miles south outside Jackson, Wyoming.

They each were wearing earbuds linked through Bluetooth to a Kryptall secure K-iPhone, which Alex had insisted they use for all communications. The phones had TLS and SRTP encryption algorithms to ensure that only the party at each end of the call could understand what was being said. Alex employed some of the best cyber professionals in the world, and this was the phone they told him to use to ensure no one could intercept his communication, not even the NSA.

"Absolutely," said Alex. "Nathan Greene's article in the Times is the spark. We need to let things develop for a week or two, but I'm confident this is what we need to initiate Phase 2 of our plan. Are you ready?"

"Of course I'm ready." Orlean's smooth radio voice hid his apprehension. Phase 2 was going to thrust Orlean personally into the limelight. While he'd remain generally behind the scenes for the immediate future, his fingerprints would be easily identifiable as the mastermind behind what they were calling Phase 2.

"Good, good," said Alex. "I'll be in touch to let you know when to start making the first calls that will initiate Phase 2." Without waiting for a reply, Alex terminated the encrypted call.

He stared out the window toward the lake and east to the pointed peaks of the Mission Mountains. Flathead Lake was the largest freshwater lake in the western United States, stretching over thirty miles in length, north to south, and fifteen miles wide. Despite the frigid weather outside, the lake itself was not frozen solid, and Alex could see the center of the lake being whipped into whitecaps by the brutal north wind. The edges of the lake were crusted solid with ice, while the gentle slope of the land down toward the lake was covered in more than a foot of snow. One of the cleanest lakes in the world, the waters were as clear as the finest-distilled vodka.

Treacher's estate was located on Cromwell Island, a 350-acre island nestled along the western shore of Flathead Lake equidistant from its northern and southern ends. Half covered in timber and half grazing land, Treacher had purchased the three-mile circumference island for more than $70 million through a nest of subsidiary companies upon the death of the island's longtime owner.

The owner had started building a monumental 45,000-square-foot lodge before his death in 2016, and Alex had immediately allocated the resources and skilled personnel to complete the building to his own specifications. Alex had also built several smaller lodges throughout the island, each secluded, secure, and well-separated from the main lodge, as well as several service buildings for equipment and other items.

Alex was very particular about maintaining the pristine natural conditions on the island, yet he knew the island and his palatial lodge would require a large workforce, including cooks, cleaners, maintenance personnel, and armed security guards. Rather than build the infrastructure to house these people on Cromwell Island, Alex purchased twenty acres on the mainland along US 93 just south of the small town of Dayton, Montana.

On this property, he built dormitories, lodges, and multiple warehouses, as well as a large pier directly opposite a similar pier on the western side of Cromwell Island. Cromwell Island's staff, with few exceptions, resided on the mainland and commuted by boat to the island for their shifts.

Alex had specifically not wanted to mar the island's beauty by carving out an airstrip, so instead built a discreet helipad with fuel and storage. He maintained two helicopters that could shuttle him north to the private jet strip in Kalispell in less than ten minutes.

A firm knock on the door to his study snapped his attention away from the lake's winter beauty.

"Come in, Sergei," Alex said, knowing exactly who had knocked.

A lean man of six feet entered the room dressed in a plain black suit and tie. With one hand, he balanced a small silver tray upon which sat a cut crystal bottle with a clear liquid and a single rocks glass. The clear bottle was shaped like a vase with the distinctive whale symbol of the Beluga Noble vodka company etched into its front. At $6,000 per bottle, the Beluga Epicure was one of the purest vodkas on earth, distilled and filtered using the purest water from a three-hundred-meter-deep artesian well located several hundred kilometers from the nearest Siberian town.

Sergei was Alex's house manager and the only person who lived full-time, all year round, on Cromwell Island. A former Spetsnaz soldier who'd served repeated tours in the Soviet wars in Afghanistan and Chechnya, Sergei was in his mid-fifties and was the first person Alex brought to Montana in 2016.

Alex trusted Sergei implicitly.

"Here is your drink, sir," said Sergei in heavily accented English. He placed the tray on the side table next to Alex and poured a healthy two fingers of the ice-cold liquid.

Divided We Stand

"Thank you, Sergei. Would you please tell the young lady that I'd like to see her at her convenience?" Alex asked.

"Certainly, sir. I will tell her now." Without further interaction, Sergei turned and exited the large study, closing the solid wooden door firmly behind him.

Alex did not need to refer to the young woman by name—she was the only other person staying on the island. Although she was constantly traveling, Alex had assigned her one of the small guest lodges on Cromwell Island, which served as the closest thing the young woman had to home.

Alex took the first sip of his drink, savoring the cool liquid's initial burn as it slid past his tongue and coated his throat with a pure fire that only Russian vodka could bring. Alex knew that other distilleries across the globe produced extremely fine vodka, but he confined himself solely to vodkas made in the Motherland.

Minutes later, as Alex savored his second sip, Sergei opened the door to his study and ushered in a young, extremely fit, muscular woman with closely-trimmed brown hair. She was wearing yoga pants and a hooded sweatshirt and looked like she had just come from the gym.

"Ah, Jasmine," Alex said, standing up from his chair. "Thank you for joining me. Can Sergei get you anything to drink?"

"No, thanks," said Jasmine, holding up a metal flask of water. "I brought my own."

"I see," said Alex, barely noticing that Sergei had departed and closed the door behind him. "My apologies if I interrupted your workout."

"Not a problem, Alex. I was just stretching. What's on your mind?"

"We're getting close to the start of Phase 2. I assume you've been following the latest news out of Florida. Professor Greene seems to have made quite a splash. I think in two weeks, the conditions will be set to initiate Phase 2."

"Yes, I've been following," replied Jasmine. She respected Alex and enjoyed his company, but Jasmine had little time for socializing and small talk. She was managing many facets of their current operation, and her mind was preoccupied.

"Where do we stand with Phase 2's moving pieces?"

"Well, I got back last week from Mexico. Team Strela is fully trained and ready to go. I turned them over to your logistics folks, who are responsible for getting them into position."

"Yes, I've received word that they are at the safe house, awaiting your arrival to activate them."

"Good," said Jasmine. "The Three Forks training program is complete. Nine of the twelve cells have returned to their staging locations, while three teams continue to wait at Three Forks. These are the D.C. teams, and we don't want them anywhere near the Capitol until just prior to kickoff."

Three Forks referred to the 1,000-acre training facility Alex's organization had established in the remotest part of eastern Oregon, just northeast of the Three Forks Recreation Site. Aside from the occasional one-off operations Alex tasked her with, Jasmine's primary mission had been to organize and train twelve six-person cells that would initiate Phase 2 of Alex's grand strategy to reshape America.

Jasmine was not concerned with understanding Alex's strategy —she was a point-and-shoot operator. Alex had proven that she could trust him implicitly, and she went where he told her to go and did what he tasked her to do without hesitation.

Jasmine was aware that her portion of Alex's strategy was a very small part of the grand master strategy, and she was content not to concern herself with aspects of the plan outside her purview. What Alex told her to do, she did. What he didn't want her to know, she did not attempt to learn.

"Excellent work, Jasmine. As usual," Alex complimented her. "I don't mean to keep you any longer. Please feel free to go back to your workout. We'll watch how things develop in the news, but I'm confident that in a week or so, we'll give the green light to commence Phase 2."

"Looking forward to it," said Jasmine, standing and heading for the door.

23

Osprey, Florida

Friday, February 23

TODAY HAD BEEN ESPECIALLY difficult for Nathan. He was proud of the Op-ed article that he'd written, both for its content and as bait to lure the perpetrators behind the St. Armands Circle bombing. However, all the attention he was garnering compounded his grief.

His article attempted to define the very essence of what had gone wrong with the federal government over the past few decades and to offer a simple path forward to excise the cancer that continued to spread through all facets of the Beltway machine. Titled "Drinking the Sand" from the famous quote of fictional President Andrew Shepard in the movie *The American President*, Nathan used irrefutable facts to show how the divisiveness of the two-party political system rewarded longevity and bred animosity between party members. The result was a completely inefficient federal government amidst a swamp of legalized corruption.

Fifteen Senators and over thirty Congressmen have currently served more than twenty years in Congress, and almost 150 more have served over twelve years. While Senators and Representatives received moderate salaries, the wealth of elected officials after spending more than ten years in DC increased exponentially—alarmingly so.

Nathan wasn't a conspiracy theorist, but he did believe that these career members of Congress were unjustly enriching themselves off the public dime. The average person making a $174,000 annual salary, which is what current members of Congress are paid, would likely have accrued a net worth of possibly a couple of million dollars at best by the end of a thirty-year career. Senators and Representatives serving in Washington for twenty-plus years were disclosing wealth increases in the magnitude of $10-20 million dollars, most of this in the final five years of their federal service.

Politicians shouldn't get rich by being politicians—that's not how the system was supposed to work.

Whether the chicken or the egg, this wealth was paired with an overwhelming advantage for incumbents in continuing to serve in Washington, D.C. In 2022, 94.5% of incumbents in the House of Representatives won reelection—in the U.S. Senate, it was 100%. 100% of those sitting senators seeking reelection were reelected! The founding fathers' vision of a citizen legislature had been replaced by a purely professional one.

Nathan's article placed the blame for this squarely on the two-party system that had developed over the last two centuries. This system rewarded individual loyalty to the party and was built entirely on a system of seniority. Consequently, everything from party dynamics to election campaign laws had been specifically designed to keep those in power *in power*.

As George Washington stated in his farewell address after he voluntarily refused to run for reelection, political parties will "become potent engines, by which cunning, ambitious, and unprincipled men will be enabled to subvert the power of the people and to usurp for themselves the reins of government, destroying afterward the very engines which have lifted them to unjust dominion."

Nathan's solution was simple: the imposition of strict term limits. His article demanded that both houses of Congress immedi-

Divided We Stand

ately propose and pass a constitutional amendment establishing term limits similar to those imposed on the President: two terms and you're out.

For decades, polls have shown that more than eighty percent of the American population fully support restrictive term limits on members of Congress. It's actually one of the very few policies both sides overwhelmingly agree on. Yet, despite its popularity, Congress has never once come close to passing such legislation. Why? Because the people elected to Congress would be, in effect, voting to limit their own ability to accrue wealth and power as members of the Washington elite.

Just after 11 p.m., Nathan noticed that his New York Times article had become one of the most popular articles in years. Nathan knew his email inbox must be overflowing, and his voicemail was full, but he refused to turn on his computer or his phone.

His goal with the article had been to put bait in the trap, and he was confident that it would work. The people behind the St. Armands Circle bombing, the ones who had meticulously plotted to kill innocent people while leaving no trace of their involvement, all had a vested interest in maintaining their power. Nathan didn't yet know who it was, but he was confident that at some point in the coming days, the perpetrators would make a move that would give Nathan a clue so he could track down his family's killers.

It was all he lived for.

He sat on the beach, in his chair, and absently watched the waves lap at the sand. The night was chilly, the gibbous moon blocked by clouds. Nathan fingered the Glock 19 in his sweatshirt pocket, wondering if he had the patience for revenge or if he'd be better off just leaving this world behind.

He decided he'd wait at least one more day—he owed his family that much.

24

Osprey, Florida

Friday, February 23

THE THREE FBI special agents crowded into the Toyota RAV4 and drove slowly up the winding, narrow road that traversed the length of Casey Key. On the northern end of the barrier island, where the Greene's home was located, the road was only a single lane that twisted and turned around and through different properties, often bisecting homes whose front yards extended all the way between the Gulf and the bay.

Special Agent Bill Halstead sat in the passenger seat and wished he were back home with his wife in Ocala. At fifty-six, he was the oldest of the three agents, which was the only reason he'd nominally been placed in charge. He had less than a year until mandatory retirement, and he wanted nothing more than to glide until his retirement date without making waves.

He'd been on the special agent fast track at one point, but that was years ago.

Alcohol and stress had ended his first marriage eight years earlier, after an especially difficult case in Detroit involving child

Divided We Stand

trafficking. He'd been a supervisory special agent then, but there had been some questions regarding the necessity to use deadly force during the apprehension of the child abductors, and he'd been quietly offered a billet in Ocala, Florida, to finish out his career.

Despite the demotion, he thoroughly enjoyed central Florida. He had married a woman twenty years his junior, had a nice house on several acres adjacent to a gorgeous horse farm, and wanted nothing more right now than to head back to his beautiful wife and home. Halstead had been one of more than a hundred FBI agents called to Sarasota to augment the ongoing investigation, and tonight, he and his two colleagues had been tasked with bringing Dr. Nathan Greene to the Sarasota airport, where an FBI plane was waiting to whisk the man to Washington.

The two other agents, Kevin Dee, who was driving, and Brian Schmidt, who sat in the back seat, were both in their late twenties and had come over from the FBI's Miami field office. None of the three had been excited about this tasking, seeing it more as an errand than as part of the investigation.

The only bright side of the tasking was that, supposedly, this was being done at the President's specific request.

The three FBI agents wore informal civilian clothes, including slacks, polo shirts, and, in Kevin's case, a dark hoodie. Given Governor Marino's executive order, they'd been specifically ordered not to wear anything that would identify them as federal law enforcement officers.

They knew nothing about Dr. Greene other than that he was a political science professor who'd written an editorial in the New York Times that was currently the leading news story across the nation. The agents were told to pick him up, but they had also been told to use any means necessary, including forcible arrest, to ensure Nathan Greene was on that plane to D.C.

Not expecting any issues, the agents slowed as they approached the Greene residence. Like the other homes on the barrier island, it was a beautiful house that must have cost many millions of dollars. While most of the houses on this part of north Casey Key had the road threaded between the house and the

Gulf, the Greene estate placed the house on the Gulf side of the road.

The Greene residence was completely dark. Not a single light was on inside the house, and all of the exterior lights had been turned off as well. Some faint landscape lighting illuminated a walkway leading to the front door, and several spotlights irradiated large palm trees spaced randomly around the property.

"Turn your lights off, Dee," said Halstead. "Just coast up and park across the front of the driveway."

"Roger," said Dee, switching off the headlights.

The RAV4 rolled to a stop, and the three FBI agents stepped out of the vehicle, quietly closing their doors behind them.

"Schmidt, you stay here in front," ordered Halstead. "Dee and I will check out the back; make sure there's no surprises. These beach houses often have big picture windows, so hopefully we can see if he's home."

"Got it," said Schmidt.

"When it's clear, I'll leave Dee in the back and come back around to the front. You and I can then ring the bell, and hopefully, Dr. Greene answers, and we can get him to the airport."

"Sounds good," said Schmidt, walking up the driveway toward the front walk.

"You ready?" Halstead asked Dee.

"Yeah," Agent Dee replied. "There's some landscape lights around to the right. Let's go that way—there looks to be a path that wraps around the house."

As the two slowly walked around the side of the house, a light breeze began to blow. The cloud cover that had hung darkly over the area all evening began to lift, and the three-quarter moon showed through. The moonlight was helpful to the agents, who could now see pretty clearly in the dark.

Dee pulled his pistol from his holster, holding it low at his side. Halstead didn't think that was entirely necessary, but it *was* dark, and they were approaching an unknown person's home with the purpose of potentially detaining him, so having a firearm ready was maybe not a bad idea.

Halstead led the way, and soon, they reached the rear of the large house, where they could clearly see a stone patio surrounding an inground pool. The windows at the rear of the house were as dark as the front, and nothing inside the home was visible. Halstead moved forward around the pool, attempting to peer into the windows from a distance, while Kevin stood on the patio and scanned toward the beach.

NATHAN WAS JARRED out of his grief-stricken trance by a scraping sound behind him. Craning his neck, he thought he saw movement on the patio.

Goddamn reporters, Nathan thought. *When will they leave me alone?*

Nathan stood up and turned to see who or what had disturbed him. He'd taken several steps toward the house before seeing the silhouettes of two men standing on his patio. The one closest to him, backlit by the low-voltage perimeter lights surrounding the patio, was wearing jeans and a dark hooded sweatshirt. He was also carrying a pistol in his right hand, holding it by his hip, pointed downward.

What the fuck?

Without thinking, Nathan's right hand pulled the Glock 19 from inside the front pocket of his hoodie.

"Gun!" The man shouted in surprise as he turned to see Nathan. The FBI agent began to raise his pistol in Nathan's direction.

Instinctively, Nathan dove to the ground, flopping down behind a low mangrove bush that grew between the patio and the beach. The man's muzzle flashed, and the crack of the gunshot pierced the night's silence.

Without hesitation, acting on autopilot, Nathan raised himself to a crouch and fired two quick rounds at the intruder. He knew instantly that both rounds had hit the man in the center of his face, and Nathan watched as the man collapsed as if a marionette with its strings cut. They were only ten meters apart, and even as rusty as he was, at this distance, Nathan knew his aim had been true.

"FBI! Drop your fucking gun! FBI! We're FBI!" yelled the other intruder on the patio, the one closest to the house.

What the—?

Nathan immediately dropped his weapon. He stood up slowly while raising his hands above his head.

"I'm unarmed," Nathan shouted. "You guys never identified yourself."

Halstead took several steps forward, his pistol now in his hand, and trained on Nathan. "You idiot!" Halstead yelled, looking down at Dee's unmoving body on the ground. He was clearly dead. Even in the dim light, Halstead could see the bullet wounds in Dee's face and forehead and the rapidly spreading pool of blood surrounding his head.

"You're FBI?" Greene asked. "You never identified yourself."

Halstead could hear Greene yelling, but all he could think of was the looming investigation this shooting was sure to bring, just like back in Detroit. He knew he wouldn't survive this one, and thirty years of pension was about to go up in smoke.

Bang! Bang!

Halstead fired without even thinking.

Both rounds hit Nathan in the chest, luckily off-center. Nathan felt like someone had slammed a baseball bat into the left side of his ribcage, and he fell backward into the sand. Something slammed into the back of his head, and for a moment, he felt like maybe he lost consciousness.

Nathan came to almost instantly—flat on his back on the sand, just at the edge of his patio.

The man who'd shot him stood directly over him.

"You stupid fuck!" The man hissed. "You didn't need to shoot him!"

Nathan tried to speak, but for some reason, he wasn't able to form words.

Halstead was highly agitated and seemed to have lost control.

"They're gonna blame it on me! All on me!" The man yelled. "You're the one who's making me do this."

As Nathan watched, the man raised his arm and pointed his pistol directly at Nathan's head. Mustering his focus and strength, his chest feeling so tight he could barely breathe, Nathan kicked his left leg out as hard as he could.

Luck was on his side, and the kick connected with Halstead's knee, causing him to lose his balance. Caught completely off guard, Halstead fell to the ground, and Nathan rolled away to his right.

My gun! Nathan thought. Miraculously, as Nathan rolled, he felt his pistol under his right thigh, which is where it must have fallen when he intentionally dropped it earlier. Nathan reached down, his fingers tightening over the pistol's grip.

Nathan looked quickly over his shoulder and could see the FBI agent fumbling for his weapon. Without hesitation, Nathan fired a bullet directly into the side of Halstead's head, killing him instantly.

In tremendous pain, Nathan let his pistol fall to the ground just as a bright light swept over him, and another man yelled, "Freeze! FBI!"

Part II

"If we are to have another contest in the near future of our national existence, I predict that the dividing line will not be Mason and Dixon's but between patriotism and intelligence on the one side, and superstition, ambition and ignorance on the other."

—Ulysses S. Grant

25

Lido Key, Florida

Saturday, March 9

THE TABLE WAS STREWN with the red and white detritus of a Chik-fil-A feast. A platter in the middle was stacked high with small white paper foil bags containing Chik-fil-A's signature chicken sandwich and several large cartons of waffle fries. Various rectangular packets of colorfully labeled sauces and condiments lay scattered about.

In front of Orlean Brumback and Benjamin King, each had two empty chicken sandwich wrappers and remnants of waffle fries. King had a half-full styrofoam soda cup of Diet Coke while Brumback sipped on a large cup of Sunjoy—the franchise's signature mix of lemonade and iced tea.

There were no Chik-fil-A franchises within a hundred miles of Orlean's home in Jackson, Wyoming, so King, a fellow fast food aficionado, had treated his guest and political advisor to a gluttonous lunch.

It was now time to get down to business.

Gregor Bout, King's personal aide, joined them at the large table in the Garden Terrace Room of King's Lido Club.

"So you're saying it's breakout time?" King asked.

"That's exactly right, Ben. I've talked this over with my entire staff, and we're all in agreement. The momentum has built significantly since the FBI raided Professor Greene's house two weeks ago. You've sealed up the Republican nomination for November, but now is the time to keep hitting the campaign trail. Raise money, sway people, and put the nail in Fulton's coffin before we even get to the convention."

The reality was that this was not Brumback's idea but Alex Treacher's. He and Brumback had spoken daily over the last two weeks since Professor Greene had been shot, and Alex had set today as the commencement day to initiate Phase 2 of their strategic operation.

Nathan Greene had survived the attack by the FBI—barely. Luckily for him, the third FBI agent, the one initially covering the front door, had immediately called an ambulance rather than attempt to sanitize the scene. Greene underwent emergency surgery at Sarasota Memorial Hospital to remove bullets from his chest and shoulder and was expected to make a full recovery.

Initially, the FBI reported that Greene had ambushed the special agents. Fortunately for Nathan, he had several Google Nest cameras positioned around the patio, complete with night vision and sound. The video showed the FBI agents did not display any credentials, nor did they announce themselves as law enforcement officers until after opening fire. Greene's actions were clearly in self-defense.

Agent Halstead's attempted execution of Greene as he lay wounded on the sand was being protested nationwide as an example of the "FBI's Gestaopo-like tactics," and the multiple bot farms controlled by Brumback's Bunker Hill Media exploited this to the fullest.

In the last two weeks, mass demonstrations had sprouted nationwide. News networks broadcast 24/7 coverage discussing Greene's Op-ed article demanding term limits, and an endless number of pundits expounded upon the virtues of both sides of the argument.

Divided We Stand

Treacher and Brumback's plan was not just about furthering their own agenda. It was about sowing discord on both sides and ramping up the intensity so that the entire country was frothing at the mouth.

"I love it," replied King. "Where do I start?"

Brumback nodded at Gregor, who had a laptop open in front of him. "Today, we are going to reach out to all twenty-seven Republican governors. In addition to supporting you in November, we need you to urge them to endorse Governor Marino's executive order exerting State's rights over all law enforcement and banning federal law enforcement within their state."

"Excellent," said King. "I mean, who's not going to go along with this after all that's been happening."

"Right you are, Mr. President," supported Orlean. "I've already spoken to several of the governors with whom I have a personal relationship. They are extremely enthusiastic about this plan and have agreed to publicly support Governor Marino's executive order by issuing a similar order for their states."

"What governors?" Interjected King's young aide, Gregor.

"Texas, Wyoming, Idaho, and Montana," replied Orleans without hesitation.

"Zane Owens in Texas is a good man," said King. "You know he's always been a supporter of mine? He's a good man. Has a terrible problem on his southern border that I hope we can help with when we get back in office."

"Yes. I spoke with him last night, and he's very much on board."

"Maybe I should call him myself," suggested King. "You know, I'll call all of them. But maybe Zane in Texas should be first."

"By all means," said Orleans, nodding to Gregor to dial Governor Owens' direct number on King's iPhone.

In seconds, the call had connected.

"Zane? This is Benjamin King. How are you this beautiful Saturday morning?"

"Great, Mr. President. Just great. I'm glad that you called."

"Well, I believe you've spoken with my good friend, Orlean, who happens to be sitting with me right now. He says you're fully on board with Governor Marino's executive order limiting the powers of the federal government."

"Absolutely, Mr. President! In fact, I've instructed my staff to draft a similar executive order for Texas, and we plan to hold a press conference on Monday."

"Excellent, excellent. And what about term limits, Zane? I'm considering pushing that as part of my campaign agenda. Congress needs to pass a term limit amendment immediately so that the states can ratify it. Would you agree with me on that?"

"Wholeheartedly, Mr. President. You know we have your back over here in Texas."

"Yes, Zane. I know you do. I know you do. Thank you. I'll be in touch."

The former President ended the call.

For the next two hours, King held similar calls with all twenty-seven Republican governors across the country, receiving full support from all but two.

Tensions across the country had ramped up considerably, especially on college campuses. Young voters were being mobilized and staging increasingly larger protests either in support of limiting federal power or against former President King's refusal to submit to the jurisdiction of the federal courts.

The Republican governors, especially those in states with Republican-controlled legislatures, were keen to act, and King and Governor Marino had given them a reason to do so.

26

Washington, D.C

Saturday, March 9

AT THE SAME time King and Brumback were calling each of the nation's Republican governors to solicit their support, Sharyn was attending a small, informal gathering in the Oval Office. The President and Vice President each sat in upholstered wingback chairs while Sharyn shared one of the two long couches with John Reynolds, President Fulton's Chief of Staff.

It wasn't often that just the four of them met, as there were almost always additional staffers or advisors present, depending on the issue being addressed. The President was departing later that morning for a few days at Camp David, and neither the Vice President nor Sharyn had been invited.

"Thanks for making time this morning, Serena," said President Fulton to his Vice President.

"Of course, Mr. President," VP Moore said, taking a sip from her cup of coffee.

"John has been keeping me informed of everything you and the

Working Group have done. It's a real mess down in Florida. It sure would have been helpful to have hosted Professor Greene here at the White House, as you originally planned."

The aftermath of the shootout at Nathan Greene's beach home on Casey Key had sent shockwaves across the country. Professor Greene had been in critical condition by the time the ambulance had transported him to the hospital, and he was in and out of surgery for the first forty-eight hours with no ability to be interviewed. Even if he'd been alert, there's no telling if the federal authorities would have even been able to question him, as Sarasota Sheriff deputies had cordoned off Greene's hospital room and refused to let anyone have access.

The FBI had initially attempted to justify their actions, but the Florida Department of Law Enforcement released video from the surveillance cameras almost immediately. The video and audio clarity left no doubt that Greene was an innocent homeowner defending himself, and Governor Marino proactively held a press conference to proclaim Nathan Greene a hero for standing up to tyrannical federal agents.

FBI Director Tracy had promptly reversed course, painting his two dead agents as rogue and undisciplined while lauding his third agent as coming to the rescue.

Amongst conservatives, this was just one more example of President Fulton's administration's misuse of their authority. Liberals, however, took to the streets, television airwaves, and TikTok to tout that this tragedy was a direct result of Governor Marino's insane executive order—if the FBI agents had been wearing FBI windbreakers and allowed to do their job properly, this never would have happened.

Sharyn had desperately attempted to contact Greene. The morning after the incident, she'd flown down to Sarasota and waited at the hospital for five days. However, no one would let her near Nathan's hospital room, and she was fairly certain none of her messages had even reached him. There was no doubt in her mind that if Nathan had known she was there, he would have wanted to see her.

Divided We Stand

On the fifth day, Professor Greene, having been declared out of danger and substantially recovered from the effects of his surgeries, had simply disappeared.

When Sharyn arrived at Sarasota Memorial Hospital to attempt to see him for the umpteenth time, she was informed that Nathan Greene had checked out of the hospital before dawn. Sharyn showed her White House credentials to the duty nurse, explaining to the nurse her personal connection to Professor Greene, and had been told that a private ambulance had arrived just after 4 a.m. and Greene had signed himself out against medical advice. Several very surly characters with lots of muscles, beards, and tattoos had transferred Greene to a gurney; that was the last anyone had seen of him.

Sources within the CIA had provided the President with information regarding Greene's location within the last few days. He'd been squirreled away to his friend's ranch on the shores of Lake Okeechobee and was apparently under the protection of several members of the Unit. As a Medal of Honor winner and former member of Delta Force, Nathan Greene had plenty of friends.

After taking another sip of his own coffee, President Fulton continued, "Despite what many are saying, I still consider myself a spring chicken and have at least ten good years left. My pops lived to be ninety-six, and my mother was driving until she passed away at ninety-three."

Sharyn tried not to smile as John Reynolds visibly cringed at the President's remarks. While it was true President Fulton's mother had driven until she was ninety-three, the President failed to mention that she died behind the wheel while going the wrong way on the interstate.

"Yes, Mr. President," said the Vice President, fully aware of the President's mother's demise. "There is no doubt in any of our minds that you are more than fit and capable as Commander-in-Chief. You're what this country needs."

"Exactly," said the President. "According to the polls, I'm the best shot this country has of keeping King from getting back to the White House. We all know what he's capable of and what he's even told us he'll do if he wins. He'll burn this city down and use it for his personal vendettas. The United States will become a laughing stock to the world, as it was when he was in office. It's our duty to stop him."

"Yes, I couldn't agree more."

"So I want you and John and young Sharyn there," the President nodded toward Sharyn. "I want you three to take the bull by the horns. Right now, King can't leave Florida without fear of being arrested. I need you all to figure out how to bring him to justice. Soon."

"Yes, Mr. President," said the Vice President, with Reynolds nodding in the affirmative as well.

"You know, Mr. President," said Reynolds, speaking for the first time. "I haven't had a chance to discuss this with you yet, but Louis sent over the latest poll numbers this morning. Bottom line: you and King still remain pretty much even, with you holding a slight lead in most polls." Reynolds paused, making sure the President and Vice President were listening. "What's most interesting, however, is the polarization of the average voter."

"What do you mean?" President Fulton asked.

"The most recent polls are showing that Americans are becoming more angry about what's happening and less likely to respect others who don't share their political views. For example, two months ago, when asked how often people feel angry or hopeful when thinking of politics, Forty percent of people said they were often angry, and sixteen percent stated they were hopeful. In yesterday's poll, seventy-two percent said they were often or always angry when thinking about politics, while only three percent stated they were hopeful."

"That's alarming," said Sharyn without thinking. She normally tried to keep her opinions to herself in front of anyone but the Vice President.

"Shocking, actually," agreed Reynolds. "Mr. President, the country has become a powder keg. The Vice President and I will put our heads together and devise a solution to resolve this crisis, but we need to ensure you're fully prepared for the campaign. The next

Divided We Stand

few months are going to be extremely taxing, and having you at your best will be paramount."

"Of course, John," said President Fulton. "You know, Serena? I was thinking. I think it's time that we, uh, we should…you know, I think, ah….Mmmm. Are we?" The President looked blankly around at the three of them. "Oh, hi, Sharyn. It's great to see you this morning."

Reynolds and VP Moore shared a grave, knowing look, with Reynolds standing up. "Mr. President, I think it's time to get ready for your trip. We'll be heading up to Camp David soon."

"Oh, great," said the President, awkwardly rising from his chair. Sharyn stood to steady the President while John went to the door of the Oval Office and signaled for the President's personal aide to escort him to the residence.

There were now just three of them remaining in the Oval Office: Sharyn, the Vice President, and the Chief of Staff.

"It's getting worse," said Serena.

"It is," agreed John. "He's on point for a period of time, but when he gets tired, he starts losing focus."

"Eight months, John. Eight months," said Serena. "Can he do it? Can we do it?"

"We have to. God help this country if we can't. King will ruin the Office of the Presidency forever. He might not ever leave!"

The Vice President looked from Reynolds to Sharyn. "We need to figure this out. King—I'm not that worried about him. It's whoever is behind his whole strategy that has me worried. We need to figure this out. It could be Marino—that little fucker is sneakier than a snake wearing slippers."

"I think it's more likely to be Brumback," said Reynolds. "He was the mastermind behind King's 2016 campaign and has the media empire to push King's agenda."

"You think?" Serena asked. "That fat asshole has been pretty quiet the last six months. I thought the threat of Congressional subpoenas seemed to shut him up, but I see your point. He's definitely smart enough and has a lot of resources." The Vice President paused for a second, thinking. "Sharyn, I want you to call Director Tracy. Tell him, from me, that you want a dedicated point person from his office with whom you can work—today. Then you and this FBI person go figure out who King's been meeting with. We need to figure this out so we can put a stop to this nonsense."

"Yes, ma'am," answered Sharyn.

27

Cromwell Island, Montana

Sunday, March 10

"THE SPRING EQUINOX. March 21st. The day we tip the dominoes," said Alex Treacher, sitting in a high-backed buffalo leather chair in front of the roaring fireplace. A cold snap had pushed down into Montana from the Arctic, and temperatures outside were hovering just above minus eighteen degrees. *Or zero degrees Fahrenheit, as the Americans would say,* thought Alex.

Joining Alex in the large living room overlooking Flathead Lake were Jasmine and two men—Luther Kojak and Wais Khan.

Luther was in his late thirties, no taller than 5'8", with a bald pate, piercing blue eyes, and a soft, pudgy body. He had the pale skin of someone allergic to sunshine, and based on his expertise, it was clear to Jasmine why Luther rarely went outdoors.

Luther was a computer expert—a hacker, cracker, and phisher. And, as Alex once mentioned, "expert" was an understatement. Luther was one of the best in the world at manipulating, penetrating, exposing, and disseminating information via computers.

Luther was to the world of the internet what Jasmine was to the world of killing. Luther provided Alex a tremendous cyber capability and ran two covert IT cells located in Iceland and Grand Cayman.

Jasmine first met Luther in Iceland over a year ago when Alex had sent her to deal with a problem created by one of the hackers on Luther's team. The hacker had been freelancing, something expressly forbidden by Alex so as not to expose his covert operations. Jasmine had been sent to eliminate the problem.

Her meeting with Luther at that time had been brief, just long enough to confirm her target, but she had come away with one conclusion about the man: he creeped her the fuck out!

As she looked over at the effeminate man sitting in a chair across from her and Alex, she focused on keeping her disgust for the man hidden from her face. She had never asked Alex any questions about Luther, but there was absolutely no doubt in her mind that Luther was a sexual predator. Little boys, teenage girls, old ladies, or small farm animals—Jasmine had no idea what Luther's sexual proclivities were, but she was 100% sure that he was a sadistic rapist. She could see it in his eyes and the smug way he looked at her.

She hadn't expressed her concerns to Alex, for she knew Luther must be extremely good at his job for Alex to keep him on the payroll. The more she thought about it, maybe it was Luther's acts of sexual deviance that made him trustworthy, for he could never go to the authorities about Alex's operations.

All she knew was that she wanted to spend as little time as possible with the man and had specifically chosen to sit in a chair as far from Luther as possible.

The second person joining Alex and Jasmine in the expansive living room of the 45,000-square-foot lodge on Cromwell Island was a man Jasmine knew much better than she did Luther, a man named Wais Khan. Other than Alex and Sergei, Wais was probably the only human Jasmine had developed any sort of relationship with since her discharge from the Marine Corps almost two years earlier.

Wais was considerably shorter than Luther, shorter than Jasmine actually, and might rise to five and a half feet tall with a thick-soled pair of shoes. He was built like a fireplug—short, stout, and made of cast iron. Now in his mid-forties, Wais had been born in the late 1970s into the Afghani royal family. His father had been appointed the Afghan ambassador to the United States shortly before the Prime Minister, his cousin, had been deposed in a bloody coup and killed with his entire immediate family.

As a consequence, Wais had spent his formative years growing up mostly in the United States but also traveling extensively as his father sought to parlay his foreign ministry experience into an international trading business. In the early 1990s, after the Soviets had left Afghanistan but prior to the Taliban taking over, Wais and his family returned to Kabul, where his father purchased a hotel and started several other successful businesses.

According to Alex, Wais successfully navigated life under the Taliban and even earned the "Fonz of Kabul" moniker for his perfectly coiffed and slicked-back hair and the 1968 Camaro convertible he drove around the city.

In addition to English, which he spoke with a New Jersey accent, Wais was fluent in six languages: Pashto, Dari, Urdu, Farsi, Arabic, and Spanish. With the ouster of the Taliban in late 2001 amid the post-9/11 U.S. intervention, Wais came to the attention of the CIA and was immediately recruited to assist America in its new Global War on Terror.

For twenty years, Wais proved an invaluable asset to the CIA and US special operations forces operating in Afghanistan, as well as in other parts of Southwest Asia. He rose steadily in the newly created Afghani intelligence apparatus and led countless operations against al-Qaeda terrorists and Taliban insurgents.

In August 2021, the Taliban began closing in on Kabul, the last holdout against the Islamist insurgency due solely to the city's bolstering by American military forces. Up until the last moments, Wais continued desperately to protect the teams of intelligence officers he had groomed over the years, working with the American military and intelligence communities to find a safe haven for those who had been so loyal during the Global War on Terror.

Wais was assured by his CIA contacts that his family was being rescued by a convoy of U.S. soldiers. He was told that his wife and three young children had been granted visas to live in the United States, and he was promised that he would be linked up with them as soon as he completed one last mission at the CIA's request.

Wais completed that mission and went directly to Kabul Airport to link up with his family. Upon arrival, he was informed that the American general in charge of evacuation had downgraded the priority of Wais' family and that an Afghan force had been dispatched to collect them instead of an American one. Unfortunately, that Afghan convoy had been attacked by the Taliban, and his family had perished along with more than a dozen Afghani soldiers. While offering his condolences, the same CIA officer who had previously promised his family would be safe nonchalantly offered Wais a seat on the next plane out of Kabul.

Fighting the urge to kill, Wais rushed back home to find that his family had never made it onto the convoy—they'd been brutally murdered in his home.

Alex had not shared with Jasmine how he had learned of Wais, but it was clear that he had recruited Wais as a broken soul, similar to how he had recruited Jasmine herself.

Unlike Luther, whom she'd only seen a few times, Jasmine had spent considerable time with Wais. Despite their age difference, the two had built a friendship based on mutual respect for each other's skills. Alex had encouraged this friendship, as their ability to work closely was critical to the success of Phase 2 of his grand strategy.

Jasmine was the operator, and Wais was the recruiter.

Aside from several multi-day strategy sessions here on Cromwell Island, Jasmine had spent most of her time with Wais at Three Forks—the 1,000-acre training facility that Alex and Jasmine had built eighteen months ago in eastern Oregon, the remotest place in the continental United States.

The geography of Three Forks consisted of rolling grasslands interspersed with small mountains, buttes, and wooded areas along the middle fork of the Owyhee River. They had been forced to bull-doze their own dirt road into the site, and the nearest town was more than an hour's drive to the northeast.

Based on the requirements of Phase 2 and the need for security,

Divided We Stand

containment, and compartmentalization, Three Forks had been designed to house twelve separate cells of up to eight individuals each. The cells, each named after a sign of the Zodiac, were provisioned with accommodations, a combination dining facility-classroom, and several storage containers for their equipment. As it was impossible to build anything in such a remote area, the sites were built using pre-fabricated buildings made from shipping containers that were capable of being transported on trucks.

The twelve sites were dispersed across the 1,000-acre property, with none within sight of any other site. In addition to the twelve compartmentalized sites for the operational Zodiac cells, they had built a state-of-the-art rifle range and some mockup facilities the cells could train on depending on their specific mission.

The genius of Alex's grand strategy was in the personnel forming the twelve operations cells. Each cell consisted of between four and eight individuals, all radicals with a similar driving focus: bringing death and chaotic change to America. Six of the cells were Muslims from several different countries, four cells were Hispanics from Central America, and the remaining two cells were Americans.

All of the Muslim and two of the Hispanic operations cells had six members each, while the two remaining Hispanic cells had eight members each. The two American cells had only four operators. Wais recruited every member of the foreign cells, while Alex supervised the recruitment of the Americans.

Aries, the first cell recruited, consisted of disgruntled American military veterans. Jasmine did not know their individual stories but had been told by Alex that the men shared two common traits. First, they all had a visceral hatred of the government in Washington, D.C., and second, their loyalty to Alex's cause was incorruptible.

Jasmine and Wais had worked with Team Aries under the train-the-trainer concept. Over the first two months, the four members of Aries were drilled in the skills necessary to train two additional teams in the skills required to initiate Phase 2, which Alex had described as "toppling the dominoes." All of the Aries members had extensive military training in special operations.

Team Taurus comprised six seasoned jihadists with experience on battlefields across the Middle East from Syria to Yemen. The leader of Taurus, an Egyptian, had cut his teeth in Bosnia as a teenager, taking a gap year before completing his engineering degree in Cairo. The others in Taurus, the first of the six Muslim operational cells, were all veterans of one jihadist group or another and had been assembled by Wais under the guise of striking a fatal blow to the infidels in America.

Team Gemini consisted of six Salvadoran MS-13 gang members who'd been given orders by their leader to complete a secret mission for their gang under penalty of decapitation should they fail. All of Gemini's members had lived at some point in the United States before returning to El Salvador and were a mix of murderers, rapists, and thugs.

The American Aries trainers always wore full-face balaclavas—knit caps with openings for the eyes and mouth—while in the presence of any of the other cell members, as did Jasmine when her presence was required. Training took place within the Taurus and Gemini team areas or at the centralized weapons range, and each of these two core teams trained for over two months before any of the other cells were brought to the Three Forks facility.

The entire training process took just over a year, but once it started, things began to fall into place rapidly. Taurus, the core Muslim operational cell initially trained by Aries and consisting of the most hardened and reliable jihadists, was tasked with the subsequent training of the five additional Islamic jihadists' Zodiac teams.

Teams Leo, Virgo, Libra, Scorpio, and Sagittarius were constituted from personnel Wais had recruited from the Islamic jihadist insurgencies throughout the Middle East and Africa. The members of Teams Leo and Virgo were Palestinian, while the nationalities of the other three teams were Iraqi, Chechen, and Somali, respectively. With the exception of Team Taurus, each team believed they were the main effort in the strike against America and had no knowledge of any other team's existence. Special care was taken never to allow teams to access the range complex at the same time, and the complex was completely sanitized after use to ensure no notes, markings, or items were left behind that could alert someone to the presence of another cell.

Similar to the process with the Islamic cells, Team Gemini took the lead in training the three additional Spanish-speaking operational cells: Capricorn, Aquarius, and Pisces.

Training for all cells followed a similar pattern that was broken into three phases. The first phase consisted of basic team-building exercises designed to solidify the cohesiveness of the cell. It also focused on attention to detail, operational security, and physical fitness. Phase two of training included advanced marksmanship, use of explosives, and close-quarters combat. Several of the cells had missions requiring snipers, and these members were trained specifically by Jasmine until they were proficient out to six hundred yards —the farthest shot any of the missions would require. The final phase was reserved for training specific to the mission of each cell, and this training continued until there was no doubt whatsoever that each cell could successfully complete its mission despite any contingency they might face.

Failure was not an option; this principle was ingrained in every cell member.

Now, eleven days before the commencement of Phase 2, Alex had assembled his key management team at the Cromwell Island lodge to ensure their plan remained solid.

"So, Luther, I assume we're all set on the cyber preparations for the 21st of March? Everything you've done so far has been impeccable, but next Thursday and the subsequent days are going to be critical to our success."

"Yes, Alex. We are ready."

"Good," replied Alex. "Jasmine? Wais?"

"Eight of the twelve Zodiac teams are already in their staging positions," replied Wais before Jasmine could answer. "With D-day now set as March 21st, the other four teams move into position between D-minus-five and D-minus-three."

"Yes," added Jasmine. "For things to kick off on the 21st, the plan requires two small incidents to occur on D-minus-two to get those specific targets into the places we want them. Those are Teams Leo and Libra, and I'll supervise those directly."

"Excellent," beamed Alex, rubbing his hands together before taking a sip of vodka.

The strategic vision behind Alex's master strategy was so grand and world-changing that Jasmine often wondered if there was a group or entity above Alex. His limitless funding and expansive logistics capabilities were on a scale she'd never experienced. Just her own travel over the last two years, often by private jet or pre-positioned vehicles with accommodations in safe houses ranging from foreign mansions to American ghetto apartments to small islands in the Caribbean, had been anonymously executed with precision and absent a single error or mistake.

As far as Jasmine knew, only the four people in this room, plus Orlean Brumback, had knowledge of Alex's master strategy. Brumback knew only about the main strategy and was not provided with any of the gritty details, especially the targeting of Phase 2. To Brumback, Phase 2 was the initiation of a social media blitz that would drive a wedge through America in furtherance of the grand strategy.

The grand strategy itself was ever so subtle, so stately, so seemingly innocent. Yet beneath this veneer, it created a mechanism of self-destruction that would cleave the United States in two, all while its proponents felt like they were actually strengthening the country.

Often referred to by Alex as "Toppling Dominos," a phrase that to Jasmine evoked an image of a boy flicking over the first small black rectangle in an endless curved row of thousands of dominos that begin to gracefully and inevitably fall in sequence, the strategy had one single purpose: to force the first Constitutional Convention since 1787.

28

Jackson, Wyoming

Saturday, March 16

"SLÁINTE!" Orlean Brumback said, holding out his glass of aged bourbon toward Alex Treacher, sitting across from him in his den. It was just after 7 p.m., and the sky was already dark this time of year, so there was no view out the wall of windows toward the Teton Range in the distance.

Alex had flown down from Montana earlier that afternoon at Brumback's invitation to an informal dinner with the governors of Wyoming and Florida. The meal had been friendly, supportive of the combined Republican governors' stalwart stance against the intrusion of federal law enforcement, and welcoming of a continued push against the perceived weakness of the Fulton administration.

At Alex's suggestion, made prior to the dinner, Brumback floated the idea of the States convening a Constitutional Convention, and both governors had jumped at the idea, although neither was terribly familiar with the mechanisms for calling for one.

Article V of the U.S. Constitution provided for two routes to amend itself. The first was for two-thirds of both houses of

Congress to propose an amendment and for three-fourths of the States to approve it. This had occurred seventeen times in the nation's history, accounting for all the Constitutional Amendments after the original Bill of Rights. This was the method that almost everyone knew from high school social studies.

A second path to amending the Constitution, a path that had never been used in over 200 years, allowed changes to be made without the approval of Congress. This mechanism required the legislatures of two-thirds of the States to call for a Constitutional Convention, at which the approval of three-quarters of the States would be required to ratify changes to the Constitution.

With the U.S. Congress hopelessly deadlocked for much of the past two decades, Alex's grand strategy encompassed jumpstarting this second path to changing the U.S. Constitution. With Alex's subtle encouragement, Brumback believed this plan was actually of Brumback's design. Orlean took tremendous pride as the architect of what would be the nation's first Constitutional Convention since the one in Philadelphia that penned the original masterpiece of democracy.

The math was simple. With fifty states in the Union, a Constitutional Convention could be called if the state legislatures of thirty-four states demanded it.

Thirty-four. 34.

After the November 2023 elections, both houses of the legislatures in twenty-nine states across the country were firmly controlled by the Republican Party. One additional state, Pennsylvania, had a split General Assembly, with its Senate being controlled by Republicans and its House of Representatives narrowly controlled by Democrats.

So, really, the number was four-and-a-half.

Four-point-five.

4.5.

The magic number to change America.

Should four additional state legislatures, plus Pennsylvania's House of Representatives, somehow become controlled by the Republican party and vote in favor of demanding a Constitutional

Divided We Stand

Convention, then the U.S. Congress would be forced to convene one. The potential havoc that this could create on the United States was beyond comprehension: should three-quarters of the States agree to any changes, the entire Constitution could be rewritten in its entirety.

"Cheers," replied Alex, taking a sip from his own glass of bourbon. The two governors had flown home, leaving Alex and Orlean alone. "Everything is in motion, Orlean. We need you to keep pressing every Republican you know on the idea of imposing term limits and to keep your social media machine churning out content."

"Understood," said Brumback. "This really fell into our lap, didn't it? I mean, we've been planning for months to push for a Constitutional Convention, but I always thought it would be around strengthening the Tenth Amendment. That's how we got King and Marino to take such a hard line on the indictments and limit the authority of federal law enforcement. But Nathan Greene, boy, did he hit a home run for us—and he doesn't even know it!" Brumback chuckled into his glass as he took another sip.

"Look, Orlean," said Alex, his tone becoming serious. "Your media machine has been pushing hard, and the country has responded. America is truly polarized. Maybe more than it's been since 1861. There are protests and riots all across the country. This coming week is going to make people do some strange things, some things we likely haven't foreseen or planned for, both good and bad. I need to make sure you're ready for that—and that you're committed to pushing forward no matter what happens."

Brumback leaned forward in his chair, mirroring Alex's serious tone. "I'm all in, Alex—one hundred and ten percent. I agree with you. This country is on the verge of erupting. And that's a good thing. I truly believe that. Maybe another civil war is exactly what we need to get this country back on track."

"That is a very distinct possibility," agreed Alex, downplaying the fact that he knew it was more a *probability* than a possibility.

"Is there anything else you need me to do? Just say the word. I'm looking forward to Phase 2 starting in a few days."

"There is one thing," said Alex. "It's just a thought, but I wanted to throw it out there to see if you agree."

"What's that?" Orlean asked.

"It's President King. I've been thinking. Right now, one of the biggest arguments fueling people's hatred of him is his refusal to submit to the jurisdiction of the federal courts. You and I know his reasons for doing this, but it's difficult for the average American, especially those not inclined to support King, to sympathize with him."

"That's an understatement. Just look at the dozens of protests seizing college campuses around the country. I mean, Jesus, it seems like you can't go anywhere nowadays without seeing a "No Justice! No King!" sign or bumper sticker.

"Exactly," said Alex. "It also creates significant risk for him on the campaign trail."

"What do you mean?" Brumback asked.

"Well, to my knowledge, King has not left the confines of the Lido Club other than to play golf on Lido Key since this began six weeks ago. The Florida primary is this Tuesday, and he's assured he'll sweep it as he has every other state so far. However, he's going to have to begin campaigning soon, and if he flies, he runs the risk of federal government F-16s forcing his plane to land in a Blue State where he'll be immediately arrested and remanded to the custody of the U.S. Marshals."

"Yes. That is a problem. What're you suggesting?"

"I think President King has proven his point. I think he's shown the American public that his indictments are purely politically motivated, and he's also galvanized the support of the Republican governors around the country. I propose that he call President Fulton and agree to be arraigned in federal court, but only with the assurance that he be released without bail or any restrictions on his travel. King will agree to attend all court hearings, but he's also free to campaign anywhere he'd like without fear of interference from federal agents."

"Interesting," said Orlean. "I think I like it, but I'm not sure

Divided We Stand

King will go for it. He's a difficult man to change directions unless he thinks it's his own idea."

"That's why you need to convince him this is his idea. My friend, I have every confidence in your subtle powers of persuasion."

"Let's say I'm successful," said Orlean, leaning closer to Alex in a conspiratorial manner. "When would you suggest this occur?"

"Immediately," answered Alex without hesitation. "Tomorrow. You should sit next to him while he calls President Fulton. And I think he should plan his first trip on Wednesday. He should visit one of the governors who's supported him. We just had dinner with Mark Howard, so maybe here in Wyoming would be a great spot. You could easily set up a rally for him."

"Yes, we could do that with no problem."

"Plus, it will have an added advantage for Phase 2 the next day."

"Okay," said Orlean. "I'll fly down to Florida first thing in the morning and make King come to this conclusion on his own. This'll work."

29

Washington D.C

Monday, March 18

"HE DID WHAT?" Vice President Moore asked incredulously. "Please tell me you're joking, John."

Sharyn was sitting on the sofa in the Vice President's office, closest to the Vice President seated behind her desk. She and Moore had been meeting late in the afternoon to review tomorrow's schedule when the President's Chief of Staff entered the office and informed them of President Fulton's recent phone call with Benjamin King.

"I'm definitely not joking, Serena," said Reynolds. "King called out of the blue. Ten minutes ago, I was sitting in my office when the President's gatekeeper buzzed me, informing me that Benjamin King was holding on Line One for the President. The President was in the Oval Office with his aide, signing everything in his documents folder, so I went in and told him that King was on hold. I urged him to let me handle the call, but you know how he gets. He just waved as if it were nothing and picked up the phone.

"And King told the President he's planning to turn himself in?"

Divided We Stand

"Exactly. King stated that he never intended to hold himself above the law. He would present himself to the federal court in Tampa tomorrow morning in the nation's best interests. All he wanted from the President was his assurance that he'd be released on his own personal recognizance and that he'd be allowed to campaign freely through the November election."

"And President Fulton agreed to this?"

"Yes. Sort of."

"What do you mean *sort of?*" VP Moore asked incredulously. "We have three branches of government for a reason, John. The President doesn't have the power to tell a federal judge how she should set bail limits."

"I know that, and you know that. But President Fulton didn't think it would be a problem. He didn't promise King anything regarding the judge, but he said he certainly wouldn't oppose it. He did promise that the Executive Branch would not attempt to arrest King during his campaign, provided that he complied with the judge's orders in the case."

"Okay, well, that's not so terrible."

"That's not all," said Reynolds.

"Dear God. What else?"

"He said he would order the Attorney General to have the Special Prosecutor agree to push any court appearances and the scheduling of a trial until after the November elections."

"Jesus Christ! He's given away any leverage we had over King's antics. This is crazy."

"I know," agreed Reynolds. "I tried to wave him off, but he kept on talking."

"Serena," interrupted Sharyn as gently as possible. "I think we need to remember that the entire concept of the Special Prosecutor is that he's independent of Main Justice. He doesn't take orders from the Attorney General, just as the federal judge doesn't. So it doesn't really matter what President Fulton agreed to."

"It's politics, Sharyn. We had leverage, and now we've given it up."

"I think you're on to something, Sharyn," said the President's Chief of Staff. "We can spin this any way we want."

"The Republicans think King was indicted solely for political purposes—when we all know the guy is a true insurrectionist and was willing to do or say just about anything to stay in power," said Sharyn, thinking out loud. "Working Group Delta has been focused on resolving King's refusal to appear at his arraignment. This solves that problem. How the President's campaign spins this new information is entirely up to them. Personally, I think they could easily get out in front of this as soon as King goes public and spin this to show the President's strength on justice and fairness towards his competitors in the political arena."

"Great idea," said Reynolds. "I'll assemble his campaign team right now. Serena, what are your thoughts?"

"As usual, Sharyn is thinking a couple of steps ahead, which is why I keep her around," replied the Vice President with a smile. "I still don't like it though. There was some comfort in knowing we had King bottled up in Florida. And let's not kid ourselves. Everything we do is political. Yes, King deserves to be prosecuted on the basis of his actions. But let us never forget that every action and every reaction is about politics, pure and simple. When you've been in this game as long as I have, it's something you come to terms with."

The Vice President paused, thinking through the situation.

"So King is going public tomorrow? Is that what he said?"

"Yes. He told the President he would be turning himself in tomorrow morning at the courthouse in Tampa."

"Okay. Look, I know we can't take the risk of reaching out directly. But maybe you could have a private word with Attorney General Krueger and drop the hint that the Special Prosecutor might want to consider adding more charges to King's indictment. It's been a while since I was a federal prosecutor. Still, I can clearly see an argument to be made that Benjamin King's refusal to be arrested by the U.S. Marshals was a causal circumstance leading to the deaths of three U.S. Marshals. Under the U.S. Code, that's the very definition of negligent homicide."

Divided We Stand

Sharyn and John Reynolds looked at the Vice President with blank looks on their face, unsure if she was being serious. The Vice President stared back defiantly, alternating her gaze between the two of them.

"Serena," Sharyn spoke softly so as not to anger her boss. "The President asked us to solve this problem. I think what you're proposing will likely make the situation much worse."

"For fuck's sake," exploded the Vice President. "This isn't a game, Sharyn. John, you know better as well. Politics is a war, and the winner is the one who takes no prisoners. If we want to be in the White House next year, we need to drive a stake in that asshole King's heart. If we don't, he's going to drive one into ours."

"But what about the American public?" Sharyn asked. "If the Special Prosecutor indicts King for negligent homicide, Republicans across the country will go absolutely crazy! Two-thirds of the country already believe that there could be violence as a result of November's election. A move like this could make small-town America literally erupt."

"And that's bad for us?" Moore asked. "Politics, Sharyn. Politics. Those people aren't voting for us no matter what we do. But how many independents will vote for a President with yet another indict-ment—and one for which any other American would be arrested? I guarantee I could find a hundred cases of people being charged with negligent homicide as a result of someone being killed after fleeing the police or refusing to submit to an arrest warrant."

"Serena," said John calmly. "You have a valid point, but maybe we should let things play out this week. I'll have a word with the Attorney General so he can inform the Special Prosecutor and the judge of Benjamin King's plans to show up in court tomorrow. It's a long campaign, and we can always look at how things go later on down the road."

"Okay," agreed the Vice President, calming down. "Let's wait and see."

30

Sarasota, Florida

Wednesday, March 20

JASMINE DROVE along Westmoreland Drive through the quiet Sarasota neighborhood several miles north of downtown Sarasota. On her right, modern, expensive houses were set back from the road. She knew from the GPS map on the Ford Bronco's dashboard that these homes were all situated directly on waterfront lots along Sarasota Bay. On her left, the houses were much smaller and dated, with many in dire need of renovation. Despite the proximity to the bay, the downside of this neighborhood was its location under the flight path of nearby Sarasota-Bradenton International Airport, commonly referred to by its airport code SRQ.

She glanced at the dashboard clock: 7:15 in the morning. Perfect. In her right ear was a single AirPod, connected through Bluetooth to her phone, broadcasting the public air traffic control frequency for the airport's tower less than 1.5 miles from Jasmine's current location on Westmoreland Drive.

Jasmine had flown down from Ohio late the previous evening, landing at the private Jumbolair airstrip outside of Ocala, about two

Divided We Stand

and a half hours drive north of Sarasota. The use of the private airstrip assured her anonymity and a new Ford Bronco Badlands SUV was waiting for her at the airstrip. She'd spent the night at a highway chain hotel along I-75 near Tampa, and this morning, she was in place to check on her team.

Team Strela.

Although not part of the twelve Zodiac teams, the events over the last eight weeks had caused Alex to add Team Strela to his master plan. Their mission was to be very limited and scheduled to occur the day before the Spring Equinox and the initiation of Phase 2.

Today was that day, and the time was almost at hand.

The four members of Team Strela were sicarios of the Gulf Cartel based out of Matamoros, Mexico. These men took their business seriously, and their business was killing. These were hard men, each a proven killer for the Gulf Cartel.

Relying upon Alex's connections with the Gulf Cartel's senior leadership, Jasmine traveled to Mexico in February and spent a week training this four-man team to meet her high standards. She had rehearsed every facet of the plan and ensured each member was proficient in using their assigned weapon.

The weapon for this mission was the 9K32 Strela-2 man-portable, shoulder-fired surface-to-air missile. Referred to by NATO forces as the SA-7, the Strela was the poor man's equivalent to the U.S. Army's Stinger missile. Using its passive infrared sensor, the missile locked onto the hot exhaust of an aircraft's jet engine and fired a 3-lb explosive warhead to completely destroy the engine and cause significant damage to the aircraft. Similar in size to a bazooka, the Strela was easily carried by one person and fired directly off his shoulder.

Jasmine turned her SUV north on Whitfield Avenue, traveling away from the water and toward Route 41, the busy six-lane road between Sarasota and Bradenton that runs north-south past the end of SRQ's primary runway. The sound of an airplane engine could be heard in the distance, and the high-pitched whine rapidly approached and increased in intensity. In seconds, the whine transitioned to a roar, and Jasmine leaned forward, craning her face up to see a Southwest Airlines Boeing 737 gliding through the sky in front of her. The plane was so low after takeoff that its wheels were still in the down position.

Houses dotted Whitfield Avenue for the first two blocks, and Jasmine wondered what it must be like to live so close to the end of the runway, constantly being startled by the roar of jet engines. As she drove, the right side of the road opened into a small neighborhood park with poorly maintained grass and several scrub trees. It was the kind of place people might occasionally let their dog take a crap, but no one would consider ever taking a child to play as there were no amenities to speak of.

At the edge of the park, positioned precisely where Jasmine had planned, at the corner of Whitfield Ave and Shepherd Street, a mere one block from busy US 41, was a white panel van with no markings. Jasmine slowed as she drove past, smiling as she saw a Hispanic male in the driver's seat. Making eye contact with the driver, who instantly recognized her, Jasmine nodded and received a slight nod in return—all according to their carefully rehearsed plan.

Jasmine concentrated on the voice in her earbud.

"Sarasota Tower, this is N757AF. Request clearance for takeoff."

A brief pause.

"N757AF, this is Sarasota Tower. You are number one for takeoff on Runway 32. Turn to 268 and proceed to 3,000 before proceeding on course."

"Thank you, Sarasota Tower. We are cleared for takeoff on Runway 32. We will turn to 268 and proceed to 3,000 feet before proceeding on course."

This was it! Game on!

Currently stopped at Whitfield Ave and Route 41 intersection, Jasmine turned right onto Route 41, heading south. Things were about to start happening.

Divided We Stand

THE FOUR SICARIOS of Team Strela had monitored the same transmission Jasmine had just heard. They knew this was the request of a twin-engine Boeing 757 jumbo jet to take off momentarily from the runway a few hundred yards to the front of their parked van.

"Vamos," the driver said calmly. They'd rehearsed the next steps dozens of times, and none of the team members seemed overly excited. The long green tubes of the four Strela-2 anti-aircraft missiles were laid neatly on the floor of the van. As the driver maneuvered between the seats to where the other three team members sat in the back, one of the team slid open the side door of the panel van and stepped outside. They each grabbed their assigned launcher. Weighing just over thirty pounds, the Strelas were more awkward than heavy. However, each man had rehearsed their movements so many times that the four moved in concert as if in an orchestrated ballet.

They could easily hear the whine of the 757's engines increase in pitch and envisioned the slow roll as the plane gathered speed down the runway. Two team members jogged to the van's left while the other two broke to the right. The trees were not a factor, and each man spaced himself ten meters apart from the others, forming a line generally perpendicular to the runway.

The safety caps had already been removed from the Strelas, and the power units had been activated. Each man now extended his sights, the long tube resting on his right shoulder, the sights aligned with his eyes, and his hands grasping the pistol grip along the bottom of the tube.

They could hear the crescendo of the jumbo jet approaching and knew the plane would take off directly in front of them within seconds. Having watched several other planes depart this morning, they knew roughly the altitude this jet was likely to be, and they stood there with their launchers pointing at this position.

Louder. Louder.

They could almost feel the vibration as the extremely loud jet reached its takeoff speed of one hundred and sixty miles per hour.

"Listo!" the team leader yelled. Despite his previous appearance, his heart was racing inside his chest.

Within seconds, a huge jumbo jet careened into the sky, seeming to fly in front of the tremendous noise of its engines. Each gunner aligned the sight of his launcher on the moving aircraft, the two men on the left aiming for the jet's left engine while the two on the right aimed for the right engine. Each man focused on their sight and depressed the trigger. This activated the seeker electronics, and each tracker attempted to lock onto a target. In less than a second, the front sight on each of the team members' missiles illuminated, and a constant buzzing noise began emanating from the missile control device.

Whoosh! Whoosh! Whoosh! Whoosh!

All four Strelas ignited almost instantaneously. The missiles fired out of their tubes and accelerated toward the lumbering jumbo jet, slowly gaining altitude and moving away from them. The heat of the jet engine's exhaust was visible to the naked eye, and the heat-seeking components of the Strela's warheads had no difficulties maintaining their lock on target.

The supersonic anti-aircraft missiles quickly overtook the Boeing 757 just as it reached an altitude of 1,000 feet. Team Strela watched as all four missiles exploded after impacting the jet. Three of them disintegrated the left engine, and one hit the right engine.

Team Strela did not wait to see what happened next. As instructed, they sprinted to the van, tossed their empty launchers in the back, and quickly drove off toward Route 41 en route to a rendezvous with Jasmine at a designated location thirty minutes north of Sarasota.

If they had been watching, they would have seen the left wing completely shear off from the body of the plane. The right wing stayed attached, which may have been worse, as the exploding engine ignited the wing's fuel tanks and engulfed the fuselage in flame. The plane took a severe dip to the left before plunging downward. While the pilots undoubtedly tried valiantly to right the plane, absent the left wing and with the right engine destroyed and flames

Divided We Stand

roaring through the cabin, there was absolutely nothing they could do in the few seconds remaining of their lives.

Nose heavy, the plane tilted forward to plow nose first into the aquamarine waters of Sarasota Bay.

There was nothing graceful about the crash. This was not a crash landing. This was 200,000 pounds of metal, fuel, and flesh slamming into the water at almost two hundred miles per hour. The explosion was so loud that it was clearly heard in downtown Sarasota, more than seven miles to the south. The water of Sarasota Bay did little to minimize the fireball created by the crash nor soften the impact.

Several boaters, out for a day on the bay of sun, fishing and doing a lot of nothing, had front-row seats to the jumbo jet crash. None of them recognized the aircraft's color scheme—it was not the familiar red, blue, and yellow of Southwest Airlines, nor did the tail have the familiar logo of American, Delta, or United Airlines. The top half of this plane was painted a dark navy blue, while the bottom was white. Every one of the eyewitnesses on the bay noticed the large American flag emblazoned on the plane's tailfin.

Only the occupants of one small fishing boat were close enough to get a good look at the single large word printed in all capital letters across the jumbo jet's fuselage: KING.

31

Jackson, Wyoming

Wednesday, March 20

"ARE you out of your fucking mind?" Yelled Orlean into the phone. "What in Jesus' name have you done?"

"Calm down," said Alex, sitting in his study, enjoying the warmth of the crackling fire and sipping the cold burn of vodka. It was almost midnight, but with the only light in the room coming from the fireplace, Alex could see the moonlight reflecting off the waters of Flathead Lake. "I'm as upset as you are."

"What the fu—," Orlean said, "I mean, I don't want to say it over an open phone line, but—"

"You can speak freely," interrupted Alex, taking another sip and enjoying Orlean's anger. "This is an end-to-end encrypted call; you can say anything you like, and no one can eavesdrop. What are you implying, Orlean?"

"I'm not implying anything! You shot King's plane down. That wasn't part of our plan! You said Phase 2 wasn't starting until tomorrow, and I never, ever authorized King's assassination. Hell,

Divided We Stand

he was critical to our plan to take back the White House and drain the swamp!"

"I had nothing to do with King's plane being shot down. I'm not sure they 100% know yet if it was, in fact, an act of terrorism, but rest assured, I was as upset as you were when I first heard about it earlier this afternoon."

"You mean to tell me you weren't behind this?"

"Absolutely not," Alex said, the lie sounding as sincere as the truth. "King had his issues, but he was important to our plan. If he was assassinated, it just goes to prove us right. This country is fractured, and people are willing to resort to violence. It's up to us, the patriots, to get the nation back on track. You see that, right?"

"Yeah, of course," said Orlean, not sounding very confident. "I just don't know what to do now that King is dead. Our entire media blitz, everything Phase 2 was supposed to accomplish, it all revolved around King's campaign for the Presidency."

"No, it didn't—and I'll tell you why. If our movement revolved around a single person, then it wouldn't be much of a movement. Our goal is to break this country wide open, to let everyone see the festering cesspool that parts of our country have become, and to build it back stronger and more powerful than ever before. Right?"

"Yes, you're right."

"Look, my team and I have been hard at work since the moment we heard about King's airplane crash. Phase 2 is still going to commence tomorrow. You need to be ready on your end. And Orlean, I think you need to be ready to step up personally."

"What do you mean?"

"I mean, you need to be personally involved in selecting the candidate to replace King. And to be honest, I think you should seriously consider that candidate being yourself."

"Are you serious?" Brumback asked. It wasn't as if he'd never thought of being President of the United States. Hell, he thought of it all the time. He just never wanted to take the risk, nor did he want to take the chance of losing.

"Dead serious," replied Alex. "Who better than you? You've

been the conservative voice of America for over twenty years. You're rich enough to bankroll your own campaign, you control a powerful media group, you have connections in every level of government, and just about every Republican elected official owes you favors. Who better than to be the 47th President of the United States?"

32

Kalamazoo, Michigan

Thursday, March 21

IT WAS Oberon Day in Michigan.

This Oberon was not in reference to the king of fairies in Shakespeare's *A Midsummer Night's Dream* but rather to the delicious, citrusy wheat ale brewed by Bell's Brewery, the most popular brewery in Michigan. The day marked the first day of Spring and the seasonal availability of Oberon beer—the best-selling craft brew in the entire state.

Lenora Carlson was a huge fan of craft breweries, and this was the third year in a row that she attended Bell's Brewery's annual Oberon Day festivities at their original Kalamazoo brewery. Not only did she attend, but she was behind the bar pouring draughts for the dozens of customers who had come out this Thursday night to celebrate.

Lenora Carlson did not work at Bell's, and this was only the second time she'd ever poured beer from behind a bar—the first time being at last year's Oberon Day festivities. Lenora was the governor of Michigan, and this was one of the events her staff planned to heighten her visibility throughout the community. As a native of Kalamazoo herself, she jumped at opportunities to return to her hometown.

For this event, she had pulled her Lieutenant Governor along with her as well as several other staff from the Governor's office, and she was quite pleased to see several prominent members of the state legislature, all members of her party, in attendance.

She wasn't naive enough to think these prominent people were here because she'd proclaimed it Oberon Day throughout Michigan. One look at everyone's attire confirmed the crowd's ulterior motive for being at the bar. Tonight was the first round of March Madness—the NCAA Division 1 college basketball tournament—and as fate would have it, Michigan State was playing the University of Michigan in Indianapolis. Neither team was expected to go far in the tournament, but this rivalry game brought tremendous excitement to all sports fans throughout Michigan.

As a Spartan alum, Governor Carlson wore a Spartan green sweater with the Michigan State Spartan helmet logo. Most in the crowd were dressed either in Michigan State's green and white or the University of Michigan's maize and blue. If she never heard another person say "Go Blue" again, it would not be too soon.

The large main room of the bar area was filled with people, but it was far from crowded. The room itself had twenty-foot ceilings, and the walls were paneled in beautiful white oak native to Michigan. Most of the tables had been cleared from the tile and wood parquet floor, and the stage on the other side of the room was currently being set up with a large screen projector and speakers so people could watch the game.

Almost everyone was sampling one of the brewery's beverages, but Governor Carlson noticed two of her State Police security detail standing off to the side at a high-top table, nursing sodas and keeping an eye on the small crowd of people. Years before, threats had been made to the Governor's life, and her security detail was always alert to anything out of the ordinary. Two other plainclothes officers stood on the other side of the room, allowing the four state troopers to spot any threats should they arise.

Divided We Stand

Done pouring, she noticed her lieutenant governor and the state legislature's Speaker of the House having a conversation at the end of the bar. She decided to walk over and bust their chops a bit before the game started in a few minutes at 6:15. Both men were Wolverine alums and proudly wearing maize-and-blue sweatshirts.

Neither Governor Carlson, her companions, nor the state troopers took any notice of the five men in yellow polo shirts working to set up the projection screen and speakers throughout the large room. No one gave a second thought as pairs of the men carried what appeared to be large floor speakers over to the corners of the room while the fifth man fished around in a large toolbox on stage.

A chorus of shouted "Allahu Akbar" filled the room a split second before the shooting began.

Governor Carlson had just enough time to turn her head from her conversation and see the dark-skinned man on stage aiming a short-barreled rifle at her, but not enough time to comprehend what was happening as a bullet from that man's rifle pierced her left eye and exploded out the back of her head along with most of her brains.

The five men, all Iraqis from Team Libra, quickly began executing their plan to perfection. The four state troopers were dispatched immediately, followed in quick succession by the key individuals whose pictures they had spent the last few days memorizing. The team members had spoken quietly in Arabic while setting up their equipment to designate targets, and they quickly slaughtered everyone standing in the room.

People rushed for the main door but were immediately cut down as they exited by the sixth member of Team Libra, who had been waiting patiently in the team's van parked in the lot out front. This sixth team member had approached and executed the lone state trooper sitting in the governor's black Cadillac Escalade and then set up in front of the brewery's main entrance to shoot anyone who tried to escape the carnage.

After the initial surge of people attempting to flee, no one else came out the front door. Like microwave popcorn finishing cooking, the crescendo of shots slowly lessened in frequency as the Iraqi shooters ran out of live targets. In less than a minute, the sixth Team Libra member outside heard only the occasional gunshot, knowing it was his teammates identifying each of the targets on their list and ensuring they were dead.

The bar's door flew open, and the members of Team Libra sprinted for their van, which was parked in a loading zone in the parking lot. They all piled in, throwing their weapons in the back. The team leader calmly drove out of the parking lot and took an immediate right turn onto Pitcher Street. The team had an additional target list and planned to hit each home on their list until the police stopped them.

Each member of Team Libra had no illusion that they would see tomorrow's dawn—hoping that they would be Allah's warriors that night and end their lives as martyrs to Islam.

33

Farmville, Virginia

Thursday, March 21

ABDEL MAINTAINED the Chevy Tahoe's speed at exactly the posted speed limit. They were passing by the campus of Longwood University on his right, and he knew the college's sports fields were coming up soon on the same side of the road. Just after that would be their target. He glanced in his rearview mirror to see his team's other SUV directly behind him.

Over the last nine months, Abdel and his team prepared, trained and waited for this very moment. The training had been intense but much easier than the waiting. For four months, he and the five members of his squad underwent vigorous military training while secluded at a training facility somewhere in the remote areas of the western United States.

Every member of his team was from Palestine, either Gaza or the West Bank, and they had quickly melded in their commitment to strike a blow against the infidels and Zionists in America. They all spoke English fluently, albeit with distinct accents, and they had each lost family members in the struggle against Israel.

Their trainers had been experienced jihadists who had fought bravely in Syria, Iraq, and Yemen. The training, though challenging, had been some of the best days of Abdel's life. His team had run long distances through an endless prairie wasteland until their bodies were hardened, and they could run for hours. They spent days on end firing AK-47 rifles, shotguns, and Glock pistols until each member of his team was declared fully proficient. His team had then practiced storming a building and killing its occupants, over and over and over, until they could almost do it in their sleep.

Exactly 174 days ago, Abdel and his five teammates had been taken to an airfield, where they boarded a private jet. They flew for over four hours before landing at another airport surrounded by rolling hills covered in trees whose green leaves were changing into hues of red, yellow, and brown. Wais, the man who had recruited all the members of Team Leo, as Wais now called Abdel's team, had accompanied them on their journey.

Upon landing, Abdel saw from the signs that they had landed in Charleston, West Virginia. Team Leo had piled into a waiting eight-passenger van, and Wais had driven them for about three hours along twisting, winding roads through the Blue Ridge mountains. Ten miles south of the small town of Covington, Virginia, the van finally turned into an unmarked gravel driveway across which hung a simple cable padlocked to sturdy fenceposts on either side of the lane. Wais handed Abdel a key and asked him to open the gate, then lock it behind the van after they'd entered.

A few hundred meters along, the gravel drive deteriorated to a rutted track through overgrown weeds, and they followed the road for more than half a mile. Upon cresting a rise, a small valley opened before them, within which sat two double-wide trailers and a dilapidated wooden barn next to a small pond. Wais parked the van in front of one of the trailers, which appeared to have seen better days, and the six members of Team Leo piled out of the van.

This valley, or holler, as Wais said the locals called it, had been Team Leo's home for the last 174 days through the long winter. The trailers had electricity, running water, and an enormous pile of cut firewood to fuel the wood stoves. Similar weapons to the ones they'd trained with at the Western training facility were in one of the trailers, with a large stockpile of ammunition, and a small indoor gym had been built in the barn next to the two SUVs parked inside. Wais gave the members of Team Leo specific rules on how to limit their target practice, ensuring they never fired on full auto, and he also gave them a regimented schedule for them to maintain their level of fitness and proficiency in various skills.

The final instruction was that they were not to leave the property under any circumstances.

For the last six months, Wais arrived every three weeks, bringing supplies, fresh food, and other sundries. Despite this, the waiting had been extremely difficult for the team, and it took all of Abdel's leadership skills to keep everyone focused. They were never told when their mission would commence, other than that Wais would give them seventy-two hours' notice before their mission was to commence.

That moment occurred seventy-two hours ago.

Wais arrived with two encrypted tablets and spent several hours briefing Team Leo on the specifics of their upcoming mission. He discussed targets, routes, procedures, and contingency options.

The team's excitement was palpable, and the last three days had gone by in a blur of preparation, final inspection of weapons, and studying the routes and locations of their various targets. Today was to be a glorious day.

With the light turning green, Abdel turned right on Griffin Boulevard before making an immediate left into the CVS parking lot. He followed the flow of the parking lot around the building to pull into a spot in front of the Verizon store, with the Tahoe facing back towards Griffin Boulevard. The team's other vehicle, a Honda Pilot, parked to his immediate right.

This parking spot offered them a perfect view of the Robert Russa Moton Museum across the street. Abdel had no knowledge of what type of museum it actually was, only that the one-story, colorfully painted building to the rear of the museum was where he was to focus his assault in exactly nine minutes.

Abdel had driven down Griffin Boulevard earlier that afternoon, on his team's arrival into the small town of Farmville, to put eyes on the target and make sure he was familiar with the routes. The team had spent that last hour parked at the rear of a busy Walmart parking lot where no one would bother them, waiting until fifteen minutes before they were expected to attack.

Team Leo watched as numerous cars entered the museum's parking lot, and their occupants walked into their target building. Parked as close as they were, Abdel could now see that the colorful painting of the building was actually a mural. The cartoonish figure of a young black girl holding a pencil was painted on the left side of the building, with various dates splashed in colorful fonts across the center of the structure. Myriad words and phrases dotted the walls but were too small to make out clearly from this distance. Written above the main entrance on the right front of the building, the doors that his team would assault through in a matter of minutes, was the phrase: The Eyes of the World Are Upon Us.

More than two dozen people entered the building over the next few minutes. They'd been told that a meeting would begin promptly at six o'clock, and they were to assault at ten minutes past the hour.

Abdel looked at the dashboard clock: 6:09.

He pushed the button to lower the passenger window, and the driver of the SUV next to him lowered his window.

"Yalla!" Abdel said, loud enough to be heard by the other driver. His teammate and driver of the other vehicle, Mohamed, simply nodded. Abdel turned to look at the two men in the backseat, men he'd trained and lived with for the last nine months.

"Hamdulillah," Abdel said sincerely.

"Allahu Akbar," they both replied simultaneously.

Abdel put the Tahoe in reverse and pulled out of the parking space. He made his way slowly to the parking lot's side entrance on Barrow Street. Directly across Griffin Boulevard was the museum's parking lot entrance, and their target building was now less than fifty yards in front of them.

Acting according to their detailed plan and rehearsals, Abdel accelerated into the parking lot and drove right up the sidewalk to the front door of the colorful building. Braking while simultaneously

Divided We Stand

slamming the transmission into Park, Abdel and his three team-mates piled out of the SUV, each carrying an AK-47 rifle and wearing a chest rig loaded with 30-round magazines. On their hips were holstered Glock 17 pistols.

The four men dashed for the glass entrance doors.

Behind him, Abdel could hear Team Leo's other vehicle come to a stop on the grass. The two men in that vehicle were to provide security in case the police arrived.

Hamza was first to the door and held it open for the other three. Abdel was first through, followed immediately by Omar and Zain. Abdel dashed down the wooden floors of a short corridor, not noticing the gift shop to his right and heading straight for the double doors to his front. He could see people sitting in folding chairs set up around a half dozen circular tables. He took no notice of the Civil Rights memorabilia displayed on the walls nor of the large banner announcing an award ceremony for this evening.

At a sprint, Abdel raised his AK-47 to his shoulder, flipped the safety with his thumb to full automatic, and sprayed his first shots into the six people sitting at the nearest table. He planned to break right toward the stage while his other three team members would break left. This would create a line of fire across the breadth of the long room, allowing them to engage targets without fear of shooting each other.

The next sixty seconds went by in a blur. Team Leo was not focused on identifying people on their target list; they were simply there to kill as many people as possible. All of their targets were adults over forty, so when possible, those were the people they aimed for first. Abdel focused on the mechanics of close combat that he'd practiced so arduously over the last nine months—aiming reflex-ively, keeping track of the number of rounds fired, smoothly changing magazines. His team made no effort to seek cover, for none of the attendees in the room were armed. Wais had once used the English phrase "like shooting fish in a barrel," and Abdel now knew exactly what Wais had meant.

In sixty seconds, there were twenty-two bodies lying on the floor or strewn across one of the tables. Two young women and a teenage boy had successfully fled to the rear of the room, disappearing in a maze of what appeared to be museum exhibits. Team Leo's instructions had been not to chase down any leakers. They were there to kill and move on.

With all of the occupants of the room wounded or dead, Abdel and his teammates quickly changed magazines and ran around the room, shooting everyone in the head at point-blank range. They ignored the pleas of the wounded and simply focused on putting bullets into heads.

With everyone in the room dead, their mission was complete.

Abdel yelled, "Let's go! Let's go!"

They had been specifically told to communicate only in English when there was potential to be overheard. With that order, Team Leo ran back down the same corridor they had entered and out through the main entrance doors.

As Abdel exited the building and sprinted for the Tahoe parked a dozen yards away on the sidewalk, he was startled to hear gunfire. Looking to his right, he could see Mohamed and Kareem, the two team members who'd remained outside, engaging a police officer across the parking lot.

A Farmville police cruiser was parked haphazardly at the entrance to the museum's parking lot, and the officer was kneeling behind the hood of his car, using his service pistol to shoot back at Mohamed. Abdel watched as both Mohamed and Kareem stitched the cruiser with dozens of bullets fired on full auto, hitting the police officer several times in the chest and face and knocking him backward.

With the police threat neutralized, Abdel and his assault mates clambered into the Tahoe. As planned, Mohamed and Kareem continued to pull security and cover the Tahoe's exit. They were going to split up for now, and it was most important that the occupants of the Tahoe get away cleanly. Abdel threw the SUV into reverse, spinning the tires a bit on the grass but swinging the vehicle into a sharp reverse turn so that the front pointed towards the exit onto Griffin Street. Abdel punched the gas pedal, and the car leaped forward toward the exit.

Abdel breathed a momentary sigh of relief as he turned onto Griffin Street, knowing he was seconds from a clean getaway. All of a sudden, the side passenger window exploded, showering Abdel with glass. He felt a warm, sticky substance on his face and wondered for a moment if he'd been wounded. Looking to his right, he could see Hamza slumped to the side, a large bullet hole just to the left of his nose. Abdel continued to accelerate and caught just a glimpse of a large black man wearing a faded green Army coat and a black baseball hat, aiming a massive revolver at Abdel's vehicle.

At the light, Abdel turned right onto Main Street, driving quickly but not speeding. He had 1.7 miles to go until he could turn onto Highway 460. If he could do that, his part of the mission would be a success, and they'd be able to seek out their next target. Mohamed and Kareem had their own targets, and Inshallah, they would all meet up back at their base of operations in twenty-four hours.

Abdel and his team had no knowledge, nor did they care, that within the twenty-two people they had just massacred, six Democratic members of the Virginia General Assembly were littered among the dead.

34

Rocky Mount, North Carolina

Thursday, March 21

TWO SICARIOS of Team Capricorn sat with their backs against the three-foot-tall brick parapet running the circumference of the roof. The sun was low on the horizon but still provided plenty of visibility. The two men had no difficulty accessing the roof of this Post Office building in the middle of the North Carolina Wesleyan College campus, as it had closed promptly at 4:30 p.m. and all of the postal workers had departed.

Sniper teams normally worked in pairs, with one person being the sniper and the other the spotter. For this mission, the terrain requirements dictated they take a different approach. The entire college campus, located in the northern suburbs of Rocky Mount, North Carolina, was as flat as a pool table. The campus itself was made up of red brick buildings and tall loblolly pines, and the three-story Post Office building with a flat roof offered the only realistic vantage point over the entrance to the Dunn Center, the modern performing arts center on the small college campus.

With the rooftop barely two hundred meters from the Dunn

Divided We Stand

Center, it was deemed too risky to place a spotter on the roof where their silhouette could be easily noticed. Instead, two snipers were now on the roof, with their spotter sitting in a vehicle in the parking lot beside the performing arts center. Connected by radio, the spotter could easily relay information directly to the snipers' earbuds, giving them directions on when to pop up and engage their target, the governor of North Carolina.

Governor Rod Chase was attending a panel seminar at the Dunn Center on the topic of converting tobacco fields to solar energy farms. The six members of Team Capricorn had no idea how their boss had learned of the governor's schedule, but it had all been in the packet they'd received the week before when Wais, their primary contact and benefactor, had briefed them.

For the last month, after completing their training, the team kept a low profile in an apartment in Greensboro, North Carolina. After receiving their orders last week, the team studied every facet of the terrain around North Carolina Wesleyan's campus, as well as the home addresses of their follow-on targets.

The six men of Team Capricorn were sicarios of the CNJG, formally known as the Jalisco New Generation Cartel. Second in power to Mexico's infamous Sinaloa Cartel, the CNJG was heavily militarized and often employed extreme violence. These men were members of CNJG's elite special operations group, and killing was nothing new to them.

Capricorn's leader sat behind the wheel of a Chevy Suburban parked at the edge of the Dunn Center parking lot, affording an unobstructed view of the center's front and side entrances. Another team member sat in the passenger seat next to him while two additional team members occupied a second Suburban parked in a lot on the far side of the performing arts center.

"It's time," the leader said in Spanish into the radio mic, which connected him to his team members. He heard clicks from his two elements in acknowledgment and turned to nod to the man sitting next to him.

Without a word, the passenger stepped out of the vehicle and began walking toward the side entrance of the Dunn Center. He'd been selected for this task because he was the youngest-looking of the six Capricorn members, spoke fluent English, and had no visible tattoos on his face or hands. Dressed smartly in jeans, a light blue Carolina hooded sweatshirt, and a half-full school backpack looped over one shoulder, the man walked directly toward the entrance as if he'd done this a hundred times before.

Pulling open the glass door at the side of the building, the sicario walked inside and sauntered slowly down the corridor. As briefed, there were small classrooms on his left, while the main corridor turned to the right, where the main performance center was located. The classrooms were all empty at this time of day.

Ducking into the second classroom, the man unslung his backpack and placed it into the trashcan by the door. He reached into the bag, forcibly jerking on a cord, satisfied with the hissing sound now emanating from the bag, and dropped the entire bag into the plastic bin. Without waiting, he immediately turned from the room and walked back into the empty corridor.

Inside his backpack was an incendiary device, and the man knew from rehearsals that it would take less than ten seconds for the bag to erupt in flames and start spewing a tremendous amount of smoke and heat. Ten seconds later, he noticed the first whisps of smoke flowing out under the classroom's closed door. Keeping exactly to the plan, the man walked back toward the same door he'd entered less than a minute previously. On the wall by the entrance, the man paused, reaching over to pull down sharply on the red handle of the wall-mounted fire alarm.

The alarm sounded instantly, blaring an obnoxious, piercing noise that overwhelmed the senses. Emergency lights along the corridor switched on, and strobes began flickering along with the sustained sound.

Reversing course, the sicario jogged down the corridor to the right, heading out toward the main entrance rather than the side entrance he'd previously used. Smoke was now billowing into the corridor. As he came to the lobby, he noticed two uniformed state police officers talking animatedly with a campus security officer.

Divided We Stand

"Fire!" Shouted the sicario. "There's smoke coming from one of the classrooms. I see flames! We need to get everyone out!"

Without waiting, the sicario ran to the series of doors leading to the main auditorium. Before he got there, several of the doors pushed open, and several dozen people streamed out of the performing arts center. Once in the lobby, everyone made for the main exit as the campus security officer began yelling for everyone to remain calm and exit the building.

The sicario turned to see a uniformed state trooper holding the governor by the elbow and leading him quickly toward the entrance. The governor was on a course to walk right by the sicario, within ten feet, and he thought for a moment of pulling the pistol from his waistband and shooting the governor in the back of the head.

That wasn't the plan; if he'd learned anything over the months of training, it was to always stick to the plan. He had confidence his teammates would do their job. Instead, he reached into the front pocket of his hooded sweatshirt and keyed his radio handset four times in quick succession.

The Capricorn team leader watched all of this happening from the front seat of his Suburban, and he kept his two snipers updated on the radio. The team leader could see strobes flashing on the side of the building, indicating the fire alarm had been tripped, and within seconds, several dozen people exited the main doors. They initially congregated outside the main entrance, but a campus security officer motioned for them to move across the street.

A large black SUV sat parked in front of the building behind a silver-and-black-marked North Carolina state trooper vehicle. The team leader knew this was the Governor's motorcade and that Governor Chase would be exiting momentarily.

"Ready, snipers," the team leader said into his radio. "Any second."

Hearing the four rapid clicks over the radio, the snipers did not wait for any verbal commands. This was the signal they'd been waiting for over an hour. Having mentally rehearsed their movements the entire time while sitting against the parapet, each sniper pivoted onto his knees, placing the stock of the barrel of their matching Remington 700 rifles onto the smooth brick of the low parapet while pressing their cheeks into their accustomed stock weld. Sighting through the Leupold scope, both men placed their reticles on the entrance doors two hundred meters to their front.

They didn't have long to wait as Governor Rod Chase walked calmly out through the center entrance door, followed close behind by a uniformed North Carolina state trooper.

Both Team Capricorn snipers gently squeezed the trigger on their rifles, neither knowing exactly which of the two rounds that bloomed red on the governor's upper chest were his. The governor crumpled to the ground, and the state trooper immediately fell on top, attempting to cover him with his body. The other trooper standing by the open door of the governor's SUV pulled his service pistol, looking around to identify where the shots had originated.

The snipers, knowing they were well out of range of the trooper's pistol, took careful aim at the prone body of the governor lying next to his SUV. The left sniper sighted on the governor's head, while the right sniper zeroed in on the state trooper.

Bang! Bang!

Two additional suppressed rounds found their mark. The suppressors on the Remington 700s weren't enough to make the shots silent, but they dampened them enough that it was difficult for anyone to pinpoint the sniper's location accurately.

"Target down," said the team leader over the radio. "Get off the roof, now," he ordered. "Team 2, hold your position."

The team leader watched as the sicario who'd ignited the fire-bomb walked quickly toward his Suburban and retook his place in the front passenger seat. The team leader immediately put the vehicle in gear and drove through the parking lot towards the access road to Tyler Drive, which would take him right beside the Post Office building. Just as he pulled up, the two Capricorn snipers, having been instructed to abandon their sniper rifles on the roof, quickly descended the fire ladder built into the side of the building that led from the roof. Within seconds, they'd made it to the Suburban and were jumping into the rear seats.

Accelerating away from the post office, the team leader turned south on Tyler Drive, heading toward Everett Gymnasium and the ball fields where the back entrance to campus was located. As the Suburban picked up speed, the team leader saw a Nash County sheriff's cruiser approaching in the oncoming lane at a high rate of speed.

Drive right by, thought the team leader. *C'mon! Keep driving.*

The sheriff's vehicle sped past their Suburban, and the team leader sighed in relief. Glancing up to the rearview mirror, the team leader's heart sank just as the men in the back started shouting. The cop car had slammed on its brakes and whipped around in a U-turn.

35

Arlington, Virginia

Thursday, March 21

THE CHECHEN TEAM leader of Team Virgo carefully watched the icons on the Life360 app move across his tablet's screen. He'd been told this software app was used mostly by parents to keep track of their teenage children, but it was proving a cheap, effective, and virtually anonymous method of keeping track of his team members in the middle of the mission.

The Chechen watched as his icons departed the Capitol Hill area of Washington, D.C., weaving through the city streets toward Independence Ave before accessing the onramp for I-395 South. The icon for Green One had just crossed the Potomac River and was approaching the left exit with signs for Crystal City. Green Two, about half a mile behind Green One, was leaving D.C. on I-395 just short of the Potomac.

Perfect spacing, thought the Chechen. *Well within our planning calculations.*

Each icon on his tablet corresponded with a vehicle being driven by one of his fellow Chechen team members, both veterans of the brutal Russian crackdown on the Islamic insurgency in Chechnya. Each of these team members was following a different full-size black SUV that had departed an underground parking garage on Second Street NE on Capitol Hill. They were not following closely, as they already knew the SUVs' ultimate destination—their role in following was purely for timing purposes.

The destination was 2231 Crystal Drive in Arlington, Virginia— adjacent to Reagan National Airport and just down the road from the Pentagon. The eleventh floor of the red stone building contained a Ruth's Chris steakhouse, with commanding views over Reagan National's runways, which was hosting tonight's intimate lifetime achievement award ceremony of the National Association of Women Judges. The occupants of the two approaching black SUVs were both past recipients of this award.

The Chechen sat at Starbucks on the first floor of the building, at the corner closest to Crystal Drive. He was dressed in business casual attire: tan slacks, a button-down Oxford shirt, and a dark green Barbour jacket. With his dark hair and beard neatly trimmed, he looked like any other professional having a cup of coffee.

A large U-shaped drive marked the entrance to the L-shaped building, with a small park built on top of an underground parking garage in the center of the U. Diners at Ruth's Chris often parked in the underground garage, but the building also offered valet services inside the U-shaped driveway, which the Chechen was confident his targets would use.

With earbuds in both ears and cradling his tablet on his lap, the Chechen took a sip of his coffee from the Starbucks cup in front of him. The hand bringing the cup to his lips was missing three fingers, and he grasped the cup expertly between his thumb and index finger.

The Chechen was an explosives expert, specifically adept at making improvised bombs. He'd first learned his trade in the basements of Grozny more than twenty years before and had honed his skills over the past two decades in the dusty warehouses and garages of Iraq and Syria. Though a devout Muslim, the Chechen's cause was not for Allah nor to bring jihad to the infidel. The Chechen lived for one thing, and one thing only—to feel the orgasmic exhilaration of watching his creations explode. There was simply no other feeling that came close to the moment his mechanical creation detonated, seemingly stopping time for that very brief moment just before colors, cacophony, and chaos overwhelmed everything in the area.

That God-like feeling, knowing that he was snuffing out human lives, was the most powerful feeling the Chechen had ever felt.

One of his creations was parked twenty yards to his front. The bomb was packed into the trunk of the sedan parked in a spot reserved for To-Go Orders, with one of his Palestinian team members at the wheel. The Chechen knew that two more of his creations were in similar vehicles strategically positioned according to their plan, one in the parking garage beneath him and another parked several blocks north of where he sat.

The Team Virgo drivers of these car bombs were three young Palestinian men from Gaza who had each lost family members to fighting with the Israelis.

"Shahid One, be alert. The first target is one minute out," the Chechen said quietly into the microphone of his AirPods. Shahid was Arabic for martyr, a callsign of great respect for the young Palestinian suicide bombers.

"Tamaam," came the reply—Okay.

"Shahid Two, you should see the SUV passing you soon. Hold your position for the second target."

All of Team Virgo's members were monitoring the open call on their encrypted phones. The Chechen's tablet showed Green One's icon approaching, and the Chechen turned to the right to see a black SUV coast to a stop on Crystal Drive, its left turn signal blinking. Two cars behind it was the gray RAV4 of his Virgo team member.

"Get ready, Shahid One," the Chechen said, keeping his voice low and watching as the black SUV made the turn into the U-shaped entrance. "There he is! You know what to do. Allah Yusallmak—May God Keep You Safe!"

Watching his team member pull out of his parking space directly

Divided We Stand

behind the black SUV, the Chechen could see the petrified but determined look on his driver's face.

"Ma'a Salama," came the driver's scared voice over the phone. "Allahu Akbar!" As he was trained, the man clicked off the call and slowly followed the black SUV as it approached the entrance to Ruth's Chris. The Chechen stood up quickly, shuffling toward the corner of the building. Knowing what was coming, he wanted to put as much of the building as possible between himself and the entrance to Ruth's Chris, about a hundred meters away.

"Shahid Two, do you—"

An enormous explosion erupted, the concussive wave knocking the Chechen to the ground even from his protected position. Debris flew everywhere, car alarm systems began blaring, and people screamed. Picking himself up off the ground, the Chechen watched two women dash from where they'd been sitting at the Starbucks, one woman's face gashed and bloody, and both with looks of pure terror on their faces.

Looking at his tablet, the Chechen quickly called to his other suicide bomber. "Shahid Two, do you have your target in sight?"

"Nam," came the reply—yes. "Allahu Akbar!" This time, the driver did not terminate the call, and the Chechen heard a man scream through his earbud just as he heard a distant explosion several blocks to his north along Crystal Drive.

With the entire area now in a panic, the Chechen followed a small crowd of people running west on 23rd Street. While these people were reacting to the explosion, this was all part of Team Virgo's plan. He would jog for four blocks before being picked up by his Green One team member, a fellow Chechen, who had been following the lead target in the car.

The Chechen took great pleasure in knowing that he had struck a blow against the Great Satan and that the U.S. Supreme Court had just lost two of its justices.

36

Las Vegas, Nevada

Thursday, March 21

THE PLAN for Nevada was the grandest of all the Zodiac team missions, which is why Wais had been tasked with personally overseeing its execution. Similar to other missions, this one had been months in the making.

At the beginning of the year, Democratic leaders throughout Nevada were invited to the inaugural Duffers for Democracy golf tournament, billed as an exclusive event pairing Nevada state senators and congressmen with Democratic donors and business leaders. It was scheduled to be held at the ultra-exclusive Arroyo Country Club on the far western edge of Las Vegas, nestled at the base of the Red Rocks Canyon National Conservation Area. The date of the event was Thursday, March 21st, and engraved invitations were sent out to dozens of Democratic members of the state legislature and local business leaders who were registered Democrats.

Luther, Alex's IT guru, had set everything up brilliantly, and Alex's support staff had ensured that all the invitations and pairings were in place. They'd even gone so far as to hire two local event

Divided We Stand

organizers to ensure everything ran smoothly—both hired virtually, having never met anyone from Alex's organization in person. They coordinated the luncheon, guest speaker, and other logistics components for the shotgun-start golf outing.

With the golf pairings set and an open-bar luncheon complete, the thirty-six Democratic state legislators headed in pairs to their golf carts and drove to their starting tee box at one of the course's eighteen holes. A brilliant part of Wais' plan had been to provide each elected official with their own golf shirt prior to the event under the guise that this would provide visibility to the many donors in attendance. These polo shirts, made of the most expensive moisture-wicking fabric, were neon blue and had the legislator's name and district embroidered on the left breast. Matching neon blue golf hats were also distributed, along with a neon blue flag mounted on each of their golf carts.

Hospitality for the event was exceptional, and the participants were somewhat in awe to find a hospitality cart at every hole. A nice man stood beside a golf cart with several coolers of ice, snacks, and an assortment of alcoholic and non-alcoholic drinks. A shotgun start required the eighteen foursomes of two legislators paired with two donors to each start at a different hole. This allowed all eighteen foursomes to tee off at exactly the same time and to progress along the course until they'd completed all eighteen holes.

The start time for this event was 3:15 p.m. Pacific Time, signaled by a loud air horn being blasted from the clubhouse by one of the temp event organizers.

Wais had positioned himself on an overlook in the foothills to the west of the country club. Although almost eight hundred meters away from the course, his elevated position provided a panoramic view over many of the course's tee boxes. Using 20-power image-stabilized Zeiss binoculars, Wais could zoom in on any one of a dozen holes to see the participants up close.

He randomly picked a hole and zeroed in on the four golfers readying themselves to tee off. At the 4th hole, as delineated by the rock at the edge of the manicured grass tee box with the large number four carved into it, a donor placed his ball on a tee and took practice swings behind it. One legislator was sitting in the cart, while another was standing next to him, drinking from a Gatorade bottle and watching the donor swing his club. Behind them, a Hispanic man sat calmly in his golf cart, two large coolers positioned next to the cart and a long slim box sitting beside him.

The air horn must have sounded, although Wais could not hear it, given his distance from the clubhouse. As the donor on the 4th hole readied himself to hit his tee shot, the hospitality man reached into the box next to him and withdrew a short-barreled AR-15 rifle. Quickly aiming, the man began firing rapid single shots at the two state legislators wearing their neon blue golf shirts. As Wais focused his binoculars, he could see the blood splotches on the men's shirts as they lay sprawled on the ground.

Wais watched as a similar sequence of events was replicated across most of the eighteen holes. It took a minute for people to recognize that the loud pops they were hearing were indeed gunshots, and then the panic set in. People began running across the fairways, hiding behind rocks and trees.

Wais watched for one more minute, satisfied that Teams Pisces and Aquarius had completed their mission successfully. Eighteen Democratic legislators needed to be removed to swing the balance of power in Nevada's Senate and House of Representatives. Wais was confident those results had been achieved.

37

Mansfield, Ohio

Thursday, March 21

JASMINE WATCHED TWO YOUNG WOMEN, likely nursing students, exit their car and walk toward the three-story red brick residence hall. One carried a full plastic grocery bag along with a 12-pack of High Noon hard seltzer, while the other delicately balanced two pizza boxes as she closed the car door.

Jasmine had driven all day and was now parked at the rear of a parking lot on the tiny Ashland College of Nursing campus. The college's one and only academic building was a hundred meters to her right, and two brick dormitories edged the parking lot where she now sat.

This was her second time in Mansfield this week, and she sincerely hoped it would be her last. It was just after eight o'clock in the evening, and the last two hours had been extremely eventful. Jasmine had been receiving updates from her twelve Zodiac teams using a specially-encrypted satellite phone that would hide her location. With only a few exceptions, the commencement of Phase 2 was going off almost exactly as planned.

ROBERT COLE

Leaving her satphone free to receive updates, Jasmine pulled her Kryptall iPhone from the cupholder and quickly dialed Alex's similarly encrypted iPhone.

"I've been looking forward to your call," said Alex without feeling the need for a greeting. "From the news reports on television, it appears Phase 2 has kicked off with a bang. Literally."

"Yes, Wais and I have heard from eleven of the twelve teams," said Jasmine. "That's quite a bit better than the fifty percent success rate we had planned."

"Excellent. What team is missing?"

"Gemini. They checked in with Wais from their safe house in Tempe this morning, but we haven't heard from them since. And I haven't seen anything on the news." Team Gemini had the task of assassinating the Governor and Lieutenant Governor of Arizona. While the legislature of Arizona was firmly Republican, removing the Governor and Lieutenant Governor, both Democrats, would pave the way for the State Treasurer, a Republican, to become governor.

"Well, that's our lowest priority mission of all Zodiac teams, so we dodged a bullet there," said Alex. "I know you've been traveling, but I assume you've been monitoring the news?"

"I've been listening to satellite radio," replied Jasmine. "I'm not sure how accurate the news reports are, but I can quickly update you on our primary targets. Four of the five gubernatorial chains have been severed. The attacks on the North Carolina governor and the Governors and Lieutenant Governors of Michigan, Kentucky, and Pennsylvania were all successful. I can also confirm that all five missions to switch the state legislatures have also been successful. The attacks in Farmville, Kalamazoo, and Dearborn were clean, with the teams getting away. Those teams—Leo, Libra, and Taurus —are now prosecuting their secondary targets."

"Okay," said Alex. "What about Capricorn? There are reports of a major shootout in Rocky Mount."

"Yes, I just heard from the assistant team leader. The team leader, with three others, was seen by the police and got into a high-speed chase and shootout. The assistant wanted to help rescue

Divided We Stand

them, but in accordance with their training, the mission came first. The two remaining members of Capricorn withdrew and are now heading to their secondary targets in southern Virginia."

"Good. You and Wais trained them well. I already know about Team Virgo and the bombing in Crystal City. CNN has confirmed that Justice Faulkner died in a suicide bombing attack and that Justice Escobar was critically injured in a separate but related suicide bombing. The informal word is that Escobar's condition is grave and that even if she survives, her injuries are massive."

"Yes, I've been in contact with Usman," said Jasmine. "He's away cleanly with the other two Chechens. The third suicide bomber, as trained, waited in the parking garage for thirty minutes and then drove up to detonate into a crowd of first responders."

"The video of that is what's currently showing on Fox News. Apparently, a couple of reporters were killed in that blast, as well as a dozen EMTs, firefighters, and onlookers."

For the next few minutes, Jasmine dispassionately reported the information she had received from each of the Zodiac teams. The primary goal of the Zodiac teams was to change the control of five states: Michigan, Pennsylvania, Virginia, Nevada, and Minnesota. The state legislatures in these states, the same legislatures that had the power to approve a Constitutional Convention, were very narrowly divided. Minnesota had one more Democrat than Republican in the Senate and six more Democrats in the House, while in Michigan, Virginia, and Pennsylvania, the numbers were less than two people difference in each house of Congress.

Teams Cancer and Scorpio had focused on Pennsylvania. Team Cancer, the second team consisting only of Americans, had earlier this evening breached the fence of the Pennsylvania governor's mansion in Harrisburg and killed the governor along with several state troopers. Team Scorpio had completed a similar mission targeting the lieutenant governor, who had no security to speak of. The two teams had then moved on to secondary targets consisting of Democratic members of the state legislature. The legislature had Session Days this week, so many of the members were in Harrisburg hotels. Teams Cancer and Scorpio would be targeting these hotels and various residences throughout the evening.

In Minnesota, the six Somali members of Team Sagittarius had been unleashed upon a meeting of state Democratic Congressional leaders at the Democratic-Farmer-Labor Party headquarters in St. Paul. The six jihadists were armed with automatic rifles and shotguns. Unlike the similar attack of Team Leo in Farmville, Virginia, two of the DFL congressmen were farmers from around Mankato, a predominantly farming community in the southern part of the state. They both had permits to carry pistols and immediately returned fire upon the assaulting members of Team Sagittarius. The result was that two team members had been killed, while a third had been grievously wounded. The two farmers/congressmen had both died in the attack, along with two state senators and five additional congressmen. In the team's latest update to Jasmine, she had been informed that the wounded Somali had succumbed to his injuries and that the remaining three members of Team Sagittarius were proceeding to their secondary targets.

The evening had been a huge success so far, and Jasmine was pleased that Alex seemed impressed after her detailed update. Looking at the dashboard clock on her Bronco, Jasmine realized it was time for her to get going. She signed off on her call with Alex and focused on the next part of her mission.

The large parking lot of the Balgreen Medical Center, directly across Marion Avenue from the Ashland Nursing College where Jasmine was parked, was mostly deserted at this time of night. Putting her Bronco into gear, Jasmine drove out of the college parking lot, made a quick turn onto Marion Avenue, and then a quick right into the side street that would give her access to the Balgreen Medical Center parking lots. She drove all the way to the rear of the Balgreen lot, parking along the edge of a grass hill that rose gently for sixty meters to a thickly wooded treeline.

Already dressed in dark cargo pants and a dark blue hooded sweatshirt, Jasmine stepped out of the Bronco and pulled a long, rectangular black nylon bag out of the backseat. Using the attached

Divided We Stand

straps, Jasmine slung the bag over her shoulder, shut the car door, and began walking up the gentle hill at a brisk pace.

In under a minute, she was in the woods and immediately turned left to follow the edge of the woods due west. Using a small lensatic compass she had brought specifically for this purpose, Jasmine changed her azimuth to the northwest. After walking through the woods for four hundred meters, Jasmin began to see the lights of a house directly to her front. Bingo!

The large home at the end of Deer Run Road was situated in a small clearing surrounded by woods. As Jasmine moved to within sixty meters of the house, she could clearly see the details of the backyard. It appeared that almost all of the lights on both floors of the home were on, as were the bright outdoor lights mounted at the rear of the house to cast their lumination over a substantial brick patio complete with patio furniture and a firepit.

Glancing left and right, Jasmine found the exact position she'd been hoping for, just a few yards to her left. She knelt on the ground in this new spot, sliding the long case off her back and placing it gently on the ground next to her. Silently unzipping the case, Jasmine removed a sleek rifle with an extra-thick barrel. The short-action Remington 700 sniper rifle was chambered in the standard .308 cartridge, also known as the 7.62 round in NATO. This was the same sniper rifle used by Marine Corps snipers from Vietnam to Iraq.

Jasmine had already loaded the rifle's internal magazine and expertly cycled the bolt to chamber a round. She extended the front bipod legs to provide a stable shooting platform and positioned herself in a proper prone firing position behind the rifle's high-powered scope. Now, it was just a question of waiting. If her research was correct, Jasmine didn't think she'd have to wait more than two hours, a mere pittance of time to a Marine sniper.

Most people believed being a sniper was about precision marksmanship. While marksmanship and camouflage were certainly requirements, they were only a small portion of a sniper's skillset. Stalking an enemy or luring a target into the kill zone was the expertise that set world-class snipers apart from the common expert marksman.

Tonight's kill zone was one that Jasmine had manufactured, even though she'd never set eyes on the target or been in these woods before. The large brick house in front of her belonged to the senior U.S. Senator from Ohio, a member of the Democratic Party. The Senator spent almost all of his time in Washington, and with everything Jasmine knew was going to be occurring that night, she did not want to be anywhere near the security crackdown that the nation's capital was now experiencing.

On Tuesday of this week, two days ago, Jasmine had spent just over an hour in Mansfield. She'd arrived at dawn and had proceeded directly to North Lake Park on the northwest side of downtown Mansfield. Wearing her usual sweatpants and hoodie pulled low over her head, Jasmine did not look out of place as she strode along the Richland B&O Trail, a former railroad line now used for biking and jogging. Relying on the intelligence provided by Wais, she recognized the man slowly jogging toward her. Late-sixties, balding, slightly overweight—there was no doubt in her mind that this was the younger brother of Ohio's senior member of the U.S. Senate. Waiting for him to jog past, confirming his face from the pictures, she simply pulled a .45 caliber Glock 21 out of her front pocket and shot the man three times in the back of the head. Twenty minutes later, she was taking off on a private jet from Mansfield Lahm Regional Airport. Jasmine felt no remorse—the man was simply part of the plan.

The Senator's brother was an inconsequential figure, completely irrelevant to Alex's grand master strategy. However, his death served an important purpose—it brought the Ohio senator back to Mansfield for the funeral.

As Jasmine patiently watched the back of the Senator's home, she hoped Wais' other intelligence would prove equally accurate. Sure enough, forty minutes later, the sliding glass door at the rear of the home slid open, and a large man stepped onto the brick patio. He was alone, and after closing the slider, he walked directly over to the patio furniture and took a seat. This was definitely the Senator.

He held several objects in his hand, and Jasmine adjusted the rifle's scope to get a better look. The Senator dipped an ivory-tipped pipe into a small bag of tobacco, then proceeded to tamp the tobacco before using a wooden match to light it.

Emotionless, with no more thought than opening a refrigerator door, Jasmine sighted the reticle of her scope directly on the Senator's temple. From sixty yards away, Jasmine knew her bullet would hit exactly where she had aimed. Gently squeezing the trigger with the tip of her right index finger, the rifle fired, and Jasmine watched as a 175-grain Sierra Matchking bullet exploded into the Senator's head, blowing chunks of brain, blood, bone, and tissue across the patio behind him.

She did not need to fire a second round to know that the Senator was dead. The thick suppressor on the end of the rifle had dampened the sound, but it still sounded like a very loud clap—the equivalent of a hammer striking a nail. While it would not alert the distant neighbors, anyone in the house would likely have heard it.

Not waiting to see if anyone was in the house, Jasmine slid the rifle back into the carrying case, slung it across her bag, and began jogging through the woods back toward the parking lot. Halfway back to the parking lot, she stopped and reached into the backpack, retrieving a black knit watch cap from a ziplock plastic bag. Jasmine looked at it briefly, then tossed it on the ground.

Two minutes later, she was driving out of town in her Ford Bronco.

38

Washington, D.C

Thursday, March 21

SHARYN HAD NEVER BEEN to the PEOC before tonight, and that was probably a good thing. The PEOC—the Presidential Emergency Operations Center—was located deep beneath the White House. It contained an exact replica of the Situation Room, which Sharyn had visited often, but there were also living quarters, dining areas, offices, and everything needed to serve as a protected command post should things turn bad on the surface.

Sharyn had no idea how deep she was underground, but based on the elevator ride, she knew it was deep.

At 6:30 p.m., Sharyn had been discussing tomorrow's schedule in the Vice President's West Wing office before she and the Vice President departed for the evening, as much of the West Wing staff had already done. Three Secret Service agents, members of the Vice President's personal protection detail, had stormed into the room, physically grabbed both Vice President Moore and Sharyn, and rushed them down the hallway to a waiting elevator. Only on

Divided We Stand

the ride down to the PEOC did the agents inform them of a potential threat against the White House.

It was now approaching ten p.m., and Sharyn was in the PEOC conference room with a half dozen members of the West Wing's inner circle. She'd been sitting there for more than three hours, mostly watching one of the large television screens on the wall. The President had participated for the first two hours before retiring to the underground bunker's special quarters set up for him and his family.

The Vice President sat at the end of the table, looking exhausted and sipping sparkling water from a can. Next to the VP, John Reynolds was watching the same television monitor as Sharyn, while next to him, Geraldine Fox was typing away at her laptop computer, undoubtedly churning out bullet points for the press briefing they were planning for the morning.

"Is this war?" Vice President Moore asked no one in particular.

"I don't think so," answered Carl Tidhams, the National Security Advisor. "If it is, who's the enemy? This seems more like a terrorist attack, but I just can't see who's behind it. Or what they're trying to accomplish."

"Two Supreme Court justices blown up by coordinated suicide bombers," said Brad Nesbitt, the deputy chief of staff whom Sharyn wished hadn't been included by the Secret Service in the personnel whisked to the PEOC as soon as the Supreme Court justices had been attacked. "The governors in four states assassinated. All Democrats. An attempted assassination on a fifth governor in Arizona, also a Democrat. Mass shootings across several states from Virginia to Minnesota—all seeming to target Democrats. I'll tell you who the enemy is, Carl. It's the goddamn Republican fascists!"

"But what do they have to gain?" Tidhams asked. "I mean, all four of those states are just going to have elections in November to install new governors. Hell, in North Carolina, the governor was term-limited and wasn't even running for re-election. And all the shootings were local Democratic party officials or members of the state legislature. They weren't powerful people, certainly not worth targeting by international terrorists. And let's not forget Benjamin King. His plane was shot down yesterday. I find it difficult to believe these attacks aren't all related somehow."

"What's the latest from the FBI?" Chief of Staff Reynolds asked, breaking his attention away from the television.

"They're conflicted," said Tidhams. "The initial indications were that tonight's violence was definitely the work of Islamic terrorists. Car bombing is a uniquely jihadist tactic. The two dead terrorists in Minnesota were definitely al-Shabaab from Somalia, and the survivors of the Kalamazoo brewery attack swear the attackers were Arabs. The FBI also says one of the survivors in Farmville, Virginia, mentioned the terrorists yelling "Allahu Akbar" as they fired their weapons. As for King's airplane, the FBI isn't saying much. There's still a major problem getting access to the wreckage as Florida law enforcement isn't fully cooperating. But everything points to the work of Islamic jihadists."

"Well, how is that conflicted?" Vice President Moore asked. "Seems pretty cut and dry to me."

"Yes, except for North Carolina. State troopers there killed four of the attackers and matched their prints to those found on the sniper rifles left behind. They're all cartel members from Mexico."

"Fuck me," said Moore, whose language when she was tired and stressed rivaled that of any sailor. "You're telling me that the Islamic jihadist whackjobs are now working together with the Mexican drug cartels? God help us."

"Serena, we don't know that, so let's not jump to conclusions," said John Reynolds calmly. "That's why Carl said the FBI is conflicted. It's too early, and the evidence is still being analyzed to reach any firm conclusions."

"What about the Pentagon or the CIA?" Serena asked. "What are they saying?"

"Well, you heard from the Chairman and the CIA Director when they were here earlier with the President," said Tidhams. "They've picked up no chatter, nor do they perceive any threat to American infrastructure. We haven't seen any major attacks since

Divided We Stand

before seven o'clock tonight. All that points to this likely being the end of it."

"Well, that's good to know," said the Vice President sarcastically.

"Ma'am?" Interrupted Sharyn. Although she had wanted to remain silent, she could no longer keep her thoughts to herself. "I think we might be looking at this wrong."

"What do you mean?" Vice President Moore sat forward in her chair, interested in what her chief of staff and closest advisor had to say.

"I think…I think maybe we're focusing too much on the *who*, when maybe we should focus more on the *why*."

"Go on," said Reynolds, also now very interested.

"Okay," said Sharyn, gathering momentum. "Put aside the perpetrators' nationality and background. Let's look at their purpose. They've conducted what has to be a highly coordinated attack across several states, some more than a thousand miles apart. Yet the targets of these attacks seem to have one common link— they're all members of the Democratic Party in some fashion. But for what purpose? They've attacked state governors and legislators. But there are almost twenty more Democratic governors and over three thousand Democratic Party members in the fifty state legisla- tures. What does killing a few governors and twenty legislators do? How does that further some Islamic jihadist cause?"

"It doesn't," said Tidhams flatly. "Jihadists aren't nuanced. They don't have ulterior motives. They tell you straight to your face what their book tells them, and they tell you what they're going to do. We just don't believe them half the time."

"So what's the purpose?" asked Reynolds. "Let's keep on this trail. What did the attacks tonight accomplish?"

"To drive a wedge between Red and Blue," answered Geraldine, pulling herself away from her laptop. "The news media is already asking questions like: are extremists targeting American liberals? Are Democratic governors safe in this country?"

Believing Geraldine was on the right track, Sharyn was about to reply when something on the television screen caught her attention. The television was tuned to CNN, and the scene had shifted from a studio conversation to show a reporter live. The harsh light on top of the camera illuminated a young African-American reporter standing in the parking lot in front of a three-story red brick building. The chyron on the bottom of the screen showed him reporting from Mansfield, Ohio.

"Wait," Sharyn said, holding up her hand. "Something's happening. Brad, could you please turn up the volume?"

With the volume up, everyone around the conference table watched as the reporter described the murder of the senior U.S. Senator from Ohio, how he was gunned down by a single rifle shot while sitting in his own backyard.

"Holy shit," said the Vice President. "This is getting out of hand. The Republicans now control the U.S. Senate, along with the House of Representatives."

39

Jackson, Wyoming

Thursday, March 21

THE CHEVY TAHOE pulled up to the front of the impressive timber lodge, whose front door opened before Alex could even open his own car door. It was just after eight o'clock Mountain time, and Alex had phoned Orlean from the jet, informing him of his imminent arrival at the Jackson Hole airport and requesting to be picked up by one of Orlean's drivers.

Orlean was upset and wanted to discuss what was happening over the phone, but Alex cut him off and told him they'd have plenty of time for discussion when he arrived shortly. Now that Alex was in the driveway, Orlean rushed out of his house to confront him.

"What the hell is happening, Alex? Things are getting out of hand."

Stepping out of the Tahoe's rear passenger seat, Alex greeted his friend warmly and took him firmly by the elbow. "It's a pleasure to see you too, Orlean. Why don't we go inside where we can have a private conversation? And maybe some of that 25-year-old bourbon, if you still have any left?"

Orlean, getting the message, nodded once and turned to walk inside, but not before forcefully yanking his elbow from Alex's grasp. Orlean walked inside to the large, brightly lit living room, fire already crackling in both fireplaces and immediately took a seat in his preferred overstuffed leather chair. Wishing to calm his friend, Alex walked over to the bar along the wall and poured each of them three fingers of the Buffalo Trace Eagle Rare 25 bourbon.

"Here, my friend," Alex said, handing Orlean one of the glasses. "It's time for a toast. Sláinte, as you say." Alex clicked his glass against Orlean's before taking a strong sip of bourbon, enjoying it for the first time.

"What have you done?" Orlean asked. "The news? It's crazy, Alex."

"You mean, what have *WE* done, don't you?" Alex replied. "We've done exactly what we said we were going to do—set this country on the right course."

"But Alex, killing governors? Supreme Court Justices? What were you thinking?"

"What did you think Phase 2 was going to entail? Posting some videos on the internet and hoping the country suddenly falls into line behind us? No, Orlean, we did exactly what needed to be done tonight. As the saying goes, you can't make an omelet without breaking some eggs."

"First King, now this!" Orlean exclaimed. "Where does it end?"

"It ends with you presiding over a Constitutional Convention, that's where it ends. Or maybe even you sitting in the White House. It's time to put on your big boy pants."

"Okay," said Orlean, taking another swallow of bourbon and beginning to calm down. He liked the sound of him being in the White House. "So, uh, is Phase 2 working? Did you, uh, did we accomplish our goals tonight?"

"Yes, so far, it's going almost exactly as planned. Tomorrow will be the true test, and that's why I'm here tonight. Tomorrow is the

Divided We Stand

day we need to do and say all the right things, push the right buttons, and at just the right time. Are you ready?"

"You know I am. Bunker Hill Media is primed. We have all the targeted materials you asked us to prepare. We just need to know when to start flooding America's social media."

"Good," said Alex. "This is your time, my friend. Don't worry about the broken eggs. That's my world. I need you to concentrate on politics. Tonight was the first shot of our Civil War—our Fort Sumter, if you will. However, unlike back in 1861, the first shots in our Civil War were not symbolic cannon fire falling harmlessly in Charleston Harbor. Tonight was a strike that completely changed the battlefield, ensuring your success tomorrow and in the coming days. Just keep the faith, my friend. Keep the faith."

40

Clewiston, Florida

Thursday, March 21

IT HAD BEEN twenty-seven days since Nathan had been shot twice in the upper chest. He had no recollection whatsoever of the first few days and had been informed that it was touch-and-go for a while in the intensive care unit. Once his vitals stabilized, his health began to improve rapidly.

At the suggestion of Governor Marino, who had successfully held off the FBI investigators until the surveillance videos had shown that Nathan was not at fault in defending himself against the FBI agents, Nathan's doctors agreed to exaggerate the severity of Nathan's injuries to keep the press at bay. This allowed Nathan to disappear in the middle of the night and travel to Spooner's ranch on the banks of Lake Okeechobee outside the sleepy town of Clewiston.

Spooner welcomed Nathan into his sprawling home, which dated back to the 1920s and had seen a handful of additions and renovations over the last century. Twice-divorced, Spooner was an avowed bachelor for life, although he did have a live-in housekeeper.

Divided We Stand

Her name was Lourdes, and over the last three weeks, Nathan had developed a close friendship with her as she helped nurse him back to health. Having emigrated from Colombia seven years previously, Lourdes spoke English fluently, albeit with a lovely Colombian accent. In her late thirties with raven hair and matching eyes, Nathan suspected there was much more to Lourdes and Spooner's relationship than just employer and housekeeper.

Lourdes lived with her adorable eight-year-old son in a suite of rooms in one of the seemingly random additions to the sprawling single-story farmhouse. While Nathan and Emily had met Lourdes on previous occasions while visiting Spooner, Nathan was unaware of the close bond his friend Spooner had developed with Lourdes and her son, Felipe. A precocious boy who was overly shy around adults, it was clear to Nathan that Spooner, who had sired no children of his own, had become a father figure to Felipe—driving him to Little League practice, helping him with his homework, and fixing the bicycle that Felipe rode incessantly up and down the farm's dirt roads.

This was a side of Spooner that Nathan had never seen, and Nathan was very happy for his friend. The affection Spooner exhibited toward Felipe was evident, as was the affection between Spooner and his housekeeper. Nathan never asked, and Spooner never commented, but Nathan was awake before dawn on several mornings and heard Lourdes quietly walking from Spooner's master bedroom to her suite of rooms on the other side of the house.

It was just before midnight, and Nathan sat in a comfortable La-Z-boy chair in the living room, eyes glued to the television set. Lourdes and Felipe had long since retired to bed, and Spooner was out for the night at the training facility conducting night training for some special operators down from Fort Bragg—or Fort Liberty as it had recently been renamed.

Nathan knew in his heart that the events unfolding tonight across the mid-Atlantic and upper Midwestern states were directly tied to the bombing in St. Armands Circle that had killed Emily and Maeve. While Nathan had no clue as to what type of reaction his family's killers would have to the New York Times article Nathan had written last month, he was 100% certain that tonight's events were orchestrated by the same killers.

This is it! He thought. *This is the break I've been waiting for! If I can just put this all together, I know I can figure out who's responsible.*

Nathan grabbed his iPad from the side table next to him and began sketching notes using a stylus. While his body was nowhere near fully recovered, his mind was as sharp as ever. He began the process of organizing the incoming data, writing down his thoughts, and seeing how everything could potentially be related.

Over the last three days, a dozen or more violent incidents had occurred involving political figures across America. First, on Wednesday, Benjamin King's plane was shot down shortly after takeoff, with all souls on board perishing. With hundreds, perhaps thousands, of protests staged across the country in reaction to King's refusal to be arraigned and the Florida governor's assertion that federal law enforcement infringed on the Constitutional rights of states, many pundits thought King's death would potentially calm the country as King's imminent prosecution became moot upon his death.

This evening, at least ten attacks had occurred, mostly targeting liberal political officials or judges. Four governors had been assassinated, along with several lieutenant governors, state senators, state congressmen, and other elected or appointed officials, almost all of whom were members of the Democratic party. Two Supreme Court Justices had been brazenly attacked by suicide bombers in the densely populated area of Crystal City, a mere three miles from the Capitol.

His mind racing and his stylus trying to keep up with his thoughts, Nathan attempted to identify the linkages.

First, the leading Republican candidate for President of the United States is killed, followed thirty-six hours later by a string of coordinated attacks against a range of Democrats. Many were speculating that tonight's attacks were reprisals for the shooting down of King's plane, and it was clear that the protests had increased in intensity rather than decreased. America was scared, but even more so, it was pissed off.

Almost everyone felt that their side was being attacked and, at the same time, also unfairly accused of attacking the other side. It was a powder keg the likes of which Nathan believed the country hadn't seen since 1861. Even the massive civil rights movement of the 1960s, with its tremendous impact on all facets of American life, did not generate the tension, fear, and animosity that had spread to every corner of the country. Whether you were white or black, young or old, multi-generational American citizen or recent immigrant, these recent polarizing events were forcing people to pick a side.

The FBI was being close-lipped about this evening's attacks, and the White House had remained completely silent on the matter. The lieutenant governor of North Carolina, a Republican, had just been publicly sworn in as the new governor after the brutal assassination of Governor Rod Chase. There had been no formal statements out of Michigan, Pennsylvania, or Kentucky, but the governor of Virginia had held two press conferences stating that they had the situation under control and that the state police and National Guard had been mobilized to hunt down the terrorists who'd brazenly attacked state legislators and others in Farmville.

The one thing the press had yet to focus on was the timing of this evening's attacks. As near as Nathan could tell, almost all of the attacks occurred within a very short period of time—between 6:10 and 6:30 p.m. As a former military officer who'd planned and executed numerous combat operations, Nathan knew that the training, logistics, communication, and command and control required to pull off such a coordinated series of attacks was incredibly difficult. So difficult, in fact, that Nathan believed that this could only have been done with government backing. Even then, only a handful of governments around the world had the resources and capabilities to execute at this level.

Nathan immediately discarded England, France, and Germany —they simply had zero reason to want to create chaos in the United States. Given the reports that at least a few of the attackers seemed to be Islamic jihadists, the next reasonable assumption was to look at

Iran, Syria, Yemen, Afghanistan, and the various groups fighting against Israel, such as Hamas and Hezbollah.

Nathan removed all of these entities from his list, with the exception of Iran. Islamic jihadist groups didn't have the resources, patience, or skill needed to pull off these attacks. More importantly, there was a very simple reason that the United States hadn't seen a large-scale terrorist attack since September 11, 2001.

While Osama bin Laden may have felt the destruction of the Twin Towers was a success, the result provided a staunch lesson learned for all of the world's terrorists. Attacking Americans *in America* was the equivalent of signing your own death certificate. While there was always some poor schmuck who could be convinced by a cultish imam to blow himself up, it was never the leaders of these organizations who put themselves in harm's way. All one had to do was look at the current leaders of Hamas living in comfortable luxury in Qatari hotels while their soldiers died by the thousands in the tunnels of Gaza to know that these current attacks on America were not conducted by an Islamic jihadist group. It would mean instant death to the leaders of those groups who enjoyed their lifestyle and their lives too much.

Setting aside Iran, Nathan crossed North Korea off the list. They had the desire and potentially the skill but didn't have the resources to recruit non-Koreans to do their bidding. So far, there'd been no indication that the perpetrators were Asian.

The Chinese could definitely pull this off. China's MSS—Ministry of State Security—was one of the best intelligence agencies in the world, rivaling America's CIA, Israel's Mossad, and Russia's SVR. While Nathan was far from an expert in international relations, everything he knew about China confirmed their firm commitment to non-intervention in the domestic politics of other countries. China expended tremendous effort exploiting the knowledge base of U.S. universities and secretly gathering technical and tactical information from the American military-industrial complex, but they had never shown interest in meddling directly in our politics. While it would not have surprised Nathan to learn that the Chinese were behind the downing of King's airplane, as they

Divided We Stand

disdained the man when he was President, Nathan couldn't fathom that China would get itself involved in killing governors and state legislators.

Reviewing his scribbled notes on the iPad, Nathan was left with four potential countries that could be behind this chaos: Iran, Russia, Israel, and the United States government itself. Iran and Russia most definitely had the resources, skill, and patience required to conduct a covert operation within the United States, although one of this magnitude and complexity would be extremely difficult to achieve.

Nathan's confidence in America's intelligence community was such that he thought it likely that snippets of intel or chatter about this operation would have been collected, but he also knew the intelligence community was no longer as capable as it had been at the height of the Global War on Terror. Both the King and Fulton administrations had decimated the intelligence community over the last eight years, so Nathan could not discount the fact that someone may not have been able to put the pieces of the puzzle together in time to thwart the attacks—similar to what happened on 9/11. In hindsight, the federal government had a lot of information about al-Queda's impending attack that fateful morning, but no one had been able to put it all together before the hijackers flew the planes into the World Trade Center.

Israel was a wild card. Ostensibly one of our closest allies, the Israelis were playing a different game than every other nation on Earth. While everyone else played a game of strategic politics, Israel was playing a game of survival. The existential threats Israelis faced on a daily basis impelled them to constantly think outside the box. Sewing chaos in America didn't seem like it held any advantage for the Israelis, but there may be an aspect of this operation that Nathan and the media did not yet see.

Lastly, the American government itself was a potential culprit. Nathan was the farthest thing there was from a conspiracy theorist, and he knew from experience that the U.S. government was by its very nature incapable of truly keeping a secret of any magnitude. The old Ben Franklin adage that three people can keep a secret only if two of them are dead was an apt description of the American government's ability to hide a conspiracy.

Looking at the clock, Nathan realized it was well past his bedtime. He wanted to get up early to watch the morning news broadcasts and see what, if any, official statements the White House and Pentagon would make. Nathan's ribs were still too sore to jog, but he had begun last week to go for long walks around the property or along the path atop the Herbert Hoover Dike surrounding Lake Okeechobee.

41

Port Huron, Michigan

Friday, March 22

JEFF VENO WALKED into Mama Vicki's Coney Island just after 11:15 a.m. and took his usual seat in a booth halfway down the narrow restaurant. Mama Vicki's had been an institution in downtown Port Huron since it opened in 1923, and Jeff loved the hometown feel of the restaurant's simple decor: a dozen booths down one side separated by a row of tables from a lunch counter with the open grills and server stations behind it. The only part of the confined restaurant not open to public view were the two small restrooms in the rear, beyond which was a back door frequented by locals in the know, as it led directly to a small parking area out back.

Jeff had used the front entrance this morning, having walked the five blocks from his office on Pine Grove Avenue. The five-minute walk each way was often the only exercise Jeff got this time of year, and he was eagerly looking forward to the annual opening of the Port Huron Country Club in just over a week. He'd put on a few pounds over the winter, as he did pretty much every winter, and hoped he'd burn the weight off this summer with a more active lifestyle—something he also told himself pretty much every spring but never seemed to accomplish. Jeff, or Waldo as his friends had called him since middle school, had always been a big guy. Standing 6'3", he'd been a star athlete in football and baseball at Port Huron Northern High School before heading off to college. He'd returned to his hometown after college, took a position in the family business, and had never looked back.

Having just turned sixty, Jeff smiled, realizing he'd turned into the creature of habit his father had once been. He'd also inherited his father's strong chin, rugged good looks, and prematurely thinning white hair. His two kids were grown, now with their own families, and he had never regretted for a second staying in the small city of Port Huron, nestled at the base of Lake Huron and at the foot of the bridge to Sarnia, Canada. The city had weathered the booms and busts of the auto industry over the decades, but it had been able to retain its quaint charm and beautiful views of Lake Huron and the St. Clair River.

Jeff's great-grandfather had been an inventor and contemporary of Thomas Alva Edison, who had also grown up in Port Huron. Recognized as a chemical genius, his great-grandfather held numerous patents for various chemical and engineering processes, which Jeff's grandfather and father had turned into a successful business—Veno Industries. More interested in business than engineering, Jeff had significantly expanded the family business to such a success that he mostly went to the office each morning just for something to do. He no longer managed the daily operations of the staff, but he enjoyed remaining involved. At one point or another he'd been the president of the local chamber of commerce, the president of the country club, and had even dabbled a bit in local politics. He was often referred to as Mr. Port Huron and enjoyed the friendly atmosphere inherent in small-town Michigan.

Almost every work day, unless he was playing golf, Jeff left the office just after eleven o'clock and sauntered down Huron Ave to Mama Vicki's for a couple of hot dogs and fries. It was probably the only place in America where a hot dog was still only two dollars. When he was feeling adventurous, he added a bowl of chili, served

Divided We Stand

in the same type of plastic bowl Jeff remembered as a young child. Jeff's dad had gone to Mama Vicki's as a young boy before World War 2, and he'd instilled a loyalty to the restaurant in Jeff, as Jeff had done with his children. It made his face smile when his son, now in his late thirties, visited with his own children and wanted to have lunch at Coney Island while in town.

Sipping on a Diet Coke while waiting for his two hot dogs—he'd passed on the chili this morning—Jeff looked up to see a man in a navy blue suit enter the restaurant, followed close behind by two uniformed Michigan state troopers. Expecting them to sit down or order at the counter, Jeff watched as they walked directly down the aisle toward his table.

"Mr. Jeff Veno?" The man in the suit asked.

"Yes, that's me," said Jeff, giving the man his full attention.

"My name is Aidan Stroud, and I'm the chief of staff for Governor Carlson. Would you please come with us, sir? It's important."

Jeff was a bit taken aback by the request, focusing more on the state troopers' presence than the man in business attire's identity. "Uh, yes. Yes, of course," Jeff stammered, sliding out of the booth and getting to his feet. "Is, uh, is everything okay? Did something happen to my family?"

Without answering, the troopers ushered Jeff toward the front of the restaurant and out the door. Jeff barely noticed that Aidan Stroud, as the man had introduced himself, had left a twenty-dollar bill on the cashier's counter as he walked by.

Jeff stopped abruptly as soon as he walked out on the sidewalk. Parked in front of the restaurant was a navy-blue Cadillac Escalade with the Michigan state seal emblazoned on the front door, behind which were parked two Michigan State Police cruisers. It was not the vehicles that had caused Jeff to stop. Two men, wearing tan tactical pants and black armored vests, held M4 rifles at the ready and nervously glanced up and down the street.

Jeff felt a hand on the small of his back, firmly pushing him forward toward the rear passenger door of the Escalade as one of the state troopers stepped forward to open the door.

"What the hell—"

"Please, Mr. Veno," said the state trooper standing closest to him. "Nothing has happened to your family, but it is urgent we speak to you. Inside the vehicle is the safest place."

Safest place? Jeff thought. *The safest place for what? Am I being arrested?*

Before he could react further, Jeff found himself sliding into the rear seat of the Escalade. Aidan Stroud had jogged around to the other side of the vehicle and was entering through the rear passenger door on that side. Just as Jeff put his feet in the SUV, the door slammed shut, and the state trooper jumped into the driver's seat. One of the men with rifles got into the front passenger seat, and Jeff watched as the other armed man walked back to the rear state police cruiser and jumped in alongside a second trooper.

The vehicle quickly pulled away from the curb, made a sharp U-turn on Huron Ave, and accelerated north.

"Enough, Mr. Stroud. What's going on?" Jeff asked sharply.

"I apologize, Mr. Veno," said Stroud, seeming a bit out of his element. "I assume you are aware of the attack on Governor Carlson at Bell's Brewery last night, correct?"

"Yes. Yes, of course," answered Jeff. "A terrible tragedy. I was planning to reach out to her husband this weekend. I knew Lenora well years ago, but we only saw each other a few times a year recently. Just a shame. How's her family holding up?"

Jeff had met Lenora Carlson on a blind date just after they'd both graduated from college when Lenora had taken a position with a firm in Port Huron. Instantly realizing they would likely be better friends than romantic partners, the two forged a deep friendship as young adults and maintained it over the years.

"I'm sorry to deflect your question, Mr. Veno, but how much do you know of the gubernatorial succession plan for the state of Michigan?"

Jeff thought for a moment. "Ah, not much, I guess. I assume the Lieutenant Governor takes over, then maybe someone from the state legislature? I really have no idea. Why?"

"Sir, Michigan's gubernatorial succession is unique. Like every

Divided We Stand

other state, there is a clear succession should the governor die or become incapacitated. And you are correct—the next in line is the Lieutenant Governor. After that, it's actually the Michigan Secretary of State, the Attorney General, the President Pro Tempore of the Senate, and then the Speaker of the House of Representatives."

"Okay," said Jeff. "Good to know. Can I ask why you're telling me this?"

"Yes, Mr. Veno. But first, it's important to know how Michigan differs from the other forty-nine states. We are the only state in the country where our state constitution requires the governor to list five additional people who would accede to the governorship should all of the people I just mentioned be unable to serve."

"My god," said Jeff. "Are you telling me that those five people have been killed?"

"Yes, Mr. Veno. That's exactly what I'm telling you. In addition to those five and others, Ms. Sarah Heckler, the former state treasurer, was also killed."

"Okay," said Jeff, still uncertain why he was having this discussion. He looked out the window and noticed their SUV was hurtling onto I-94 West. "Where are you taking me."

"To the State Capitol in Lansing, Mr. Veno," said Stroud.

"The State Capitol?"

"Mr. Veno, if you'll give me just one more moment, I think everything will become clear."

"Okay," said Jeff, "Please go ahead."

"Sir, were you aware of Governor Carlson's list? The five people she listed to succeed her, should the others not be able to serve?"

"No, Mr. Stroud. I had no idea there even was such a list. Why?"

"Well, sir. You are the second person on the list—a list signed, notarized, and sealed by Governor Carlson."

"Wait. You're saying…you're saying that—"

"Yes, Mr. Veno. You are about to be sworn in as the 50th governor of the State of Michigan. I wish it were under different circumstances, but the six people above you on the gubernatorial succession list were killed last night. When we arrive in Lansing, you will take the oath of office administered by the Chief Justice of the Michigan Supreme Court."

"Jesus," said Jeff.

"Sir, with all due respect, I don't think Jesus has been anywhere in Michigan the last twenty-four hours."

42

Staunton, Virginia

Friday, March 22

"AT EASE. PLEASE TAKE YOUR SEATS," said Colonel Robert Clark as he breezed into the brigade headquarters' conference room and took a seat at the head of the table, around which were arrayed his subordinate commanders and staff officers.

The room was adorned with memorabilia from the 29th Infantry Division and the 116th Infantry Regiment, including guidons, plaques, and mementos from the battles of Normandy to more recent ones in Iraq and Afghanistan. Those around the table in uniform wore a patch of the yin-yang symbol, colored in blue and gray, depicting the unit's lineage as Union and Confederacy veterans.

Most people think the 116th Infantry is most famous for storming the beach at Normandy on June 6, 1944, as the regiment was the first wave ashore at Omaha Beach and suffered more than 800 killed, wounded, or missing in action on that day. However, a unique aspect of the unit's lineage that most people were unaware of was that it still retained eleven Confederate campaign streamers earned fighting for the South during the Civil War. While President Fulton's recent Renaming Commission voted to recall all Confederate streamers along with renaming more than a dozen installations, it was impossible to erase the lineage of the "Stonewall Brigade" with the penstroke of some do-gooders in Washington D.C.

Clark was a dichotomy to all who met him, almost all of which truly enjoyed the man's company. He was an extremely proud Virginian, although his grandparents had emigrated from Ireland at the turn of the last century, and he considered himself a Civil War buff as well as a staunch supporter of state's rights. For Clark, despite what most scholars he admired might say, the "War of Northern Aggression" was more about states' rights than slavery. Clark, however, was by no means a bigot. He'd been happily married for the past twenty-four years to the love of his life, a Black woman from Zimbabwe whom he'd met while attending Longwood University, and he was proudly raising four mixed-race children.

Looking around at the fifteen or so people gathered in the conference room, Clark noticed that about a third were wearing civilian clothes, while the other two-thirds wore the standard woodland camouflage Army Combat Uniform like Clark was wearing.

"Thank you all for getting here so quickly. I realize some of you came directly from work." The 116th Infantry Brigade Combat Team was a unit of the Virginia National Guard, whose members, except a very few, were part-time soldiers. One weekend a month and two weeks in the summer, the recruiters had said. Twenty-six years and four deployments later, Clark thought maybe they hadn't been telling the entire truth.

The men and women around the table nodded to Colonel Clark.

"I've just gotten off the phone with the Division Commander and the Governor. They are activating all six battalions of our 116th Infantry Brigade Combat Team. Initial activation is for a period of sixty days. They're giving us as much leeway as we want regarding exceptions, as their goal is to be as minimally disruptive as possible. However, they are anticipating significant use of our assets, with

Divided We Stand

missions including riot control, checkpoints, critical infrastructure protection, and support to law enforcement."

Clark paused to look around the room. All of his soldiers present were either officers or senior NCOs. In addition to two infantry battalions, the Stonewall Brigade consisted of a single battalion each of mounted cavalry, field artillery, engineer, and support soldiers. All in all, he had almost 4,000 soldiers under his command.

"You've all been watching the news," Clark continued. "So you know what this is about. In addition to the attacks in Farmville and up in Northern Virginia, the protests at several universities have turned deadly. Gunfire has erupted at UVA, Virginia Tech, James Madison, and VCU. At least a dozen people have been killed across these campuses. The level of animosity is ramping up to such a degree that the Governor wants to mobilize the capability of our brigade to help local and state law enforcement deal with these compounding issues, especially as things seem to be getting more violent.

"Lastly, the Governor mentioned that there is a strong likelihood that states may start taking sides—either Blue or Red. You'll remember that when the Florida governor outlawed federal law enforcement in his state, quite a few other Republican governors followed suit. Despite the fact that the Virginia governor is a Republican, our state has stayed neutral on this issue, most likely because we probably have about 30,000 federal agents living in the state, not to mention the FBI training center and all the military investigative services located up in Quantico."

Several people chuckled around the table. Colonel Clark knew the chuckles were from those who knew Clark's civilian job. When he wasn't the commander of the 116th Infantry Brigade Combat Team, Robert Clark was a supervisory special agent with the Naval Criminal Investigative Service, a position he'd held for over twenty years after several years as a police officer for the Metropolitan Police Department in Washington, D.C.

"For those of you who aren't in on the joke, let me enlighten you as I think it will prove important over the next few days. I have been

253

a member of the Virginia National Guard since being commissioned in 1996. Since 2000, I have also been a special agent for NCIS. I serve two bosses—the governor and the director of NCIS. There is a very strong likelihood that those two bosses will be on opposite sides of the storm that is gathering and that I will be caught in the middle.

"I say this not for your sympathy but because many of our troops, and maybe even some of you in this room, will be caught in a similar dilemma. The governor understands this and assured me that he would not hold it against anyone, no matter their decision. I will share with you that the governor specifically told me he appreciated all that I had done for Virginia but that if I felt it necessary to choose NCIS over the 116th, he would fully support my decision and that he'd have a job open for me when this whole thing blew over."

Clark paused to look around the room, his eyes settling on two of his subordinates.

"Jim, you work for the DEA, right? And Tonya, you're with federal corrections, if I remember correctly." Both officers nodded affirmatively. Major Jim Fritz was the battalion executive officer for the 3rd Battalion 116th Infantry, while Captain Tonya Strickland was the assistant S-4—supply officer—for the Brigade headquarters. "Both of you may have to make a difficult decision should the governor decide to ban federal law enforcement from the state. He did not share his plans with me, so I don't know any more than you do."

"Sir? If I may?" The question was posed by the only person in the room older than Colonel Clark, a man sitting in the back of the room, dressed in ACUs adorned with several badges, including a Combat Infantryman's Badge, Ranger Tab, and Master Parachutist wings. The man's name was Terry Ramsey, and he was the Brigade Command Sergeant Major—the senior enlisted soldier in the brigade and Colonel Clark's right-hand man.

"Of course, Sergeant Major, please go ahead."

"Folks, this here is fixin' to be one giant shit sandwich, and we're all gonna have to take a bite. The focus right now needs to be on mobilizing. You all need to get to your armories ASAP and get your

Divided We Stand

people accounted for. Have your senior NCOs list all personnel failing to make muster and anyone whose civilian job may make being activated an extreme hardship. And I don't want to hear about Private Snuffy worried about getting fired from his *sandwich artiste* position at Subway. Real problems, people. Otherwise, get control of your people and wait for further instructions. Things are going to change quickly, and when Colonel Clark says jump, we all need to be ready to jump." He looked around the room, making sure everyone understood. "Sorry, Sir, that's all I had."

Colonel Clark tried to hide his chuckle. *Leave it to the Sergeant Major to tell it like it is*, he thought.

"Okay, folks," Clark said out loud, wrapping up the meeting. "I know some of you have a long drive to get to your armories. I'll likely be around to visit, but I am prepared to receive orders at any time. The governor is on edge and believes this thing is going to get exponentially worse very quickly. Thanks for coming."

Colonel Clark stood, and his executive officer yelled, "Attention!" Everyone in the room came to attention while the Colonel walked back to his office.

43

Washington D.C

Friday, March 22

THE MOOD in the Oval Office was dour. President Fulton had just completed his noon press conference, and while it had gone reasonably well, the questions that were being asked had left everyone speechless. The shouted questions, almost all of which President Fulton ignored, could be summed up in one: is the country at war?

Sharyn was sitting at the end of one of the Oval Office's two sofas. Beside her were Brad Nesbitt and his boss, John Reynolds. On the couch opposite her were National Security Advisor Carl Tidhams, CIA Director Gwendolyn Novak, and FBI Director Barry Tracy. To her right, sitting in one of the wing-backed upholstered chairs, was her boss, Vice President Moore. In the other chair adjacent to the vice president sat General Jack Vine, an Army four-star general and Chairman of the Joint Chiefs.

The President was sitting at his desk and currently staring out the window. Everyone agreed that the President had been rock solid at the press conference, forceful when needed, and ad-libbing several lines that he wanted to add at the spur of the moment. He'd

Divided We Stand

answered one reporter's question before exiting the stage and had done so with alacrity and precision. Watching him now, with everyone gathered in the Oval Office at his request, Sharyn worried for a moment that he might be having one of his lapses in concentration.

As soon as President Fulton pivoted in her chair, her fears were allayed.

"I'm concerned, folks," he started. "The situation out there is getting more violent, and there is no doubt at all that we are under attack. Director Tracy, I need your best estimate right now on whether this is the work of a foreign government or domestic terrorists."

Everyone in the room stared at the FBI Director, who was now in the hot seat.

"Mr. President, that is very difficult for me to say at the moment. Our analysts are——"

"Cut the malarkey, Barry. I know it's difficult. If it were easy, I wouldn't need you now, would I? C'mon, give it to me straight. I know you don't have any certainty—but what's your best estimate?"

"Sir, there is no doubt that the car bombings of Justices Faulkner and Escobar were the work of Islamic jihadists," said Director Tracy. "The Israelis have helped us positively identify the three suicide bombers, all Palestinian members of Hamas. TEDAC—the FBI's Terrorist Explosive Device Analytical Center down at Redstone Arsenal in Alabama—has identified the unique signature of the bombmaker. This has allowed us to narrow it down to a dozen or so terrorists who've had recent activity in Syria and Yemen."

"What about the other attacks?" asked Vice President Moore, causing Director Tracy to pivot on the couch. "We have four dead governors, plus almost two dozen state legislators and senior state officials. Are these Islamic jihadists as well?"

"Not all of them, no," answered the FBI Director.

"Then who are they?" asked President Fulton, causing Director Tracy to ping pong back toward the President behind the Resolute Desk.

257

"We know that one group was Hispanic, and indications are that they may be members of a drug cartel. One other group was Somalis from al-Shabaab, and yet another were members of the MS-13 gang and appeared to be illegal immigrants from El Salvador."

"You mean *undocumented immigrants*," voiced the Vice President.

General Vine gave VP Moore a withering look that she failed to notice. Director Tracy chose to ignore her comment as well.

"Lastly, Mr. President," said Director Tracy. "During your press conference, I received notice that we obtained a hit off the DNA results we analyzed from a knitted cap found in the woods near the sniper position from which someone killed the Senator from Ohio."

"More Islamic terrorists, I assume?" asked the President.

"No, Mr. President. The DNA was a match to a convicted felon and former Navy SEAL. A member of a right-wing white supremacist cell based in the Florida Panhandle that's affiliated with the Three Percenters."

"Who the hell are the Three Percenters?" Vice President Moore asked.

"They're a loosely affiliated group that espouses gun rights and resistance to the federal government. Their national headquarters disbanded after the January 6 insurrection, but dozens of small cells still remain active. This individual, Mike Yancey, served seven years as a Navy SEAL before being convicted on federal gun charges and dishonorably discharged. We don't have any other evidence yet to place him in Ohio, but we are certain hair fibers in the hat found in Ohio are a 100% match to his DNA."

"My god," said Chief of Staff Reynolds, speaking for the first time. "This is a complete mess. We have at least five groups of terrorists, maybe more, and all from different countries and with different ideologies. This is an absolute political nightmare."

Before anyone could answer, a Secret Service agent opened the recessed door to the Oval Office, and in walked a harried-looking Geraldine Fox. Looking around the room and choosing to remain standing, the White House Communications Director addressed President Fulton directly. "Mr. President, we have a major issue

Divided We Stand

brewing right now that has the potential to significantly raise the stakes, if that's even possible."

"What is it, Geraldine? Please, have a seat and join us."

Geraldine ignored the president's request to sit. "Sir, Reuters reported thirty minutes ago that they have credible documentation showing that several of yesterday's attackers entered the United States seeking asylum and without any documentation. They were processed through an entry point and paroled into the United States."

"What?" Asked an incredulous Carl Tidhams, the National Security Advisor. "How can that be?"

"I don't know," said Geraldine. "But it gets worse. Two minutes ago, Mr. President, reports were made to a news affiliate in New York City of three men storming a city-run shelter for asylum-seekers in Queens. Initial reports are that more than forty people have been killed. That story is competing with an emerging video from Liberty University in central Virginia, where a prayer vigil was interrupted by gunmen. At least a dozen dead are being reported, but I've been told that figure could go up significantly."

"My lord," said President Fulton.

"Jesus H. Fucking Christ," echoed the Vice President much more colorfully than the President.

Director Tracy looked like he'd swallowed a frog, and everyone else just stared in silence. Sharyn thought of speaking up, but John Reynolds beat her to it.

"Mr. President, everyone, we need to stay focused for a few more minutes, and then everyone can get back to their offices and begin working on solving these problems. Barry, the President's initial question is what we need to answer here and now. Are we under attack from foreign terrorists or a foreign country? We have to know that because it drives everything else."

"As I said, John, the—"

"Excuse me, Barry," interrupted Gwen Novak, the director of the CIA. "I think it's clear some of the perpetrators are foreign, but I can unequivocally tell you that the intelligence community has not picked up any, and I mean *ANY*, chatter regarding attacks on the

United States. No signals intel, no human intel. None. Additionally, we've had several remarkable conversations with intelligence officers from Iran, Syria, and China, informing us in an underhanded way that their countries had nothing to do with yesterday's attack despite any information to the contrary. The way these contacts were made suggests they are extremely concerned about being blamed for something they didn't do."

"Mr. President," said General Vine, speaking just a touch louder than everyone else—Sharyn wasn't sure if he was hard of hearing or if he wanted his voice to dominate the room. "The Department of Defense concurs with Gwen's comments. We've seen nothing to indicate this is a foreign incursion."

"Okay, thank you, everyone," said the President, wanting to wrap this up. "For now, based on everything that's been said here, we should proceed as if this is a domestic threat. Director Tracy, the FBI has the lead, and everyone else will support you. We need to put every asset we have into finding out who is behind this and preventing any more attacks from happening."

"Yes, Mr. President. We will do everything we can. I know all the other federal law enforcement agencies are working closely together. However, we are hitting some obstacles when it comes to cooperating with state and local authorities. I'm worried that more governors may follow Florida's lead and keep our special agents from doing their jobs."

"Barry, you call me directly the first time your agents hit a roadblock. John, let me know, and I will call that governor immediately and yank him through the phone if I have to."

"Understood, Mr. President. And what about Mr. Yancey, the Navy SEAL down in Florida? Our normal protocols would be to send in agents to arrest him immediately and question him regarding the murder of the Senator."

"Do so, Barry. Do so immediately."

44

Dearborn, Michigan

Saturday, March 23

KEITH JEFFRIES HAD BEEN GLUED to his couch since Thursday, unable to break away from the continuous news coverage of the events unfolding across the country. At twenty-seven, he was too young to remember 9/11, but he couldn't help but think this was his generation's call to action, as 9/11 had been for his parent's generation. Even though Keith was a toddler at the time, the events of September 11, 2001, had irretrievably changed the lives of Keith and his wife Hanna.

As violent attacks and protests continued to unfold across America, Keith now felt as if a revolution were occurring. A middle school English teacher at Dearborn's Woodworth Middle School, Keith wondered if these were the same sensations felt by people watching world-changing events unfold in Berlin in 1989, Tehran in 1979, or even Paris in 1789.

Keith had spent his entire life in Michigan, with the exception of the one year he'd worked abroad teaching English at a school in the northern Iraq city of Erbil. That year had been the high point of his life—he had explored a new culture, escaped his mother's overprotective umbrella, and met his wife, Hanna. At the time, almost five years ago, he'd been a recent graduate of Eastern Michigan University and hellbent on putting his own mark on the world. Now, after four years of dodging the politics and parents of middle school teaching, Keith felt like he was on a slow train to nowhere—as if he'd wake up one day forty years from now and realize he'd done absolutely nothing with his life.

> *Gather ye rosebuds while ye may,*
> *Olde time is still a flying;*
> *And this flower that smiles today*
> *Tomorrow will be dying.*

Keith recited the stanza in his head from the Robert Herrick poem made famous by Robin Williams in *The Dead Poet Society. Carpe Diem and all that*, he thought. *Seize the day.*

Keith's father had seized the day when he was Keith's age, answering the call to arms after 9/11 and the initiation of the Global War on Terror. His father had deployed with the 101st Airborne Division to rid the world of the ruthless dictator Saddam Hussein and had been a true American hero, or so Keith had been told. When Keith was six, his father had returned from Iraq in a flag-draped aluminum box.

With the news channel on a commercial break, Keith walked over to the apartment's galley kitchen and grabbed a cold beer from the fridge and two more slices of pizza from the box on the counter. It was just after seven o'clock in the evening, and Hanna wasn't expected home until morning. His wife was a dispatcher with the Detroit police department and had volunteered to work a double shift, given all that was happening.

As Keith walked back to his chair, he caught a glimpse of himself in a reflection of the sliding glass door leading to their small balcony. Standing just under six feet in his stocking feet, Keith had short dark hair and a swarthy complexion, which allowed him to grow a beard almost instantly. He'd always been

Divided We Stand

athletic—a running back in high school and also an avid ice hockey player—but lately, he'd been putting on a few pounds. He could still run three miles and often did with his wife on the weekends, and he vowed to hit the apartment complex's gym in the morning.

This was spring break, and he was off school the entire week. He and Hanna had talked about catching a cheap flight down to Florida or maybe even driving somewhere. Hanna had been talking a lot about visiting Nashville, so he thought maybe he'd research that and see if they could get a good deal on a hotel.

The news station was back from a commercial just as Keith sat down and took a bite from his slice of pizza. A flashing banner popped up on the television screen, alerting viewers to a special alert. Keith watched as the news anchor described another attack on undocumented immigrants, this time at a hotel in downtown Chicago. Keith watched television with his iPhone in hand, scrolling rapidly through Instagram Reels. He was amazed at how many videos he saw of protestors and violence, but he thought nothing of the algorithm that was feeding him this content.

Glued to the television and his phone, Keith became angrier and angrier. *How dare these fascists attack innocent people searching for a better life,* he thought. *What happened to 'give me your tired, your poor, your huddled masses?' And that clown down in Florida, who the hell in their right mind thinks a governor can tell the President of the United States what to do?*

Speaking of the Florida governor, Keith perked up as the news anchor cut away to a live shot of a press conference in Tallahassee. Governor Marino was standing at a podium with a uniformed state trooper, an Army officer, and several men in suits standing behind him.

"Good evening," Governor Marino said solemnly into the camera. *"At a few minutes after four o'clock this morning, several dozen members of the FBI's Hostage Rescue Team conducted a raid on a homestead in a rural part of the Florida Panhandle near the small hamlet of Munson. They did not announce themselves but instead arrived in two Blackhawk helicopters and assaulted multiple homes on the property by force. The property owners, fearing they were under attack, attempted to defend their homes against these unlawful*

263

intruders. A firefight ensued, and I'm sad to say that eleven people were killed, seven of them women or children under the age of eighteen.

"The FBI has no authority here in Florida and has not since my executive order on February 5th. Upon the arrival of the first deputy sheriff from Santa Rosa County, the FBI agents trained their guns on this peace officer and forcibly disarmed him. As additional deputies arrived, along with members of the Florida Highway Patrol, a standoff ensued between Florida law enforcement and the unauthorized invaders from the federal government. In the interest of taking care of the wounded, the FBI team was allowed to board their helicopters and depart, taking their wounded personnel with them. Florida law enforcement secured the scene, where they found eleven people killed by the FBI, as well as several wounded children. Every adult on the property had been killed by the FBI, including four veterans of America's armed services."

Keith, visibly frustrated, threw his empty beer can against the wall.

"That fucking lying weasel!" Keith shouted. "You know damn well the FBI doesn't attack innocent people! What the fuck is happening?"

Full of adrenaline and energy, Keith stood up and did twenty pushups, the last five of which were extremely difficult. He then switched to burpees but stopped after the second one, completely winded. *I've got to do something,* he thought. *What's happening down in Florida is going to happen here in Michigan. They killed Governor Carlson already—who's next? I need to stand up and fight for what's right!*

Keith sat back down in his chair and grabbed his iPhone, opening Snapchat. He scrolled through the long list of friends, looking for one in particular. This guy was a real activist back at Eastern Michigan that Keith had been somewhat friendly with. Rumors were that he was part of Antifa during the George Floyd riots. He'd know how Keith could get involved.

45

Jackson, Wyoming

Sunday, March 24

THE NINE MEN and three women stood in the private lounge of Bunker Hill Media's secluded conference center located on Orlean Brumback's picturesque property overlooking Jackson Hole. Each had a drink in hand, although some had opted for a non-alcoholic beverage, and they chatted idly while awaiting the arrival of their hosts. Everyone in the room was familiar with each other, although none would claim any other as a close friend. They were powerful people and were not used to waiting.

Watching on monitors connected to a hidden surveillance system, Orlean Brumback sat behind his desk in an office on the other side of the conference center. The Center, as it was referred to, was a 10,000-square-foot timber frame facility that included a small amphitheater, two conference rooms, several offices, smaller meeting rooms, and a private lounge that rivaled the highest-end clubs. The Center sat atop two subterranean floors that housed Bunker Hill Media's staff offices, media studios, and server farm.

Florida Governor Vince Marino and Alex Treacher sat with

Brumback in chairs facing his desk. While Orlean was the host of today's meeting, Governor Marino had extended the invitation to each of the twelve people socializing in the lounge. It had been Alex's idea to have Brumback and Marino wait until everyone was gathered before making their entrance—a subtle technique to assert dominance.

"Okay, gentlemen," said Alex. "I think you're on. You each have a folder outlining the plan; the key is getting everyone to agree. I don't think it's helpful for me to show my face at this point, but I'm happy to have a quiet conversation with anyone who appears reluctant. I'll be watching."

"Let's do this," said Marino. He and Orlean stood and made their way down the hall, leaving Alex to watch on the monitors.

Minutes later, after greeting their twelve guests and ushering everyone into the conference room, they sat around a sequoia wood conference table with exactly fourteen high-backed leather swivel chairs. A slim leather folio had already been placed before each chair.

"Welcome," said Orlean. "It is truly an honor to have all thirteen of you as my guests. I recognize how highly unusual it is for all of you to meet like this, but these are unusual times. The fact that thirteen Republican governors deem it important enough to gather and discuss the future of our nation is a testament to the trying times we are facing. Governor Marino has been at the forefront of confronting the continued over-reach of the Fulton administration, and as our time is valuable, I will turn the floor over to him."

Vince Marino looked around the room, making eye contact with each governor sitting at the table. He knew all of them, some as acquaintances and some as closer friends. Today would decide how much he could count on his fellow Republican governors.

"Thanks, Orlean, and thank you for hosting us. This is truly a spectacular property, and it was the one place I thought of where we could all meet outside the prying eyes of the media and the federal government. Rudy," Vince said, nodding at the governor of Wyoming. "Thank you as well for securing the airport and providing transportation for everyone."

Divided We Stand

Vince paused to build the solemnity of the moment. "Our states are at war. We can say we're not. We can keep our heads in the sand. But America is not going to let us do that. The people are speaking—we are seeing it all over the country. The federal government has reached too far. They've taken over every facet of our state and local communities—layers upon layers of taxes, telling our kids what books they can read and what food they can eat in the cafeteria, mandating which pronouns are acceptable, allowing men to compete as women, forcing us to deal with illegal immigrants that are overwhelming our facilities, outlawing conservative thought and indicting those politicians who speak out.

"Yesterday, the federal government attacked and killed eleven Florida citizens, American citizens. They did so without presenting a valid warrant and without coordinating with state or local law enforcement. There is a serious question as to who was responsible for shooting down President King's airplane. It's unclear whether President Fulton gave the order for King's assassination, but he's made his position very clear by not allowing federal buildings to lower their flags to half-mast in recognition of the passing of a former President. This is unconscionable and pure partisan politics. It's a respect for the office, not for the man—something Fulton is all too quick to point out when it applies to himself but not to his Republican predecessors.

"This is not a war of secession. Unlike what the liberal media would have us believe, conservative America has no interest in splitting off from the United States. We ARE the United States. This is a war for control, pure and simple. Its battles will not be fought with guns in the streets. The battles will be fought in the voting booth. This is a war we cannot lose. To lose will mean the end of America, the end of our Forefather's dream of one nation, under God, with liberty and justice for ALL."

Stunned silence ensued, with most either looking at Marino or staring down at the table, lost in thought. In the back office, Alex Treacher was grinning from ear to ear. *You nailed it, Vince*, he said to himself. *Absolutely nailed it.*

Ada Patterson, the female governor of Alabama, began to clap slowly. Soon, everyone around the table, including Orlean and Vince, was clapping.

"You're 100% right, Vince," said Ada, who had known Vince for several years. "I assume you brought us all here because you have a plan?"

"No beating around the bush, Ada," smiled Vince. "Yes, we have a plan. If you would, please open up the leather folio in front of you."

He paused to allow everyone to look at the first sheet in their folio: a draft of the demand for a Constitutional Convention to pass the 28th Amendment. "This is a demand from both Houses of the Florida State Legislature to hold a Constitutional Convention for the purpose of enacting a Term Limit amendment that would limit U.S. Senators to being elected to two six-year terms, and Members of the House of Representatives to three two-year terms. The Convention would be held in Omaha, Nebraska, on July 4, 2024."

"This has never happened in history, Vince," said Luke Decker, Virginia's governor. "Doesn't two-thirds of Congress have to approve an amendment?"

"Yes, two-thirds of Congress must approve an amendment, but they have no say in holding a Constitutional Convention, Luke. That's the beauty. Not to get into a deep history lesson, but the Founding Fathers provided two mechanisms to amend the Constitution. The first way, the only way our country has ever done it, is for two-thirds of Congress to pass an amendment and three-fourths of the States to ratify it. At this point, the amendment becomes part of the Constitution."

Vince paused to take a sip of water. "The second method is for the States to call directly for a Constitutional Convention. This bypasses Congress completely, and it also bypasses the governors, I might add. If two-thirds of the States demand a Constitutional Convention, then Congress is forced to convene one."

"Two-thirds is thirty-four states," added Orlean, sitting next to Vince.

"Exactly," said Vince. "If thirty-four state legislatures demand this, then it happens. Last Thursday morning, both Houses of twenty-nine of the fifty state legislatures were controlled by the Republican Party. After the unfortunate attacks on March 21st, thirty-four state legislatures are now firmly controlled by the Republican Party."

The reaction across the room was instantaneous. "Wait a second!" Tennessee governor Clark Hahn shouted. "That can't be a coincidence. Are you telling me you helped assassinate four governors? Rod Chase was a dear friend of mine. This is utter—"

"Stop!" Vince commanded as others in the room were chattering as well. "Please! Of course, I had nothing to do with those attacks. My staff put together the concept of moving for a Constitutional Convention more than a month ago, but I tabled it as I didn't think we had the votes across the state legislatures. On Friday morning, my staff brought this to my attention. I've been thinking about it all weekend and bounced some ideas off of Orlean here; as you all know, he's the foremost conservative strategist in the country and was Benjamin King's closest advisor.

"This is an opportunity. We didn't create the opportunity, but it's one we can't pass up. Frankly, I'm convinced it was Fulton's follies that likely led to foreign terrorists attacking the country. He's been such a milquetoast, especially after abandoning Afghanistan to the Taliban, and our southern border is a sieve—it's no wonder we've been attacked. It's already been three days since the most recent terrorist attacks, and Fulton hasn't done a single thing other than send the FBI to kill Floridians!"

The tenor of the room immediately calmed. Alex, watching from the back office, noticed quite a few of the governors nodding their heads as they read the complete text of the proposal for the Constitutional Convention.

"I like it," said Zane Owens, the charismatic leader of Texas. "We have to do something, and quickly. You all really don't have the full picture of what's happening at the border. The federal government admits to daily border crossings of up to 14,000 people per day. Folks, those are *encounters* with the Border Patrol. *Encounters!* That means people the Border Patrol interacts with. In the best case, there's an additional twenty percent; in the worst case, it's more like fifty percent more. That is *SIX MILLION* people illegally entering our country in a 365-day span. *SIX MILLION!* The population of Arizona is just over seven million people. Think about that."

Zane paused. "And think about the fact that the Fulton administration is doing nothing. Strike that, they *are* doing something—they're taking me to court to keep me from protecting the borders of my state."

"Shameful," agreed Avis Reid, the attractive, vivacious governor of South Dakota who'd been considered a frontrunner for Vice President on King's 2024 ticket.

"So, step one," said Vince, attempting to steer the meeting back on track. "Step one is to meet with your senior party leaders and get state Congressional approval of this document."

"What's step two?" Tennessee governor Hahn asked.

"Glad you asked, Clark. Step two is the issuance of this draft executive order," said Vince, holding up a second piece of paper. "You'll note that this is very similar to the executive order I issued a month ago and that quite a few in this room have already issued. Given the FBI incursion into Florida yesterday, I modified this executive order and will publicly issue it at 9 a.m. tomorrow morning. It forbids federal law enforcement activity outside the confines of federal installations, buildings, or airports and authorizes state and local law enforcement to arrest federal agents displaying a badge or in a marked vehicle for the felony of impersonating a law enforcement official. Deadly force is authorized to apprehend these individuals, as it would be for any armed person committing a felony."

Several governors around the table smiled or smirked.

"You think this is funny?" challenged Vince.

"Not at all," said Tim Davis, the blue-collar governor of Idaho. "I think it's about time we stick it to these fuckers. I love it."

"You're an important voice for the conservative cause," interjected Orlean, wanting to present himself as the strategist behind this movement. "And it's more than just sticking it to the Fulton administration and their progressive agenda. With all of you in this room, plus the other Republican governors, we have a real opportunity to take back America. For the last decade or more, we've all

Divided We Stand

seen the slide we've been on, the erosion of our morals, of our principles, of what makes America the greatest country in the world. It's our chance to stop that slide and to lead America forward."

"Absolutely," agreed Vince. "So step two of the plan is for all of us, and for those Republican governors not in attendance, to issue this executive order tomorrow. Step three is partial to full mobilization of your state's National Guard. Some of us, like Luke in Virginia, Zane in Texas, and myself in Florida, have already substantially activated our Guard forces. In order to stand strong against federal law enforcement and whatever reaction President Fulton may have, we need to mobilize our resources."

"Who's paying for all this?" Asked Claude Jennings, the long-time governor of South Carolina. "Mobilization is not cheap, and I can't imagine we'd be receiving any federal funds."

"That's true," said Vince. "It will not be inexpensive, but it will be worth it. The November 5th election is 226 days from today. I don't think we'll need to have the Guard mobilized after the Constitutional Convention convenes, but between now and then, we need to have this capability. You've all seen the news, and most of us are dealing with some pretty crazy situations in our states right now. Violent attacks are on the rise, initiated from both the left and right, and it is very likely to get worse. If President Fulton declares martial law and attempts to lock down our states, we need to be prepared."

"He can't do that," said Zane. "Under the Posse Comitatus Act, the President has no authority to use military troops in our states."

"Exactly," agreed Idaho's governor. "The Idaho Constitution specifically forbids federal troops or federal law enforcement from being used to put down civil unrest."

"Not to rain on anyone's parade, but I think we're forgetting the Insurrection Act of 1807." This last comment was made by Janette Hunter, the recently elected governor of Arkansas who'd once held a senior position in the King administration and was also an attorney. "Under Sections 252 and 253, the President can deploy troops without the state's permission to enforce federal law. Are we planning to go up against armored tank divisions?"

"That's not going to happen," replied Vince. "This is not an insurrection, nor is it sedition or secession. We are doing our jobs under the rights given to us by the U.S. Constitution as well as our state constitutions. If Fulton deploys the U.S. military under the Insurrection Act, it will be tantamount to starting a new Civil War."

"But Vince, you started this meeting by stating that we are already at war," said Janette.

"I did. And I mean it. But I'm not suggesting that we engage in open armed conflict against our fellow citizens. Our plan is to take back control of our country through legal means and based strictly on the words of the U.S. Constitution. The Supremacy Clause is bullshit, and the Supreme Court never should have allowed half of Congress' laws to be enacted as they are in direct violation of the Tenth Amendment. If President Fulton wants to rely on a law from 1807 and deploy troops against us, he's going to find out that seventy percent of the country is staunchly on our side."

"Gentlemen, ladies, I'd like to add one small bit of information," said Orlean. "You know I have contacts pretty much around the world. I have it on good authority that the Pentagon has openly discussed this possibility, and there is little chance that they will allow themselves to be used for domestic issues short of an outright attack on the Capitol."

"That's right," said Vince, not having heard this before but wanting to sound like he was in charge. "And this brings us to the final point, step four. Step four entails a mass migration plan. Simply stated, we need to encourage the movement of conservative voters to key locations around the country. The first priority is ensuring we have enough conservatives in the thirty-four Republican-controlled states; we will be assured control of the White House next January. The second priority is gaining control of the state legislatures in four additional states. This will give us the needed thirty-eight states, or three-fourths of all fifty states, to ratify the changes we enact at the Constitutional Convention. The third priority is to make sure we have solid Republican candidates running for the U.S. Senate and House of Representatives so that we can also gain control of that branch of the federal government. If we do this, the next four years will allow us to get this

Divided We Stand

country back on track. We can balance the budget, expand the economy, control our borders, and allow our nation to flourish once again."

"Here here," said Zane Owens, and every governor on the table either clapped or pounded their hands lightly on the table.

"What about deciding who is going to take King's place for the nomination?" asked Janette Hunter, known for her bluntness. This was the elephant in the room since the moment King's plane was shot down, and several governors thought they were in line for this position. Orlean and Alex had discussed this in detail, and Orlean knew just what to say.

"Governors, if I may," Orlean began. "As the senior Republican strategist for the last four Presidential cycles, I would ask that you table that question for the moment. You are all here under a cloak of secrecy, and it is critical that you get back to your home states as quickly as possible. I think it would be detrimental to have this discussion with just the thirteen of you when this is more appropriate to have at a meeting of the Republican National Party where all voices can be heard and there is no potential for conspiracy theorists to believe we've been up to something nefarious. The issues we've addressed here today are all specifically relevant to your individual states, while the Republican nomination for President is a much broader issue. I hope you'll agree with me."

Orlean paused to look around the table. A few governors didn't look pleased, but they all seemed to recognize the logic of his comments. Seeing this, he decided to push on.

"Your folios contain detailed information about the migration plan. I hope to get an opportunity to discuss this with each of you privately in your home capital cities, as each state has unique issues. Rest assured, the entire force of Bunker Hill Media is behind you on this. We will assist with marketing, social media campaigns, and influencing. We've outlined some strategies to attract conservatives to your states, and we'll be targeting conservatives in specific Blue states with algorithm-driven campaigns encouraging them to move to certain places. For example, engineers in southern California may have their social media feeds oriented toward opportunities in

Phoenix, while conservatives in Washington state may be shown the benefits of Nevada, Georgia, or New Hampshire.

"As Governor Marino stated at the outset of this meeting, this is a war, and all of us here are on the war council. We will need to continually refine our operational strategy to ensure success, and like any plan, we must be prepared to adapt to the Fulton administration's actions and overcome the obstacles they put in our path. Governor?" Orlean concluded, handing the floor to Vince.

"Thank you, everyone. I know some of us have long flights home. Please stay in touch."

46

Washington, D.C

Monday, March 25

REPUBLICAN GOVERNOR PRESS conferences were popping up like popcorn across the country without notice. At last count, thirteen governors had condemned President Fulton's actions, issued executive orders prohibiting federal law enforcement activities within their state, and mobilized elements of their National Guard. More press conferences were expected throughout the day, as many as a total of thirty.

The White House was in full crisis mode, and the President had called for a meeting of the entire Cabinet. With all the principal Cabinet members sitting around the exceptionally long conference table in the Cabinet Room, Sharyn was relegated to a chair along the side wall immediately behind the Vice President. Unlike other meetings where the President sat at the head of the table, for Cabinet meetings, he sat directly in the middle of one side. The Vice President sat immediately opposite him, and the various Cabinet officials were arrayed down the sides, often in descending order of importance in relation to their distance from the center of the table.

President Fulton was visibly angry, as angry as Sharyn had ever seen him. He also looked tired. The stress of the last few days had begun to take its toll on everyone, but many of the White House staff were whispering about how exhausted the President seemed.

"I am tired of these two-bit governors thinking they can tell us what to do. The law is clear, as is the Constitution. Neil, I want to declare an emergency under the Insurrection Act. Today." President Fulton was looking straight at his Attorney General. "No pussy-footing around. Enough is enough. I don't know if it's just a blanket executive order or if we have to pick a specific state. If you have to pick one, let's make it Florida—Marino's the one who started this whole thing with King. They're both insurrectionists as far as I'm concerned."

Sharyn watched John Reynolds cringe from his seat across from her. She had been in a closed-door meeting with the Vice President and Chief of Staff earlier that morning when the President had first proposed using the Insurrection Act. Reynolds had strongly urged the President to use restraint and let things develop a bit more, while her boss, Vice President Moore, was inclined to agree with the President.

"Enough is enough," were the Vice President's exact words. It was not lost on Sharyn that President Fulton had just used the Vice President's strong language verbatim.

Sharyn herself was conflicted on the issue. On the one hand, she completely disagreed with what the governors were doing and firmly believed the Constitution's Supremacy Clause was the glue to making the United States work. However, this would not be some symbolic use of the 101st Airborne Division to guard black students integrating into white schools. The widespread violence and the significant approval ratings in support of the Republican governors meant a real possibility that this could lead to an all-out civil war.

"Ah, yes, Mr. President," said Attorney General Krueger. "I'll contact the National Security Advisor, and we can have something drafted within the hour."

Divided We Stand

"Good," said the President, looking around the table and settling on the Secretary of Defense and Chairman of the Joint Chiefs. "Melvin, General Vine, I would like you to draw up plans for how best to leverage the military in support of my forthcoming executive order. I think we should immediately nationalize the National Guard in those states, which will remove them from their governor's control. I also think the deployment of active-duty soldiers to each of the state capitals, as well as other areas that are seeing violent uprisings. I'll leave it to you to provide a detailed plan."

"Yes, Mr. President," replied Secretary of Defense Melvin Boyd. Boyd had never served in the military and had come up through the civilian side of the Defense Department after having been a former professor at Harvard.

"Mr. President," said General Vine. "I have spoken with all six service chiefs, as well as the NORTHCOM and SOCOM combatant commanders. We are all in agreement that U.S. military personnel and equipment should not be deployed against our citizens, nor for political purposes. The potential for civil war is simply too great, and the degradation this would cause to our armed services is immeasurable. The military is fully prepared to protect federal infrastructure across the country, but being used to enforce federal law against so-called "insurrectionists" is not something the military will do."

The room went completely silent, and Sharyn actually felt like the temperature had dropped several degrees. The President stared hard at General Vine, who maintained eye contact with his Commander-in-Chief. While it was clear General Vine wasn't comfortable disagreeing with the President, it was also clear that the General felt his stance was righteous.

Sitting directly behind her boss, Sharyn couldn't see the Vice President's face, but from the Vice President's rigid posture, she knew her boss was boiling. Looking across the table, Sharyn watched as President Fulton's face turned a deep shade of red. His hands were shaking as he attempted to hold the note cards in front of him.

The President took several deep breaths, gathering his thoughts before speaking.

"General Vine, as Commander-in-Chief, you are hereby relieved. I will appoint your, ah, I will appoint your successor immediately. I, uh, I want you to—"

"I stand relieved, Mr. President," interrupted General Vine in his booming voice, immediately popping to the position of attention. The Secretary of Defense had turned pale, as did most around the table. The general pushed back his chair and turned to leave.

"Sit down!" yelled President Fulton. "I'm not finished with you." The President put both hands on the conference table and pushed himself to his feet. He seemed a bit wobbly on his legs, and his face had turned an even deeper shade of crimson, alarmingly so.

"Secretary Ca—, ah, Cccarrter," the President stuttered, pointing his finger at Secretary of Defense Melvin Boyd. "I, uh, I ddddon't knnnnow what type of outfit you're running at the Pentagon, but, but, but, no officer will, will ever speak—."

The President paused in mid-sentence after struggling to form his words. He seemed to be looking over the Vice President's head directly at Sharyn. He stood there, legs trembling but otherwise unmoving. Five seconds. Ten seconds. President Fulton's face remained beet red.

John Reynolds stood up and began walking around the table to assist the President.

Suddenly, the President seemed to snap out of his trance. His eyes refocused, and he took a deep breath. He continued to look toward Sharyn, and Sharyn felt confident he was making eye contact with her. Everyone else must have felt the same way as they all turned toward her to see what President Fulton was looking at.

"Why, hello there, young lady? What's your position?" President Fulton said. Sharyn looked on, horrified. This was almost exactly what the President had said to her last month in a meeting in the Roosevelt Room.

John Reynolds had reached the President's side by this point, and he gently put his arm around him, leaning in to whisper something in President Fulton's ear.

Divided We Stand

"Okay, John," the President said in full voice. "I was just going to have an ice cream with that young lady there." Reynolds pulled the President's chair back and gently guided him behind those sitting at the table. Brad Nesbitt, Assistant Chief of Staff, jumped up from his seat along the wall and darted out the door. In seconds, two Secret Service agents and the President's bodyman came rushing in. They gingerly held the President by the elbow and walked him out of the room.

Everyone around the conference table sat in stunned silence.

Sharyn waited for the Vice President to begin speaking, as did most around the table. Some had seen the President have brief episodes where he seemed to lose his train of thought, couldn't find the right word, or even stumbled to the ground, but no one had seen this level of incapacity.

"I guess I'll be the first to address the elephant in the room," said Secretary of State Brent Snowden. "Do we need to have a discussion of our obligations under the 25th Amendment?"

"You'll do no such thing," said the Vice President, forcefully snapping out of her silence and taking charge of the room. "President Fulton has had a very long day and has been up most of the night over the past week while he leads this country through one of the most trying times in history. Bill Fulton has our full support, and I will not entertain any discussion to the contrary. If you read the 25th Amendment, it requires the Vice President to agree that the President is unable to discharge the powers and the duties of his office, and I am not prepared to do that based on a minor lapse due to fatigue and stress. Is that understood?"

Everyone around the table nodded but remained silent.

"General Vine?" The Vice President asked, turning to the Chairman of the Joint Chiefs, who had remained standing throughout this entire debacle.

"Yes, Ma'am."

"I and the President continue to have full confidence in your abilities as Chairman of the Joint Chiefs of Staff. To clarify, you have not been relieved, and I will not accept your resignation. Please have a seat."

General Vine looked for a moment as if he were going to speak, then thought better of it and sat down.

"Ladies and Gentlemen, our nation is under attack. These are both ideological and political attacks, as well as violent attacks by people we have not yet been able to identify fully. Two members of the Supreme Court have been assassinated, as well as a U.S. Senator and multiple state governors. All were members of the Democratic party. We, in this room, have a duty to lead this country, and we also have a duty to win this political war. Place yourselves and your departments on a war footing. I will be meeting with small groups of you throughout the day to convey the President's plan. We must stick together and keep focused on winning the November election, which will ultimately allow us to win this war. I thank you for your time this morning and your discretion. It goes without saying that nothing that has occurred in this room today is to be divulged to the press. Thank you for your time."

Without waiting for a response, the Vice President stood up and walked out of the room.

Part III

"I can't remember what all Frank had fighting in the jar that day, but I can remember other bug fights we staged later on: one stag beetle against a hundred red ants, one centipede against three spiders, red ants against black ants. They won't fight unless you keep shaking the jar. And that's what Frank was doing, shaking, shaking, the jar."

—Kurt Vonnegut, *Cat's Cradle*, 1963

"Pay no attention to that man behind the curtain!"

—L. Frank Baum, The Wizard of Oz, 1900

47

Clewiston, Florida

Thursday, April 11

NATHAN CLOSED the gate behind him and walked across the gravel parking area. He dropped his weighted vest on the porch and entered the house through the front door. He'd just completed a six-mile hike down the levee, before which he had done an hour of circuit training. His ribs were still sore, but he could work out a bit harder each day and was rapidly approaching being back to 100%. He was sweating profusely, but that was mostly due to the heat of Florida in April rather than his own exertion.

He still slept little and spent most of his time watching the news, continuing to cull and organize data for his investigation, and spending long hours on the pistol range. He hadn't spent this much time shooting since his time with the Unit over fifteen years ago, and he thoroughly enjoyed having Spooner put him through the paces. He was nowhere near as quick or as sharp as he once was, but he gave himself a respectable B+ grade considering his advanced age of forty-seven.

Bypassing the shower, Nathan ducked into the spare bedroom

he and Spooner were using as their operations room. He sat down in one of the two swivel chairs and gazed at the walls before him. Several large maps hung on the wall, one of the entire United States and others depicting the mid-Atlantic states and Florida. Various pieces of paper and photographs were pinned to the walls, as well as countless small Post-it notes in a variety of colors. Red and blue string connected the papers and photos to specific locations pinned to the map. Nathan stared at the wall as if the chaotic data had some meaning—which it actually did.

He felt like he was getting close to finding the Cabal, but he'd felt like this before, only to realize he was on the wrong track. It had been just over a month since Emily and Maeve had been killed, and Nathan continued to be driven by his sole focus of avenging their senseless deaths.

He and Spooner cataloged every piece of available open-source information on the various attacks and also queried contacts in the CIA, FBI, and a couple of state police forces to gather intel not available to the public. From all this information, they believed they'd identified nine separate hit squads that had been operational starting on March 21st, ten if you count the assassination squad that shot down former President King's Boeing 757.

Of these, at least six teams had been neutralized—although this information wasn't yet publicly available, and Nathan wasn't quite sure if any single government agency had put it all together. The press certainly hadn't.

Four dead Hispanic males had been found shot dead in the middle of an orange grove in Wimauma, Florida, on the afternoon after Benjamin King's plane was downed. Although they appeared to be Hispanic males, with indications that they were likely from Mexico, the Florida Department of Law Enforcement had so far been unable to identify these individuals. However, they did find traces of an explosive residue on some of their clothing. The FDLE forensics lab had no experience with these specific contaminant compounds, so a curious technician queried the University of Rhode Island's Explosive Database, one of the largest repositories for analytical data on explosive and energetic compounds. While the

Divided We Stand

query did not return an answer, it did garner the attention of a CIA analyst with backdoor access to the URI database. The result was the CIA's ability to match the specific compound to the residue of a Strela-2 surface-to-air missile. The CIA shared this with the White House but not with Florida's FDLE.

The terrorist cells in St. Paul, Rocky Mount, and Phoenix were neutralized at the site of the attack, although evidence shows one or more of each cell may have escaped. The cells in Virginia, Pennsylvania, and Michigan were each tracked down over the last several weeks following the wave of destruction in their paths and were eventually killed by a combination of police and National Guard forces.

That left four of the cells remaining free, and it was anyone's guess what their next target would be.

Through his detailed analysis, Nathan had come to several conclusions. First, the terrorist cells were not all foreign. Yes, several definitely consisted of Islamic jihadis, but the fact they were from all different countries added to Nathan's conclusion. Palestinians and al-Shabaab Somalis had nothing in common and would not be recruited by the same people. At least one cell was American—the former Navy SEAL killed by the FBI raid in the Florida Panhandle —and Spooner had been able to gather some classified intel that there were indications some of the other cells were Americans. For example, the attacks on the governors of Pennsylvania and Kentucky were almost assuredly American—the tactics and techniques that were used reeked strongly of former U.S. Army Special Forces. Several of the follow-on sniper attacks at various university protests also had eyewitnesses who swore the perpetrators were American.

The second conclusion Nathan reached was that these terrorist teams were not ideologically focused, and therefore, the Cabal did not belong to one of the sides in the looming civil war. Nathan had traced the likely path of destruction for each of the ten teams, and some of the teams attacked both liberal and conservative targets. It was almost as if their goal was to cause agitation and disruption rather than to further a specific ideological agenda. The significance of this for Nathan's primary mission could not be overstated—he wasn't searching for a Cabal who was wed to a single side; he was looking for a group that benefited from the chaos, not the win.

Lastly, Nathan had always known that the Cabal was well-funded, but each piece of the puzzle made him revise his estimates upwards as to how much funding the Cabal must have. Nathan now believed the Cabal had resources in the hundreds of millions of dollars in order to recruit, plan, and conduct an operation with such disparate cell member compositions and under complete secrecy. The logistics infrastructure to move people, weapons, and explosives was incredibly pricey—and all under the nose of the greatest intelligence and law enforcement machine the world had ever seen.

It was time to poke his nose under the circus tent and see what he could learn. Spooner had encouraged Nathan to wait a few more weeks, until at least the first of May, in order to heal completely, but Nathan couldn't wait any longer. Things were happening too fast, and he needed to figure things out before the country devolved into complete chaos.

Nathan also considered heading back to Casey Key or possibly somewhere new. He had the resources to live just about anywhere, and maybe a change would do him good. He'd been discussing this with his brother-in-law, a commercial realtor with lots of contacts.

Nathan turned on his iPhone, which he had kept off with few exceptions since his family had been murdered. He pulled up the contact for the first person he wanted to speak with, and she answered on the first ring.

"Nathan? How are you?" Said Jessica Dwyer, managing editor of the New York Times and one of the very few people Nathan had kept in touch with over the last month.

"Doing well, Jessica. How about you? Things still as crazy as they seem on television?"

"Crazier, if you can believe it. It's like nothing I've ever experienced. The level of animosity has reached unfathomable proportions, and it's not the people you think. You expect the ultra-conservative and super-progressive to be the most aggressive and even college students looking for a cause, but that's not the case. Yes,

Divided We Stand

those groups are agitated, but so are the senior citizens and the teenagers, the working-class and the business owners, the home-owners and the homeless. You can walk down the street right now and hear ordinary people talking heatedly about the potential for a Constitutional Convention or discussing the nuances of the Supremacy Clause. The average American had no clue about these concepts a month ago, and now it's part of our everyday lexicon."

"Kind of reminds me of the story of Joe Kennedy before the stock market crash in 1929. He knew as soon as the shoeshine boys were discussing stocks, it was time to get out of the market."

"Exactly!" Jessica remarked. "Except it's worse because people aren't talking about investing. They're talking about dismantling the government or possibly even going to war."

"What's the gossip in the newsroom? What are people saying about who's behind all this?"

"You know what, Nathan? You're the first person to ask me this question. The precursors to all this—the governors being assassi-nated and the state legislatures being tipped to Republican control —that's all water under the bridge. Now you're either Red or Blue. You believe term limits are critical and the states need to take back control, or you believe the federal government is the best entity for managing the issues America is facing. No one is asking if anyone is behind it—as each side believes they're the ones who came up with the idea."

"So the country is dividing into Red states and Blue states?"

"No, that's the crazy part! The country has always been divided into Red states and Blue states—but the reality is that most states are fairly evenly split, with the majority being just fifty-five percent or so favoring one side or the other. Even the Bluest and Redest states, Vermont and Wyoming, are only 70% majority to 30% minority. But this will show how crazy things are. Vermont, who voted 70% for Fulton in the last election—they have a four-term Republican governor who wins with more than 75% of the vote! Crazy, right?"

"Yeah, I was gathering research on just this issue before my sabbatical," said Nathan. "Contrary to what people want to believe, there is no North-South geographical divide like the Civil War in 1861. You can look at a map and see Red and Blue states, but the mix of people who favor Red or Blue in every state is at the neighborhood level."

"Well, you're the Constitutional expert. Why don't you tell me what's going to happen?" Jessica asked.

"The people are pawns in a political game of chess where the goal isn't to win. It's to keep playing long enough to enrich yourself. We have Congressmen being investigated for sex with underage girls who are considered the moral compass of their party. We have judges who are legislating from the bench not based on matters of law but because they don't personally agree with whatever issue they are sitting in judgment. The President cares only about gathering power to win the next election—but the Governors are doing the same thing at the state level. That's not including the handful of governors who dream of sitting in the White House and who push a state agenda for the sole purpose of launching their bid for President."

"Go on," said Jessica.

"The rigidity of the two-party system has taken hold in recent years and paralyzed the federal government. Because most Americans are actually moderate on the grand political scale, there's always been respect between the parties and the ability to change your party affiliation throughout your life. I can speak personally— there've been times in my life I've voted Democrat and times that I've voted Republican. I don't think I've ever actually voted a straight ticket in any election, and I would venture to say the majority of people have the same experience.

"But today, with the stalemate between the parties and the use of social media to influence everyone, each party's slim but radical faction actually has the most power. A few rabid Republicans can swing the vote on who's Speaker of the House. A few progressive Democrats can force the President to adopt an agenda that even the majority of his own party doesn't support. This party rigidity has caused each party to become a coalition of various factions, and the

Divided We Stand

smallest, most radical faction now wields a tremendous amount of power."

"And term limits will solve this?"

"To a large extent, yes. At a minimum, term limits will eliminate the career politician, the person who's in Washington not to help their constituents but to build a career. But that won't solve the current crisis."

"What will?"

"The American public is being manipulated, Jessica. And until we all figure out who's shaking the jar, we'll continue down this road of animosity and hatred."

"Shaking the jar? What do you mean?"

"Haven't you heard the old saying about a hundred red ants and a hundred black ants in a glass jar? They're content to live peacefully, going about their business with no issues. But if someone shakes the jar, they suddenly start attacking. The black ants think the red ants are the enemy causing the disruption, and the red ants think it's the black ants."

"Interesting. So, who's shaking the jar? The Red or the Blue?"

"That's my whole point, Jessica. Neither. The Red and Blue are *IN* the jar. Someone else is doing the shaking. That's who killed Emily and Maeve, and I'm going to find them."

Jessica said nothing for a few moments. "This is crazy, Nathan. If you're right, this is absolutely earth-shattering."

"I agree."

"Hey, I have a serious favor, Nathan. And you can feel free to say no, okay?"

"Okay," said Nathan, not liking where this was heading.

"Can I quote you on this? On all the stuff you just said."

"No."

"C'mon, Nathan. Pleeease! What you just said makes more sense than anything I've heard in the last month. Your term limit Op-ed has become the single most-read article on the New York Times website *ever*, and your tweet has been re-tweeted more than any other tweet. The American people need to hear what you just said."

"Look, Jessica. I owe you a lot, so I'm not going to say no to you. But I'd prefer if you kept my name to a minimum or just kept me out of it altogether. But under no circumstances can you use that very last part. You can't mention to anyone that I'm trying to find out who's shaking the jar. Deal?"

"Deal! Thanks, Nathan. Good luck."

Nathan said goodbye. He was already exhausted, and he had two more calls to make. He hoped to make these much quicker.

48

Clewiston, Florida

Thursday, April 11

NATHAN MADE HIS NEXT CALL, listening as the phone rang four times before being connected to voicemail. He hung up without bothering to listen to the greeting, let alone leave a message. Before he could decide what to do next, his phone started vibrating in his hand. The caller id was the person he'd just been trying to reach.

"Hello, Sam. How are you?" Nathan asked in greeting.

"I'm well, Nathan. Thank you so much for returning my call. I know I've left an ungodly number of messages, but the Governor and I have been trying to reach you. How is your recovery going?"

The man on the other end of the line was Sam Stryder, Nathan's former pupil from long ago and the current senior advisor to the Florida governor. Nathan didn't know exactly how many times Sam had tried calling, as he almost always kept his phone turned off, but he did know there were at least a dozen voicemails from the man.

"It's going well, thank you. Not quite back to 100%, but getting there. And no worries, Sam. I've had my phone off for the last month or so. I see that you and Governor Marino have been quite busy."

"That would be an understatement. It's exciting times, truly exciting times. Vince was hoping that you might be able to come to Tallahassee for a visit. He's happy to send a plane for you, but he has several urgent matters that he'd like to discuss with you."

"That would be great, Sam. I was actually going to ask you about the potential for meeting with the governor, so this works out well. Is he free tomorrow? I don't need transportation, and I can be there anytime that's convenient for the Governor."

"How about noon? We could have lunch at the residence. It's a bit more private than his office in the Capitol Complex."

"Sounds good," replied Nathan. "Hey, Sam, I did have one quick question for you. I was thinking of reaching out to Orlean Brumback. Would you happen to have his direct number?"

"Oh, absolutely. I'll text it to you right now."

"Do you see much of Orlean?" Nathan asked innocently.

"Funny you should ask. He's coming to town this weekend—he actually has a full bedroom and living suite on his private 737 jet. He rarely stays in hotels. He and the Governor are spending the day together on Sunday going over strategy. I'm sure it will be something the Governor will speak with you about tomorrow."

"I look forward to it," said Nathan. "And Alex Treacher? I remember him from the meeting at the Lido Club. He seemed like he was pretty close with Orlean."

"Yes," said Sam, a bit warily. "I'm not sure about the exact relationship between Alex and Orlean. I haven't seen Alex in over a month."

"I'm sure you're busy. I won't keep you, and I look forward to seeing you again tomorrow."

"See you then," said Sam, disconnecting the call.

49

Clewiston, Florida

Thursday, April 11

THE LAST CALL Nathan had to make was one he'd been dreading. This young woman was like a second daughter to him, and he had intentionally ignored her attempts at outreach after the St. Armands bombing that had killed Emily and Maeve. Nathan knew it wasn't her fault, but he couldn't help feeling animosity toward the woman's employer.

Given how busy he knew this person was, he half-expected his call to go straight to voicemail. He was surprised when she picked up on the first ring.

"Nathan?" the woman said in greeting.

"Yes, Sharyn. How are you?"

"How am I? My God, how are you?" Sharyn Gray asked, and Nathan could hear the emotion in her voice. "I'm so sorry, Nathan. I'm so, so very sorry." The woman started sobbing over the phone.

Nathan tried to hold back his own tears, crying not for his family but for how he had evaded contact with someone he cared deeply for, and thereby made her grieving that much more difficult. Nathan had lost his wife and daughter, but in his own grief, he forgot that they were important to others who were also grieving their loss. He felt selfish and ashamed.

"No, I'm the one who should be sorry. It's inexcusable that I shut you out. You're an important person to our family, and I'm sorry for not reaching out to you. I basically shut down after Emily and Maeve were killed. I stopped dealing with everyone and everything. I, I don't know. I think I—"

"Shhhh," said Sharyn. "It's okay, Nathan. Honestly. I understand."

"Thank you," said Nathan, getting his emotions under control.

"How are you doing? I tried so many times to reach you—first about Emily and Maeve and then about your injuries. How are you healing?"

"I'm doing well, thank you. It's a long process, but physically, I'm regaining my strength and endurance. Doing a lot of walking."

"That's great. Where are you? I heard you checked out of the hospital and haven't gone home to Casey Key."

Nathan became instantly guarded. "Who's asking? My friend Sharyn, or the chief of staff to the Vice President of the United States?"

"Nathan!" Sharyn replied, the hurt evident in her voice. "You don't think I had anything to do with what happened to you, do you? Those FBI agents were out of control."

"I know you'd never wish me harm. I understand that. But let me ask you—did you know the FBI was going to my house? Did you try to warn me? Because that's what friends do."

The silence on the other end of the line was deafening. Unwilling to be the first to break the silence, Nathan waited. At first, there was not a sound, but then he heard sobbing and then crying. Nathan's fears were confirmed. *She knew,* he thought. *Sharyn knew they were coming to get me.*

After thirty seconds, the crying stopped, and Nathan heard a few sniffles.

Divided We Stand

"Is that what you think of me, Nathan?" Sharyn asked, her emotion-filled voice barely above a whisper. "Is it?"

It was Nathan's turn to be silent.

"Yes, I knew," said Sharyn, and Nathan thought he heard guilt in her voice. "The Vice President gave the order personally to have you brought to the White House. She didn't want you arrested, but she did authorize the FBI to use any means necessary to get you on the plane to Washington." Sharyn paused. "I left that meeting, Nathan, and I called you. I called you seventeen times. I even used the Secret Service to find your sister-in-law's phone number and called her. No one returned my calls. No one called me back!" Sharyn was crying again. "I tried to warn you, Nathan. I tried. No one called me back."

Nathan put his head in his hands, wondering how he could be so wrong about someone—someone he cared deeply about and trusted. Shaking his head, Nathan realized he was no different from all the agitated people choosing the Red or Blue sides. He was an ant in a jar, and someone was shaking it, causing him to react rather than act. This caused him to question his loyalties, shun his friends, and judge before knowing the facts.

"Sharyn, shhh. Please calm down for a second," said Nathan. "I'm sorry, Sharyn. Please accept my apology. I can't believe I would ever question your loyalty to me and our family—and I do consider yourself part of my family. I may have forgotten that for a few weeks, but I assure you, I never will again. Can you forgive me?"

Sharyn sniffled. "Of course I forgive you. There's nothing to forgive. I understand how you could think what you did. It just hurts. I miss Maeve. I miss Emily. Maeve used to text me funny pictures of all of you just hanging out at the house. You probably didn't know that, but it made me feel close to you."

Nathan remembered all the evenings at Stanford when Sharyn came over to play a game with Maeve before sitting down to a family dinner. They tailgated at football games, Sharyn took Maeve to the theater on campus, and Sharyn even accompanied them on several family vacations, once to Yosemite and a couple of times to

Lake Tahoe. He'd been selfish in his grief, disallowing any empathy for how others might feel after losing Emily and Maeve.

"I've been thinking of coming to visit you, Sharyn, but honestly, I'm a little worried about traveling to the District. Not sure your boss is still on the lookout for me, and I'm still a bit concerned about the FBI."

"Nathan, you shouldn't come here," Sharyn said, intentionally lowering her voice to a whisper. "This place has gone completely crazy. I think you'd be safe, but sometimes I just don't know anymore."

"What's going on? I mean, I've been following the news, but what's happening in the White House."

"Nathan, can I call you back in five minutes? I'd like to be frank; right now, I'm in my office at the EEOB. It might be a good time for a walk."

Nathan told her he understood, and Sharyn agreed to call when she got to a more private location. Five minutes passed, and Nathan began to worry; at ten minutes, he was downright concerned.

Sixteen minutes later, Sharyn called.

"What happened?" he asked as he answered the call.

"I'm sorry. The deputy chief of staff came by my office just as I was walking out. It took me a while to get rid of him."

"Anything important?"

"Actually, yes. I'm not sure how much you're aware of this, but Vice President Moore is making quite a few of the decisions in the White House these days."

"Is it that bad? I know Fulton seems pretty frail on television, but I thought a lot of that was just rumor."

"Definitely not a rumor, and it's gotten quite a bit worse in the last three weeks. March 21st was almost too much for him to handle, and he hasn't been quite the same since."

"I did see the quote from an unnamed source who was supposedly at the Cabinet meeting where Fulton had a breakdown or maybe even a stroke."

"Yeah, it's basically true. I don't think there's been any medical

Divided We Stand

diagnosis, but Fulton lost it. He just froze and then seemed to have some temporary dementia."

"Does he do this frequently?" Nathan asked.

"No. Well, yes, kind of," answered Sharyn. "I mean, it's not that frequent, but he's definitely done it before. John Reynolds, the President's Chief of Staff, makes sure the President gets plenty of rest. When rested, he's normally pretty sharp. It's just under extreme stress, and when he's tired, he sometimes seems…I don't know…he just kind of seems old. Too old."

"What about the 25th Amendment?"

"Serena doesn't want to do that, not only because she respects Fulton but also because, right now, he still seems to offer us the best chance to win in November. Currently, she's almost 100% focused on the brewing civil war and letting President Fulton worry about the election."

"Civil war?"

"You have no idea, Nathan. The media is only reporting a fraction of what's going on. Frankly, with the Red states keeping federal law enforcement out, we probably don't even know half of what's going on in these states. What we do know, however, is alarming. More than alarming."

"How so?"

"Well, state governments are basically making people pick sides: Blue or Red. This week, several governors have changed their state driver's licenses and license plates to reflect one's party affiliation.

"What?"

"Yeah, the license plates have an R for Republican, a D for Democrat, and an N for no party affiliation. The same goes for your driver's license."

"The star of David," said Nathan, immediately seeing the significance.

"Exactly! While some say it's a pride thing, the reality is trying to find ways to identify which team everyone is on. And it's not just Republican governors doing this. It started in Idaho and Montana, but Oregan fired back, trying to shame the minority of Republicans in their state.

"And all thirty-four state legislatures have passed laws making it illegal to drive in their states with licenses granted by the other sixteen states, as these states all allow undocumented immigrants to obtain a driver's license. Two of these Red states, Utah and Virginia, had to repeal their own laws as they had previously allowed undocumented immigrants to get a license."

"Yeah, well, it always seemed strange to me to allow people here illegally to get a driver's license," said Nathan. "especially when that license and a utility bill get you access to all sorts of state and local services."

"Look, I don't disagree that it was a progressive push that went too far. But now, we have cops pulling people over because they have an out-of-state license plate. It's severely curbing interstate travel."

"Maybe that's their intent," said Nathan.

"Who's intent?"

"The people shaking the jar," replied Nathan. For the next few minutes, he used the analogy of ants in a jar to explain his theory of an external force manipulating the American people.

"Well, they're doing a good job, whoever these people are shaking the jar," admitted Sharyn. "The sheer volume of violent incidents around the country far exceeds anything the press is reporting. If anything, the media seems to be downplaying it."

"What do you mean?"

"Homeland Security is cataloging more than a thousand incidents a day of politically motivated violence or intimidation. It's happening in all fifty states, in large cities and small towns alike. Everything from targeted assassinations of elected officials to brawls with baseball bats at college protests to intimidation of people registered to vote for the minority party to get them to move out of state."

"Does the White House have any clue as to who's behind all this? Who's shaking the jar, so to speak?"

"Not a clue," said Sharyn. "The CIA has mentioned that they believe the Russians could have a hand in stirring the pot, but honestly, the CIA sees a Russian behind every tree. Twenty years ago, it was an Islamist behind every tree; today, it's a Russian. The

FBI is pretty sure everything is currently homegrown. There's definitely evidence of Islamic jihadists and drug cartels behind the March 21st attacks, but since then, they believe it's been all domestic groups."

"You need to be careful, Sharyn. Seriously, this all seems to be getting out of hand," Nathan said.

"Don't worry about me. I'm always careful."

They said their goodbyes, promising to be in touch more often.

50

Port Huron, Michigan

Friday, April 12

GOVERNOR JEFF VENO sat on the slate patio porch in front of his lakefront home on Conger Street in Port Huron. Conger Street was his favorite street in the world, even if you discounted the fact that this had been his childhood home, and he'd lived on this street most of his life.

Conger Street wasn't really a street. It was a sidewalk. Running just under a half-mile in length, the sidewalk set back a hundred feet from the shores of Lake Huron at its very southern tip, with views of Sarnia, Canada, less than a mile across the aqua-blue waters. On one side of the sidewalk were manicured lawns leading down to the sandy beach, each lot delineated by a row of small shrubs or a few larger trees, while on the other side of the concrete path were the houses. Most were built in the 1930s as summer residences for wealthy Detroit families. These large homes weathered the passage of time, some being renovated dozens of times while others retained their original appearance.

What made Conger Street so unique was its inherent lifestyle.

Divided We Stand

The front doors of all the homes faced the sidewalk and the lake, with their garages in driveways to the rear. The postman still walked the sidewalk street, a large mailbag slung over one shoulder as he slid mail into the slots of the colorful front doors. Paperboys and papergirls rode their bikes while delivering "old-fashioned" newspapers, often ringing a bell on their handlebars to alert pedestrians out for a morning stroll. Mothers pushed strollers, while in the summer months, it was common to see children with inner tubes running up Conger to jump in the lake at Lakeside State Park and float down the lake along with the current to get out at Lighthouse Beach under the looming framework of the Bluewater Bridge.

Jeff loved this street. This was his home. So despite the upheaval of the last few weeks—the chaos, sleepless nights, and feelings of having been thrown into the deep end with concrete shoes—Jeff insisted that he spend a long weekend at his home.

Three weeks ago today, Jeff was whisked off to Lansing to be sworn in as the 50th governor of the State of Michigan. He was entirely unprepared for the role but quickly settled in, learning who he could trust and who was up to no good. Governor Carlson had assembled a top-notch staff, and Jeff saw no reason to make any changes. Aidan Stroud had proved a capable chief of staff, and Jeff had come to rely on him heavily.

The other person he had become close with was Lieutenant David Ortiz of the Michigan State Police, the man in charge of the governor's protection detail. Ortiz was not quite as tall as Jeff's 6'3", but he was built like a pitbull—narrow hips, broad chest and shoulders, bald head, and a look on his face like he was just itching to take a bite out of someone. With a name like David Ortiz, he'd been nicknamed Big Papi after the famed Red Sox slugger since his first days on the force fifteen years ago, and he insisted the Governor call him Papi.

As his predecessor had been killed in the attack on Governor Carlson, Papi was new to the leadership of the governor's personal protection detail. Papi kept tight reins on Jeff's travel and appearances. If it were up to Papi, Jeff would be secluded in the Governor's Mansion and never leave it.

That wasn't possible, especially since Jeff had graciously allowed Lenora Carlson's widower and children to remain residing in the Governor's Mansion until the end of the year. Jeff had no intention of disrupting any more lives, and it was the least he could do. The Governor's Office was in the George W. Romney Building across from the State Capitol, and Jeff took a room at the Doubletree Hotel just a block down from his new office. Papi preferred that Jeff ride in the governor's armored SUV for the twenty-second trip, but most days, Jeff insisted on walking.

It was a gorgeous Spring morning on the patio, and Jeff was enjoying his morning coffee. Jeff attempted to ignore the bullet-proof glass guard shack Papi had brought in and placed on the corner of his lawn, with a state trooper manning this 24/7 to keep an eye on anyone approaching. Looking out at the lake, Jeff watched a large Great Lakes freighter approaching, seemingly just several hundred yards offshore, the brick red hull and white bridge structure reminiscent of the Edmund Fitzgerald. In Jeff's youth, this part of the lake would have hundreds of American and Canadian recreational fishermen floating in their small boats in search of walleye, but in recent years, there were usually less than a dozen in view.

Watching the freighter pass, Jeff was interrupted by the approach of Aidan Stroud, his inherited chief of staff.

"Good morning, Governor," Aidan said.

Jeff still had a difficult time being referred to as the governor, but no matter how many times he asked Aidan to call him Jeff, Aidan never complied.

"Morning, Aidan. What's the news overnight? Things getting any better?'

"Worse, I'm afraid," said Aidan. "There were fatalities associated with protests in Lansing, Ann Arbor, and Ypsilanti. I don't think we can wait any longer on a decision to fully mobilize the National Guard."

Jeff had spoken almost daily with the state's Adjutant General, a two-star Army general in charge of the Michigan National Guard. Jeff had been reluctant to mobilize the state's entire Army National Guard, even though one of his first orders as governor had been to

Divided We Stand

mobilize one Guard unit, the 177th Military Police Brigade, to support law enforcement throughout the state. As the crisis continued, it appeared likely that Jeff was going to be forced to mobilize additional soldiers.

"Okay, get me the paperwork and schedule another call with the Adjutant General this morning. I think I should do a blanket mobilization for a minimum of ninety days. It's better to have too many resources than not enough."

"Yes, sir. The other item we need to decide on this morning is the Constitutional Convention. The new Republican leadership in the State Senate and House of Representatives has already passed joint legislation demanding the U.S. Congress call a Constitutional Convention, but you need to decide if you're going to sign it, fight it, or do nothing."

"We've been over this, Aidan. I'm not a Democrat. I've been an Independent my entire life and don't feel comfortable changing my party affiliation. It wasn't my idea for Governor Carlson to put me on her list, knowing I wasn't a member of the Democratic Party. While I don't necessarily agree with the risks associated with a Constitutional Convention, I think the term limit idea is pretty good. Brilliant actually. I mean, we already limit the number of terms Michigan Governors, Senators, and Congressmen can serve, so it only makes sense for the Constitution to be amended so the federal government can do the same. I know you've told me the Supreme Court says term limits for the U.S. Congress are unconstitutional, but they also said slaves were once property and the whole separate but equal thing. Times change, and so should the Supreme Court. "

"So you're planning to sign the bill?" Aidan asked, knowing that the new Republican leadership had been pressuring Governor Veno to do just that.

"No, I'm not going to sign it either," said Jeff. "I'm not a lawyer, thank God. But I've certainly listened to enough of them over the past three weeks. This isn't a bill that requires the governor to sign. They passed a resolution demanding that the U.S. Congress call for a Constitutional Convention as required under Article V of the U.S.

Constitution. This is a process restricted to the state and federal legislative branches of government. The governor has no part in it. So, I'm not planning to endorse it, nor do I want to use state resources to fight it. It's not our fight."

Aidan disagreed with Jeff, wanting the Governor to fight it, but he understood that Jeff had made up his mind. Like a good staff advisor, he knew when to move on.

"How about the recognition of out-of-state driver's license bill? The new Republican legislature is due to vote on the bill early next week. It follows similar laws enacted by a couple of dozen Republican states already, which doesn't recognize the licenses issued by states who allow undocumented migrants to receive driver's licenses."

"That seems ridiculous, doesn't it?" Jeff asked.

"Absolutely," said Aidan. "I can't believe they've even introduced the bill."

"No, I mean that states are giving driver's licenses to illegal immigrants."

"You mean *undocumented*, right, Governor? I know it's semantics, but the outcry should someone hear you speak like that—"

"Look, Aidan, I really do appreciate and value your advice, but I'm not a politician. I'm not going to run for election in November. I'm willing to do this job because Lenora Carlson thought I would be good at it for some reason, and I'm willing to devote 110% to doing the best job that I can. But *undocumented* versus *illegal*, I think the semantics is a bit ridiculous. Frankly, if states issue undocumented immigrants driver's licenses, wouldn't that now make them *documented*? I mean, they're really not undocumented. They have passports and birth certificates. They just don't have permission to be in this country *legally*. So, in my mind, the most accurate term is *illegal* immigrant."

"I didn't realize you held such conservative views," said Aidan.

"Aidan, this here is part of the problem. And I hope we can have a frank discussion. You should always feel free to speak your mind. But labeling me conservative because I think the proper term for someone being in this country illegally is to refer to them as an

Divided We Stand

illegal immigrant doesn't make me conservative. It just means I don't ascribe to all the craziness that's been going on the last decade or so. For Pete's sake, Aidan, I'm about as liberal as anyone I know my age. If I had the power, I'd grant amnesty to every immigrant in this country and start fresh at the border by making everyone enter legally. I believe the government can and should do great things. Federal and state governments are obligated to help people not as fortunate as others, to make sure no child gets left behind, and to provide affordable healthcare. Benjamin King was an utter embarrassment as President. Does that make me a conservative? Or is it just because we disagree on an issue?"

Aidan looked hard at Jeff without speaking, seeming to absorb what Jeff had just said. "I see your point, Governor. I also see how labeling and putting people in a box can escalate the situation. Thanks for clarifying."

Not sure if Aidan was agreeing with him or appeasing him; Jeff just wanted to move on to the next issue. "Good. What's next?"

Before Aidan could answer, Papi walked out from the interior of the house. In his hands, he held an iPhone and an iPad.

"Sir," Papi said, addressing Jeff. "Your phone has been blowing up. I think you should watch this." Jeff took both devices from the leader of his security detail, having purposely left his phone on the counter to enjoy a few minutes of solitude on his front porch.

Jeff held the iPad so both he and Aidan could watch while Papi stood behind them and watched over their shoulders. The screen showed a reporter standing on a sidewalk, emergency vehicles visible behind her, along with a burning building. The chyron on the bottom of the screen read: Islamic Mosque Attacked; Dozens Feared Dead.

"Jesus Christ," said Aidan as he saw what was happening. Although not amusing, Jeff couldn't help but notice Aidan's colloquial use of the phrase, as Jeff knew Aidan to be Jewish. Jeff's eyes were drawn to the building in the foreground, just on the edge of the camera's frame. In one of those rare moments when you see something you know is about to go viral, Jeff zoomed in on the small building right at the edge of the sidewalk where the reporter had decided to broadcast. The white sign had red lettering in Arabic script, and below this, the words: Gateway to Heaven.

Jeff turned up the volume.

"—this morning, not more than thirty minutes ago. As you can see, firefighters and EMS are on the scene, as well as investigators from the Dearborn Police Department. We have not received any official comments, but it appears that at least fifteen people were shot while fleeing the burning building, and fire officials fear that additional people remain trapped inside by the smoke and flames and may not be able to get out.

"If you're just joining us, I'm Amelia Hernandez with WXYZ News in Detroit, and we are on the scene of what appears to be yet another terrorist incident. An explosive fire erupted inside a Dearborn mosque this morning, the building you see in the distance behind me, and eyewitnesses say that an unknown number of assailants began shooting at worshippers fleeing the mosque. As you may know, Friday is the Islamic day of worship, and I'm being told the mosque was quite full, with more than a hundred in attendance."

Jeff clicked the button to turn off the iPad, placing it face down on the glass patio table next to his now cold cup of coffee.

"Do I need to go back to Lansing?" Jeff asked his chief of staff.

"I don't know. Let me get some people on the phone and find out more about what's going on."

"This is going to escalate, Aidan, if we can't do something. The government is here to solve problems, not create them. If we aren't seen as helping things get better, they are going to get worse. A lot worse."

"I know, Governor. Let me see what I can find out."

51

Tallahassee, Florida

Friday, April 12

"YOU SURE DO KNOW how to get yourself on the cover of the New York Times," said Governor Vince Marino, sitting down with Nathan and Sam Stryder in the living room of The People's House, the governor's mansion in Tallahassee.

"That was about the farthest thing from my intention," Nathan sheepishly replied. He'd awoken that morning to find that Jessica had indeed quoted him, and the article was the lead story in Friday's morning edition of the New York Times.

"We appreciate you coming up to Tallahassee to meet with us," added Sam. It was just after ten o'clock in the morning and one of the governor's stewards had served them coffee and biscuits. The large sunroom they were sitting in looked like it had been decorated in the 1960s, which it probably had, and looked out over the garden and the pool. Governor Marino was wearing khakis and a polo shirt with the Florida crest on the breast, while Nathan had opted for a linen blazer and open-necked dress shirt.

"It's my pleasure," said Nathan, taking a sip of coffee. He had his own agenda for the meeting, but he was curious about why Marino was so eager to meet with him.

"Based on your comments in the Times, it appears you've been following the situation across the country closely. It's great to see you looking healthy. How's the recovery going?"

"It's going well, and I do try my best to keep informed." Nathan was wondering when the small talk would end, knowing the governor had little patience.

Setting his own cup down on the coffee table between them, Governor Marino rubbed his hands together in the universal sign for getting ready for business. "The Republican governors and various party leaders have been meeting regularly over the last few weeks since President King's assassination. It's been decided that the Republican National Committee will put forward my name as the candidate they endorse to receive all of the primary delegates President King earned through the majority of primaries across the country."

Interesting, thought Nathan. *But not really a surprise.* Marino had become the face of conservative action across the country.

"Congratulations, Vince. I'm sure you'll represent the Republican party well."

"Thank you, Nathan. I appreciate that. While the Republican Convention isn't scheduled until late July, with all of the momentum gained by the move toward a Constitutional Convention on July 4th, the party has requested that I consider naming a running mate sooner rather than later. I'm considering selecting you as my Vice President."

Surprised, Nathan could only think of taking a sip of coffee as an excuse to gather his thoughts.

"That's quite an honor," said Nathan. "To be honest, I'm not sure it's an honor I'm qualified for or even worth."

"You let me be the judge of that," said Vince.

"Nathan, there's no one I can think of that is more qualified and worthy than you," added Sam. "It's why you're Vince's number one choice."

"What does Orlean Brumback have to say about me?" Nathan

Divided We Stand

asked. "He seemed pretty influential with the King campaign, and I'm curious as to how he plays into all this."

"Orlean is one of your biggest fans," said Vince. "But I haven't told him about this running mate decision. I wanted to speak with you first."

"I'll be honest, Vince. I'm not a registered Republican, and I'm not sure I agree with all that's been happening the last couple of months, beginning with Benjamin King's refusal to face his charges in court. Some of the Red states' recent initiatives seem to me to potentially make the situation in this country worse, not better."

"Well, I value your opinion," said Vince, clearly gritting his teeth. "But maybe you don't have the full picture. Our nation's under attack. Our borders are being overrun, and the progressives in Fulton's administration are ruining the very fabric of our nation. I've read your take on someone shaking the jar. I can assure you, I'm the one shaking the jar, and I make no secret about that."

Nathan looked at Vince for a moment. "I don't think you are. I think you're an honorable man trying to do what you think is right. But I don't believe you ordered the assassination of five Democratic governors and two Supreme Court justices."

"Of course not," blurted a frustrated Marino. "Those were Islamic terrorists. There's evidence to prove that."

"But who sent them, Vince? And they just happened to attack the day after King was shot down? Speaking of which, who shot down King's plane? Someone is manipulating our political process."

"Nonsense. I can assure you. I've been in all the relevant political discussions at the national level, and there's no one pushing our buttons."

"Not Brumback? Hasn't he been in all these meetings as well?"

Vince laughed. "You think Orlean Brumback killed President King? They were friends for God's sake."

"What about the governors and Supreme Court justices? It's no secret he despises liberals."

"It doesn't mean he goes around assassinating them!" yelled Vince. "Brumback is a very wealthy, very powerful conservative media mogul. But he plays within the rules. He has some forward-looking strategies, and he definitely is helping to shape the conservative movement across this country, but he's not advocating killing people. Trust me, I meet with him all the time, sometimes several times a week. He's harmless."

"Someone is behind this, Vince. Someone with a lot of money, a lot of resources, and very little scruples is shaking the jar. They're sitting back and manipulating us so that our nation continues to fracture. We're killing each other. You have to see that, right?"

"Nathan, the conservatives in this country didn't create this mess, but we are damn sure going to clean it up. If you have the personal conviction to do what's right for this nation, I think you'd be a strong addition to our team. If not, don't let the door hit you in the ass on the way out." Vince was clearly pissed off, but so was Nathan.

Nathan showed no emotion, and he locked eyes with the Governor. Vince realized, not for the first time, that Nathan was a man capable of great violence.

"Governor Marino, I believe I warned you during our first meeting about questioning my personal conviction."

Without saying another word, Nathan stood up and walked out of the room.

52

Dearborn, Michigan

Friday, April 12

KEITH SAT in stunned silence as he watched the news. The flatscreen television was showing footage of the attack on the Dearborn mosque, which was located not five miles from where Keith currently sat. With the television announcer reviewing the death toll, now up to fourteen, Keith's right thumb flicked through various TikTok videos on his phone. The memes and videos from this morning's attack on peaceful worshippers were already cascading through social media.

Tuesday and Wednesday, April 9th and 10th, had been school holidays in celebration of Eid al-Fitr, the Muslim celebration of the end of Ramadan. Keith had elected to use two sick days and take off Thursday and Friday as well.

After his despair at the events of March 21st, Keith had reached out to a friend from his college days at Eastern Michigan University. Sparky, as everyone called him, but Keith had no idea why, lived on the same dorm floor with Keith during freshman year, and they had remained social throughout their four years of college. Sparky, a tall, lanky redhead, was a student activist during their four years in Ypsilanti, participating in protests for anything with a progressive cause. Keith had lost touch with Sparky after graduation but had heard from mutual friends that Sparky had been kicked out of Navy boot camp and had subsequently become very involved in the Black Lives Matter protests after the killing of George Floyd in 2020. There were rumors Sparky had become a member of the nefarious Antifa.

Sparky had been happy to hear from Keith, although skeptical of the purpose of Keith's call. When Keith asked for information about getting involved with Antifa, Sparky became instantly aloof but agreed to meet for a drink at a local tavern. Sparky was already at the bar when Keith arrived, and Keith was taken aback when Sparky immediately patted him down, searching for a hidden wire.

"You can never be too careful," Sparky had said. "It's good to see you, Keith, but I needed to make sure you're not a narc."

They had talked for over an hour, with Sparky asking most of the questions. Seemingly satisfied with Keith's honest resolve to get involved, Sparky invited Keith to meet up several nights later, near a large protest at the University of Michigan in Ann Arbor. When Keith had arrived at the meeting site, a small parking lot at the corner of Huron and Division Streets, Sparky was gathered with a half dozen men and women wearing hooded sweatshirts and surgical masks. Everyone was introduced using nicknames, and Sparky introduced Keith as Gilligan—a moniker that Sparky admitted he just came up with on the spur of the moment.

Keith was handed a surgical mask and a canister that Keith initially thought was spray paint. It wasn't until several minutes later when Sparky was briefing the small group, that Keith realized the canister was actually bear spray. Several blocks to the south, on the corner of one of the University of Michigan's main quads, a peaceful vigil for the assassination of the Michigan Governor and Supreme Court Justices was being drowned out by a large group of conservative activists demanding a Constitutional Convention. Tensions between the two groups, currently numbering several hundred on each side, provided the kindling, and it was Sparky's intention to light the match.

Divided We Stand

What followed over the next thirty minutes was perhaps the most exhilarating thirty minutes of Keith's life. Spraying bear repellant into the eyes of Nazis, punching and kicking those who got in his way, and at one point holding down a man wearing a Benjamin King t-shirt and spitting in his face caused an adrenaline rush within Keith, the likes of which he'd never experienced. He was finally making a difference! He had a cause, and he was finally doing something about it!

That had been almost three weeks ago, and it had only been the beginning. Keith found himself spending more and more time with Sparky and his group, learning that they were just one of many so-called Antifa cells that were very loosely organized and operating around Michigan and across the country. Each mission they went on seemed to get a bit bolder.

This past week, Sparky had invited Keith to go on what he said was a top-secret mission, one where they'd be committing felonies. Keith was all in.

Four of them met at 10 p.m. at the Willow Run Airport in Ypsilanti. They boarded a Cessna 208 eight-seat single-engine airplane piloted by an unknown man and flew northwest. Keith watched the lights below as they flew over Lansing, then Grand Rapids, and then the black darkness of Lake Michigan. They landed at a small runway several miles west of a large lake just under two hours after takeoff.

Keith had learned not to ask questions but had been told they were at an airfield outside Appleton, Wisconsin. Keith had never even heard of Appleton and had absolutely no clue why they were flying into this deserted airfield in the middle of the night. Sparky grabbed a duffel bag from the plane, and the four of them piled into a beat-up SUV that reeked of gasoline and was waiting for them at the end of the airstrip. Sparky drove and seemed to know exactly where he was going. Keith noticed the sign as they exited the airfield —Brennand Airport.

It all meant nothing to him until Sparky started briefing them as he drove through the dark night, the SUV's aged yellowing headlights barely illuminating the road.

"The fucking John Birch Society!" Sparky had exclaimed. "We are going to fuck them up."

"Who's the John Birch Society?" One of the other cell members asked.

"A bunch of goddamn Republican Nazi white supremacists, that's who," Sparky answered. "They're all over the country— mostly old white men who think we're still fighting communism. They hate anything liberal, and it's time we showed them who really runs America."

"Why Appleton, Wisconsin?" Keith asked, breaking his rule about not asking questions.

"Their headquarters is here. It's just a symbolic building, but it will get some coverage for our cause."

Ten minutes later, they drove through the small city of Appleton and were heading north on Westhill Boulevard.

"I'm not going to slow down," Sparky said. "But the building is coming up on the right. It's a one-story brick building; you'll see the name on the side."

They drove past the national headquarters of the John Birch Society, and Sparky continued for another block, turning right and driving past a Sam's Club, then turning right again before pulling into a narrow lane between rows of warehouses. He parked and shut off the lights.

"Okay, listen up," Sparky ordered. "Me, Warlock, and Drifter are going to break into the rear of the building. There's gas cans and lighter fluid in the back. We want to be in and out in less than two minutes. I have bolt cutters and a sledgehammer in the bag. We'll cut the cable and telephone lines and hope it kills the alarm, but in any case, we'll be out in two minutes. Gilligan, your job is to go out front. Did you see that big American flag? Your job is to lower it, flip it upside down, then raise it back up again. These fucking fascists will lose their goddamn minds when they see that. Everybody got it? We just need to go through those bushes in front of us, then turn left and follow the grass about a hundred yards down to the back of the building. I'll throw the match to light it on fire; then everyone beats feet back to this vehicle. We'll be flying home in thirty minutes. Okay, let's do this!"

"No Pasaran!" Warlock had yelled. Keith had learned this was one of Antifa's trademark phrases—meaning "they shall not pass." It stemmed from a battle cry in the fight against the fascists during the Spanish Civil War in the 1930s.

Minutes later, slightly winded, Keith found himself kneeling at the side of the one-story brick headquarters of the John Birch Society. Hoodie pulled tight and wearing gloves and a surgical mask, Keith looked up and down Westhill Boulevard to make sure no cars were coming. It was midnight, and the street was clear. Behind him, he heard the clear sound of glass breaking and knew it was time to get moving.

He wasn't sure he'd ever lowered a flag before, but when he got to the flagpole, he realized it was pretty simple. Undoing the thin halyard wound around a brass cleat, Keith figured out which end to pull and began lowering the flag. Once he had it on the ground, he unhooked it from where it was attached to the halyard and flipped it upside down.

As he stood atop the large flag bunched on the grass, he had a quick flash to second grade, where his class had been taught never to allow the flag to touch the ground. He wondered what his mom and dad would think if they saw him now—actually, he didn't need to wonder. He knew they'd be severely disappointed in him—not in his cause, but in his actions. Mentally shoving this aside, Keith refastened the flag with the stripes above the stars and began hoisting it back up to the top. He felt the rope hit the end in seconds and quickly tied it off to the cleat.

As he ran back to the rear of the John Birch building, Keith saw Sparky coming out of an open door, the window panes smashed. "Run," Sparky said as he lit a rag with his lighter and tossed it into the open doorway. Keith noticed his two other compatriots running north along the narrow grass strip behind the buildings and sprinted after them.

The four young men laughed hysterically, high on adrenaline, as they heard numerous sirens wailing in the distance. Sparky drove north along a circuitous route, and the ride back to the airfield took over thirty minutes. Smiles never left their faces the entire ride. They boarded the waiting Cessna for the return trip, with the four sleeping most of the way back to Ypsilanti.

That had been Monday night, just four days ago. Keith's wife, Hanna, continued to work nights as a dispatcher for the Detroit Police Department, so he'd been able to engage in Antifa without her knowledge. He knew he had to tell her at some point, but he wasn't sure of her reaction.

Keith woke up Tuesday to a text from Sparky inviting him on an overnight trip. "Important training," the message had said. Keith knew he'd be able to get away as Hanna was working a double shift again that evening, so he met Sparky as instructed. Tuesday and Wednesday had been days he'd never forget.

It was the same four cell members as the trip to Appleton, and Sparky had driven them an hour north of Detroit to a rural farm somewhere near the small town of Capac. There, they'd been introduced to a woman wearing a black balaclava that covered her entire face with the exception of her deep brown eyes. J, as the woman was introduced, was wearing cargo pants and a tight Under Armor long-sleeved shirt that accentuated the definition of her muscular upper body—Keith thought she was the fittest woman he'd ever met. Over the next thirty-six hours, he'd come to believe she was also the most capable woman he'd ever met.

They spent the first day familiarizing themselves with the Glock 19 pistol and the AR-15 rifle. Keith had only fired a pistol once and never a rifle other than a pellet gun. After hundreds and hundreds of rounds were fired through both weapons, Keith realized two things. First, he wasn't a very good shot—although he wasn't as bad as Warlock. Second, he absolutely loved shooting guns! The feeling of power and invincibility was indescribable.

On Tuesday night, J had focused the training more on tactics. She taught them how to set up an ambush, assault a position, and clear a room. They practiced well into the night, not using bullets until J seemed somewhat satisfied that the four of them could work as a team.

Divided We Stand

After getting just a few hours of sleep, two vans and an SUV arrived at the farm on Wednesday morning. J had given each of the four of them a navy blue balaclava to put on. Interestingly, the occupants of each vehicle exited while wearing similar full-face balaclavas, albeit in different colors. The six people from one van wore burgundy, while those from the other van wore dark green. The four men in the SUV wore black balaclavas, identical to what J wore.

"Okay, everyone, gather round," J had ordered. Everyone assembled around her, with the exception of the four men in black, who stood together a short distance behind J. "You're assembled here today because you share a single cause, and it's now time to band together to strike a blow upon our enemies."

J looked around at the sixteen assembled Antifa cell members. "Your three cells are going to conduct a joint mission, but for operational security, it's important to keep your identities hidden. You can use your monikers with each other, but your cells will be referred to by the color of your balaclava: red, green, blue. Those four gentlemen behind me? You can call them Aries. They helped train some of you, but they will be leading this mission."

J briefed all of them for the next thirty minutes on their upcoming mission. They then spent the next eight hours rehearsing it until everyone was comfortable that they would succeed. Tired and sore, Keith was incredibly proud of himself and eager to conduct the mission scheduled for Saturday evening. He understood how soldiers must have felt on the eve of a big battle.

Now, sitting in his apartment living room on Friday morning and watching the coverage of the burning mosque, Keith was sick to his stomach at the innocent lives that had been taken so unnecessarily by these ignorant fascists. Who would attack innocent people worshipping? They weren't harming anyone, and according to the newscaster, there were at least seven women and children who had been killed in the Dearborn mosque bombing. Keith looked forward to tomorrow evening when he would finally be able to strike a meaningful blow against the fascist machine.

No more disrupting protests. This was going to be a real target.

Keith's thumb kept flicking through short TikTok and Instagram video clips on his phone, each one making him even more angry. He loved the videos of people like himself, young Americans standing up for what they thought was right. He also couldn't believe how ignorant some people could be—banning the FBI? Governors telling the President what to do? Attacking innocent people new to this country?

As he kept absorbing the social media content, his anger increased, and he thought, when will it end? Only when we make it end. No Pasaren! They shall not pass!

53

Washington, D.C

Friday, April 12

THE SITUATION ROOM WAS CROWDED. In addition to the members of Working Group Delta, the conference room included the National Security Advisor, Secretary of Homeland Security, Secretary of Defense, Chairman of the Joint Chiefs, several deputies, and general officers.

The Vice President sat at the head of the conference table, chairing the meeting, with the President's Chief of Staff, John Reynolds, to her left and the others arrayed around the table. Additional chairs had been brought in, but everyone seemed able to squeeze around the table, barely.

The President was absent and had been seen less frequently over the past few weeks. He'd formally authorized the Vice President in writing to respond to and resolve the crisis erupting across the country through expanded powers granted to Working Group Delta. Sharyn was privy to the private conversations with the Vice President and Chief of Staff, in which this Presidential authorization was a politically viable solution that allowed them to get things done without having to use the 25th Amendment and declare President Fulton unfit. The plan was still to have President Fulton run for reelection, as this was deemed the most likely path for everyone in the administration to keep their job.

The Republicans had yet to declare a replacement nominee for Benjamin King, but Sharyn suspected it would be Florida Governor Vince Marino. Vice President Moore had very low approval ratings nationally, especially in the Red states, and the fear was that no one in the current administration could win against a Republican nominee with the support of all the Red states. Bringing in a Democratic outsider, like the governor of California, or possibly a liberal Senator, would mean that the entire Cabinet and the Vice President would be replaced.

Working Group Delta now met daily, but this meeting had been moved to the Situation Room in response to the attack on the mosque in Dearborn earlier that morning. The images were upsetting to everyone, and the Vice President felt a decisive move was vital. Sharyn had attempted to temper the Vice President's anger but was afraid she hadn't been successful.

"Thank you all for coming. I know we weren't scheduled to meet until later this afternoon, but given this morning's events, I wanted us to meet as soon as possible. I'll be blunt. What we are currently doing is not working. Chaos and violence continue to increase across the country, and all indications are that we are moving ever closer to a civil war.

"I see that Professor Nathan Greene has gotten himself back on the front page of the New York Times. That guy gets better press coverage than the President!" She said jokingly to a few wary smiles around the table. "He should probably be in a federal jail cell after killing two FBI agents, but that's a problem for another day. The Times article does quote him as making some very profound statements regarding external intervention in our domestic issues—perhaps some entity actually creating this chaos across America by, quote, shaking the jar, unquote. Do we have any evidence to the validity of this, Barry?"

"No, Madame Vice President," answered FBI Director Barry

Divided We Stand

Tracy. "At the current time, while we know foreign agents were involved in the March 21st attacks, we don't have any proof that any external group or country is involved in the recent violent events happening all around the country."

"Okay, keep working that angle," said VP Moore. "But I agree. This is most likely a conservative conspiracy with some or all of the Republican governors. They have too much to gain; all they've done is encourage the chaos, not prevent it.

"That said, we need to take some affirmative, concrete steps to prevent this nation from sliding into civil war. Secretary Melendez, what is the update from the southern border? I've seen various reports, both from your office and on television, but I'd like to hear the latest from you."

Marcellus Melendez, Secretary of Homeland Security, looked down at the sheaf of papers he had laid out before him. "Illegal border crossings are down eighty percent in the last ten days. Instead of the more than 10,000 undocumented immigrants we have been averaging over the last year, we have seen this number dwindle to less than 2,000. Almost all of these are along the Arizona and California borders, as crossings into Texas have decreased almost to zero."

"And is there an official estimate as to the reason for this decrease, Mr. Melendez? I've seen the news articles, but I'd like to hear it directly from you."

"Yes, ma'am. I spoke with the Senior Official Performing the Duties of the Commissioner of Customs and Border Protection, and he told—."

"Wait," interrupted the Vice President. "I'm sorry to interrupt, Marcellus, but what kind of title is the Senior Official Performing the Duties of the Commissioner? Is that like the *acting* commissioner?"

"Yes, ma'am, that's exactly correct."

"Then why the long title?"

"Madame Vice President, we received a memo from the Presidential Personnel Office last year stating that this was the correct title, as Tim Mason has been in this interim position for over two years."

"Serena, if I may," said John Reynolds. "This is something the President has been working with Congress on. We can discuss it offline if you'd like."

"Very well," sighed the Vice President, not wanting to derail her meeting any further. "Please continue, Marcellus."

"Ma'am, cutting to the chase, the reason behind the severe drop in border crossings into Texas is a direct result of the engagement orders issued by the Governor of Texas to his National Guard troops arrayed along the border."

"You mean his shoot-to-kill order?"

"That's what the media is calling it, yes, ma'am. He's ordered his Guard commanders to stop any incursions into Texas that are not at an official crossing point. His orders authorize the use of deadly force to protect the sovereignty of the Republic of Texas, and there have been several incidents where Guardsmen have fired upon groups of people attempting to enter Texas from Mexico."

"With more than thirty people killed or wounded, is that right?"

"Yes, ma'am. I believe the official numbers as we know them to be sixteen immigrants killed and twenty-one wounded and requiring hospitalization."

"All the immigrants were unarmed?"

"Yes, ma'am, as far as we know. The Mexican government has lodged an official protest with the United Nations. We believe that the drug cartels are continuing to move illegal drugs across the border, but the mass migration of immigrants into Texas has virtually ceased. People are afraid that they will be shot. The recent attack on the CBP bus transporting asylum seekers from the border up to our detention facility in Dilley—that too has had a significant impact. Asylum seekers don't trust that they will be protected."

The Vice President just shook her head. "It's a sad day when people who just want to come to America fear for their lives. Okay," said the Vice President, switching gears. "General Vine, I know you disagreed with President Fulton on the use of military forces, even under the emergency powers of the Insurrection Act. It's my recollection and hope that this was more of a philosophical disagreement over a hypothetical situation.

"At ten o'clock this morning, President Fulton signed an executive order invoking Section 253 of the Insurrection Act of 1807. In part, this section allows the president to deploy troops to suppress *any insurrection, domestic violence, unlawful combination, or conspiracy* in a state that *opposes or obstructs the execution of the laws of the United States or impedes the course of justice under those laws.* The legality of this power is not in question.

"While I don't think it's yet necessary or prudent to place active-duty troops in positions where they may exacerbate the situation in many of these hotbed areas, I do think it's critical that we reposition forces so as to be best able to respond should the situation require."

Vice President Moore pulled a sheet of paper from a folder in front of her. "I am ordering the immediate repositioning of the 1st Ranger Battalion from Hunter Army Airfield, Georgia, to Fort Devens in Massachusetts. I am also ordering the repositioning of the 75th Ranger Regiment Headquarters, the 3rd Ranger Battalion, and the Special Troops Battalion to the Great Lakes Naval Training Center north of Chicago, Illinois. These are some of our most capable and responsive units, and we need them to be outside the geographic boundaries of these Red state governors. I'm also issuing the Secretary of Defense a warning order to be prepared to deploy the Second Marine Expeditionary Force to Fort Dix, New Jersey, and the First Marine Expeditionary Force to Las Vegas, Nevada."

Secretary of Defense Boyd and General Vine shared a knowing look.

"Madame Vice President," said Jack Vine in his natural booming voice. "In my capacity as Chairman, I am the senior military advisor to the Commander in Chief. I am informing you that the United States military should not be used in any capacity to resolve the current tensions, crises, and chaos that are occurring throughout the country. Our primary goal, as has been for the last hundred years, is to provide a deterrent to America's foreign enemies and to deploy internationally in response to external threats to our country. I am prepared to tender my resignation to President

Fulton if my counsel is no longer desired, but I urge you in the strongest possible terms not to order the deployment of U.S. troops inside the United States."

"I understand your position, General Vine. I spoke with the Vice Chairman, Admiral Bischoff, at the last meeting at which you were not present, and he seemed more open to using our active-duty forces domestically."

"With all due respect," countered General Vine. "Admiral Bischoff has spent his entire career in the Navy. The Navy and the Air Force have nothing to do with the Insurrection Act—unless you're planning to bomb American cities or surround Florida's coast with battleships. What you're talking about, ma'am, is deploying soldiers and Marines to handle politically sensitive situations that they aren't organized or trained to handle. Our military is trained to kill bad guys, pure and simple. The surest way to escalate the current situation into a full-blown civil war is to introduce our active-duty forces into the equation."

General Vine looked at all of the faces around the table. "Madame Vice President, you have 150,000 federal law enforcement officers at your disposal. They are trained and have the authority to deal with the situations we are facing in cities across the country. Red state governors have prohibited these federal agents from doing their jobs, but how do you think they will react to Army Rangers or a battalion of Marines attempting to take over parts of their states?

"The Red states have a significant National Guard capability, and they've begun joint operations to allocate resources across different states. My subordinate commanders—and I've talked to most of the Brigade commanders and above throughout the Army and Marine Corps—unanimously agree that they should not be deployed domestically. The fear of widespread mutiny and desertion is very real, and the consequences of that are ones that we cannot put back in the bottle."

Serena Moore was not used to people not obeying her orders. Her initial reaction was to accept General Vine's resignation and move forward with her plan after appointing the Vice Chairman to fill General Vine's position. She looked at the Secretary of Defense for support. After all, the Chairman technically worked for him.

Seeing her looking at him, Secretary of Defense Melvin Boyd spoke first. "Madame Vice President, I, too, have met with many of the leaders at the Pentagon. There is a clear consensus that involving the military in this domestic political squabble would have disastrous consequences for the nation. Let the Defense Department focus on deterring external threats while the President and the governors sort out this mess. That is my strongest recommendation. And similar to General Vine, I'm prepared to tender my resignation to the President should my advice no longer be desired."

Sharyn watched her boss for a reaction. She knew the Vice President absolutely hated losing an argument or being shown up in public. However, at this level of politics, it was critical to know when one was holding a losing hand of cards, especially if one wanted to spend four more years in the White House. Thankfully, Sharyn could tell by the Vice President's expression that she was not about to go nuclear.

"Okay, gentlemen," said the Vice President calmly. "I disagree with you, as I think we are appeasing these power-hungry governors. However, I recognize that you are the experts, and I will accept your recommendation until I have a chance to speak with President Fulton again. Given that, we need solutions. Now." She looked around the table. "Let's hear some. What are our biggest problems, and what are their solutions?"

54

Cromwell Island, Montana

Friday, April 12

"CHAMPAGNE SEEMS TO BE IN ORDER," said Alex magnanimously. "You've done a truly remarkable job, Orlean. Truly remarkable."

"Thanks, Alex. That means a lot," said Orlean Brumback, talking loudly so he would be heard through the speakers of his encrypted iPhone. "It was a team effort, though. We absolutely could not have done any of this without your vision and resources."

Alex was sitting in his office on Cromwell Island. The snow had finally melted except in the mountains, and the land surrounding the lake was sprouting green with spring bloom. It was a beautiful April day, and Alex could see several boats out fishing on Flathead Lake. The views across Wild Horse Island at this time of year were truly spectacular, and Alex loved just staring out at the browns and greens of the ponderosa pines and the rugged shoreline across the bay.

"The reconvening of the Nevada Legislature and the Minnesota Legislature's narrow vote this morning approving the demand for a

Constitutional Convention gave us the 34th state approval. That's the requisite two-thirds majority we needed and will force Congress to call a Constitutional Convention."

"Yes," said Orlean. "This is all virgin territory as we've never had a Constitutional Convention after the very first one in 1787. Now, having Republican control of both houses of Congress gives us the ability to get some things done, and with the secure knowledge that the Supreme Court will favor our agenda, I don't think there are any more obstacles to a July 4th start to the Constitutional Convention in Omaha."

"Good to hear, good to hear," said Alex. "It's about time to initiate Phase 3. Do you have everything in place?"

"Yes, of course," replied Orlean. "Bunker Hill Media has been preparing this for months, and over the last two weeks, I've spent almost every day visiting and speaking with Red state governors to make sure they're on board. The November election is the real prize in all this. Everything else is a distraction."

"Exactly," replied Alex. Phase 3 was the culmination of the grand strategy Alex had put together over the last few years, and he felt confident that all the moving pieces were positioned to begin executing. This phase had four key components.

First, it was imperative to keep escalating the violent protests and attacks across the country. This did very little to further Alex's cause, but it did keep the federal government focused on these issues rather than trying to figure out Alex's real plan.

Second, they would initiate a massive Red-to-Blue campaign focused on tilting the partisan balance of eight key states. Alex had divided these states into three separate battleground campaigns: the Western campaign, including Arizona, Nevada, and New Mexico; the Mid-Atlantic campaign of Pennsylvania and Delaware; and the New England campaign of Maine, New Hampshire, and Vermont. Other states, such as Georgia and Wisconsin, would also receive an influx of registered Republican voters, but Alex did not anticipate these as being true battleground states as these state legislatures were firmly under Republican control.

The Red-to-Blue initiative was straightforward, although

required a tremendous amount of foresight and resources. Simply stated, Bunker Hill Media would blanket targeted conservative populations, especially residents of predominantly Blue states, and incentivize them to move to these battleground states. For example, hardscrabble Republicans in California and Oregon would be offered payments, jobs, and housing to move to Reno, Nevada. Similar initiatives would be unveiled for Texans to move to New Mexico and staunch Republicans from southern states to relocate to Delaware, Vermont, or Maine.

Each of these states required less than one hundred thousand new Republicans to change the partisan majority to Republican, and in four of these states, the margin was less than thirty thousand. This seemed like a lot, but Alex had virtually unlimited resources bankrolling his grand strategy, and he had already laid an extensive foundation for these initiatives. Local councilmen had been bribed; numerous trailer parks had been established or purchased, and secret arrangements had been made with RV dealerships to provide Red-to-Blue volunteers with sweetheart deals with no up-front payments until after the 2024 elections. This would basically allow people to move for free and, in some cases, even to be paid.

The third component of Phase 3 was the intimidation of existing registered Democrats within these battleground states. Both the carrot and the stick would be used to accomplish this task. Democrats would find an easy pathway for new jobs, affordable housing, and some under-the-table cash payments to leave the state, while at the same time, those who insisted on staying would face gangs of angry, violent white supremacists or other ultra-conservative groups that made staying in their home states difficult and dangerous.

Alex knew that these initiatives would be like pushing a car down a gentle hill. Moving the stationary car would take maximum effort, but once it was rolling, it would quickly gather steam and require almost no energy to keep the momentum.

The last component was arguably the most important, but it was also the easiest when the other three components had been put in place. Alex's grand strategy focused on dominating the November

Divided We Stand

elections with candidates who were beholden to him, whether they knew it or not. This last component of the plan consisted of identifying and bankrolling local, state, and federal candidates, and the ultimate candidates would be the Republican nominees for President and Vice President of the United States.

"What is everyone saying about replacing Benjamin King?" Alex asked Orlean over the encrypted phone. "Are there any challengers to Marino?"

"Not really," said Orlean. "I'm a little concerned about the governors from Virginia and Tennessee—they both see themselves in the White House—but I think they realize this is not their time."

"Good," said Alex. "And Vince? I know he wants it, but do you think we can be assured he'll listen to us?"

"He's a bit hard-headed, but ultimately, his desire to be President makes him pretty pliable. We want to have a couple more frank discussions with him, but he understands that I am pulling all the strings now that the King is dead, pun intended."

"Good. That's exactly what we need. I'll text you later tonight, and we can set up a sit-down with Vince in the next few days. Get ready for Phase 3. I have to review a few items, but I think we can start the big push as soon as next week."

"I love it when a plan comes together," said Orlean.

The two men said their goodbyes, and Alex ended the call. He pressed a button on his desk, and fifteen seconds later, the door to his office opened, and Sergei poked his head in.

"Yes, sir? How can I be of service?"

"Sergei, please send in Wais and Jasmine and three glasses of champagne."

"Yes, sir. One moment, please."

In less than a minute, Wais and Jasmine entered the study and took seats across the desk from Alex. Just as the two settled into their chairs, Sergei entered while balancing three delicate champagne flutes filled with bubbling pale gold liquid. Without being told, Sergei served a glass to each of them before departing silently from the room.

"Congratulations are in order," said Alex, lifting his glass in a toast. "The thirty-fourth state demanded a Constitutional Convention under Article V, so that is now on the agenda for July 4th. We are celebrating a very successful Phase 2 and toasting the start of Phase 3."

The three raised their glasses, and each put the glass to their lips. Jasmine didn't really enjoy champagne, and Wais almost never drank alcohol. Alex noticed that both of their glasses were still mostly full but did not comment. It wasn't that he respected their choices. It was more that this reinforced his belief that subordinates did what their superiors told them to do. Alex was fully aware that neither of his lieutenants drank alcohol, but this was another small test of their commitment to comply with his directives. As usual, they both passed without even knowing.

"Jasmine, how are things progressing in Michigan?"

"Excellent," she replied. "Team Aries is on the ground and linked with all the cells on both sides. They're planning an Antifa raid tomorrow night in Indiana with three cells and another one on Monday with the Three Percenters. I'm heading back in the morning to supervise the first raid."

"Good, good," said Alex. "And you, Wais? Still heading to New Mexico?"

"Yes, Albequerque tonight, then over to PA tomorrow to give the final mission orders to Team Cancer before flying up to New Hampshire. There's a lot of work still to be done in northern New England."

"You've both done an outstanding job so far, but the next six months will decide the future of the United States for a very long time. I need you both to keep to the plan, but also to stay flexible. Things may happen that I need your specific skills. Honestly, this has all gone just a little too smoothly."

55

Lake Station, Indiana

Saturday, April 13

LIEUTENANT BUTCH KREMER sat on his green army cot on the free-throw line of the black and red ancient wooden floor of the Gary Armory in Gary, Indiana. This was his seventh day in Gary, and he was bored out of his mind.

Butch was not in Gary as the leader of the Sarasota County SWAT team. He was here in his reserve capacity as a master sergeant in the Florida National Guard. Upon leaving the Navy SEALs years ago and returning to Sarasota to become a deputy sheriff, his old boss had convinced him to take a lateral transfer into the Florida National Guard. Butch's six years on active duty would continue to accrue, and the Sheriff's Office was extremely supportive of members of the Guard.

Never being one to do anything half-assed, Butch transferred and immediately volunteered to become a member of the 20th Special Forces Group, whose 3rd Battalion's Charlie Company was headquartered in Wauchula, Florida, less than an hour from Sarasota. Butch completed Special Forces Assessment and Selection his first summer in the Florida Guard and then attended the year-long Q-Course. Now, he was the Team Sergeant for Operational Detachment Alpha 292, which had been activated by Governor Marino two weeks ago.

After just under a week of training up at Camp Starke in central Florida, Butch's team was deployed to Gary, Indiana, with orders to support the highway interdiction and protection effort along interstate highways I-65, I-90, and I-94. Normally, an A-team consists of twelve Special Forces soldiers, led by a Captain, with a Warrant Officer or Master Sergeant as second-in-command. Due to staffing shortages and conflicts in mobilization, Butch found himself the team leader with eight additional members in his team.

Butch and ODA 292 had been assigned as the Quick Reaction Force in support of the 2nd Battalion, 151st Infantry Regiment, members of the Indiana National Guard based in South Bend. The battalion's mission was to establish checkpoints on the three interstate highways and to monitor all traffic coming from the neighboring state of Illinois. Orders had been issued to turn around anyone with an Illinois driver's license unless they also had a valid U.S. passport for all occupants of the vehicle.

Butch thought this was a bit overkill, but who was he to judge the orders of his superior officers. There was plenty in Iraq with the SEALs that he'd disagreed with. *Theirs not to reason why, theirs but to do or die.*

Being the battalion's QRF—Quick Reaction Force—sounded exciting, for it was their mission to respond by helicopter to any situation requiring immediate reinforcement. The men of his ODA were fully kitted out with combat loads, and they'd rehearsed moving to the UH-60 Blackhawk helicopter on the helipad outside and getting airborne in less than two minutes.

The reality was that Butch and his team sat on their cots in the armory's gymnasium. Some of his men read books, some watched the small television in the corner, and some watched videos on their phones.

The bell sounded, jarring Butch out of his daydream, and for a second, he thought he was back in high school. The armory had a bell that was just like the bell used in schools to signal the end of a period. This sound meant trouble—and that Butch's QRF was needed.

Butch's team immediately jumped up and started putting on their armor-plated vests and helmets before grabbing their weapons. Butch noticed the two pilots and crew chiefs already running out of the armory's back door, beyond which was parked their UH-60 Blackhawk helicopter. A staff captain from the 2/151st came rushing in from the battalion Tactical Operations Center, located elsewhere in the building.

"Sergeant Kremer!" The Captain shouted as Butch was fastening his helmet, his heavy chest rig with ceramic plates already cinched to his upper body. "This is not a drill! Checkpoint Saturn is under attack, and we have reports of multiple casualties. Wheels up as soon as you can. It's a four-minute flight."

"Roger, sir," said Butch, grabbing the piece of paper the battle captain was holding out for him. "These the call signs?"

"Correct, Sergeant. It's Bravo Company's checkpoint, so the commander is Bulldog 6."

"Roger," said Butch, already walking to the back door and following his guys. "I'll check in with the TOC once we're airborne."

"Good luck! And Godspeed!" said the Captain.

Godspeed? Thought Butch as he jogged out to the Blackhawk, the whine of its engine getting louder as its four overhead rotor blades began to turn. *I wonder how long that Captain was waiting to say Godspeed to someone? Jesus, these guys watch too many movies.*

The thumping of the speeding rotors was palpable. They'd removed the helicopter's seats, and the nine men of ODA 292 piled in on the floor, the two crew chiefs serving as door gunners from their seats on each side of the aircraft immediately behind the pilots. Butch had always loved this moment—the feel of the rotors thumping through your body, the dump of adrenaline hitting your bloodstream, and the look on everyone's face witnessed only by those about to experience imminent combat. It was part excitement, part fear, part anticipation, and part hoping you would perform well for your team.

Butch grabbed the radio headset the crew chief held out for him and checked in with the pilots. The decision had previously been made to fly with the doors closed, as they could be slid open immediately before landing. Butch gave the pilots the all-clear, and he felt the nose of the bird tilt forward and accelerate.

In seconds Butch watched the buildings flash by underneath. They were over I-65, heading northeast toward Checkpoint Saturn, which Butch knew was located at the point where I-90 and I-94 crossed over each other. It was a natural chokepoint, and it allowed Bravo Company to control traffic on two major routes that left the Chicago area.

"Bulldog Six, this is Panther Two-Six," Butch said into the radio mic wound into his helmet. This was the ground radio net, not the headset he used to speak with the pilots.

"Panther, this is Bulldog Six, what's your ETA? We're taking heavy fire." Butch could hear sustained bursts of automatic rifle fire in the background as the company commander for Bravo Company answered him.

"Four minutes, Bulldog Six. Where do you want us to land? Gimme a sitrep on the enemy situation."

"LZ is Ade Plaza. We're taking fire from McCutcheon Plaza. Estimate twelve to fifteen tangos, no heavy weapons. They got the drop on us from behind, but we have at least some of them pinned down. If you land at Ade, we'll have them in a crossfire, as my men are on the overpass."

"Roger, two mikes outs," said Butch, his voice calm. *Mikes* were military shorthand for minutes.

Butch held up his two fingers to his men, signaling two minutes. He then keyed his radio handset for the squad network, which all eight of his soldiers were monitoring. "Listen up, guys—twelve-to-fifteen tangos, small arms only. We're coming into LZ Ade, and the enemy is on LZ McCutcheon. This will be a hot LZ. I say, again, hot LZ. Let's get to cover, and then we'll assault through by fire team, on my command."

Everyone nodded. They'd rehearsed this several times, and each man had poured over aerial imagery of all six battalion checkpoints and the various landing zones—or LZs—where the QRF might be called to land.

The crew chiefs held up their hands, thumb and forefinger held an inch apart. "Thirty Seconds!" everyone yelled. Two of Butch's men slid open the doors, and looking out, Butch saw they were flying just over the tops of houses and trees. A small pond flashed beneath them, and Butch felt the Blackhawk brake sharply, its nose tilting upward twenty degrees while the aircraft descended rapidly.

The helicopter landed hard, and its rubber wheels did little to cushion the impact. Barely noticing it, Butch's men piled out both doors and laid flat on the ground. The bird took off less than three seconds from the time the wheels hit the ground.

The rhythmic bass of the helicopter's rotors was immediately replaced by the sharp cracks of rifle fire, followed by the deep boom of a .50-caliber machine gun blasting away in six-to-nine-round bursts. The helicopter had dropped Butch's A-team in front of the George Ade highway travel plaza along I-90, the interstate highway that ran from Boston to Seattle. Immediately to his front were the eastbound lanes, then the westbound lanes, and finally, the McCutcheon Travel Plaza on the far side of the highway. It was open ground, with a grassy median between the two highways, but there was plenty of cover for his men to assault forward.

Butch could see flashes of gunfire coming from the backside of the small building in the McCutcheon Travel Plaza, which appeared to be a 7-Eleven store just over a hundred yards away. Butch was sure the tangos had seen the helicopter landing, but as of yet, no enemy fire had been directed toward his team.

"Listen up," Butch yelled, not bothering with the radio. "I want Alpha team to bound into the median and take up a position in that swale. Once you can cover us, Bravo team, we're going to bound all the way to the right side of the building. Those two Amazon trucks? That's where we're headed. Alpha, if anyone starts shooting, light 'em up, but no need to give our position away until they see us."

Everyone nodded or said, "Got it." Butch's two team leaders,

Staff Sergeant Brody and Staff Sergeant Zamarripa—otherwise known as Brody and Z—readied their teams. In seconds, Brody and his three men were sprinting into the median while Z's team covered them.

Still no shots heading their way.

"Bulldog Six, this is Panther Two-Six," said Butch.

"Go ahead, Panther Two-Six," said the Bravo company commander.

"We're assaulting the travel plaza now. My first element is in the median, and my second is heading for the trucks in the parking lot. We'll pop smoke when we get there. You make sure your guys shift fire to north of the building. We will not go north of the building."

"Good copy. Shift to north of the building on your smoke."

Butch watched Z's team start running, and he decided he'd go with them all the way to the eighteen-wheelers. This would give him a better vantage point to see what they were up against.

Sixty yards into the hundred-yard dash, Butch realized he was too old for this shit. He kept himself in peak condition, but at forty-two, he now understood that combat was a young man's game. *Goddamn!* He thought, pretty winded by the time he slid up behind one of the large tires on the Amazon trailer.

They could hear sustained rifle fire coming from the far side of the building. It sounded like 5.56 rounds, so probably from an AR-15 or M4, and Butch estimated five or six rifles were firing. It was difficult to tell for sure without seeing.

Whack! Whack! Whack!

Three rounds ricocheted off the trailer undercarriage directly in front of Butch.

It appears the tangos knew the QRF had arrived.

Sergeant Brody's fire team immediately opened fire, and Butch could see they were directing well-aimed shots into the entrance doorway of the travel plaza. Butch could now hear sustained bursts of fire coming from inside the travel plaza.

Holy shit! Butch thought. *There's fucking civilians in there.* He looked around, noticing a dozen cars and probably two dozen tractor-trailer trucks parked throughout the parking lot.

Divided We Stand

"Sergeant Z!" Butch yelled to his team leader about ten yards down behind the tires of another trailer. "They're killing civilians. We need to stack up on the door and hit it. Now! Go!!!" Butch pulled a smoke grenade from a pouch on his vest and tossed it toward the front doorway of the 7-Eleven, both as a signal to Bravo company but also to help mask the movement of Z's team.

Without a word, Z's fire team began moving forward, attempting to use the cover of the trucks and trailers to get as close as possible to the door.

"Brody!" Butch said into the radio. "They're killing civilians. Lay down a base of fire on the front door, and Z's team will stack up on the right. As soon as we enter, sprint like hell and come in the same door behind us."

Butch didn't bother waiting for a reply and sprinted after Z's fire team, the four men who were already standing alongside the brick wall tucked back from the glass doorway at the front of the building.

Z's team positioned themselves in the classic stack formation, each man covering a different arc to ensure no enemy could approach them undetected. Z was the designated breacher, and Sergeant Aidan Rogers—callsign Buck—had his left hand on Z's shoulder, telling him by squeeze when the stack was ready.

Butch fell in at the rear, becoming the fifth man in the stack.

Z threw a flash-bang grenade through the open door of the 7-Eleven. The team readied itself. The brilliant flash accompanied by the 170-decibel bang of the grenade had a debilitating effect on anyone inside the building. Z surged around the corner as soon as it detonated, and the entire stack followed him inside.

Carnage. That was the only word Butch could think of as his eyes searched the open floor plan of the store and cafeteria area for tangos. Three men, each wearing a red balaclava over their face with AR-15s slung across their chests, stood immobilized near the entrance—evidently stunned by the flash-bang grenade. Z and Buck fired multiple single shots into each of the tangos, dropping them to the floor.

The two Green Berets in front of Butch peeled off to the left to clear the corridor leading in that direction while Z and Buck continued moving into the main part of the store, dashing between the aisles to clear them of tangos. Butch looked to his right and saw another man in a red balaclava kneeling behind a table and taking aim at Z facing the other way. Without thinking, Butch raised his M4, placed the red circle of his EOTech holographic sight on the chest of the man, and pulled the trigger twice. The man fell to the ground, and Butch zeroed in on the red fabric of his balaclava, putting another two rounds directly into the tango's head.

"Clear!"

"Clear!"

Butch heard his two team members who had rushed down the corridor yell that the bathrooms and kitchen area were clear. *What a bloodbath,* Butch thought, his mind racing. In the aftermath of the gunfire, Butch could now hear the sobbing and cries of some of the wounded patrons in the store.

"Brody, secure the front of the building," Butch said into his radio. "Send Doc in here. Hurry."

Butch looked up to see Z's team disarming the tangos and ensuring they were dead. "Z, get two guys covering the back door. Don't go outside, but make sure no one gets in. Doc is on his way in to deal with the wounded."

"Roger that," said Z.

"Bulldog Six, this is Panther Two-Six. Building secure. What's the status behind the building?"

"Panther, we have multiple attackers down in the parking lot. It looks like most of them just bugged out through the woods to the north. I've sent two squads in up-armored Humvees to try to cut them off on Melton Road, but we think they're gone. One gunner reported seeing them loading into SUVs back off Clem Road behind the parking lot."

"Okay, Bulldog Six. I need you to have your men hold their fire. We are going to clear the parking lot. CEASE fire!"

"Affirmative, Panther Two-Six. We have ceased fire."

"I need you to send your company medic down here; we have multiple civilian casualties. At least fifteen, maybe more."

"Ah, Panther, our medic is busy with our own wounded at the

Divided We Stand

moment. We have multiple KIA. I've called Battalion and requested a medevac."

"Break. Break. Panther Two-Six, this is Nighthawk Six." Nighthawk Six was the battalion commander, who typically did not monitor this company radio frequency.

"This is Panther Two-Six, over," answered Butch, realizing the Battalion Commander was probably already en route to this location.

"We've been monitoring your net," said the Battalion Commander over the radio. "I have several medevac birds en route and a reinforced platoon on the way. ETA is ten mikes. Birds will be on station in five mikes, but will wait for your call that the LZ is cold."

"Roger, Nighthawk Six," Butch said, realizing that in about ten minutes, everyone and their brother would be descending on this location. *Good*, he thought, *but right now, I have a parking lot to secure so we can get these wounded taken care of.*

Butch grabbed Z and went out front to where Brody was kneeling by the front of the store. "Okay, guys, here's the plan. It's a shitshow inside there, but the cavalry is coming. Reports are that the tangos out back have bugged out. We need to confirm. Brody, take your team around the east side of the building and get overwatch over the rear parking area. Pay attention to where the dirt road at the back comes in—supposedly, that's where the tangos had their vehicles. Z, you and Buck pop out the back door when Brody is in position. We'll catch anyone back there in a crossfire."

The two sergeants nodded, being the quiet professionals that they were, and moved out to ready their teams.

Three minutes later, the parking lot was secure. Brody confirmed that there appeared to be six tangos KIA, all wearing a mix of green or red balaclavas over their heads. Several had been shot by the .50-cal gunner, and there wasn't much left of them. There were no wounded or any sign of the tangos who had fled.

Hearing the eggbeater sound of approaching helicopters, Butch went back to check on Doc and help get the wounded ready for transport. The brass would be showing up soon, and as a Sheriff's deputy, Butch knew that there was going to be a lot of attention paid to what had occurred here. He had no doubt television news crews would be arriving any second. He was just glad that he was the QRF team sergeant, and hopefully, they'd be back on their cots at the armory shortly.

56

Wakulla Springs, Florida

Sunday, April 14

THE LODGE at Wakulla Springs opened in 1937. Situated twenty miles south of Tallahassee on a crystal clear spring and built by financier Edward Ball, this grand hotel takes a voyage back in time to Florida's "land boom"—those glorious days when money and people flowed into the Sunshine State, braving mosquitos and gators with an eye to future fortunes.

The lodge's ambiance is reminiscent of the 1930s, with parquet floors, decoratively painted cypress ceilings with whirring ceiling fans, and the world's longest marble bar. The springs behind the lodge were the set for numerous Hollywood movies, including the original Tarzan movie starring five-time Olympic gold medal swimmer Johnny Weismuller. The lodge's twenty-seven rooms had housed countless celebrities over its eighty-seven-year history.

Today, the lodge's ornate library had been reserved by the Florida governor, who was hosting several very private meetings away from the prying eyes of Tallahassee.

Orlean Brumback had flown his retrofitted Boeing 737 through the evening from Wyoming to Tallahassee to participate in these meetings with his new pal, Vince Marino. They'd become very close over the last few months, with a shared vision for America and their own powerful futures in it.

Orlean loved his bespoke 737, which he had dubbed his "flying fortress." He had chosen the Boeing 737 over other luxury private jets for its proven ability as a workhorse plane, capable of flying almost constantly with the proper maintenance. This was evident in the fact that many of the original models built more than fifty years ago are still in service today, albeit with third-world airlines.

Brumback had personally designed the interior of his plane, which he'd divided into three sections. The first half was the living area—more than a dozen luxurious lie-flat chairs, several couches, and a dining table that doubled as in-flight workstations. The back half contained a small, ornate conference room paneled in mahogany that doubled as Orlean's office. It had every electronic device one would expect of the chief executive of the world's most powerful media empire. The rear section was Orlean's living suite, complete with a king-sized bed and bathroom with a full shower.

Orlean had spared no expense in retrofitting the plane and was glad he had, as he estimated he spent well over one hundred nights a year living on the jet. Several years ago, Alex offered to help Orlean manage his logistics, and ever since, Orlean had found flying a breeze. Pilots and crew were always ready, a chauffeur-driven SUV was always waiting on the tarmac when he landed, and a great ground support crew was always available to meet Orlean's needs. Orlean's new assistant handled many of these details, but he was not naive enough to think that it wasn't Alex's expansive logistics network they were relying upon.

The cleaners on the ground support crew were Orlean's favorite part of the entire travel experience. At sixty-six, Orlean had been very happily married for over thirty years—albeit to four different women. His current wife, Isobel, was a former model and anchorwoman who'd been married to Orlean for eight years. Isobel enjoyed the perks of the marriage, perhaps more than she enjoyed Orlean, but she had little interest in politics and was content to

Divided We Stand

spend most of her time at their beachfront home in Malibu. This arrangement worked well for both of them, and they truly enjoyed each other's company, but they found they enjoyed it most when it was only a few times each month. Isobel had one very close female friend who stayed with her in Malibu, keeping her company—and satisfied—as Isobel's discretion was also part of the arrangement.

Among the other aspects of logistics, Alex had arranged for a special cleaning crew at each airfield, and Tallahassee had become one of Orlean's favorites. The crew were always women and often a variety of ethnicities. Sometimes alone, but often in pairs or triples, they were available as soon as the plane touched down and would clean the plane as often as Orlean desired.

The Tallahassee cleaning crew involved two Eastern European beauties in their early twenties. Oksana was a statuesque blonde, while Iryna wore her brunette hair in a bob and had the body of a gymnast. They each arrived carrying a small bag, but Orlean was certain no cleaning supplies were inside. Not unless lingerie, vibrators, and restraints were now considered cleaning supplies.

Orlean and Vince had just finished a two-hour meeting with senior members of the Republican National Committee, including its chairman. Everyone was pleased with how the Republican governors and state legislatures had banded together to push for a Constitutional Convention. The RNC was quite concerned at the escalating level of violence throughout the country, but their goal was to push forward toward November with an overwhelming surge of American patriotism sweeping Republican candidates into office at the local, state, and national levels.

The RNC Chair told Vince that he was the current darling of the Grand Old Party and formally asked him if he would accept the Republican nomination to be on the November presidential ballot. Vince graciously accepted, which led to a detailed discussion of how Benjamin King's delegates would be reallocated to the Marino campaign.

The meeting had closed with a discussion of who would be the best running mate for Vince. The RNC Chair had tossed Nathan Greene's name in the hat, but Vince informed him that he'd already spoken to Nathan and that he was definitely not a good candidate for Vice President.

Vince threw out Orlean's name as the best possible Vice Presidential candidate. The RNC Chair smiled, not having previously considered this. He answered non-committally that it sounded like a great idea but wanted to run some polls to ensure Orlean added value to the Marino ticket, especially as Orlean had never previously held elected office. This was precisely what Vince and Orlean had envisioned would be the reply, and all agreed to keep working towards finalizing the ticket with the intention of going public by the end of the month.

A few minutes after the RNC group departed, a new individual joined Orlean and Vince in the Lodge's library. Alex Treacher entered without fanfare and took a seat in one of the mission-style leather and wood chairs. Alex had flown into Tallahassee International Airport that morning from Montana specifically for this meeting, his private jet departing Kalispell well before dawn.

"Good morning, gentlemen," said Alex. "I appreciate you both finding time to meet with me."

It was not lost on anyone that meeting with Alex was never optional and that "finding time" was a euphemism for "doing as you're told." Vince was just now beginning to see how long Alex's tentacles reached, but Orlean was blissfully aware, for despite how wealthy Bunker Hill Media had made Orlean, he didn't have a fraction of the wealth that Alex Treacher could tap into. It wasn't just Alex's own checkbook; it was the contacts and resources that the man had access to, and it was offered seemingly without any strings. When Alex said he could do or get something, it simply happened.

"I take it congratulations are in order, Vince," said Alex, referring to the expected nomination as the Republican candidate for President. "I can think of no better person to lead this country forward than you, especially with Orlean as your running mate."

"Thank you. It's not public yet, but it should be by the end of the month. I floated Orlean as a running mate. They were open to the idea but wanted to confirm some feedback with polls before making a firm decision."

Divided We Stand

"Just noise to make them feel important," said Alex, sweeping his hand in a brushing motion to show the RNC's opinion was meaningless. "I've no doubt their polls will show them exactly what we already know—the combination of the two of you is unbeatable. Plus, it's ultimately the candidate's decision." Alex made a mental note to speak with Luther, Alex's clandestine IT guru. Alex knew that Luther had access to the RNC's computer systems, and he also knew that most of the nation's top pollsters were secretly on Luther's payroll, many without even knowing who was funding them. There was no doubt in Alex's mind that the polls would show exactly what he wanted them to show.

"What can we help you with this morning?" Vince asked. He enjoyed Alex's company but found the man had little time for chitchat and almost no sense of humor.

"I understand from speaking with Orlean yesterday that we may have a problem with Nathan Greene. Is that correct?"

"Well, possibly," answered Vince, wondering if Alex would be upset to learn that Vince had offered the Vice President slot to Nathan. "We were discussing whether he had any interest in being part of my campaign, and he started to ask some alarming questions."

"Such as? Please be as accurate as you can recall."

"Well, some of it was the same nonsense he was quoted in the New York Times on Friday—this idea of an external influencer shaking the jar and causing all us *ants* to get riled up so that we can be better controlled. He then started asking some very pointed questions about my history with Orlean and Orlean's potential involvement with Ben King's plane crash."

"Did Greene ever ask about me?"

"Not to me directly, but he did mention you to Sam Stryder, my senior advisor."

"And what did he say to Mr. Stryder?"

"He asked how often you interacted with Orlean or me."

"Interesting," said Alex. "Very interesting."

"Do you think Nathan Greene is going to be a problem for us?" Orlean asked.

"I don't know if he will, but he certainly could be," replied Alex. "He's a very capable man, this Professor Greene. He has a tremendous social media following and clearly has connections at the New York Times. He seems to be quick to throw stones, but perhaps he lives in a glass house. Whatever happened with the investigation into the shooting with the FBI agents?"

"It was deemed justified under Florida's Stand Your Ground laws," said Vince.

"A pity," said Alex. "Wouldn't it be convenient if he were brought in for questioning or perhaps even arrested? Maybe the investigators missed a critical piece of evidence?" Alex stared directly into Vince's eyes as he made these comments, forcing Vince to look away like a pet dog being dominated by his master.

"I understand," said Vince.

"Do you?" Alex countered.

Vince looked coolly at Alex, not used to being questioned and somewhat taken aback. "Yes, Alex, I just said I understood."

"Well, just to ensure there's no miscommunication going forward, what is it that you understand you are to do?"

Vince shifted uncomfortably in his chair. Never one to shy away from a confrontation, Vince suddenly felt a bit vulnerable. He hadn't realized until this moment that maybe he and Alex were not peers.

"Well, Alex," Vince started. "I'm going to speak with the senior member of my protective detail, a twenty-year Florida Department of Law Enforcement veteran. I'm going to let it be known that Professor Greene should spend some time in jail while the investigation into his shooting of two FBI agents is more thoroughly investigated."

Alex kept his eye contact with Vince, pausing a few seconds before answering as if he were evaluating Vince's solution. "Excellent, Vince. Excellent," said Alex. "You definitely understand correctly."

Orlean intentionally stayed out of this conversation. He could tell that Alex was testing Vince, and it seemed that Vince had passed the exam. As powerful as Orlean thought he was, he had always

Divided We Stand

known Alex was infinitely more powerful. Alex was a man who could help Orlean get to where he wanted to go, but he was not a person Orlean would want to cross.

Hopefully, Vince's innate hubris would not prevent him from seeing this as well. Orlean had no doubt that Alex would launch them both into the White House and knowing the details of the upcoming Phase 3 of Alex's grand strategy, Orlean was looking forward to riding the wave for the next six months.

"Alex?" Vince asked. "There is one question I'd like to ask of you.

"Okay," said Alex, non-committally.

"What is it that you get out of all of this? You've been involved in all these conversations going back to campaign and legal strategies with Benjamin King. Now, it seems you're getting involved in my campaign. And while I'm grateful for the support and consider you a friend and close ally, I'm curious as to what you get out of all of this. You're spending ungodly sums of money, and you seem willing to spend even more. So what's in it for you?"

Alex sat back in his chair, his eyes calmly assessing both Vince and Orlean. After several moments of contemplating his answer, he said simply, "Whatever I want, Vince. Whatever I want."

57

Staunton, Virginia

Sunday, April 14

COLONEL ROBERT CLARK sat reclined in his cheap, high-backed swivel chair and with his boots propped up on his desk. He'd just attended the shift changeover briefing in the Brigade TOC— Tactical Operations Center—and he was utterly exhausted.

Catching catnaps on the army-issue aluminum and nylon cot he stashed in the corner of his office and showering in the neighboring gymnasium's locker room for the past three weeks, Clark was feeling every one of his fifty-two years. He sat reading the latest report of daily incidents prepared by his S-2—the Brigade intelligence officer.

In the last twenty-four hours alone, his area of operations had seen forty-seven incidents categorized as domestic security threats. These ranged from intimidation and harassment all the way to home invasions, sniper fire, and vehicle ambushes. Eleven people had been killed, with scores more wounded.

Clark had spent yesterday in Richmond attending marathon meetings with the Governor, Adjutant General, and other commanders in the Virginia National Guard. The situation throughout the state was deteriorating rapidly, and from all indications, the same thing was happening in other states across the country. Clark's brigade, the 116th Infantry Brigade Combat Team, had initially been tasked with helping provide security for Virginia's elected officials and also to augment law enforcement in high-profile situations, such as the protests expanding on college campuses throughout the state.

Last week, based on Clark's recommendations to the governor, his orders had been modified. He'd detached his field artillery battalion to Richmond to provide security for the governor and Capitol. Clark's remaining two infantry battalions and cavalry squadron had been deployed around the state's three largest universities and several smaller ones to dampen the violence occurring on these campuses. There were only two weeks left of school, and at that time, it was hoped that he could use his forces elsewhere.

Clark had already had four soldiers killed since their activation three weeks prior. Two soldiers had been felled by sniper fire, one at the University of Virginia and the other at James Madison University. They'd been killed instantly.

In one case, the perpetrator had gotten away cleanly, but in the other, his soldiers had returned fire and cornered the sniper, killing him in a shootout in an alley behind a dorm. The sniper had been a young college student from Northern Virginia, who'd taken his father's hunting rifle without his knowledge, returned to school, and shot a 20-year-old soldier from the window of his dorm room. The student/sniper had been radicalized by social media posts he'd been watching that called for his generation to stand up against the evil fascists preventing free speech on campus.

Colonel Clark had rushed to both scenes and had been at the morgue when the parents of both the shooter and the soldier had come to see the bodies of their sons. The sadness in both fathers whose dreams for their child were now gone forever was identical, as was the grief of the sobbing mothers inconsolable at the loss of their offspring.

The deaths of his other two soldiers were even more tragic. Both soldiers had been granted a forty-eight-hour pass to visit home after ten straight days on duty. Both had been killed by neighborhood thugs—not gang members in the traditional sense, but part of the new breed of violent bullies revved up by ideological motivation to strike out at others. One case involved a group associated with Antifa, while the other was actually good old boys from Virginia who mistakenly thought the National Guard soldier was part of the "federal police."

Clark put down the incident log and picked up his notes from yesterday's meeting with the Governor. Clark's brigade had been given new orders, and at the last shift change, Clark had gathered his staff and issued them the information they needed to begin planning. On Wednesday, the 116th Infantry Brigade Combat Team would redeploy and establish blocking positions in northern Virginia along the borders with Maryland and Washington, D.C. Checkpoints would be established on the major highways, with occupants searched, citizenship verified, and purpose for entering Virginia confirmed.

The mantle of command was lonely, especially in Staunton, Virginia.

Robert was vexed by these new orders. On the one hand, he fully supported his governor and Adjutant General and believed in the cause of Virginia First. However, as a staunch conservative all his life, he admired the entire U.S. Constitution, including the parts that stated citizens should be allowed to travel freely between the states and not just the parts of the Constitution that favored the states over the federal government.

He was not an attorney, so he sat forward and touched the keyboard of his laptop to bring it to life. For the next thirty minutes, he researched everything he could find on the internet regarding this issue. After reading dozens of scholarly texts, including the relevant clauses in the Constitution and Articles of Confederation, as well as several of James Madison's *Federalist Papers*, Clark felt much more knowledgeable on the subject but no less confused. He could definitely see how the average person was easily swayed by social media and the press.

The right of American citizens to travel freely between the states

Divided We Stand

was generally accepted under the Privileges and Immunities Clause of Article IV, Section 2 of the Constitution. However, the same Article specifically stated that the federal government would protect states against invasion and intervene in domestic violence only "on Application of the Legislature, or of the Executive (when the Legislature cannot be convened)."

For Clark, this meant that the federal government had an obligation to keep illegal immigrants out of the country and could only intervene in a state when the state formally requested such assistance. As a career veteran of NCIS, Clark prided himself on his knowledge of the law but had always had difficulty understanding the politics at the southern border. On the one hand, it seemed about as straightforward as it gets—allow people into the country according to the law, but don't allow people to cross the border illegally. On the other hand, America had always been proud of its status as a safe haven for the world's downtrodden, and there seemed to Clark to be a middle ground where those less fortunate should have a process for reaching the United States and pursuing their own "American Dream." Everyone knew the U.S. Congress was woefully broken, but their inability to pass new legislation didn't mean that an administration could simply ignore previous legislation. If visa limits had expired, then they'd expired—no one but Congress had the right to authorize new limits.

Yet the more Colonel Clark read, the more frustrated he became. He fully understood why the average American was upset that they could never get a straight answer out of anyone, whether politician or pundit. The issue of undocumented immigrants and asylum-seekers was foremost in the news, especially with what was occurring at the Texas-Mexico border. Clark read several articles by immigration attorneys on the rights of refugees, how the "first safe country" principle was fictitious, and how refugees were not only allowed to enter the United States illegally but that the Geneva Convention prohibited their deportation.

He remembered how difficult it was for his wife, born in what was then Rhodesia (now Zimbabwe), to emigrate to the United States after having first fled her country to South Africa. She'd been specifically told that the only path to America was by applying through the U.S. Embassy in Pretoria. Any attempt by her to enter the U.S. without a visa or asylum approval would result in her immediate expulsion.

Clark decided to read the 1951 Geneva Convention document himself. He was shocked at what he read, as it seemed contradictory to the media's presentation of the issue. Even the introduction written by the United Nations High Commissioner for Refugees seemed to selectively interpret articles in favor of its political stance on the issues—stating that asylum seekers may not be penalized for illegal entry nor may they be expelled, even when the specific articles say otherwise.

Yes, it was true that Article 31 of the 1951 Geneva Convention, titled "Refugees Unlawfully in the Country of Refuge," states that countries may not penalize refugees on "account of their illegal entry or presence." However, that sentence contains several clauses that are conveniently not mentioned by the media, including that the refugees must be "coming directly from a territory where their life or freedom was threatened" and that they must "present themselves without delay to the authorities." The clause about being threatened is further referenced to the Article 1 definition of a refugee, which narrows these threats to those of political persecution and not fear of crime or poverty.

Even more alarming to Clark was the text of Article 32, titled Expulsion. Under this article, countries "shall not expel a refugee lawfully in their territory." Seems clear enough. Utilizing the same reverse logic the U.S. Courts have always applied to the Constitution, Article 32 could be restated that countries *may* expel a refugee who is *unlawfully* in their territory—using Article 31 as a point to define "lawful" refugees as those who either entered legally or may have entered illegally from a territory where they were not being politically persecuted or had not presented themselves immediately to the authorities.

As Mexico was a democratic country and not accused of politically persecuting its citizens or undocumented immigrants, it was difficult for Clark to understand how the current administration was

Divided We Stand

allowing such rampant illegal behavior along the southern border. There were over 40,000 border patrol agents for a reason, yet when they failed to accomplish their mission of protecting the border, those in violation seemed to be getting a free pass under a clearly intentional misinterpretation of the 1951 Geneva Convention. To Robert, a career law enforcement officer, it was akin to telling car thieves that if they're caught in the act, they'll be prosecuted, but anyone who initially gets away clean can keep the car and register it legally after a short waiting period.

All this research hurt his head, and he realized he probably wasn't doing anyone any favors. He was a colonel in the Virginia Army National Guard, and these issues were way, way above his pay grade. *Who gave two shits what I think about the border crisis?* He thought. *My job is to do what I'm told, accomplish the mission, and keep my troops safe.*

58

Clewiston, Florida

Monday, April 15

CARLY BRUNO DROVE down the long shell driveway. The two Florida Highway Patrol vehicles behind her maintained a good distance back due to the dust cloud billowing up as the tires of her vehicle crunched over the dried, broken shells. This April seemed especially dry, and rain would be welcome.

Beside her sat Mike Peppers, a fellow senior investigator with the Florida Department of Law Enforcement based out of Fort Myers. They were both members of a statewide investigative task force responding to the various violent incidents that had occurred over the past month, and while based in Tallahassee, both had spent the last month living out of a suitcase. First, they'd spent a week in Sarasota helping investigate the former President's plane being shot down into Sarasota Bay, and then they'd both been shifted to Miami-Dade County to assist with all of the violence surrounding protests in that part of the state.

Yesterday afternoon, they received notice to participate in a conference call with the senior advisor to Governor Marino. On the

Divided We Stand

call, they'd been instructed to serve an arrest warrant on Nathan Greene as part of the re-opened investigation into the shooting deaths of two FBI agents in Sarasota County. Both Carly and her partner were familiar with the shooting, as they suspected everyone in America might be, and she was also very familiar with Professor Nathan Greene. Not only had she read his Op-ed article in the New York Times and the more recent piece last week, but she also followed his Twitter account—one of his more than sixteen million followers.

"You ready?" Carly asked her partner as they approached a large gravel parking area in front of a sprawling one-story ranch home. Two pickup trucks were parked in the driveway, but there was no sign of any people. "Greene seems like a good guy. Hopefully, this will go smoothly."

"Ya think?" Peppers said next to her in his usual smart-ass voice. "I wonder if those FBI agents said the exact same thing when they pulled up to his house on Casey Key?"

Carly drove up and parked their unmarked SUV immediately behind and perpendicular to the two pickup trucks. This not only prevented the two trucks from leaving, but it also provided additional cover for her and her partner should things go sideways. The two Highway Patrol vehicles pulled up on the flanks of the open parking area, affording them visibility over the front and sides of the homestead.

Carly and Peppers slowly stepped out of their vehicle. Carly turned to see the Highway Patrol officers doing the same, except each officer held an M4 carbine in his hands and stood shielded behind their cruisers.

Adrenaline surged through Carly's body, and she willed herself to calm down. Beside her, Peppers drew his sidearm.

"Put it away or stay in the car," she said. "I understand he's a murder suspect, but if we truly thought he was gonna put up a fight, we shoulda brought a tactical team. There's a reason the governor sent us. Let's try the easy way first."

Peppers stopped and looked at her for a moment. She was the senior officer, but that didn't mean she was correct. "Okay, Carly.

But remember, if you're wrong and we get killed, I'm blaming you. Okay?"

"Yeah, I got it," she said, not knowing if he was serious or not. Peppers was sarcastic about everything, but with the adrenaline flowing through her veins, Carly wasn't sure at the moment.

Seeing her serious look, he said, "Hey, lighten up. I'm teasing." He smiled. "Well, half-teasing." At which point, he broke into a chuckle.

"C'mon," she said, "Let's go be nice and see what happens."

They walked up to the front porch without incident and proceeded to knock on the door. No answer. They rang the bell, knocked some more, and waited a full sixty seconds.

"Check the back?" Peppers asked.

"Yeah, let's stick together." She turned and signaled to the Highway Patrol officers their intent to walk around back. Five minutes later, having checked two outbuildings and peeked in the windows, it was clear that no one was home.

"Okay," said Carly once they got back to their vehicle and were joined by the two troopers. "It looks like we're going to sit here and wait for a while. Why don't one of you head into town and bring us back some lunch? I'm buying. It could be a long day."

59

Ferrisburgh, Vermont

Monday, April 15

NATHAN WOKE up later than usual on Monday morning. It was the first night in his new bed, and it was probably the best sleep he'd had in weeks. He lay awake in the large king-size four-poster bed and admired the westerly views across Lake Champlain to the New York shoreline in the distance.

Valhalla.

That was the name of his new home—estate might be more apt. Situated on 345 acres, Valhalla was a copper-roofed French Colonial Revival-style 3-story mansion with 10,000 square feet of elegance and built of Panton stone quarried directly from the site. The property was located along the shores of Lake Champlain, due west of the small hamlet of Ferrisburgh, Vermont. Comprising a small peninsula jutting into Lake Champlain with the main house, three smaller homes, a large dock, and a private 9-hole golf course, this was one of the most expensive properties in the entire state of Vermont.

Nathan had contacted his brother-in-law last Friday and asked him to find an estate in Vermont that they could lease for up to a year. He'd consider purchasing a place, but the one caveat was that he had to be able to move in immediately—and by immediately, he meant yesterday.

Nathan wanted as much land as possible with several homes on the property, but he didn't care about the details. And with his current net worth after Emily's death, he didn't care what it would cost. Dave, his brother-in-law, had found Valhalla, which had been on the market for almost three years. He struck a deal leasing the place for a year for $300,000, all of which could be applied to the purchase price if Nathan decided to buy it.

Nathan had chartered a private jet to fly himself, Spooner, Lourdes, and Felipe to Vermont yesterday morning. This morning, the same plane was bringing some of Spooner's staff from his firearms and tactics academy, along with crates of weapons and equipment. Nathan felt that he was getting very close to taking on the Cabal directly, and it was time to begin preparations.

The main house had eleven bedrooms, so Nathan had invited Spooner, Lourdes, and Felipe to make themselves at home. Nathan had taken the master bedroom at the top of the main staircase for himself, while Spooner had moved into another of the ensuite rooms located on the far side of the mansion near the back staircase. Lourdes and Felipe had decided to occupy the entire third floor, where they'd have three bedrooms and a sitting area all to themselves.

Finally getting out of bed and throwing on a pair of jeans and a faded green Dartmouth sweatshirt, Nathan headed down to the main floor to see who was awake. Spooner was a notorious early riser and often liked to make breakfast. The house was new to Nathan, but Vermont was not. He had grown up on the Seacoast of neighboring New Hampshire, attended Dartmouth University as an undergraduate, and spent two summers during college living and working in Burlington, Vermont's largest city with a booming population of just over 40,000 residents.

Nathan found his way to the kitchen, stopping once to admire the gorgeous views of the manicured garden down toward the edge

Divided We Stand

of the water, with the deep blue of Lake Champlain contrasting with the dark green of New York in the distance. Nathan then followed his nose to find Spooner hard at work in the kitchen making pancakes. While stocking up on supplies at the grocery store yesterday evening, pancake mix and fresh Fancy Grade A Vermont maple syrup were two necessities.

"Good morning," Nathan said, greeting his friend.

"Well, look what the cat dragged in. You're finally up!" Spooner replied, speaking to himself as no one else was in the room. "I was actually just about to wake you. Lourdes and Felipe have already enjoyed my famous flapjacks."

"Hey, man, this is Vermont—they're called pancakes. Flapjacks are what you make in Florida."

"Same difference," said Spooner, smiling.

"Yeah, pretty much. Just about thirty IQ points, I'd say." The two men had been in a perpetual argument over North vs. South since they'd met almost twenty years ago. Spooner, a Florida native and proud Southern man, constantly ribbed Nathan about his Yankee heritage while Nathan did the same.

"Okay, Yank. Whatever you say. Three *pancakes* coming right up."

"I told you, Spooner. You can call me a Yankee, but I prefer the term The Victor; it's more accurate."

Spooner smiled, flipping pancakes onto a plate and delivering them to Nathan, who had just sat down with a freshly poured cup of coffee.

"You eat, I'll talk," said Spooner. "That issue that you thought might happen has happened."

Nathan stopped eating, his fork halfway to his mouth, and suddenly, a serious look on his face. "When?"

"About thirty minutes ago, one unmarked vehicle with two detectives plus two Highway Patrol cars knocked on the door, walked around the house, and are now sitting in the driveway." Spooner handed over an iPad tablet whose screen was divided into views from four static surveillance cameras. In two of them, Nathan could clearly see the police vehicles at Spooner's house in Clewiston.

"I take it Terry, Mitch, and Roy made their flight without issues?" Nathan was referring to the three men from Spooner's training business, all three former Special Forces and Delta operators, who were due to fly up this morning on the plane Nathan had chartered.

"Yes, no problem at all. They're actually due in Burlington in about two hours."

Nathan looked at his watch—9:51 a.m.

"Okay, let me finish these pancakes, and let's go down to the Bunker. I worked late last night setting everything up, and I want to get your opinion on a few things."

After wolfing down the delicious pancakes, Nathan led Spooner down to the basement. Valhalla had been built from stone quarried right on site, and one of the added features Nathan loved about the house was the two-level subterranean basement that had literally been blasted and carved out of granite rock.

The main basement was absolutely massive. Nathan estimated its dimensions were thirty by one hundred feet, providing approximately three thousand square feet of space divided into multiple rooms. A large storage room filled with shelves and supplies was at the very far end, taking approximately one-third of the entire basement. It looked like the previous owners had prepared for doomsday and had left most of the supplies in place. A back stairwell led directly up from this part of the basement into the house's prep kitchen and pantry area.

The middle section of the basement contained a hallway with a large room on one side and two smaller rooms on the other side. The large room was a utilitarian office with a drafting table in the middle and lots of overhead lighting. The other two rooms were smaller storage ones, one of which was the house's IT hub.

As soon as Nathan had made arrangements to lease the property, he'd reached out to an old friend who he hadn't seen in almost thirty years. During the two summers Nathan had spent in Burlington while in college, he'd lived in a fraternity house at the edge of the University of Vermont's picturesque campus. Nathan's best friend from high school was attending UVM, and a brother in

Divided We Stand

the fraternity. The fraternity, Lambda Iota, was one of the oldest in the country, and Nathan had made fast friends with the brothers who spent the summer in town. John Wadder was one of these fraternity brothers, and Nathan knew he owned a successful IT security firm in Burlington. John had been willing to come out to Valhalla yesterday and ensure the house had everything it needed regarding internet connectivity, security, and communications.

The final third of the basement was a comfortable living room with a home gym in one corner and a ping-pong table on the other side. Multiple couches and chairs were arranged in the middle, facing an eighty-five-inch flatscreen television.

Nathan didn't bother showing Spooner the sub-basement at this time. Under the storage third of the basement was another full-height basement, maybe 1,000 square feet total. With a stone staircase that doubled back on itself, this sub-basement made an ideal fallout shelter, and the previous owners had clearly agreed. This space contained several cots and additional supplies.

Nathan led Spooner to the utilitarian office in the middle of the main basement.

"Whoah," said Spooner, walking in the door. "Someone's been doing their homework."

Both men walked into the room, and Spooner did a slow 360-degree turn to take in Nathan's handiwork. Similar to the war room they'd set up in Spooner's Clewiston house, this room was twice the size, and Nathan had already mounted maps, cork boards, documents, photographs, and colored string connecting everything. Three laptops were open on the desk, several monitors were mounted along one wall, and a high-speed color printer was in the corner.

"This is the Bunker. It's where you'll find me for the next week or two. We're close, Spooner. Really close. Those police at your house were there to arrest me, and that could only come directly from Marino. Had to be."

"Yeah," said Spooner, dropping into one of the swivel office chairs and twirling to look at Nathan's handiwork on the wall. "I agree with that. Based on the bait you dangled the other day, they seem to have taken it."

"Exactly. I specifically asked questions about Brumback and Treacher. Those guys are both shady as far as I'm concerned, and they have the means and the motive to be the Cabal. They also don't answer to anyone, and that makes them even more likely to be involved."

"I still think the Cabal has to be government-sponsored," said Spooner. "They've been too successful and too well-hidden to have this be their first rodeo. The Cabal has institutional experience in covert operations, and that points back to Fulton's administration."

"Yeah, I see your point. I'm going to speak with Sharyn in the Vice President's office this week and maybe see about a visit if I can get a guarantee not to be arrested."

"Okay, I like it," agreed Spooner. "We just need to keep working the angles and collecting intel. The picture will paint itself, and the Cabal will be revealed." Spooner glanced at his watch. "We probably need to get going soon to the airport to pick up the boys. By the way, you're confident you're safe here in Vermont, right? Is there any chance Marino can get you arrested up here?"

"No, I don't think so. It's public knowledge that Governor Glenn hates Marino. Even though Glenn's the Republican governor of Vermont, the Vermont legislature is firmly Democrat, so Glenn has to be pretty careful. He can't just join the other Republican governors, or he'll have a vegan mutiny on his hands. They'd probably revoke his right to drive a Subaru." Nathan chuckled at his own joke. "But seriously, I think I'm good. Plus, I'm not sure anyone is even going to know we're here. I had my brother-in-law put everything under the name of a shell corporation he purchased—there's nothing in writing that ties me to this place."

60

Dearborn, Michigan

Monday, April 15

KEITH WAS startled awake by someone sitting at the end of his bed.

"We need to talk, Keith," said Hanna, his wife.

"What time is it?" Keith asked groggily, not wanting to wake up.

"We need to talk, Keith. It's almost noon." Hanna stood up and began pacing in the small bedroom. Keith immediately knew something was wrong, as Hanna normally snuggled into bed with him or at least lay down and started talking. She'd been working double shifts consistently, and while the overtime pay was great, she basically came home only to sleep.

He knew Hanna was probably angry at the state of their apartment and that he was off work. He'd taken another personal day today. Keith had been pretty freaked out after returning home late Saturday night from the raid in Indiana. He hadn't bothered cleaning anything. The sink was full of dirty dishes, piles of pizza boxes littered the counter, and his dirty clothes were strewn all over the bedroom floor. He was usually fastidious and assumed Hanna was pissed.

He sat up, shirtless, and leaned against the pillows. "Come sit down, Hanna. I know the place is a mess. I'll get——." He stopped talking, noticing the AR-15 rifle propped against the wall for the first time. He was certain he'd put it at the back of his closet.

"What is this?" Hanna asked. "Where did you get a rifle? You know how I feel about guns."

Hanna worked as a police dispatcher for the Detroit Police, yet she abhorred guns. This was one reason Keith had never fired one before last week. His mind raced to come up with a good explanation.

"Uh, one of the guys I went to college with, Sparky, took me to the range yesterday. He asked me to clean it before I gave it back to him."

"What?" Hanna asked, incredulous. "And he gave you this too?" She reached down to the foot of the bed, where Keith couldn't see, and picked up the chest rig he'd been given. The rig was simple nylon and canvas straps with pouches full of empty thirty-round magazines. Sticking out of one pouch was his navy blue balaclava.

Keith stared back, saying nothing.

"I'm not stupid, you know. I know you've been up to something. I looked at the laptop, and you've been searching some crazy stuff. Antifa? Fascism? What have you gotten yourself into? You've changed."

"How would you know? Huh? You've been at work for the last two months. How would you know if I've changed?"

"Keith, please, just tell me. Please tell me you had nothing to do with the mosque shooting on Friday."

"The mosque shooting? In Dearborn?" Relief flooded through Keith. "Of course not, honey. I would never do anything like that. Those are the people we're fighting against!"

As soon as the words came out of his mouth, Keith knew he had fucked up. Badly.

Hanna stopped pacing and stared at him. "Fighting against? What is going on, Keith? You're a teacher. You don't fight."

"I, uh, I didn't mean it like that. I meant that those are the

Divided We Stand

people we hate. They represent everything that's wrong with this country."

"And you're fighting them? Are you part of this Antifa? They brief us about that at work, you know. I'm not stupid. No one gives someone a machine gun to clean. And they certainly don't give them pouches that only soldiers carry." Hanna was getting worked up, almost hysterical. "Tell me! What are you doing?"

"Okay. Okay," said Keith, trying to buy some time to think his way out of this. "It's not what you think. Yes, I've been hanging out with some friends who are against what's happening in this country. In Michigan. We went to some protests, but that's it. Just protesting."

"Then why the machine gun?"

"It's not a machine gun, it's just a rifle."

"I don't care what the fuck it is! I don't want it in my house. And I don't want a husband who would bring it into my house." Hanna was losing control, and Keith knew from experience that there was no calming her down. It would only get worse, and this was as heated as he'd ever seen her.

"Okay. I'm sorry. Maybe I should go visit my mom for the day."

"You haven't answered my question. Why do you have a gun?"

"In case, Hanna. In case things get worse."

"What? You're going to protect us now? By wearing a ski mask and dressing up like a soldier? I'm not stupid."

"I just—."

"Get out. Take your gun and get out. I need time to process this. Don't plan on coming back today."

Hanna stormed out of the room and shut herself in the bathroom. Keith knew there was no reasoning with his wife at this point. He'd screwed up in not hiding the guns properly, and he was going to have to let her cool off while he figured out how to talk himself back into her good graces.

He grabbed a long duffel and started throwing clothes into it, enough for several days. He then put the rifle and chest rig inside and finally grabbed the Glock 19 pistol that he'd hidden in one of his boots in the closet.

He said goodbye to a closed bathroom door, telling it that he'd call later tonight and that he'd be at his mother's new house.

Minutes later, Keith was in his car, approaching the onramp to I-94 and heading north toward Port Huron. Keith had grown up in Novi, a suburb northwest of Detroit, but his mother had moved to a small cottage near the lighthouse in Port Huron. It was a perfect spot for her. She had a good job working in the front office of a doctor's office, and she loved walking down to the beach and taking pictures of the sailboats, freighters, and sunrises. While winterized, it was a very small two-bedroom cottage, but his mother had turned the second bedroom into an office. He knew she wouldn't mind if he stayed on the couch for a few days.

61

Burlington, Vermont

Monday, April 15

NATHAN PULLED his rental Ford Explorer into the parking lot of Al's French Frys on Williston Road in Burlington. In the back seat sat a wide-eyed Felipe. He'd never been out of the small town of Clewiston before, let alone a small city in Vermont. They'd just picked up Spooner's three employees and their equipment, rented two additional vehicles, and loaded everything in them for the trip back to Valhalla. Nathan had let everyone go ahead and decided to show Felipe the real Burlington, Vermont.

Nathan hadn't been to Al's since college, but during his two summers there, he ate there probably four days a week, sometimes twice a day. It was a classic Fifties-style diner complete with chrome siding, checkerboard tile floors, and filled with red vinyl booths. Their burgers were pretty good, but their fries were fantastic.

Honestly, Nathan couldn't remember if the food was really any good—he just loved the ambiance and the price. It was a classic joint, and he had always loved joints. The food was fresh, greasy, and cheap—and that spelled delicious in Nathan's book.

Thirty minutes later, Nathan was satisfied that little had changed at Al's. The place looked pretty much the same; the menu items were still cheap, and the food was greasy and delicious. Felipe was a huge fan and couldn't stop eating the French fries.

It was another beautiful Spring day in Burlington, and Nathan and Felipe took their time walking to the car parked in the rear of the busy lot.

Bang!

The sound of a gunshot not more than twenty yards away made Nathan jump. His hand instantly went to the Glock 19 in an inside-the-waistband holster under his sweatshirt as his eyes scanned to identify the threat.

Two pickup trucks on oversized tires were blocking several other cars just down the lot. Outside one of those cars stood a family of four, the parents and two teenagers, one boy and one girl. Even from a distance, Nathan could tell they looked Hispanic. Arrayed in front of the pickup trucks were five young men who looked to be in their early twenties. Scruffy beards, tattoos, and a penchant for flannel shirts seemed to be their schtick. Two of the men held baseball bats while another pointed a semi-automatic pistol in the direction of the family.

Nathan knew he should leave, but he couldn't bring himself to do so. "Run back inside the restaurant," Nathan instructed Felipe. "Tell the girl at the counter to call 911 and then go sit in a booth until I come to get you."

Felipe dashed the few yards back to the restaurant.

Turning toward the threat, Nathan walked quickly. His pistol was still in its holster, and the men were angled such that they didn't see him approaching as their focus was on the Hispanic family of four.

Nathan could hear them clearly now, the hatred dripping from the voice of the man with the gun.

"You fucking wetback scum. Go back to fucking Mexico. Maybe stop in D.C. and take Fulton with you. We don't want you in Vermont."

The Hispanic man, clearly the father, had both hands held up

Divided We Stand

in a placating gesture. He was wearing a Western-style cowboy shirt tucked into tight Wrangler jeans held up by a wide leather belt and an enormous, shiny buckle. On his feet were cowboy boots. Straight out of central casting. The teenage boy, who looked to be about sixteen, was dressed similarly. The mom and the teenage daughter, who was likely the older sister at around eighteen, were dressed stylishly in clothes purchased from any American mall. Their car was a new Toyota RAV4 with Massachusetts license plates.

"We're sorry. We meant no disrespect," said the man, without a hint of a foreign accent. If anything, it sounded to Nathan as if the man had a Texas drawl.

"You're goddamn right. You are sorry," screamed the angry young man with the pistol. "And being in Burlington is disrespectful. You fucking aliens make me sick. I should fucking shoot you right here. If our Governor had any balls, it would be legal to shoot you."

"Mister, please. We were just leaving," pleaded the man.

"You don't want to do this," said Nathan calmly but forcefully, interrupting the scene.

The five young men turned toward Nathan, while the one guy, really just a kid barely out of his teens now that Nathan could see him up close, was now pointing his gun at Nathan. Nathan stayed completely calm.

"Sir," Nathan said to the man with the family. "Get in your car."

The young man wavered, not sure what to do. He couldn't look at both Nathan and the Hispanic man at the same time.

The kid turned toward the car.

Bang!

The kid fired a shot that exploded the driver's side mirror of the car. The Hispanic man jumped back in fright, and the gunman's friends started laughing.

In an instant, before anyone could react, Nathan had taken five quick steps forward while simultaneously pulling the Glock 19 from his holster.

"Drop the gun," said Nathan, in the same calm voice as he firmly pressed the muzzle of his pistol into the side of the young man's temple. "In two seconds, you're dead. I won't ask again. Drop—."

The kid's pistol clanged onto the ground.

Keeping his Glock pressed against the side of the man's head, Nathan looked around at his four friends. None seemed like they wanted to fight, and one looked like he'd just pissed his pants.

"Gentlemen," Nathan said quietly, just loud enough to be heard. "I'd ask you to apologize, but none of you are worth the effort. I'm going to give you five seconds to get in your trucks and get out of here. I have your license plates, so I strongly recommend you drive straight to the nearest police station and turn yourself in. Go!"

The five men scrambled for their trucks. Within seconds, they'd peeled out of the parking lot. Nathan could hear sirens approaching in the distance.

He looked over at the family standing there. "Are you all right, sir? I'm terribly sorry that this happened to you."

"Yes, thank you," said the man. "We're from Texas. My daughter is here to visit the University of Vermont. We've been getting dirty looks from people everywhere we drive. It must be the license plate."

"Yes, I'm afraid so," said Nathan. "Intolerance is becoming commonplace nowadays."

"I actually work for the Border Patrol," said the man. "We had no idea it was going to be like this here. It's one reason Mary, my daughter, wanted to go to school here. We flew into the Burlington airport and had no idea the rental car company would give us Massachusetts plates. I've never even been to Massachusetts. Or Mexico, for that matter. I'm a third-generation Texan!"

The sirens were getting louder. Nathan holstered his Glock and reached down to secure the pistol the young bully had dropped.

"I'm sure the police will be here any moment. They'll definitely want a statement from you."

62

Port Huron, Michigan

Monday, April 15

JEFF SAT in his living room and looked out through the window at the lake. The north wind had picked up, the sky slate gray, and the lake full of whitecaps. It was a raw April day, but Jeff could always appreciate the beauty of Lake Huron.

He'd gone to Mama Vicki's Coney Island for lunch today—the first time he'd been back since that fateful day on March 22nd. Despite ordering the same meal he always did, it just wasn't the same. Two state troopers sat in the booth in front of him, and he could see the idling SUV at the curb with an armed state trooper standing guard. While Jeff had somewhat gotten used to the protection detail, what had really changed was how people treated him. The waitress was nervous and gushing, the cooks kept glancing his way, and people he'd known all his life kept coming up to say how proud they were of him.

He felt like saying, *Hey, I didn't do anything to be proud of. A close friend of mine, who went on to become governor, put my name down on an offi-*

cial piece of paper, and suddenly, I'm Governor of the State of Michigan. It's not like I earned it.

But instead, he smiled politely and said nice things, nodding and shaking everyone's hand. *Jesus*, he thought, *I've become a politician!*

He left a big tip for the waitress and was sad as he left, realizing he'd likely never be able to go back to Mama Vicki's and have the experience he'd grown accustomed to—the quiet anonymity and friendly banter he'd always enjoyed. Being governor was certainly interesting, but he'd trade it in a heartbeat to regain his old life.

Sitting in his living room, he waited for Aidan to bring him something to do, something to sign, some decision to make, some person to call, some funeral to attend. He'd been going to quite a few funerals lately. First, it was politicians, and then lately, it was police officers and National Guard soldiers. The violence across the state was escalating significantly, and he felt powerless to do anything to stop it. Every good idea his advisors had seemed to result in more casualties, and he was aware that people across the state, young and old alike, were becoming more and more radicalized.

Hell, his son had called and texted him several times last week, spouting absolute nonsense. It was clear to Jeff that social media and the press were strongly influencing everybody, and the algorithms were such that once one started down the slide, it was so slippery it was impossible to slow the descent, let alone even think of climbing back to neutral.

A bit concerned about his son, who had a six-month-old baby boy at home, Jeff's wife Debbie had driven over to Battle Creek to stay with his son and daughter-in-law for a few days. Jeff wished he could go as well, but he didn't want to put that type of pressure on his children.

63

Port Huron, Michigan

Monday, April 15

KEITH ARRIVED at his mother's cottage and let himself in with his key. He'd phoned his mom during the hour's drive from Dearborn, and she was happy to have him, although she had plans after work and wouldn't be home until eight o'clock that evening.

Keith tucked his duffel bag in his mom's office and sat on the couch, scrolling through his phone's social media apps. His feeds on TikTok and Instagram were full of video clips showing protesters being battered by police and soldiers. In some of the southern states, people who looked Hispanic or who had out-of-state license plates were being pulled over and accosted. Some of the videos said women were being raped at some of these checkpoints and that two soldiers in Virginia had raped a six-year-old girl and had yet to be arrested.

The world was getting crazier by the day!

Keith never wasted time reading any of his news apps anymore. It was just easier and faster to watch the videos.

Several of the clips showed masked crusaders striking back

against uniformed soldiers. One series of clips was just sniper shots targeting soldiers strung together in a row against the backdrop of Lee Greenwood's *God Bless the USA*. The clips looked almost like a video game despite the blood and gore. *That's what I'm talkin' about,* thought Keith. *That's why we're fighting back. This is America, and we won't let these governors ruin our country. Ruin two hundred years of history. No way!*

Keith's smile vanished when he thought of his own experience in Indiana two nights ago. He really hadn't let himself process everything that had happened, instead spending all of his awake time the past two days scrolling through social media clips.

The raid on the highway checkpoint in Indiana had started out as an absolute blast. They had left as a three-vehicle convoy from their training grounds outside Capac, and it had taken just over four hours to get to Lake Station, Indiana. They stopped just short of their target in an empty warehouse parking lot and double-checked their weapons and equipment. Guys were high-fiving each other, and it felt like a locker room before a big game.

Keith was nervous, but not overly so. He enjoyed the pump of adrenaline, and Warlock played the song *Seven Nation Army* by White Stripe on a loop at full volume. They were getting pumped, and they were going to fuck some people up!

Everything was fine until they took their first casualty. Shooting at the soldiers was exhilarating, better than any video game, and he even thought it was cool when he could see his bullets hit one of the soldiers in the chest about 150 meters away. Even when the soldiers started firing back—the rounds cracking overhead like bees buzzing, followed by the crack of a whip—that was still cool. When one of the guys in green balaclavas standing about ten meters to Keith's left took a bullet through his eye—that was when it started not to be cool anymore.

Keith watched as the bullet seemed to go right through his teammate. It was weird. The bullet never slowed. It went in through his eye and then immediately came out the back of his head, bursting blood, tissue, and pieces of green knitting into the area. The man,

Divided We Stand

who Keith never even knew his name, simply stopped moving and dropped to the ground. Definitely not cool.

Keith's team kept up their firing for maybe a minute or two, enough for Keith to burn through four magazines, firing single shots at a time. It went from *not cool* to *let's get the the fuck out of here* as soon as the soldiers brought a Humvee with a massive machine gun to the overpass and started shooting down at them. Sparky yelled for their team of four to run back to their vehicle.

Keith didn't need to be told twice. Keith had no clue what the other teams were doing, but he had seen some of the red team enter the 7-Eleven store.

As the four of his blue team retreated, they could hear the booming chatter of the .50-caliber machine gun firing. Warlock cried out next to him and fell to the ground. Warlock's face looked stunned, but Keith helped him stand up—only for Warlock to fall down again immediately. Keith looked down and would never forget the sight for as long as he lived. Warlock's leg from the thigh down was simply gone. Keith looked back and saw the lower half of Warlock's leg lying in the parking lot. A .50-caliber round had hit him cleanly just above the knee and instantly severed his leg.

Sparky dashed over, and he and Keith grabbed Warlock under the armpits and dragged him to the car, which was less than fifty yards away at that point. Warlock didn't say anything; he just gulped air with his mouth like a fish out of water. Keith knew now that Warlock had been in deep shock, but he didn't think anything at the time.

They tossed Warlock into the back seat of the SUV, and Drifter climbed in with him. Keith took the passenger seat while Sparky drove. They heard a helicopter landing behind them and continuous fire by all types of weapons. Sparky tore out of there, heading for home.

About ten minutes later, Warlock died. Drifter was covered with blood, but they didn't have any medical supplies, and none of their training had been in first aid.

Warlock had simply bled out, dying without fanfare, ribbons, or a ticker-tape parade. His death wouldn't be heralded on the news, and it seemed the ideals they were fighting for had become a little less clear.

The four-hour drive back to Capac had been made entirely in silence. It was most definitely not as fun as Keith had thought it would be.

Keith didn't like to think about it as he sat on his mother's couch, so he kept scrolling through TikTok. After a while, those videos made him so angry that he wanted to lash out at someone. America was going down the toilet. The fascists were telling people what to think, preventing them from speaking their minds and preventing hardworking people from achieving their American dream. It just wasn't right!

Finally, Keith decided to go out for a walk.

It was a chilly afternoon, so Keith went to his duffel and grabbed an EMU sweatshirt. Seeing his Glock sitting there, he decided to grab it as well. You never know when something bad might happen, especially in today's violent world. He didn't have a holster, so he decided just to tuck the pistol into the back of his jeans, as he'd seen countless times on television.

His mother's cottage was located at the corner of Ballentine and Omar Streets, just one block from the water. Heading out the front door toward the water, Keith started to turn to the right to head toward the Fort Gratiot Lighthouse and views of the Blue Water Bridge. Stopping, he realized he'd done that walk the last time he visited his mother. Maybe this time, he should try walking north.

64

Port Huron, Michigan

Monday, April 15

THE SOUND of a revving chainsaw ripped through the living room, cutting through the silence between the governor and his chief of staff. Jeff was holding firm on not signing an executive order that would unilaterally extend Michigan's state of emergency for another thirty days, as Aidan was pressuring him to do.

It wasn't that Jeff didn't want to continue the state of emergency. Under Michigan law, the governor could only declare a state of emergency for thirty days, after which the state legislature must renew it through a joint resolution. The issue now, with the first 30-day state of emergency due to expire in less than a week, was that the new Republican leadership of the legislature was playing hardball with Jeff, thinking him a pushover as he had no political experience.

In a classic quid pro quo, the Republicans offered to extend the state of emergency and the expanded powers this gave the governor and his executive branch in return for Jeff agreeing to outlaw federal law enforcement throughout Michigan, as all Red states had done. Aidan's solution was to ignore the state legislature and simply sign a new 30-day extension, something the previous governor had done on several occasions, including the response to COVID-19.

This was "politics as usual," as Aidan had said.

The problem was that Jeff did not intend to be a "politics as usual" governor, even for the short time he would be in office. His conscience wouldn't let him do it, and he was committed to doing things correctly. Hence the silent standoff with his chief of staff.

The sound of the chainsaw was a welcome diversion, and Jeff looked out the front windows to see what was happening. There, in the front yard where the grass met the beach, Ted Thompson was cutting up the limb that had fallen several weeks back in his neighbor's yard. Good ole' Ted Thompson!

Jeff excused himself with Aidan and walked out the front door into the yard. The sound of Ted's chainsaw was much louder outside, and as Jeff approached, he could smell the pleasant scent of freshly cut wood. Jeff noticed the state trooper standing in his glass security cubicle at the edge of the sidewalk and was vaguely aware that someone, likely Big Papi, the leader of his protection detail, had trailed Jeff out of the front door.

Ted was bent over the fallen oak limb by the stone wall separating Jeff's property from his neighbor Don's. Older than Jeff by a few years, Ted was now in his mid-60s but still had a full head of blond hair and his famous blond handlebar mustache. If Ted had any personal protective gear, such as a helmet, goggles, or protective pants, he had left them at home. Still extremely fit as always, Ted was expertly using the chainsaw to carve the large fallen limb into manageable pieces, likely to be used on his farm for firewood.

Jeff's best friend growing up, and still his best friend, was his neighbor Don. They were the same age, their parents were friends who vacationed together, and they'd spent their entire childhoods in these two adjacent houses on the lake. Don's older brother, Mike, had been best friends with Ted Thompson, and Jeff and Don were always in awe of the two free spirits who were several years older than they were. Ted was in a band; Ted had a motorcycle; Ted had the hottest girlfriend; Ted had beer; and Ted had weed. For most of

Divided We Stand

Jeff's teenage years, it was always Ted this, Ted that, hey, did you hear what Ted was doing? The guy was an absolute legend, and his presence always brought a smile to Jeff's face.

Ted's presence on his lawn stripped away all of the stress of the past few weeks. Here was a guy Jeff could talk to who could care less about his appointment as governor.

"Hey, Ted!" Jeff yelled so as to be heard above the din of the chainsaw. "Ted!"

Ted looked up upon hearing his name. A smile broke out under the waxed handlebar mustache, and Ted shut off the chainsaw. "Well, if it isn't Jeff Veno! Hey, brother, how've you been?"

Ted walked over to shake Jeff's hand. There was no need to remove any protective gloves, as Ted had apparently left those at home as well.

"Hey, Ted, great to see you. Don finally has you cutting up this limb for him?" While Jeff and Don had both purchased their family homes on the lake, Don had moved away years ago to Massachusetts, now using his childhood home as a vacation home. Ted did caretaking jobs for Don when needed.

"Yeah, yeah, he finally called me about it. Apparently, the dang tree service was gonna charge him four hundred dollars to remove it. I said, hell, Don, I'll do it for a hundred bucks if you let me keep the wood." Ted and Jeff both laughed, knowing Don was notoriously stingy with a buck.

"Good for you, Ted."

"Yeah, yeah. I woulda done it just for the free firewood—that stuff's like gold nowadays—but I figured what the hell, it's not every day you can get a hundred bucks outa Don with him feeling like he saved money!" Jeff laughed. No one could match Ted's sense of humor or ability to tell an engaging story. "So, waddya been up to, Jeff? I hear you're governor now. How's that going?"

Jeff smiled. Only Ted Thompson could ask about being governor in the same tone as he'd ask about Jeff buying a new bicycle.

"It's going good, Ted. A lot of work, but so far never a dull moment."

"Yeah, yeah. I can imagine. I bet you have to go to Lansing all the time now, huh? Did I ever tell you the time Mike and I went up to Lansing to party with a few girls from a sorority? Oh, man, that's quite a story. Nothing at all to do with the sorority girls—has to do with a white horse we found."

Jeff smiled, trying not to laugh. Good old Ted Thompson—he could put a smile on anybody's face and always made the day just a bit brighter. Jeff had indeed heard that story before—a classic tale that ended with Ted and Mike loading a white horse into an old Pontiac convertible, two hoofed feet in the front and two in the rear, and driving around the countryside in the middle of the night searching for the horse's owner.

KEITH WALKED SLOWLY up the sidewalk, not in any hurry. He'd never been down this sidewalk before and admired the large houses on the left side of the walkway, envious of their unspoiled views out across Lake Huron to Canada. Keith liked the fact that some of the houses were newly remodeled, but others had kept their original charm and character and looked more like old beach houses rather than small mansions.

It was a chilly day, but Keith inhaled deeply, savoring the smell of Spring alongside the lake—the deep, earthy scent of the land combined with the fresh, airy breeze coming off the lake. In the distance, Keith could see two large freighters, but they were too far away to tell whether they were coming or going.

Keith stepped aside and said hello to an older gentleman walking toward him with two small dogs on a leash. The pistol at the rear of his waistband kept feeling like it was going to fall, so Keith found himself continually adjusting it through his sweatshirt.

A hundred yards ahead, Keith could see what looked like a plexiglass portapotty, but with a guy standing inside the small booth. Off to his right, near the lake, two men were chatting over a downed tree limb. One of the guys, the big guy with white hair, looked vaguely familiar to Keith.

As Keith continued along the sidewalk, he could tell the man in the glass booth was a policeman. Cops always made Keith nervous. He felt the Glock pistol in his waistband begin to slip again and reached back to adjust it as he walked past the booth.

"Gun!" Keith heard someone say from his left. He never saw the man in the blue blazer standing just off the front porch of the large house. Keith's initial reaction at hearing someone yell "Gun" was to reach for the pistol in his waistband.

The next thing Keith knew, he was looking sideways at shiny black shoes and the cuff of gray pants right at his eye level. He had the sensation of grass on his cheeks, but otherwise, he was just cold. A deep, piercing cold emanated from his arms and legs and pushed inwards toward a burning fire he felt in his chest. He couldn't focus on the shoes, but more shoes came into view, and he thought he heard people yelling.

The cold kept coming closer and closer to his core, to his heart. Keith felt frigid icicles piercing his chest, his soul. Then he felt—.

65

Ferrisburgh, Vermont

Sunday, April 21

THE INTRICATE WEB of blue and red string was supposed to paint a picture, but the more Nathan stared at it, the less he understood. It was nine o'clock at night, almost a week after his confrontation at Big Al's Frys in Burlington, and he'd been working in the basement bunker since after lunch earlier that day.

Felipe had been a bit shaken by the events of the previous Monday, but an ice cream sundae had gone a long way toward bringing back some normalcy. The Burlington Police had taken Nathan's information, but they didn't seem terribly concerned once they realized no one was injured. This was one of many calls regarding shootings or violent confrontations, and the police were rushing off to another call of shots fired.

Lourdes was doing an amazing job turning Valhalla into a home for all of them, while Spooner spent his days getting his team and equipment settled into the four-bedroom Bancroft House located at the entrance to the estate's property and enhancing security around the perimeter of the 345-acre estate.

Divided We Stand

Nathan continued to collate all the information and intelligence he and Spooner had been able to collect, but it just wasn't adding up to anything actionable. He could feel they were close, and he definitely suspected Orlean Brumback and possibly Alex Treacher were involved in the Cabal or could lead him to the Cabal, but he currently had no definitive information upon which to act.

He took a sip of Diet Coke and continued to analyze the maps, photos, and connecting string.

A quick knock at the door startled Nathan. "Knock, knock," said Spooner, slowly pushing open the door to the basement office where Nathan sat. "Any progress?"

"None," said Nathan. "I feel like we're so close, but there's so much information we still don't have access to."

"Did you speak with Sharyn Gray down in D.C?"

"Briefly. She was caught up in some drama, so we agreed to speak at length tomorrow. What about you? Everyone settling in?"

"Yes. Terry, Mitch, and Roy are all settled into the farmhouse at the entrance. That place is off the hook. Nicer than probably any home I've ever been in—excluding this one, of course."

"I know. Pretty crazy, huh?" Nathan agreed. "Twenty years ago, we were both living in tract housing outside the back gate of Fort Bragg. Now look at us."

"Yeah, it's definitely been a wild ride."

"Hey, I was thinking," Nathan said. "We need to beef up our team a bit."

"Okay," said Spooner, wary of Nathan's often unconventional ideas. "What did you have in mind?"

"I was thinking we need our own intelligence cell here—more than just you and me. Someone who can access things and connect the dots in ways we can only dream of."

"Okay, I like it."

"Remember Ruby?" Nathan asked.

Of course, Spooner remembered Ruby. Who could forget Ruby?

Ruby was an intelligence analyst who had been seconded to support Task Force 121 in Iraq. She was an information exploitation expert whom Nathan and Spooner's Delta Force team had worked with extensively during many missions and came to respect.

A fiery redhead standing no higher than 5'0" tall, Ruby was rail thin, had the physique of a 10-year-old boy, and a penchant for red licorice and foul language. She could do amazing things with computers and technology and was the fastest computer hacker Nathan had ever seen. No one was ever really sure what agency Ruby was originally from, with most bets on her being from the National Security Agency—NSA—the ultrasecret U.S. Intelligence agency tasked with all things related to signals intelligence.

"Yeah, you mean the Ruby who told General McManus to go fuck himself with a pool noodle?"

"Yeah," laughed Nathan. "That Ruby."

"No one forgets *that* Ruby," Spooner replied.

"We need her here. She could crack this open for us in weeks, maybe days."

"Okay, and how do you propose we find her?"

"That's your job, man," said Nathan, smiling. "I'm the good idea guy. You're the get it done guy."

Spooner rolled his eyes, but his mind was already searching for contacts who might know how to contact Ruby directly.

Nathan stood up with his empty glass of Diet Coke. "I'm going up to the kitchen for more Diet Coke and a snack. Need anything while I'm up there?" Spooner shook his head negatively. "Okay. Do your best to find Ruby by the time I get back."

"It's nine o'clock at night," said Spooner.

"I know, but I have confidence in you."

NATHAN RETURNED to the basement office with two cans of Diet Coke and a full glass of ice. He'd waited fifteen minutes in hopes that Spooner had made some progress in the search for the elusive Ruby. Spooner was just finishing up a phone call when Nathan sat back down in his swivel chair.

"Well," started Spooner. "I've got good news and bad news."

"Okay," said Nathan. "I'll bite."

Divided We Stand

"The good news is that I tracked down Ruby. She *was* with the NSA when we knew her in Iraq, but she's subsequently gone private and is now a private contractor with the NSA, picking and choosing the jobs she works on."

"Okay, that's the good news?" Nathan asked.

"Kind of. The actual good news is that I found someone with Ruby's direct phone number, and he informed me she's currently between contracts. Which means she's available to freelance for us."

"That *is* good news," said Nathan. "And the bad news?"

"The bad news is that she's in Koh Lipe—a tiny island off southern Thailand with more beaches than people. She's apparently cut herself off from the world and told everyone she won't be back until the end of the year. I have her direct satellite phone, but there's no telling if she'll answer."

"What time is it in Koh Lipe? Where the hell is that, anyway? By Phuket?" Nathan had been to Thailand before but had never made it south of Bangkok. He and Emily often talked about visiting Phuket once Maeve started college. Nathan realized, not for the first time, that all those dreams were ancient history. He'd never see Phuket. His sole focus was on avenging his wife and daughter, and after that, he still had no intention of continuing the pointlessness that life had become.

Spooner typed for a few seconds on the laptop in front of him. "It's eleven hours ahead of us. So eight-thirty in the morning their time."

"Excellent," said Nathan. "Dial her up."

Spooner referred to his notes and dialed the number on his iPhone. He put the phone on its external speaker setting and placed it on the table in front of Nathan. The phone rang in that unmistakable fast double-ring that was common to overseas telephones, even though, in this case, it was a satellite phone they were calling.

"Speak," said a woman answering the phone on the other end.

"Ruby? This is Nathan Greene. We worked together—."

"*The* Nathan Greene?" Ruby interrupted, speaking over him. "*Professor* Nathan Greene? Medal of Honor winner Captain Nathan

Greene? *The* Nathan Greene who shoots FBI agents? That Nathan Greene?"

Oh shit, Nathan thought. *Ruby hadn't changed.*

"Ah, yeah," he said. "That Nathan Greene."

"Oh my gosh, my panties are so wet right now," Ruby squealed in her fakest imitation cheerleader voice. "What can I do for you, Professor?"

Nathan could hear Ruby chomping away at something, and he could picture her chewing on the end of a long piece of red licorice. In the year that they'd worked together, he'd never seen her without licorice, almost always red. She had boxes of it flown in from the Netherlands, he'd once been told.

Nathan began to wonder if reaching out to Ruby had been a mistake. He decided to just be blunt.

"I need your help, Ruby. I'm trying to find my wife and daughter's killers, and I need your help. It's an off-the-books operation, privately funded, but I need you to help me find them so I can kill them."

Ruby was silent for a moment. "Who's car we gonna take?"

Nathan laughed. Leave it to Ruby to crack a joke, quoting the famous scene from Ben Affleck and Jeremy Renner in the movie *The Town.*

"I'm dead serious, Ruby. I know you don't value small talk, but that's the mission."

Ruby's voice changed, reflecting her change in demeanor. "I was very sorry to learn of your wife and daughter's death, Nathan. I'm sorry for giving you shit at the start of our conversation. I've been waiting for your call for the last ten minutes, so I thought I'd have some fun. Where do you need me to be, and when do you want me there? I'm in."

"Thanks, Ruby. But I haven't even told you what I need you to do or how much it pays or for how long."

"Nathan, you're the most noble warrior I've ever worked with, and in the year we worked together, I never once saw you ask for help. If you're asking for my help now, I'm in—it doesn't matter

Divided We Stand

what it is or for how long. And for the record, I'm extremely expensive, but I heard you can afford it."

Nathan had to chuckle. "Burlington, Vermont. Buy a first-class seat that gets you here the fastest, and text us your flight number and anything else you need. This is Spooner's phone. I'll reimburse you when you get here."

"Hi, Spooner!" Ruby shouted. "And all I need is red licorice and Dr. Pepper. Oh, and I'm bringing a friend. Her name is Opal. See you soon." Ruby disconnected the call.

Nathan just sat there, staring at the silent iPhone.

"Ruby has a friend named Opal? Are you telling me we're gonna have two women here named after gems? God help us. What have we just done?" said Spooner, only half joking.

66

Washington, D.C

Monday, April 22

THE MORNING HOMELAND Security briefing was just wrapping up in the Situation Room, and the President's Chief of Staff had asked the Vice President and Sharyn to remain for a private discussion once everyone else had cleared the room. At the Vice President's order, these meetings were being held daily with all relevant officials in attendance to keep everyone updated on the deepening crisis taking America by storm.

Noticeably absent from these meetings was the Secretary of Defense, Chairman of the Joint Chiefs, or anyone representing the active-duty military. The active-duty military had initially provided static security for federal buildings, courthouses, and installations across the country. However, last week, soldiers were forced to defend against more than a dozen attacks across the country, resulting in several soldiers being killed. Secretary Boyd and General Vine had expressed their displeasure at what they perceived as a misuse of the military and had offered the Vice President a solution. They proposed that since the southern border crossings had significantly dried up everywhere but in California, border patrol agents should be redeployed to protect federal property alongside the U.S. Marshals. With over 40,000 border patrol agents, moving 10,000 to provide static security should not pose a problem.

The Vice President hated the idea, resenting General Vine's refusal to capitulate, but ultimately gave in and acquiesced. Since that meeting, with the military having successfully removed themselves from homeland security functions, no one from the Defense Department attended these daily meetings.

Today's briefing included more of the same alarming news as the previous briefings. The nation was turned on its head, and as things worsened, Sharyn could see a real path toward an all-out civil war: Red States and Blue States. In fact, the Secretary of Homeland Security, Marcellus Melendez, had recently begun using a briefing map of the United States that actually used red and blue color designations for the fifty states. Sharyn was reminded of historical maps of the 1860s that showed the Union in blue and the Confederacy in gray.

Thirty-four state legislatures had officially demanded a Constitutional Convention. In Sharyn's discussions with Congressional leaders, there seemed no question that the Congress, now with both houses narrowly controlled by the Republicans, would authorize the first Constitutional Convention since 1787. The Convention would be held in Omaha, Nebraska and commence on July 4, 2024.

There remained numerous questions regarding the delegates and voting at the Convention, and these were all being worked out between the state legislatures and the U.S. Congress. Some proposed delegates apportioned similarly to the Electoral College, while others said each state should get one vote. The current consensus seemed to be to allow each state to determine its own number of delegates but that each state would get only one vote at the Convention. Despite Sharyn's deep misgivings about convening the Convention, she understood this one-state-one-vote approach as, ultimately, for any changes to the Constitution to be made, thirty-eight states would be required to ratify the changes.

There were currently sixteen confirmed Blue states, and each of these states was pretty firmly in the control of the Democratic Party, her party. As she looked at the map, she felt certain that twelve of the sixteen Blue states could never be turned Red. The four western states—California, Oregon, Washington, and Hawaii—each had close to seventy percent of their population as registered Democrats. The same was true for Illinois and the six states along the Eastern Seaboard from Massachusetts to Maryland.

This left only four possible states with any potential to be turned Red. Colorado and New Mexico had traditionally been Republican strongholds during the mid-20th century. New Mexico had periods where it flipped back and forth every couple of decades, but Colorado had been firmly Republican from the 1920s through the 2004 election. It was only in 2008 that it turned fully Blue.

Vermont and Maine were the other two potentials. Located in northern New England, each has a very small population; it would not take much to swing these states over to Red. Vermont, the second smallest state by population with only 650,000 residents, voted Republican in every election but one between 1856 and 1992. Maine, slightly larger, had 1.3 million people and had a similar election history of voting Republican. Blue didn't run very deep in any of these four states, and if Sharyn were advising the other side, these are where she'd be focusing her efforts.

That said, no one was asking Sharyn's opinion of how this potential civil war would progress, and her job was to advise the Vice President and not comment on civil war strategy.

The most alarming aspect of each daily briefing was the escalating level of violence across the country, Red and Blue states alike. It was clear that people were angry. They were not only angry but also felt like they had either the right or the obligation, or perhaps the freedom, to inflict harm on those who disagreed with their point of view. Freedom of assembly was being replaced with freedom to fight; freedom of speech was being subsumed by freedom to hate.

All fifty states had activated and mobilized all or some of their National Guard units to help quell the violence. Universities across the country had either already suspended on-campus activities or shortened their Spring semester and moved their graduations to this

Divided We Stand

past weekend. School boards throughout the nation were discussing options for stay-at-home learning, similar to what occurred during the COVID-19 pandemic.

Every day, more and more people were being killed over ideology, rhetoric, and partisanship. Geraldine Fox presented the assembled staff yesterday with a study tracing the current social media content and usage shift. The figures were absolutely staggering. Everyone, from children to senior citizens, was spending more and more time watching television, viewing social media, and posting online. CNN, Fox News, and MSNBC were seeing ratings similar to those during the first few days after 9/11. Not only were exponentially more people viewing Facebook, Instagram, X (formerly Twitter), and TikTok, but they were spending double the amount of time as compared to three months ago.

It was a chicken-and-egg conversation as to whether social media content drove the algorithms or the algorithms drove the content, but the result was the same. Content was becoming more divisive, more instigatory, and more hateful. People felt incited to act, and the result was that thousands of people had been senselessly killed over the last six weeks.

The Vice President adjourned the meeting, and the participants exited without fanfare. Everyone had a busy schedule ahead of them, and no one wanted to linger and chitchat. Before long, only the Vice President, Chief of Staff, White House Communications director, and Sharyn remained in the Situation Room.

"Thank you all for remaining behind for a few minutes. Serena, I know you're exceptionally busy today, but I thought this would be a good time for us all to huddle for a few minutes and make sure we're all on the same sheet of music," said John Reynolds.

"Sure, John," said the Vice President. "What has you concerned?"

"Everything has me concerned. But what I'm specifically referring to is President Fulton. We've done a commendable job covering for him these last few weeks, but at some point, it's not going to be feasible. If this crisis keeps getting worse, the President will need to speak directly to the American people. I'm not as worried about campaigning, as it's basically the same speech and same routine over and over, but at some point, we need to address the long-term prospects on whether President Fulton can fulfill the obligations of the office of the President for four more years."

"I had a very good conversation with him yesterday," interjected Geraldine, the Communications Director. "He was totally engaged and had some very interesting insights."

"Look," said John. "The President has all his faculties, and his doctors say he's extremely healthy for his age. The issue becomes one of capacity, almost like an old battery. When fully charged, the President is great. But he wears down quickly, at which point we don't know which Bill Fulton we're going to get. That's why we have these daily meetings in the morning and have the President attend the first fifteen minutes. He's sharp as a tack when he first wakes up, but at some point, whether it's fatigue or information overload, he just seems to lose concentration and have a bit of snap from reality. After these morning meetings, Brad takes him to the Oval Office to sign documents and make a few phone calls. Then, after resting in the residence and having a good lunch, he's normally good for another hour or two of meetings in the Oval each afternoon—at least on a good day."

"So what are you suggesting, John?" Vice President Moore asked.

"I don't know, Serena. I just want us to have a plan for how best to proceed. Marino will most likely be the Republican nominee for the November election. President Fulton still polls extremely well against Marino—the majority of moderates can't stand the guy."

"The majority of Americans think Governor Marino's a little Napoleon," said a smiling Geraldine. "It doesn't hurt that our social media advocates keep churning out memes showing how short Marino really is."

"This growing crisis could actually help with Bill's campaign," offered Moore. "As the security situation continues to deteriorate, it will become more likely that the candidates will be unable to travel as much as they have in past elections. This will allow us to manage

Divided We Stand

the media's access to the President while still allowing the campaign engines to keep working full speed in every state."

"That's a good point, Serena," said John. "But do we truly think it's in the nation's best interest for the President to have four more years in office?"

"It's certainly better than having Marino in office," said Geraldine. "The guy can't get past his *anti-woke* agenda to even begin discussing the real issues facing this country."

"Keeping Marino out of the White House isn't the real issue, Geraldine," stated Moore. "John, you and I both know the only way for us to keep our jobs is for President Fulton to get re-elected. If I were to launch a campaign myself, it wouldn't even get off the ground. We've talked about this, but no viable Democratic candidate, other than Bill Fulton, currently polls high enough to beat anyone the Republicans will nominate. And if Bill is re-elected, we can keep our jobs and then have a discussion about invoking the 25th Amendment."

Sharyn tried to keep the concerned look off her face. She greatly respected the Vice President. Serena was a strong, intelligent, charismatic Black woman who was committed to America's best interests. Lately, however, Sharyn had come to see a side of Serena that wasn't as admirable, a side that was more about gathering and retaining power and status. Sharyn supposed every politician at this level had this same hubris and rabid self-interest, but sometimes it was disappointing to peek behind the curtain.

"Look," said John. "I'm all for beating Marino, and I don't necessarily think it will be difficult, even with the country as divided as it's becoming. The more Marino puts his goofy, child-molester smile on television, the more America dislikes the guy. The question for me becomes: at what point are we perpetuating a fraud on America by hiding Bill Fulton's limitations? It's one thing to protect him until the end of his term. It's a whole 'nother story to pull a Weekend at Bernie's and try to get him re-elected."

"Enough!" Serena snapped. "Talk like this is not helpful, John. America needs us—and I mean the four of us in this room. We are the ones keeping the barbarians from storming through the gate. A

Republican presidency would be the end of American leadership in the world and quite possibly the demise of democracy around the world. If I thought another Democrat, or even a reasonable Republican for that matter, would do a better job, then I would gladly step down. But we've seen the polls, John. We've read the analysis. It's Bill Fulton, or it's doomsday. And as for fraud, I never want to hear talk like that again. You saw Bill this morning—he was engaging, witty, and sharp as a tack. Does he have weak moments? Sure. Does he need to rest more frequently than he did a couple of years ago? Absolutely. But he's still President of the United States, and if he gets re-elected, we have four years to sort it out while keeping America on course."

"Okay, Serena, I see your point," said John, somewhat sadly.

67

Ferrisburgh, Vermont

Friday, April 26

THE GOLDEN RETRIEVER had fallen asleep with her head across Nathan's lap and was snoring lightly. He lazily stroked the dog's fur, unsure how he'd gotten himself into this predicament. *I've never even owned a dog, so why is she becoming attached to me?* He thought with a smile.

Nathan had just finished a five-mile run along the dirt roads of Ferrisburgh and currently sat on the wide stone steps leading down from Valhalla's back deck to the expansive lawn running down to the shores of Lake Champlain. With a frosted white muzzle indicative of her age, the golden retriever had sauntered up, plopped down gracelessly next to him, and nuzzled his arm for a pet. In minutes, she was fast asleep across his lap and snoring.

It had now been just over two full days since Ruby had arrived, having flown into Burlington International Airport on the last arriving flight of Tuesday evening. Spooner had finagled security passes for himself and Nathan, apparently telling the airline staff that his sister Ruby was mentally challenged and needed assistance.

The woman was skeptical, but something must have changed her mind when she looked Ruby up in the system. She immediately issued passes to both Nathan and Spooner to allow them to go through the TSA screening point.

Ruby was the first passenger up the jetway, with Opal walking next to her. One look at Opal had Nathan smiling from ear to ear, realizing that Ruby had once again surprised him. The female friend Ruby had insisted on bringing was a golden retriever.

"Well, look at you two degenerates," Ruby said, smiling and tightly hugging Nathan and Spooner in greeting. "Boys, meet Opal. Where I go, she goes."

As they walked to baggage claim, Spooner asked, "I'm surprised you were able to get Opal in the cabin with you. I thought you had to put dogs in crates."

"Not when they have their own first-class ticket," said Ruby, chuckling. "Opal thanks you for that, Nathan."

"My pleasure," said Nathan, not caring in the least and glad to have Ruby and Opal in Vermont. He knew in his heart that Ruby was the answer to their missing link. If anyone could find the Cabal, it was Ruby.

Ruby had been awed by Valhalla's grandness, but once she saw the "bunker"—what they had begun calling the large office in the basement—she wanted to get right to work. Nathan thought Ruby would be jet-lagged, but she showed zero signs of being sleep-deprived after her almost thirty-hour flight ordeal.

At midday on Wednesday, a large panel truck arrived from Boston. The inside of the truck was chock-full of computer gear: servers, hard drives, flat-screen monitors, laser printers, and myriad other electronic devices and contraptions. The two delivery drivers had spent all afternoon shuttling boxes to the basement and helping Ruby set everything up.

Spooner had wondered what that all cost, but Nathan didn't care. He could feel them getting closer to the Cabal, and money was not an issue.

Since then, Nathan had only spent several hours in Ruby's company. She'd requested his presence Wednesday evening in the

Divided We Stand

bunker, and he and Spooner had gone down to explain to Ruby everything they'd tried up to that point to find the Cabal. Even though Ruby had been living on one of the most remote islands off the coast of Thailand, she had kept up with current events in the United States. She did, however, ask Nathan a significant number of questions about all of the terrorist attacks he'd been tracking, especially those occurring on March 21st.

After the lengthy question-and-answer session, Ruby said, "Okay, boys, that's all I need. I'll let you know when I have something. Could be days, could be weeks, but don't disturb me 'til I let you know I have something."

Since then, Nathan had been bored out of his mind. Spooner had his team of ex-Delta operators and worked tirelessly on improving security at Valhalla. Lourdes was focused on managing the operations of the house, as well as being a mom to Felipe. Felipe had made friends with several local boys and was having a blast playing on a Little League team in the nearby town of Vergennes.

That left Nathan to work out in Valhalla's gym, jog all the trails on the property and adjacent dirt roads, and generally attempt to keep his mind occupied without going stir-crazy. Opal had taken to following Nathan around the house, probably because he slipped her pancakes under the table each morning, and the two had become fast friends. It was nice to feel close to someone, and he enjoyed and envied her sleeping on his lap, not a care in the world.

"Stealing my dog?" Came a voice from behind him.

Nathan turned to see Ruby standing in the doorway at the back of the house. She was wearing yoga pants and a bright green form-fitting tank top that matched her emerald green eyes. Now in her mid-thirties, she still had zero curves to her body. Nathan wondered how she kept so thin on her steady diet of red licorice. Ruby's long red hair was pulled back in a ponytail, and with the freckles across her cheeks, Nathan couldn't help but think of Pippy Longstockings.

As soon as Opal heard Ruby's voice she perked up and slowly got to her feet. The dog's rambunctious years were definitely in the rearview mirror, and it was clear Opal's age encouraged her to be a bit more methodical about her actions.

"Good morning, Ruby. Just enjoying another beautiful Spring morning in the sunshine. How's everything coming?"

"Good," she said, never one to waste words. "I'm ready to show you what I've found. Grab Spooner and come down to the bunker. But take a shower and wash your stinky ass first. I can't have you fouling up my bunker." Ruby turned and walked back into the house without waiting for his reaction.

Opal looked at her owner and then glanced back at Nathan as if to say, "Should I follow her or stay with you?" Nathan reached out to give her a quick pet, which seemed to sway Opal's decision, as the retriever promptly sat down on the warm stone steps.

"Feel free to stay out here, girl, and enjoy the sunshine. Looks like I have to go shower."

FIFTEEN MINUTES LATER, Nathan and Spooner were sitting in chairs across the drafting table from Ruby. The oversized drafting table and the one wall of maps Nathan had put together were the only things in the room recognizable from before Ruby took over the bunker. One entire wall was now a computer screen, as Ruby had seamlessly connected a dozen very large monitors to make one integrated screen upon which various graphs, charts, maps, and images were displayed. The back wall had a computer workstation upon which a 57-inch curved computer monitor sat in front of a red leather SecretLab Titan gaming chair. This was clearly where Ruby performed her magic. The last wall had been turned into a floor-to-ceiling corkboard, upon which Ruby had tacked dozens of printouts and photographs.

"Okay, Ruby, what've you got for us?" asked Spooner.

"I don't have shit for you, you Neanderthal," said Ruby smiling. "But for Captain Medal of Honor here, I have quite a bit."

Both Spooner and Nathan shook their heads, attempting not to laugh. Although they hadn't seen much of Ruby since she'd arrived, as she'd spent almost every waking minute sequestered in the bunker, the time they did spend with her was filled with amusing expletives, imaginative nicknames, and sly retorts.

Divided We Stand

"Okay, Ruby," said Nathan. "We're all ears."

"Speaking of which, Spooner-man should consider shaving his." Ruby typed quickly on the wireless keyboard in front of her, and the wall of computer screens went black before transitioning to display images along the perimeter of various terrorist attacks conducted over the last two months.

"Okay, I'll speak slowly so you two knuckle-draggers can understand, but please try to keep up," Ruby began. "First, the FBI has no clue who's behind these attacks. They aren't even positive that they're all linked. They know that some were conducted by Islamic jihadists, and they also have confirmed evidence that at least two of the attacks were perpetrated by drug cartel thugs. None of the eighteen U.S. intelligence agencies have put any puzzle pieces together. The leads they are following from the attackers they've killed have been deadends, and so has any forensic evidence recovered from the scene. Fingerprints, weapon serial numbers, vehicle registrations—none of these has produced any viable threads upon which to pull and unravel the mystery of who's behind these attacks."

"Please tell me this isn't all you've found," said Spooner.

"Hey, Spooner, when I want something out of you, I'll squeeze your head. Otherwise, zip it," Ruby teased, drawing her fingers across her lips in a zipping motion. While likely joking, Spooner did keep his mouth shut.

"Relax," Ruby continued. "I'm telling you all this to show you what the government has found, which is basically zilch. I, on the other hand, am not the government, and by that I mean that I actually get shit done."

She typed a few more keystrokes, and a full-size map of the United States popped onto the center of the wall's video screen. Dozens, maybe hundreds, of small dots and lines connected various cities across the country.

"I took a much different approach than the FBI and law enforcement investigators. First, I started with the St. Armands Circle bombing and then created a list of every known terrorist incident. Not just the March 21st incidents but also violent protests, murders, or home invasions that appeared to be, one, politically motivated, and two, executed by someone with some form of military training or expertise. Basically, I discounted everything where it was a shooting by some right-wing nutjob or vegan Antifa freak.

"I gathered all the information I could find and used several analysis platforms to find patterns—anything that might help point us in the right direction. And I got nothing. Bupkis. Nada.

"But then I read a news article on the latest attempted assassination of the new governor of Michigan. Some guy named Jeff Veno, who apparently isn't even a politician. Anyway, it sounded like a completely amateur effort—some young guy who'd been radicalized by too much social media walking by the governor's home and trying to pull a gun out of his waistband and shoot him."

"So what's that got to do with the Cabal?" Spooner asked.

"Absolutely nothing. At least, that's what I thought at first. But reading the article made me want to tap into the Michigan State Police investigation files 'cuz you never know how badly the press screws up a story nowadays. Anyway, I crack into their server and start reading the files they've put together. This guy, his name is Keith Jeffries, is kind of a misguided young man who was radicalized after March 21st. But the attack on the governor isn't his first shindig. When they searched his mother's house, they found a rifle. The ballistics of that rifle, a short-barreled AR-15, led the investigators to a recent raid on a National Guard checkpoint in Indiana two weeks ago. Killed a bunch of National Guard guys and resulted in a few dead Antifa terrorists. A fingerprint on some piece of equipment found in Indiana led investigators to some whackjob named George Crenshaw, aka Sparky. The State Police rolled up on this guy, and he gave up everything he knew—the most juicy tidbit being the presence of a very fit woman who trained their teams on some land outside Capac, Michigan. He had dates for their training.

"So I now added this information to the database that I had built with all this other information on St. Armands Circle, the shooting down of King's plane, and the attacks on March 21. Bingo! One little hit, but like a tiny little thread on a massive wool blanket, it keeps getting bigger and bigger once you start pulling on it.

"I started adding to this dataset and focusing on transportation.

Divided We Stand

If the Cabal does, in fact, exist, and I agree with you, Nathan, that it does, they must be moving their people around. If they can recruit and train Islamic jihadists, drug cartel sicarios, and misguided Michigan English teachers, they have to be able to somehow rapidly transport their trainers and recruiters around the country. And given the distances involved, they have to fly.

"Knowing that the FBI has already exhaustively searched the airlines for any links to the dead terrorists, I looked at private planes. While there's no central database, numerous databases collect various data on tail numbers and flight information. Even a couple of top-secret programs have clandestinely implemented surveillance systems at private airfields to capture this data where people think no one is looking.

"The other thing I focused on was the information in the state law enforcement databases. Ever since the Red States told the FBI and U.S. Marshals to pound sand, quite a few states stopped sharing information with the various national law enforcement databases. By hacking into the files in each state, I basically built what is probably the most comprehensive dataset related to all of these incidents."

Nathan had to shake his head. Whatever Ruby was going to charge him for her services wouldn't be anywhere near her full value. She was simply priceless.

Ruby continued her briefing uninterrupted. "I built a program that collates the relevant information from all of these databases and datasets. I then refined the software with artificial intelligence and queried it to find any commonalities. Lo and behold another bingo! This time: winner-winner chicken dinner. I was able to tie several tail numbers of planes that arrived or departed within twenty-four hours and from an airfield within two hundred miles of an incident. It may not seem like much, but you'd be surprised at how few planes that entails. And you'd be even more surprised that I can link the corporations that own all of those tail numbers."

"Holy shit," said Spooner.

Nathan leaned back in his chair, unable to speak. *I've fucking got you!* He thought to himself. He began to feel the emotions surging forth and had to will himself to keep them at bay.

"So, what's that mean?" Nathan asked. "You have the corporation behind the Cabal?"

"No, not exactly," said Ruby. "It's complicated, but whoever is behind this has incredible resources. Maybe more than anyone other than the U.S. government itself. Layers of shell corporations, single-purpose entities, and false identification documents were used to purchase or charter these aircraft. There isn't any single entity at the top of the pyramid, but I've basically been able to define what is more like an octopus—lots of tentacles that all seem to connect to each other in an amorphous head. While I can't define exactly who or what the Cabal is, I do believe I've narrowed down where their headquarters is."

"Where?" asked Nathan.

"I have two places of significant interest. The first is Kalispell, Montana. Do you know anyone operating out of Kalispell that fits your profile for the Cabal?"

"Not offhand," replied Nathan.

"From what I've gathered and using AI, Kalispell appears to be ground zero."

"You mean there are private plane flights from Kalispell to the various terrorist attack locations just on or before the attacks?" Spooner asked.

"No, you fucking moron. That's not what I'm saying," said Ruby. "Even the FBI could figure that one out."

Spooner didn't take Ruby's harsh language personally. It was a part of her personality that he'd become used to a dozen years ago when they first started working together when Ruby was a child prodigy barely twenty years old.

"This Cabal is not only well-financed, they are incredibly smart," continued Ruby. "Although not smarter than me. Without artificial intelligence, this web of private flights likely wouldn't be possible to unravel. However, with the computing power you've just purchased, Nathan, and I'm sorry to say it's several hundred thou-

Divided We Stand

sand dollars of equipment you've just bought, I can now connect the dots in a way that's never been possible."

"Okay," said Nathan. "I told you I don't care about the price tag. Please continue."

"The connections are not directly between Kalispell and airports near the terrorist incidents. This is a web of flights using hundreds of airfields, dozens of aircraft, and an even greater number of corporate entities. I've been able to generally define this amorphous web from the ether and identify visible links. Nothing that would ever stand up in a court of law, but definitely actionable intelligence like the good old days back in Iraq."

"And Kalispell, Montana is the hub?" Nathan asked. "Can you pull up a map?"

Ruby clicked a few keys, and the on-screen map zoomed in to an area encompassing northwest Montana, centered on a small city at the northern tip of Flathead Lake. "It's the closest thing we have to a hub. I can't trace any information about passengers, but it does seem to be a terminus of some sort to quite a few of the trips."

"Any other place of interest?" Spooner asked, somewhat gunshy about how Ruby might reply.

Ruby passed up the opportunity for more insults and said, "Yes, good question. There might be a connection with Jackson, Wyoming. Based on the analysis you and Nathan already put together, which I admit was pretty good for a couple of mouth-breathers, I had the software program emphasize connections initially with Sarasota but also with Tallahassee. One hotspot that immediately became evident was Jackson, Wyoming."

"That's Orlean Brumback," said Nathan. "Has to be. Bunker Hill Media is headquartered in Jackson, and there's no telling how many times he's flown between there and Florida to meet with Benjamin King and Vince Marino. But you're saying there's a connection between Jackson and Kalispell?"

"Yes, and it seems to mostly be one specific private jet, tail number N891TS. It belongs to a single-purpose entity out of Cayman, which is then owned by an entire series of shell corporations. Without AI, this would be impossible to unravel, but AI has found several connections to the ownership of other aircraft involved in the web of tentacles I just described."

"What do you mean by *several?*" Nathan asked.

"I mean that it is statistically impossible for Kalispell and this specific jet not to be directly tied with the terrorist events of March 21st. I can't say in what capacity that link involves, but I can tell you with certainty that there's a link. If this were Iraq, we'd be revving up the Blackhawks and sending you D-boys out to kick in doors and determine the link."

Nathan smiled, and it was not lost on either Spooner or Ruby that this was the first time they'd seen him truly smile.

68

Jackson, Wyoming

Saturday, April 27

ORLEAN PLACED HIS FORK DOWN, unable to eat another bite. The elk steaks had been seared to a perfect rare, lightly charred on the outside and deep pink on the inside. The lean meat was one of Orlean's favorites and he thought it appropriate for his big dinner with Vince Marino to celebrate the upcoming press conference where they would announce their Presidential and Vice Presidential ticket to America.

Eating the elk, Orlean couldn't help but think about the adage that successful predators eat what they kill. He considered himself an apex predator—sitting on top of the food chain, manipulating the people under him, and enjoying the spoils. It failed to cross Orlean's mind that he hadn't killed the elk he'd just eaten, it was a gift from a neighboring landowner in Jackson Hole. Likewise, it never occurred to him that maybe he wasn't the one doing the manipulating and that there might be a true apex predator above him.

Vince Marino enjoyed the meal as well, although the meat was a bit underdone for his liking. He couldn't remember ever having eaten elk, but like a lot of things recently, he was adding it to his list of new experiences. Vince wasn't one hundred percent thrilled with Orlean Brumback as his running mate, but he did recognize Orlean's value in building conservative support throughout the country and acting as a shield against some of Marino's personal criticisms that were now likely to be redirected toward Orlean.

"That was a truly delicious dinner, Orlean. Thank you for sending your plane to bring me to Jackson. This really is one of the prettiest spots I've ever seen."

They were having a late lunch so that Vince could fly back to Florida, and the views of the Teton Range through the large bay windows were truly spectacular.

"My pleasure, Vince. I didn't previously have a chance to give you the full tour of Bunker Hill Media's operations, so I thought it appropriate to have you out here before our campaign schedule gets hectic and show you around. I also wanted you to know that every capability I have now belongs to you. The full force of Bunker Hill Media is going to be behind our campaign, and frankly, I'm confident we'll be unstoppable."

"Thanks, and I completely agree. I can't believe the Democrats are still committed to running Fulton for a second term. The country is facing its biggest crisis in decades if not centuries, and the President is nowhere to be seen. His staff is using every excuse in the book, but America recognizes that Fulton is no longer fit for the job. Do you think there's any chance the Dems will roll someone else out? They have until their party convention in early August to make the change."

"I haven't heard any rumblings," said Orlean. "The Vice President seems to have everything locked down at the White House, and from what I'm hearing, she only cares about retaining power for herself. Fulton's reelection is her only chance of staying in the White House."

"There is one question I've been meaning to ask you," said Vince. "What's your relationship to Alex Treacher? And how well have you vetted him? My people can't find out anything about him

Divided We Stand

other than he's a self-made billionaire, mostly through some venture capital firms and hedge funds he's been involved with since he was young—parlaying a seven-figure inheritance into a nine-figure empire. Other than that, the man's a bit of a mystery."

"He's a very powerful guy," answered Orlean. "Much of King's success was due to Alex's advice and support. He and I have been friends for quite a few years, and he's someone I've come to trust implicitly. If he says he's going to do something, it gets done. And every time he asked me to do something, it turned out to be enormously beneficial for me."

"Okay," said Vince, not fully satisfied with Orlean's answer.

"Guys like Alex are part of playing the game at this level. They come with the territory. Of all the guys like Alex I've ever met, I'd definitely choose him. He's a true patriot. Lives and breathes red, white, and blue. So far he's never steered me wrong, and his pockets are so deep I don't know if there's a bottom."

"Good to know," concluded Vince. "So what's on the agenda this week?"

"I'm headed to Richmond tomorrow for a meeting with Governor Decker. On Monday, I'll be down in Tallahassee for the big announcement, and then after that, I thought I'd go to D.C. and make the rounds with all the talk shows. That is unless you want me elsewhere. After the announcement on Monday, my full attention is on supporting your campaign."

"No, your schedule sounds good. We can talk on Monday to refine the campaign strategy."

69

Alexandria, Virginia

Sunday, April 28

NATHAN TOOK a long pull from the cold pint glass of Hefeweizen. He closed his eyes, letting the taste take him back to the carefree time when he was studying for his PhD at Georgetown and he and Emily lived just a few blocks up the road on Prince Street.

He was seated in the familiar red leather booth of the Union Street Public House. Nothing had changed since he was last here more than a decade ago, and the cold Hefeweizen with the slice of orange went down as smoothly as he remembered. *God, I wish Emily was here. I never even had a chance to take Maeve here. There's so many things she'll never experience.*

Nathan shut down his thoughts like a steel trap. He placed the beer on the table and started paying attention to the conversation between his tablemates—Spooner and Sharyn Gray. They'd flown down that morning to meet with her and were planning to complete another mission task while they were in the area.

"I know when you're lying," said Nathan after listening to a few seconds of Sharyn answering one of Spooner's questions.

Divided We Stand

"What do you mean?" replied Sharyn. She leaned back and crossed her arms across her chest in a classic defensive pose. "Why would I lie?"

"I didn't say I know *why* you're lying," said Nathan. "But I can tell when you *are* lying. Or at least covering something up. What was Spooner's question?"

"I was asking her about Fulton and why we never see him on television," said Spooner. "I would think the President would want to get out in front of the crisis that's erupting all across the country."

Sharyn was quiet, and Nathan looked at her calmly. "Sharyn, we're friends. You don't have to answer our questions, but you certainly shouldn't feel the need to lie to us. Spooner, maybe this is something Sharyn doesn't feel comfortable divulging."

"Yeah, well, I guess that would answer my question then, wouldn't it. Does he at least remember his own name?" Spooner asked.

A defiant Sharyn leaned forward, "Hey, he's my close friend," she said to Spooner, pointing at Nathan. "You're not. So I don't feel the need to take shit from you about what you think you know about the President of the United States. I work in the White House. Maybe I actually know something about the President's state of mind."

"I'm sorry," said Spooner. "No offense meant."

"Hey, hey, hey," added Nathan. "Let's all take another drink. Sharyn, Spooner was just asking an innocent question. Honestly, I'm surprised he knows the President's last name. But there are a lot of rumors going around. How's that impacting your job? Everything okay?"

Wanting to allow Sharyn and Nathan to speak freely, Spooner excused himself to go looking for the restroom.

"It's not good, Nathan. I wish it were, but it's not. The President is a great man. He's done so much for this country. And most of the time, he's fine. He just gets tired more often, and sometimes his staff worries that when he gets too stressed, he kind of mentally checks out."

"I'm sure that's hard on you."

"Yeah, although, to some degree, it's moved me up in the decision-making process. Vice President Moore makes pretty much most of the decisions right now, especially regarding the Red versus Blue crisis. As her chief of staff, I'm involved in almost every substantive discussion. It's a difficult time in the White House, though, that's for sure. So, you're heading to Richmond?" Sharyn asked, trying to change the subject. "Spooner says you're driving because you don't want to fly into a Red state."

"Yeah, Marino down in Florida tried to pull a fast one on me. He issued a warrant for my arrest when I pushed back at him after I told him I wanted no part of being his Vice Presidential running mate."

"Wow," said Sharyn. "That's crazy. Be careful. Governor Decker is pretty close to Marino. You don't want to come up on his radar and have him throw you in jail and extradite you to Florida. This whole Red State / Blue State thing is really out of control."

"We'll be fine."

70

Fredricksburg, Virginia

Sunday, April 28

SPOONER DROVE while Nathan sat in the front seat of the Cadillac Escalade. It was a much bigger vehicle than they needed, but it had been the one waiting for them at the very small Maryland Airport located in Indian Head, Maryland, just south of the National Harbor. The pair had left lunch with Sharyn in Old Town Alexandria and were now heading on a mission to Richmond, Virginia.

Traffic was light on I-95, and they were making good time heading south to Richmond. It was just over a hundred miles, and the trip should take less than two hours with continued light traffic. Forty-five minutes into their drive, just before Fredricksburg, traffic slowed. They could see brake lights ahead, and it appeared all vehicles were coming to a stop. Nathan wasn't sure if this was an accident or one of the checkpoints he'd seen on the news.

Soon enough, as traffic came to a standstill, they saw several flashing road signs declaring a checkpoint ahead and narrowing traffic down to one lane. Thankfully, they should be through the checkpoint in less than ten minutes, with traffic as light as it was.

As they drew closer to the checkpoint, Nathan admired the tactical sense of the unit's commander. The checkpoint was located on the far side of the long, straight bridge high above the Rappahannock River. This provided a great defensive position for the soldiers manning the checkpoint and severely limited the options available to approaching vehicles. There was no place to exit, and anyone not wanting to go through the checkpoint and attempting to make a U-turn would be easily spotted by the soldiers sitting atop armored Humvees positioned on each flank of the barricades.

Spooner was armed with a Glock 19 pistol carried in a concealed holster inside his waistband. He had a valid concealed carry permit issued by the State of Florida, which was recognized by Virginia. Nathan still had a California driver's license, not having had time to change it to Florida, so he kept his pistol unloaded and locked inside a box in the rear of the Escalade.

Spooner rolled down his window as they approached the checkpoint. A soldier, outfitted in full battle gear, including a helmet, armor-plated vest, and M4 rifle, stood next to the open window and peered inside. On Nathan's side of the vehicle, another soldier attempted to peer in through the passenger-side windows.

"Sir, I'm going to have to ask you to pull over to that inspection point to your left. Please remain inside your vehicle and keep your hands on the steering wheel."

Spooner glanced at Nathan, shrugged, and then slowly proceeded to the inspection point, which was nothing more than an area designated by two rows of orange cones and a handwritten plywood sign declaring it as Inspection Point #1. Spooner placed the transmission in Park and kept his hands on the wheel.

A different soldier approached, and Nathan could see this soldier was a Staff Sergeant by the chevrons and rocker insignia pinned to the front of his uniform. The NCO carefully looked over their vehicle as two other soldiers approached Nathan's side of the vehicle. Behind the sergeant, about thirty yards back, was an up-armored Humvee. In the turret was a very alert soldier manning an

Divided We Stand

M240B machine gun, which seemed to be aimed in the general direction of the Escalade but pointed downward toward the ground.

"Sir, please turn off the ignition. By executive order of the governor of Virginia, we are authorized to inspect your vehicle and the nationality of all passengers. Please pass me the driver's licenses for you and your passenger."

Spooner looked at the soldier, who looked to be in his late twenties. "Excuse me?"

"Sir, please hand me your driver's license and turn off the vehicle."

Spooner looked at Nathan, who shrugged as if to say *what're you gonna do?*

Spooner turned off the ignition and handed the soldier his license.

"Sir, this is a Florida driver's license, yet your vehicle has Maryland plates. Could you please explain?"

Spooner had heard enough. "Look, Sergeant, I understand you're just doing your job. I've been there. But what do you care where I'm from? My license is valid, and I'm not breaking any laws. Are we free to go?"

"No, you are not free to go, sir," said the NCO. "What is the citizenship of your passenger? Does he have a Florida driver's license as well?"

"Why don't you ask him yourself," said Spooner.

The Sergeant, clearly either used to dealing with difficult people or very well trained in doing so, simply nodded and walked around to the vehicle's passenger side. As Nathan rolled down his window, he heard the Sergeant tell the two soldiers standing there to put down the stop-sticks. Nathan turned his head to watch the soldiers drop long plastic tubes in front of and behind the Escalade's tires. These tubes were filled with spikes and specially designed to puncture tires should a vehicle drive over them. They were effectively blocked in. *Smart,* thought Nathan. *Whoever was in charge of this checkpoint knew what they were doing.*

"Sir, in what state do you currently reside?"

"Vermont," answered Nathan.

"Could I please see your driver's license or some form of identification? A passport if you have one."

Nathan pulled out his wallet and handed the soldier his California driver's license.

"Please step out of the vehicle, sir."

Now, it was Spooner's turn to shrug back at Nathan. Not wanting to escalate the situation unnecessarily, Nathan slowly exited the vehicle.

"What seems to be the problem, Sergeant?"

"Sir, it says on your license that you reside in Stanford, California. Under the governor's executive order, we are required to confirm the citizenship of all people entering the Commonwealth of Virginia. Because your state is one of the states that provides licenses to illegal immigrants, we cannot let you enter Virginia until you can prove you're an American citizen."

"Well, Sergeant, if you look closely, you'll see that the word Veteran is stamped on the front of my license. That should answer the question for you."

The Sergeant looked somewhat perplexed as if unsure how to proceed. "I'm sorry, sir. I have been told that does not necessarily mean that you are a citizen."

"But it should suffice to let you know that I have a right to be in this country, right? I mean, if I can defend the country, I have a right to travel freely throughout all its states, don't you agree?"

"Sir, ah, sir, it's not up to me, sir. I'm just following orders."

"I get that, I really—"

"Sergeant, do you have any idea who you're speaking to?" Spooner said in a commanding voice. Spooner had exited his side of the Escalade and had walked around to stand behind Nathan. "If you want to follow orders, Sergeant, you and your men should be saluting this man."

"Spooner—"

"I've got this, Nathan, and I'm tired of this bullshit. Sergeant, go get your commander and first sergeant. Now! This man's a recipient of the Medal of Honor, for Christ's sake."

Divided We Stand

COLONEL ROBERT CLARK was speaking before a small group of soldiers from his 1st Battalion's Alpha Company. His brigade was currently manning fixed checkpoints along a line that stretched from Fredricksburg to Winchester, effectively creating a cordon around Northern Virginia. His mission, straight from the governor, was to keep Blue people out, especially anyone suspected of being in the country illegally.

Clark lived outside Fredricksburg and had finally been able to make it home this weekend to see his wife and four children. He had decided to come out this afternoon to inspect Alpha Company's checkpoint across I-95 South before driving over to Culpeper, where he'd temporarily established his brigade's tactical operations center.

Alpha Company's commander had just finished giving Clark a tour of the checkpoint and was briefing him on several ongoing issues they were being forced to deal with. A few of the company's senior NCOs were gathered around at Clark's request, as Clark enjoyed taking these opportunities to hear from his NCOs how things were going at the point of the spear.

Suddenly, the company commander reached down to toggle the radio handset clipped to the front of his vest. "This is Alpha-Six, say again, over."

The commander and several of the NCOs in the group were listening through their earbuds, but Colonel Clark could not hear it.

"Roger, Two-Two. I'll be right there."

"I'm sorry, sir. We have an issue at the checkpoint. Some clown from California claims to be a Medal of Honor winner. I'm sick and tired of these whackjobs. I should be back in a few."

"I'll tag along if you don't mind, Captain. Maybe I'll learn something."

Clark followed the Captain and his First Sergeant, the senior NCO in the company, out to the checkpoint about a hundred yards up the road. Colonel Clark felt a little out of place as he was the only soldier not wearing a helmet, vest and carrying a rifle. He did have his sidearm in a shoulder holster worn over his ACUs.

As soon as they arrived at the checkpoint, the squad leader in charge walked up to the company commander and handed him a driver's license. Twenty yards distant, Colonel Clark could see a Cadillac Escalade with two civilians standing next to it, loosely guarded by two soldiers. The men appeared in their mid-to-late forties, and both were physically fit. One man was clean-shaven, while the other had shaggy hair almost to his shoulders and a long fu-manchu mustache.

"I don't give a fuck who this guy says he is. We have orders from the governor. If he has a license from a Blue State and can't prove his citizenship, then turn him around."

"Ah, yes, sir. Sir, do you think we should check to see if he's actually a Medal of Honor winner?"

"You don't *win* the Medal of Honor, Sergeant. And from the looks of them, I doubt either one has ever served. The closest they've probably been to combat is a cross-fit gym."

Colonel Clark wasn't really paying much attention to the Captain's conversation with his squad leader, as something about one of the men seemed familiar. He couldn't quite place it. Maybe someone from television? Someone from college?

Just as the squad leader was turning to go back to the inspection point, Colonel Clark said, "Hey, Sergeant. What's that guy's name? The one on the left."

The sergeant looked down at the driver's license in his hand. "Greene, sir. His name's Nathaniel Greene."

Clark smiled. "Well, I'll be a son of a bitch." Without saying a word to the company commander, Colonel Clark began walking briskly toward the two men at the inspection point.

NATHAN COULD SEE the sergeant talking to what Nathan assumed to be the company commander. An older soldier stood behind them, dressed only in ACUs and a soft cap, and Nathan knew this had to be a senior officer. By the man's age, several years older than Nathan, it was likely a colonel or general officer.

Shit, he thought. *This thing is getting out of hand. We need to get to Richmond.*

Suddenly, the senior officer started walking directly towards him. *Goddamnit!* Nathan watched the man approach.

With the senior officer about five yards away, the man said, "Greene? Is that you?"

Nathan squinted, trying to read the man's rank and name tape on his chest. *Holy shit! It's Bobby Clark.* "Bobby?"

Clark rushed forward, and the two men embraced in an emotional bear hug. Everyone, from Spooner to the company commander to all the soldiers watching, was completely stunned.

"What are you doing here?" Clark asked.

"I should ask you the same thing!" Nathan replied. "Who was dumb enough to make you a colonel? Please don't tell me you're in charge of this clusterfuck."

Robert and Nathan were both laughing, holding each other by the arms and looking each other up and down.

"Jesus, man, what's it been? Twenty-five years?"

"Yeah," said Nathan. "Almost exactly twenty-five years. Hey, excuse my manners. Spooner! This is Bobby Clark. We went to IOBC together—the Infantry Officer's Basic Course—down at Fort Benning back in the day. Bobby here was with me on the road trip when I met Emily." Nathan's mood turned suddenly somber.

In 1998, Nathan Greene and Robert Clark had been newly commissioned second lieutenants attending the six-month Infantry Officer Basic Course at Fort Benning, Georgia, just outside Columbus. The two had been assigned to the same squad and had become fast friends, especially as both of their rooms had been down the hall from each other in the massive Bachelor Officers Quarters on post. Bobby was a bit older, having been previously enlisted before attending college, but they found they had a lot in common and spent most of their free time together. Bobby was a Reserve officer who was assigned to the Virginia National Guard, while Nathan was in the Regular Army with an initial assignment to the 101st Airborne Division at Fort Campbell, Kentucky. During one of the course's long holiday weekends, Bobby and Nathan drove down to

Pensacola, Florida, to have some fun at the beach. While bar hopping, they'd met a group of attractive young women from the University of Pennsylvania. One of these lovely young ladies was Emily Harkness, whom Nathan would fall madly in love with and marry two years later.

"I'm sorry, Nathan. I followed what happened in the newspaper. I sent you a note and thought of coming down, but I figured you had tons of people around and wouldn't want to see someone from twenty-five years ago."

"Thanks, Bobby. I'm sorry, too. I left my house pretty soon after the incident with the FBI, so I haven't had a chance to see my mail. But I sincerely appreciate the sentiments. So? Full colonel, I see. Brigade commander? What brings out to I-95 on a Sunday afternoon?"

"Yes. I'm the commander of the 116th Infantry Brigade Combat Team. We have checkpoints established from here to Winchester. This is all part of the governor's plan to protect the integrity of the Commonwealth of Virginia."

"I feel like we're crossing the DMZ, going from north to south," said Nathan.

"Well, it seems like that's maybe what it's coming to. I've lost more soldiers in the last month than both of my battalions when we deployed to Iraq and Afghanistan. This is getting crazy, Nathan. I fear it's going to get a lot, lot worse before there's any chance of it improving."

"I know, Bobby. I can't say I've seen anything to dispel that notion."

71

Richmond, Virginia

Sunday, April 28

SPOONER AND NATHAN sat in the Escalade outside the Richmond Jet Center, a fixed-base operator at Richmond International Airport. From their location, they could clearly see the large Boeing 737 aircraft parked just on the other side of the chain-link fence. It was nearing eleven o'clock at night, and the woman had yet to depart.

After a brief chat with Colonel Clark and a sincere commitment to stay in touch, they arrived in Richmond shortly after seven o'clock in the evening. They made a quick stop at Walmart for some necessary supplies, then headed directly to their current location. They'd had eyes on the 737 since their arrival and had watched the lithe Asian woman arrive just before nine o'clock.

Immediately after Ruby's intelligence breakthrough on Friday, Nathan knew precisely the significance of Jackson, Wyoming. It had to be Orlean Brumback. He was the only common denominator in everything that had happened since early February.

With Spooner's help, Nathan had dispatched two of Spooner's guys, Terry and Mitch, to Jackson. They brought all the necessary equipment on the private jet, and their mission was to hike up above Brumback's home and establish a hide position where they could keep eyes on Brumback's estate for at least a week. If they needed to do it for longer, Spooner would send reinforcements. Their specific task was to photograph and report all people who arrived at Brumback's lodge in the Tetons.

At the same time, Ruby began a deep dive into Orlean Brumback. Within hours, she'd gathered some very interesting and useful information. A plan began to form in Nathan's mind. Ruby could access the secret NSA databases containing a tremendous amount of personal information about average Americans. Almost every phone call and text message ever transmitted was stored in the NSA's massive data vaults. By law, accessing this information could only be done under very specific parameters as defined in the Patriot Act. By the U.S. Constitution, American citizens were protected by the 4th Amendment against unreasonable searches, and consequently, a court order was required before the NSA could access information about its own citizens. However, as Edward Snowden pointed out, this wasn't always the case.

In Ruby's case, there was no doubt that she was breaking the law. The information she quickly assembled, however, was truly astounding. Although the data she accessed was months, sometimes years old, she quickly put together a program to pull all data related to Orlean Brumback and scrub it through her AI software programs. The result was a portrait of Brumback that was anything but flattering.

One thing that jumped out at everyone was Brumback's communications with what appeared to be a network of high-end call girls. At almost every airport, Brumback would coordinate with these women to arrive at his plane at a certain time. Ruby found it strange that the women texted him first on the day Brumback was to arrive, and she assumed this meant Brumback had someone behind the scenes who was making the initial bookings and also the

Divided We Stand

payments, as Brumback's contact with the ladies was simply to coordinate their arrival time. Ruby vowed to look into this further.

Another interesting fact was that Brumback had an encrypted Kryptall iPhone and a significant portion of his calls were fully encrypted. Neither the NSA nor Ruby could crack these, but they could see when and for how long the encrypted call had been made. Again, Ruby vowed to delve into this deeper.

Learning that Brumback would be in Richmond this Sunday evening, a plan was quickly hatched that involved Nathan and Spooner traveling down to Richmond. Which was why they were sitting in the FBO's parking lot watching Brumback's airplane.

Lights were on throughout the plane, but the shades were drawn for privacy. A canopied movable stairway had been positioned at the large jet's front door, but the plane's fuselage door was shut.

Just before midnight, the jet's door opened, and a petite Asian woman pulled the door closed behind herself and descended the stairs. There was no sign of Brumback. Nathan and Spooner watched as the woman entered the FBO main building. Seconds later, she came out through the main entrance and walked briskly to her car.

They waited five minutes, then both Nathan and Spooner exited the Escalade. They were now both wearing button-down blue workshirts, the kind worn by air conditioning repairmen, plumbers, and electricians. In addition, each of them wore a bright orange reflective vest, and protective ear muffs were slung around their necks. Spooner reached in and grabbed a metal toolbox from the back seat while Nathan carried a small nylon tool bag. Each of them had an identification badge hanging from a lanyard around their neck.

Without hesitation, both men walked directly to the main entrance to the FBO. Even at midnight, the lobby was completely lit. However, there was only one attendant on duty—a young man sitting behind the guest services counter watching a movie on his iPad. Spooner pulled out his phone, pressed it to his ear, and began a loud conversation with a make-believe person from work. Nathan and Spooner walked swiftly through the lobby, heading directly for the doors leading out to the tarmac. Nathan gave a quick nod to the man behind the counter, but otherwise, they just breezed on through the lobby.

Nathan learned years ago that the key to penetrating security was to act like you belonged. Low-paid security guards or front desk personnel didn't want to confront someone who obviously knew what they were doing. The worst thing you could do was look lost. Put a toolbox or a manila folder in your hand, quicken your step like you were in a hurry to get somewhere important, and almost no one would stop you.

Nathan and Spooner found themselves on the open tarmac with Brumback's 737 parked about thirty yards to their front. They walked directly to the stairway and quietly ascended the stairs. At the top, Spooner gently lowered the toolbox, which was empty, and tested the door to ensure it would open. In all likelihood, Brumback would be alone on the plane and in the rear bedroom area. However, it never hurt to be cautious.

Nathan pulled his pistol from the holster by his appendix as Spooner opened the thick aircraft door as quietly as possible. As soon as Nathan turned down the main entryway, he could see no one else on the plane. Spooner quickly followed him in, gently closing the door behind him.

The two walked toward the back of the plane, careful to place their feet gently so as not to create a vibration that might alert Brumback. The door to Brumback's bedroom suite was mostly closed but not latched. Nathan thought of trying to peek through the one-inch opening but decided it wasn't worth giving up the element of surprise.

Shoving the door open, they saw Brumback lying in bed, completely nude, thumbing through his phone. Brumback literally almost jumped off the bed when the door crashed open.

"Good evening, Orlean. I trust you've had a pleasant night so far?" Nathan said, stepping into the room. Spooner surged past him, walked over to the bed, and snatched the phone from Brumback's hands before he had a chance to text or call anyone. Nathan had

Divided We Stand

put the pistol back in its holster but was aware that Brumback could still see its butt poking up from his waistband.

"Greene? What the hell are you doing here? You scared the living shit out of me!"

"I think it's time we had a little talk, Orlean. I know about your role in the St. Armands Circle bombing. It's time to come clean."

Orlean just stared directly at Nathan. "Professor Greene, I have no earthly idea what you're talking about. That was a terrible tragedy, and I ache for your loss, but whatever misguided information you think you have, I can assure you I know absolutely nothing about the bombing at St. Armands Circle."

Nathan had participated in his share of battlefield interrogations over the years as both a member of the Unit and an operations officer with the CIA. He felt confident he could tell when a suspect was lying. Looking at Brumback, Nathan was certain the man was telling the truth. *How could that be possible? We tracked the Cabal to Jackson Hole.*

"Stop the bullshit, Brumback. We know. It was difficult to piece together, but we now know. Shooting down King's plane? Killing four governors? Assassinating two Supreme Court Justices?"

There! He'd seen it.

A flash of fear in Brumback's eyes as Nathan mentioned the killing of the governors and members of the Supreme Court.

Nathan smiled. "You just gave yourself away, Orlean. I got you now." Nathan turned to Spooner. "Why don't you go out in the main cabin and keep an eye out in case anyone comes? I'm going to have a little chat with our friend here."

Spooner nodded and walked toward the front of the plane.

"Why?" Nathan asked Brumback. "You had everything going for you. Why did you have to resort to these cowardly attacks?"

With Spooner out of the room, Orlean felt a bit less intimidated and began to think more clearly. Deny, deny, deny—the golden rule of big-boy politics. "Nathan, I understand you've been under an enormous amount of pressure these last two months—the loss of your family, the attack on your house by the FBI, and the attempted arrest by the Florida police. These are things that would break almost any man. I can assure you that I have never participated in anything related to a terrorist attack. It's not who I am. I'm a radio host, for God's sake. I don't plan military operations; I interview people and talk about things to get people riled up—people who are too dumb to know any better. I don't bomb or kill people."

"If you had nothing to do with any of these, then how'd you know about my attempted arrest? I'm not even supposed to know about that. Only someone who gave the order to arrest me would know."

Brumback's face contorted, realizing he'd been caught in a trap. He decided to follow the second rule of big-boy politics—when you find yourself in a hole, stop digging. Orlean remained silent, staring blankly at Nathan.

"What about Alex Treacher?" Nathan asked. "We know about his base in Kalispell and how he's behind all this?"

There it was again! This time, instead of a flash of fear, it was a look of pure panic.

"I, ah, I think…look, Nathan, you need to be careful. Alex Treacher is not a man one should trifle with."

"But you think I am? You and Alex don't seem to have a problem *trifling* with me. I can assure you, Brumback, I'm definitely not a man to *trifle* with."

In his head, Nathan was keeping track of the time. They had agreed to spend less than five minutes aboard Brumback's plane. It was critical that they get away undetected by anyone but Brumback.

Brumback just stared back at Nathan, and Nathan knew at this point there was very little else Brumback would admit to. He'd had a chance to get his wits about him, and short of resorting to some very unsavory enhanced interrogation techniques, Brumback was going to stick to his story. *That's okay*, Nathan thought. *We got what we came for.*

"This isn't over," Nathan said loudly. "I'm going to show up when you least expect it, and you're going to answer for your crimes."

Spooner had been standing outside the partially open bedroom door and now came back into the room. He walked straight up to

Brumback and shoved him in the chest, pushing Brumback backward into his pillows. "Not a word of this visit to anyone! If you do, you'll read all about your airport hookers in the paper. The media will eat that shit up."

Without another word, Nathan and Spooner turned and walked out of the plane. In minutes, they were back in their Escalade and heading north toward their airplane in southern Maryland.

72

Cromwell Island, Montana

Sunday, April 28

THE PHONE RANG as Alex sat in his study, sipping from another ice-cold glass of vodka. He rarely slept more than four hours per night, and lately had found himself sitting in his favorite buffalo leather chair in his darkened study and staring out over Flathead Lake. He enjoyed these moments of quiet solitude. He often thought of his grand strategy as a mental chess game, and this alone time allowed him to move the various pieces in his mind and see the merits and pitfalls of various moves he might make to further his grand strategy.

The caller ID on the phone showed the call was from Orlean. It was unusual for him to call at this time of night, especially as Alex knew Orlean was in Richmond where it was well after midnight.

"Hello, Orlean," said Alex.

"We have a bit of a problem, Alex."

"What kind of problem? Please be specific."

"Is it okay to talk on an open line?" Orlean asked.

Divided We Stand

"I told you. These Kryptall iPhones have end-to-end encryption. You can say anything you like."

"Okay," said Orlean. "I just received a visit from Nathan Greene. He accused me of being part of a conspiracy behind the March 21st attacks."

"I see," said Alex, taking a sip of vodka. "That is a problem, isn't it."

"Yes, I thought you should know right away."

"What else did Professor Greene have to say? Did he have any specifics? Did he mention Marino?"

"I don't think he has any specifics. He was accusing me of all sorts of things, including the St. Armands Circle bombing that killed his wife and daughter. He never mentioned Marino at all."

"That's good. Anything else?"

"He mentioned you."

The blood in Alex's veins turned cold, as cold as the vodka in his glass. "What did he say about me?" Alex asked, his voice barely above a whisper.

"He said he knows about your base in Kalispell and insinuated you and I were both part of this conspiracy."

"And what did you say to that?"

"I told him he was crazy, and that while I understood he was under considerable stress, that still gave him no right to make these unfounded accusations."

"Okay," said Alex. "Anything else? Did he threaten to do anything? Go to the press?"

"No," said Orlean. "He just walked away."

"Thank you for calling, Orlean. I will handle this." Alex terminated the call.

He sat calmly in his chair for a moment, looking out at the moonlight reflecting off the lake below. Alex picked up his glass of vodka, taking a gentle sip. As the burn of the liquid coated his palette, a surge of anger bloomed through his body and he hurled the glass against the stone fireplace, where it shattered into hundreds of pieces.

He took a minute to mentally move some of the chess pieces in his mind before smiling. He then pressed a button on his phone, summoning Sergei to bring Wais and Jasmine to his office.

73

Ferrisburgh, Vermont

Monday, April 29

THE MISSION to Richmond had been a resounding success, and Nathan spent the plane ride back to Burlington thinking about how close they were getting to unmasking the Cabal. The real purpose of visiting Brumback had nothing to do with questioning the man, as Nathan knew it was highly unlikely Brumback would say anything incriminating. No, the real purpose had been to gain access to the man's cell phone.

As Nathan was questioning and accusing Brumback, Spooner was in the other room, attaching a special device Ruby had given them just for this mission. This device served two functions. First, it downloaded everything on Brumback's phone—text messages, emails, contacts, call history, the works. Second, it embedded code that would allow Ruby to access real-time data about the phone's usage and location. The Kryptall software was too good to penetrate, so there was no chance of cracking into the encrypted calls, but the code would allow them to hear Brumback's side of the conversation, as well as to see the phone numbers that he called.

Ruby assured Nathan that with this information, she should be able to quickly identify the Cabal members and their locations.

Spooner had also hidden several tiny microphones around the plane, including one in Brumback's bedroom. As Ruby assumed Brumback regularly electronically swept his plane for bugs, these special devices remained completely dormant, undetectable by any sweep. However, Ruby could activate them remotely, at which point they would begin transmitting.

All in all, Nathan was extremely happy with their trip.

He was just finishing lunch when Spooner came in from outside.

"Hey, man, how's everything going?" Nathan asked.

"Good. I was just down at the Bancroft House meeting with Roy. Mitch and Terry are doing well out in Jackson, but I'm sending two more guys from the farm down in Clewiston to relieve them. I'm also bringing four additional men up here. After meeting with Brumback, I feel like we need a few more security personnel here. Right now, it's just Roy."

"Okay," said Nathan. "Whatever you think's best. No one knows we're even here, so I'm not too worried about the media."

"You can never be too careful, man."

Nathan finished his sandwich, thought for a moment, then decided this was as good a time as any. "Hey, Spooner, speaking of being careful, I wanted to have a quick chat. It's not a big deal, but with all that's going on, I wanted to make sure you were taken care of financially."

Spooner looked at his friend. "Hey, man. Money doesn't mean anything to me, you know that. The property down in Florida is worth a bit, and the training center is profitable. I also have my pension from Uncle Sam. So, you can keep your big bucks. I mean, I'm enjoying flying private jets everywhere, don't get me wrong. But I don't need money, Nathan. We're friends."

"I know that. And you're right, it's not a big deal. But just in case something happens to me, I want you to know I had my brother-in-law draw up some documents last week. The mortgage on your family property has been paid off, and Dave opened an account in your name with enough money that you don't have to

Divided We Stand

ever worry about money. I also opened a college fund for Felipe—so when he's in high school, he can go to any college he likes and doesn't have to worry about paying for anything."

"Jesus, Nathan. You didn't have to do that. I'm serious, I don't need your money. Felipe? Well, I thank you for that, and I know the boy and Lourdes will be eternally grateful. She doesn't have a lot, and she works hard, but I also started saving a bit for his college."

"It's done, Spooner. If you don't want the money, then don't spend it. But it's already yours. I was going to put something in an account for Lourdes as well, but I realized I don't have any information on her. The 529 college fund was easy, as you're the administrator and Felipe is the beneficiary. But I need Lourdes' personal information to open an account."

Spooner got a dark look on his face, clearly troubled by something.

"What is it?" Nathan asked, knowing his friend normally kept his inner demons bottled up.

Spooner looked at Nathan, his best friend in the world, and decided to divulge something he promised he'd never would. "Lourdes is in the United States illegally." Spooner paused, wondering how much he should divulge. "Her father was a colonel in the Colombian police, and her husband was a police officer in a special unit her father commanded. They were both murdered by FARC guerillas just after Felipe was born. She took an opportunity that presented itself to get to Miami, and she never processed an asylum application. At the time, she probably didn't even know the process for seeking asylum. But by the time she looked into it, she realized the U.S. Government would send her back to Colombia for the same amount of time she'd been in America illegally, and only after waiting this time in Colombia could she reapply for asylum."

"Ah, man, that explains a lot. I'm sorry, Spooner. I didn't know."

"I promised not to tell anyone—even you."

Nathan's heart ached for Lourdes and Spooner. Everything you see on television about illegal aliens or undocumented immigrants, and at the end of the day, it really came down to individual people making decisions to provide a better life for themselves and their families. Were there criminals entering the United States illegally? Undoubtedly, and probably by the thousands. But for tens of thousands, even millions of people, the United States offered a dream to elevate one's family to achieve anything they wanted to achieve. Politics was never easy, but when you looked at Lourdes and Felipe, the answer was different than what was portrayed on the news. This didn't mean a country didn't have the right to close its borders and to allow only those immigrants they desired, but each immigrant had their own unique story.

"I won't tell anyone," said Nathan. "But I will say this: I think you should make an honest woman out of her, Spooner. You clearly love each other, and Felipe sees you as his father. It's easy for anyone to see—even Ruby made a comment about it. It's up to you, but you seem happy. Maybe you should consider it and discuss it with Lourdes? A summer wedding at Valhalla would be quite an event."

Spooner smiled, and Nathan was glad his friend had confided in him.

"Thanks, man. Seriously." said Spoon, with the closest thing to tears in his eyes that Nathan had ever seen."

"So, what's the plan for the rest of the day?" Nathan asked.

"Felipe has a dinner with his Little League team down at Rockers Pizzeria. You're welcome to come if you'd like."

"I appreciate it, but I'll let you guys have all the fun. Maybe you could bring a pizza back for Ruby and me. I love their Jonny Rocker!"

"Will do," said Spooner as Nathan stood up to head upstairs. "Hey, Nathan?" Nathan turned in the doorway. "Thanks, man. I mean it. I appreciate all you've done for me."

"You're welcome. But it's you who's done everything for me." Nathan turned and walked upstairs, not wanting to show emotion in front of his friend.

74

Ferrisburgh, Vermont

Monday, April 29

THE SUV ROLLED ALONG Interstate 89 across the green hills of Vermont. Jasmine drove so Wais was free to look out the window and admire the passing scenery. It was very different than Montana and certainly very different from his homeland, Afghanistan.

After meeting with Alex last night and receiving their orders, Wais and Jasmine had prepared their weapons and equipment before boarding a private jet to Lebanon, New Hampshire. Alex didn't want them flying into a Blue state, and the Lebanon airport was right along the Vermont-New Hampshire border, less than a two-hour drive from their target in Ferrisburgh, Vermont.

Valhalla. That was the name of the estate where their target was living. Hall of the Slain—Wais had looked up the meaning of Valhalla, and that's what it meant. How appropriate, he thought.

Professor Nathan Greene. Former U.S. Army Captain in the elite Delta Force and recipient of America's highest military award, the Medal of Honor. As Wais watched the green mountains of

Vermont pass by, he couldn't help but remember the last time he'd approached an esteemed professor holed up in a remote estate.

It was sixteen years ago now, thought Wais. Actually, it was almost seventeen years. He'd been the commander of an Afghani intelligence unit that was working closely with American commandos to root out the last of al-Qaeda's strongholds in Afghanistan. The target that day had been al-Ustadh—the Professor, or the Master as some translated. This was the nom de guerre of a man calling himself Abdullah al Nadim, an Egyptian history professor from the University of Cairo who had become the number two man to Osama bin Liden in the al-Qaeda network.

The Americans had gleaned actionable intelligence that al-Ustadh was hiding out in a remote fortress north of Jalalabad nestled into the foothills of Nuristan National Park. Wais was to be the lead element for the raid, approaching the fortress as a local Afghani and gaining access to the front gate before the helicopters swooped in carrying the American commandos. Wais had been told that al-Ustadh was suspected of holding two American hostages at this location—female members of a humanitarian non-profit organization that had been kidnapped outside Jalalabad several weeks prior.

Over the previous few years, Wais had worked very closely with the American forces. In some cases, he'd developed very strong friendships forged in the heat of combat. The team that was to fast rope into al-Ustadh's compound that day was a group of American Special Forces that he had worked with extensively over the last six months, and this was to be one of the most important raids of the war—possibly second only to finding Osama bin Laden himself, who at the time was still on the lamb.

Things had started well on that operation, with Wais easily gaining access to the fortress under the guise of being a local Taliban commander paying his respects to the esteemed Professor. Wais had even been shown the two female hostages, and that's when things had gone FUBAR, as the Americans liked to say—fucked up beyond all recognition. The helicopters swooped in over the compound, dropping their ropes and discharging a dozen or more

Divided We Stand

commandos. The Professor had immediately figured Wais was a traitor, and before he could even pull his weapon, the Professor's guards were shooting at him. Wais was able to shuffle the hostages into another room, but not before taking a bullet in his upper arm.

The battle raged around him, bullets flying, grenades exploding, and people crying out in pain. He huddled with the two hostages and then saw an opportunity to rush to the protection offered by yet another room in the dusty mountain compound. The American commandos were close, but the al-Qaeda guards were even closer. Finding himself in a room with the two hostages behind him and a rabid Professor in front of him, he knew the jig was up when al-Ustadh pulled a grenade from beneath his cloak. Just as the Professor pulled the pin, a commando rushed into the room and fired a hail of bullets that riddled the Professor's upper torso. Wais recalled the grenade falling to the floor and the heroic commando pushing him and the hostages to the ground.

Wais woke up the next day in a Kabul hospital. His injuries were significant, but nothing that wouldn't fully heal in a couple of weeks. The war had a long way to go, and he would be back in shape to continue the fight. He'd received a medal for his bravery in the attack, but he'd never seen those particular American commandos again as they rotated back to the United States and were replaced with a new team for Wais to work with.

Jasmine also seemed somewhat preoccupied during the drive, and the two spoke very little during the journey. In two hours, they found themselves driving along Fort Cassin Road, just two kilometers south of Valhalla's main house. Because Valhalla was an estate with almost 350 acres, they had planned to park their vehicle well south of the property and hike through the woods.

It was early afternoon, and they had no problem finding a suitable place to hide their vehicle along a dirt path off Fort Cassin Road. Grabbing their weapons and backpacks, Wais and Jasmine began walking north. They were both well-versed in the plan, and there was little small talk as they walked. They'd been briefed that there were four people staying at the main house: Professor Nathan Greene, a male friend, and a woman and her young son.

Their mission was to reconnoiter the property and kill Nathan Greene. They also planned to kill anyone else in the house.

In less than an hour, Wais and Jasmine had found a suitable position approximately 150 meters south of Valhalla's large house. They had set up a hide position in the woods that offered unobstructed views across what appeared to be the fairway of a golf course. A smaller house was several hundred meters to their right. From their position, they had a complete view over the front of the house—the side not facing the water—and the large parking area in front of it where several vehicles were parked.

Both Jasmine and Wais possessed patience in spades, and they settled into a routine of switching off and on while watching the house. Unless something changed, they planned to wait until dark and storm the house. From what they'd seen so far, none of the house's occupants appeared to be armed.

At 5:30 p.m., Jasmine watched the Professor's male friend, the woman, and her son get into a full-size SUV and depart down the long gravel driveway. Wais had caught glimpses of Nathan Greene earlier that afternoon and knew that he was in the house. The three individuals' recent departure meant Greene was the only one left at home.

Jasmine looked at Wais. "He's the only one left. I think we should go now. What better time?"

Wais was somewhat reluctant. He'd had a sour feeling in the pit of his stomach about this mission from the moment Alex had told them their target. "I don't know."

"C'mon, this is it, Wais. You know that. Strike when you get the shot. That's the first rule of being a sniper. We have the shot—let's go get this done."

Unable to come up with a good excuse, Wais agreed.

In minutes, they stealthily approached the front entrance through the woods. They'd left their packs at the hide site and carried only their weapons—suppressed M4s and Glock 19s with silencers attached.

As they neared, Wais' mind flashed back to that mission long ago. This estate was nothing like that one. There was no dust, no

Divided We Stand

mud-brick wall creating a compound around the old structures, and no armed bearded guards looking at the world through deadened eyes. Looking up, Wais couldn't help but admire how nice the Valhalla property was, from the manicured lawns to the intricate granite facade and colored shutters of the main house.

In no time, they had reached the edge of the narrow copse of woods within twenty yards of the house. This was their last covered and concealed position.

"Cover me while I run up to the side of the front door," whispered Jasmine. "I didn't see them lock the door, so I think it's likely unlocked. When I get there, you come up, and we'll enter."

"Okay. I'm covering you."

Wais watched as Jasmine sprinted to the front door, weaving to her right in an effort to use the large F-150 truck parked in the driveway as a bit of cover for her movement. She knelt next to the front stairs, three granite steps that led up to the colorful wooden front door. Wais followed Jasmine's path, and the two knelt next to the house.

Wais could feel the adrenaline spiking and see Jasmine getting amped up.

"Let's go," she said.

She jaunted up the stairs and gently tested the front door's handle, one of those large handles that opened the door by pressing down on a lever with your thumb. The thumb latch depressed fully, signifying the door was unlocked, and Jasmine firmly but gently pushed the door inward. Wais held his M4 at the ready, the stock welded to his cheek, and his eye looking through the glass of the EOTech holographic sight mounted to the top of the rifle.

The door opened into an expansive entryway that led straight back to what appeared to be a large kitchen at the back of the house. A large open room with a wide archway opened off to the left, while several open doors led to rooms on the right. Wais covered the left room as Jasmine quietly pied off the corners to the rooms on the right. She basically kept her weapon pointed into the room, then slowly moved toward the center of the doorway, allowing her to see more and more of the room as she moved to her left. This was known in close-quarters combat as slicing the pie.

With the two rooms on the right clear, Jasmine motioned for them to move toward the kitchen in the rear of the home. As they approached, they could hear the sound of a television emanating from somewhere off the kitchen, what sounded like a news broadcast. Knowing that there was likely someone in this room, Jasmine and Wais stacked up at the entrance to the kitchen.

Wais squeezed Jasmine's shoulder. She immediately stepped forward and whipped around the left side of the entryway. Wais followed closely behind her and moved to clear the right side of the room.

Bang!

"Don't fucking move!"

With his half of the room clear, Wais whipped his head around to see Jasmine approaching Nathan Greene, who was sitting in an overstuffed leather chair, his feet up on an ottoman. Jasmine had been the one to fire her weapon, and her round had splintered the top of a small side table next to Greene, upon which sat a Glock pistol.

Jasmine walked into the family room area adjacent to the kitchen, keeping Greene in her sights as she moved in front of him.

"Well, if it isn't the great Professor Nathan Greene," she said. Wais was somewhat taken aback, as Jasmine was normally not one for small talk.

Nathan looked from Jasmine to Wais, then back to Jasmine, a look of recognition crossing his face.

"Do you remember me, Professor? University of Florida? Spring Semester 2018?"

Nathan sat there calmly, not even bothering to remove his feet from the ottoman. He was focused on Jasmine but kept glancing over at Wais.

"Jasmine, isn't it? Jasmine Ortiz? If I remember correctly, you were leaving school to join the Marine Corps."

Jasmine was clearly shocked that Greene recognized her. This

Divided We Stand

was the first time Wais had seen emotion on her face in the two years he'd known her.

"You…you remember me?" Jasmine asked, thrown for a loop.

"Of course," Nathan replied. "I don't remember all my students, but I tend to remember the bright ones. It seems the Corps didn't work out for you. I'm sorry to hear that. You had a very bright future. Who sent you now? Marino? Or that fool Brumback?"

Wais was now conflicted. He'd been waiting to see if Jasmine was going to pull the trigger, but now he wasn't sure that she would.

"I'm sorry, Professor Greene. I'm not sure what you've done to anger my boss, but I have a job to do, and he believes in me. So I can't let him down." A look of resolve had replaced Jasmine's look of uncertainty.

Greene steeled himself with a similar resolve, a part of him welcoming what was about to happen and glad that Spooner, Lourdes, and Felipe weren't around. "I understand, Jasmine. We all have missions to accomplish, and loyalty is important."

Not sure there was anything more to say, Jasmine slowly began squeezing the trigger.

Bang!

The suppressed round was still loud to Wais' ears. He looked down at the leather chair where Nathan Greene sat, a pool of blood spreading across the wooden floor and beginning to pool under the ottoman.

Jasmine lay on the ground, her eyes open in death, and the gaping wound in the side of her head the source of the expanding pool of blood. Wais looked down at Nathan Greene, still sitting in the chair, the pistol next to him untouched. A small wisp of smoke emanated from the end of the suppressor on Wais' M4. It had been he who had shot Jasmine.

Jasmine seemed to know Nathan Greene and kept calling him Professor. But to Wais, Nathan wasn't Professor Green. He was Captain Greene, a man Wais hadn't seen since Greene had selflessly thrown his body atop Wais and the hostages in that dusty building in the eastern mountains of Afghanistan.

"Wais?" said Greene.

"I'm sorry, Nathan. There was nothing I could do. I wanted to warn you."

"Wais Khan? What are you doing here? Do you work for the Cabal?"

"The Cabal?" Wais asked. He was now thoroughly confused; everything in his world turned upside down. "I'm sorry. We have so much to discuss. There's so much I need to——."

Bang! Bang! Bang!

Three crimson holes appeared on Wais's upper chest as he crumpled to the floor next to Jasmine. Nathan jumped out of his chair, grabbed the pistol off the side table and turned to face the new threat. Bringing the Glock up to a firing position, he saw Ruby standing there in the kitchen, a Glock pistol held awkwardly in her hand, a look of shock on her face.

"Is he dead?" She said. "I've never shot anyone."

Nathan walked to Ruby and took the pistol from her grasp, not trusting her to be safe with it. He then rushed back over to his friend, a friend he hadn't seen in a very long time.

Wais lay gasping on the floor, unable to catch his breath. Two of the rounds had penetrated his upper chest on one side—serious but likely not fatal. One round, however, was dead center of his breastbone, and Nathan knew this shot had likely done irreparable damage.

"Get me some towels," shouted Nathan as he knelt next to Wais, pressing down on his chest wound in an attempt to slow the bleeding. Turning to his gravely wounded friend, Nathan said, "Hang in there, Wais. We'll get you to a hospital in no time. Just hang in there."

Ruby tossed Nathan two dish towels, and he immediately pressed them hard into Wais' chest. He knew it was futile, but it was all he could think to do.

"My family…" Wais gurgled, barely able to speak as his throat filled with blood. His aorta had likely been severed, and his entire chest cavity was filling with blood.

"Shhh," said Nathan. "Hang on, my friend. Hang on."

Divided We Stand

"I'm sorry...." Wais gasped. "Cromwell..."

Nathan pressed down harder, but he could see the light fading in Wais' eyes. Suddenly, the gurgling and gasping stopped, and Wais was still.

"You called him your friend," said Ruby, standing over Nathan, who was now covered in Wais' blood. "How could this guy be your friend?"

"A long time ago, Ruby," said Nathan sadly. "A long time ago on a different battlefield."

"He said *Cromwell*," said Ruby. "I know what that is."

75

Ferrisburgh, Vermont

Friday, May 3

NATHAN SAT on the covered stone patio at the back of Valhalla, enjoying the bright sunshine of the unseasonably warm May day on the shores of Lake Champlain. He'd been told his visitors would be arriving momentarily.

The events since the attack on Valhalla had been significant, but somewhat unfulfilling. Ruby had immediately connected the dots with Wais' final utterance and the large island on Flathead Lake less than thirty miles south of Kalispell, Montana. She'd been tirelessly searching for connections related to Kalispell, so when Wais said the name *Cromwell*, she instantly recognized its relevance.

After the Vermont state police had left, the bodies of Jasmine and Wais had been removed, and Ruby had found the links to Cromwell Island, Nathan and Spooner had spent the first couple of hours planning their own raid on the island. They could realistically muster the equivalent of a full Special Forces A-team from the seasoned personnel Spooner employed or that they were close

Divided We Stand

friends with, and Nathan had the resources to get them there quickly.

However, with the information Ruby was able to provide, it was impossible to tell exactly what threats they would face on the island. Based on the size of the lodge and the large compound on the mainland adjacent to Cromwell Island, it was estimated that they could be facing upwards of thirty armed individuals and possibly defensive emplacements with heavy weapons. A dozen retired Special Forces, no matter how good they might have once been, were no match for a professional, well-armed guard force triple the numbers of the attackers, which was most likely what they'd be facing.

Believing that discretion is the better part of valor, Nathan made a call to Sharyn Gray and filled her in on what his team had been able to put together about the Cabal. She'd alerted the Vice President, who had ordered the FBI Director to launch a raid to seize the island. Armed with all the incriminating evidence that this could be the mastermind behind the March 21st attacks, the FBI Director reached out to Montana's governor who reluctantly agreed to authorize a joint state-federal raid on the island.

However, in the time it took them to put the raid together, Cromwell Island had been abandoned. The FBI found very little value and nothing that could connect Cromwell Island to any of the terrorist attacks.

While unsatisfying, Nathan knew that he had found his Cabal. He'd found the man who was responsible for killing his wife and daughter, and he wouldn't stop until he'd found him.

Alex Treacher.

Nathan knew that with the help of his friends, he would find the man very soon.

The door opened from the back of the house and out stepped Sharyn Gray. She immediately ran to Nathan and hugged him warmly, pressing her head tightly to his chest.

"I'm so glad you're safe," she said, trying to keep her emotions in check.

Nathan hugged her back, rubbing his hands along her back in

fatherly comfort. Looking past her, he watched a distinguished gentleman step onto the patio. He was medium height with wide shoulders, a thick neck, and the remnants of cauliflower ears. Although they'd never met, Nathan recognized him instantly from television.

Disengaging himself from Sharyn, Nathan stepped over to greet the man. "Mr. Reynolds, it's a pleasure to meet you. I'm Nathan Greene. Welcome to Vermont."

"Please, Nathan, call me John." Reynolds shook Nathan's hand with an iron grip, leaving Nathan no doubt the man had once been a champion collegiate wrestler and was not one to tangle with. "Thank you for agreeing to meet with me."

"It's my pleasure," said Nathan graciously, even though he had reluctantly agreed to the meeting only as a personal favor to Sharyn. "Can I get you two something to drink? Lemonade? Iced tea? Something stronger?"

"I'd love a beer," said John.

"Same," echoed Sharyn.

"Coming right up." Nathan dashed into the house and grabbed three beers and pint glasses. He was back in a minute, and the three poured their own beers into glasses.

Reynolds was the first to raise his glass in a toast, "To the future," he said. "May we no longer stand divided."

The three clinked their glasses, and each took a deep pull on the yellowish, copper-colored beer. It had a citrusy taste with a hint of sourness, which was very refreshing but also a bit unexpected.

"Hmm," said Reynolds, enjoying the taste and picking up the bottle to read the label. "Lost Nation Brewing, huh? How apropos."

"I thought you might enjoy that," said Nathan, leaving them to guess whether he was referring to the beer's taste or the brewery's name.

"Well, Nathan," John began. "There's no sense wasting time with small talk, so I'll get right to the point of my visit. Sharyn has informed me of some of her conversations with you and that you generally understand President Fulton's current physical and mental condition."

Divided We Stand

"Yes, she's told me some things. In confidence, of course."

"Of course," said John. "We are concerned, Nathan, and by we, I'm referring to the President's closest advisors and cabinet secretaries. We're concerned that President Fulton will not be fit to hold office for another term. Hell, we're concerned if he's fit to hold office now."

"I see," said Nathan, unsure what an appropriate response to this admission should be.

"We are even more concerned about the deepening crisis occurring across America. This red-versus-blue civil war that everyone seems to be gearing up for is being led by Vince Marino, the newly announced Republican nominee for President.

"Yes, I share your alarm. And I agree that Governor Marino is most definitely attempting to use the crisis to propel himself into the White House."

"Good," said John. "So we're on the same side of this."

"Well, I don't know if I'm on any side, John. I've always been pretty apolitical. But I am opposed to Vince Marino holding any office higher than the chief bottlewasher in his own family's kitchen. He has his own private agenda to gather personal power and is not fit for public service."

"That definitely puts us on the same side, Nathan. That's why I'm here," said John, pausing to choose his words carefully. "There's no real easy way to ask this, Nathan, so I'll just say it. The United States is at a crossroads, and we need serious leaders for the serious job ahead—leaders who will place the future of this country ahead of their own personal ambitions. No one exemplifies this more than you. On behalf of a grateful nation, I'm here to ask if you would consider accepting the Democratic Party nomination for President of the United States for this November's election."

Nathan divided his look between John and Sharyn, suddenly at a complete loss for words. When Sharyn had asked for Nathan to meet with President Fulton's Chief of Staff, never in a million years did Nathan think it was to ask him to run for President.

Still at a loss for words, Nathan blurted out the first thing that came to mind. "But, I'm not a Democrat."

John and Sharyn both smiled.

"Well," said John. "If that's your only reservation, I think we can solve that one pretty quickly."

"I'm serious," said Nathan. "I've always registered as either an independent or with no party affiliation, and I'll be honest—I've almost always voted for the Republican nominee. I consider myself a moderate conservative, and I'm not sure that's compatible with the current Democratic Party."

"We need you. Your country needs you. I'm happy to get into all the details, but the bottom line is that the Democratic Party has no established leader willing to stand up and lead this country forward. The fringes in this country are just that—fringes. We need someone to lead from the center. We need to resolve this pending civil war and then repair the damage that the divisiveness has done across all fifty states, Red and Blue alike. It's going to take someone new to Washington but someone the people can believe in. You're that person, Nathan. If you don't trust me, trust Sharyn."

Nathan looked at Sharyn. "It's true, Nathan. You're the best this country has to offer. The fact you have zero interest in being President is exactly the reason why you will be so good at the job."

"What's your boss have to say?" Nathan asked her.

"She doesn't know," admitted Sharyn sheepishly.

"Serena would absolutely lose her mind if she knew we were having this conversation," admitted John. "But Serena has become part of the problem, not part of the solution. She's too busy trying to keep her job and loses sight of what's required to *do* her job."

"Please, Nathan, please consider this," said Sharyn. "Please consider being the nominee for President. You would win in a landslide."

"Okay," said Nathan, putting his beer down on the table.

"Okay?" Sharyn asked. "As in, okay I'll accept the nomination?"

Nathan smiled. "Okay, as in, I'll consider it."

Epilogue

Havana, Cuba
Saturday, May 4

ALEX TREACHER SAT on the wide balcony overlooking the Gulf of Mexico, sipping coffee in the morning sun. The past few days had been disappointing, but he considered it only a minor setback.

While forced to flee his lair on Cromwell Island, his reins controlling Orlean Brumback and Vince Marino remained firmly in place, and the Constitutional Convention would commence in two short months. The pieces of his grand strategy continued to move forward, and the United States continued to fracture. It was only a matter of time before he controlled the White House and the United States became his pawn.

This balcony he sat on was on the third level of the mansion he owned on Cuba's north shore, a short distance west of the capital city of Havana. Similar to his lodge on Cromwell Island, the views were astounding, and he had to give Cuba two thumbs up when it came to hospitality. Whereas he had limited staff on Cromwell Island, here in Cuba, Sergei managed dozens of workers both inside and outside the massive villa on the shores of the Gulf of Mexico. While he'd miss the lodge on Cromwell Island, the ornate villa in the sun would serve just as ideal to continue maneuvering his chess pieces inside America.

Alex's guest would be arriving soon—a person he communicated with often through encrypted electronic means but someone he had not seen in person in almost five years. Despite Alex Treacher's seemingly unlimited wealth and resources, everyone had a boss, and Alex was no exception.

He heard the man enter the balcony behind him and stood to greet him. The man was stooped yet walked with an assurance that belied his physical frailty. Appearing to be in his mid-seventies, with whisps of gray hair on his balding head and long jowls on his narrow face, the man's piercing blue eyes were lively and intelligent. The man's name and title struck fear in the hearts of millions, but very few had ever met him in person, and even fewer had the honor to host him for lunch in a tropical setting.

This man had literally created the person Alex Treacher had become.

"Zdravstvuyte," said Alex, formally saying hello to the man in Alex's native tongue, a language Alex had not used in many years.

"Dobroe utro—good morning," said Alex's esteemed guest and boss, the director of the SVR, Russia's foreign intelligence service.

Join Nathan's Continued Hunt for the Cabal

Does the United States continue on its path to civil war?

Will Russia be successful in influencing the November elections?

What is the outcome of the Red versus Blue ideological fight?

Join Nathan Greene on his hunt for the Cabal and see how America's first Constitutional Convention in 230 years has the potential to reshape the country.

UNITED WE FALL

Book Two of the Fractured Union Series

Coming Summer 2024

Thank You

Since you've made it this far, I wanted to take a moment to thank you for reading *Divided We Stand*. It was a fun and interesting novel to write, and I sincerely appreciate the time you've invested. I hope it has provided you with some entertainment.

As I mentioned in the preface, it is not my intention to use this novel to make a political statement. Rather, I hope readers will enjoy a fresh look at some unique aspects of our complex, fluid federal system of government woven into an enjoyable story. If you appreciated the story and are left with more questions than answers, then I believe I've achieved my goal.

If you enjoyed *Divided We Stand* or any of the four previous Matt Sheridan novels, it would mean the world to me if you would take the time to leave a review on Amazon. The goal of any author is to increase the readership of their books, and leaving a quick 5-star review on Amazon greatly impacts the algorithms that allow new readers to find this book. So, I would like to personally thank each of you in advance for taking the time to leave a quick rating.

If you're considering leaving a 1-star review (or even a 2- or 3-star one), why not email me directly instead at Robert@Official

Thank You

RobertCole.com? I personally read every email and always welcome feedback from readers, positive or negative. If any of you have specific comments or questions, please don't hesitate to reach out.

Best regards,
 Robert Cole

Acknowledgments

The idea for the Fractured Union series of novels stems from a conversation in November 2000, when an uncle visiting from Ireland commented on the recount process in Florida after the close Presidential election between George W. Bush and Al Gore. Only in the great democracy of America, he stated, could such a close election be resolved peacefully, for every other less mature democracy would surely resort to armed conflict. As I read an article about Donald Trump's indictments last summer, I wondered what would happen if he simply refused to acknowledge them—what could happen?

I was very unsure of whether to write this novel, as America's fractiousness has reached the point that a book on this topic, despite being entirely fictional, was bound to anger just about everyone. But then I realized something—this was an interesting story that I wanted to tell, not because I thought others would enjoy it, but because I thought I, myself, would enjoy it. I would enjoy researching and writing this story because it's exactly the type of novel I would enjoy reading.

That said, I would like to personally thank all of you who have taken the time to read *Divided We Stand* and had the personal wisdom and restraint not to use the Amazon comment section to espouse your personal political views. For those of you who feel compelled to make a political comment rather than a literary one—when you look in the mirror, understand one thing: you're the problem, not the solution.

While I have attempted to make this work of fiction seem as real as possible, any factual errors are entirely mine. In some cases, the errors are intentional, while others are likely due to ignorance - but in all cases, the fault lies entirely with me.

A special thank you to Jeff Wine, Steve Clark, and Butch Klemeyer, who each agreed to read and comment on the first draft of the novel. Your insightful comments, constructive feedback, and support mean the world to me.

Another huge thank you to all my extended family and friends who have encouraged and supported me on this journey as a novelist. I have attempted to weave bits and pieces of your personalities into the various characters, and I hope you have enjoyed some of these special moments.

Thank you to my parents for their endless encouragement and for passing on their love of reading.

Thank you most of all to my wife and children. Your love and support are what makes everything worthwhile. I appreciate the sacrifices you make in allowing me to spend so much of my time writing, and your interest, insight, and suggestions make writing extremely enjoyable.

Every author needs a critic and an editor, and thankfully, my wife and son fill these roles. To my wife, Melanie— thank you for enduring numerous evenings listening to various ideas on new plotlines and characters. Your advice is always sage, perceptive, and helpful. To my son, Liam—this journey as an author would not be half as fun without you by my side, and I cherish the time we get to spend working together on these novels.

About the Author

Robert Cole is a political science professor and former U.S. Army infantry officer who has served in several of the Army's rapid deployment forces, including the 101st Airborne Division and 75th Ranger Regiment. He is the Amazon best-selling author of the Matt Sheridan series of post-apocalyptic thrillers that follow the Sheridan family as they attempt to survive a realistic terrorist scenario that decimates the world.

To learn more about Robert, please visit his website at www.officialrobertcole.com. If you subscribe to the newsletter on his website, he promises not to inundate your inbox, but will keep you apprised of future novels.

<u>The Matt Sheridan Series</u>
    Cataclysm
    Breaking Contact
    Standing Ground
    Bounding Overwatch

<u>Fractured Union Series</u>
    Divided We Stand
    United We Fall - coming Summer 2024

facebook.com/officialrobertcole
x.com/robertcolebooks
instagram.com/robertcolebooks

Made in the USA
Monee, IL
24 October 2024

68605228R00270